**Every woman sees the appeal of a strong man, a sexy man who can take charge, but, after working hours, even the boss has to ask for what he wants… Of course, he can make a special request…**

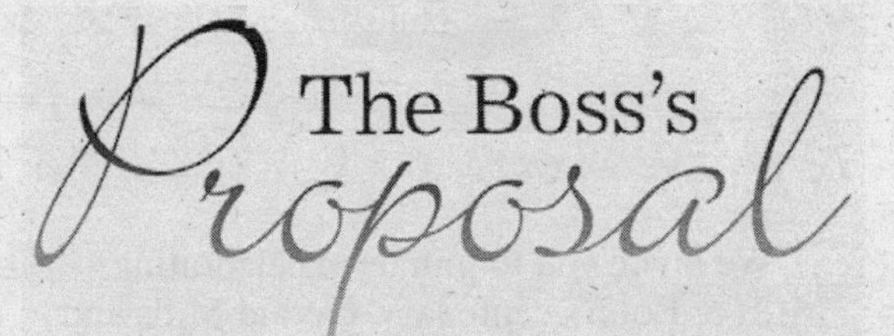


"Margaret Way's latest is a great story with lots of emotion and passion to keep you entertained."
—*Romantic Times* on *Strategy for Marriage*

"Jessica Steele's latest is a delightful read. The characters' chemistry and depth add to the romance."
—*Romantic Times* on *A Paper Marriage*

"Ms Thayer leaves no emotion untapped as her multifaceted characters make you laugh, cry and even get burned by the passionate heat of true love. Keep the tissues handy!"
—*Romantic Times* on *Nothing Short of a Miracle*

# *100 Reasons to Celebrate*

We invite you to join us in celebrating Mills & Boon's centenary. Gerald Mills and Charles Boon founded Mills & Boon Limited in 1908 and opened offices in London's Covent Garden. Since then, Mills & Boon has become a hallmark for romantic fiction, recognised around the world.

We're proud of our 100 years of publishing excellence, which wouldn't have been achieved without the loyalty and enthusiasm of our authors and readers.

*Thank you!*

Each month throughout the year there will be something new and exciting to mark the centenary, so watch for your favourite authors, captivating new stories, special limited edition collections...and more!

# The Boss's Proposal

Margaret Way Jessica Steele
Patricia Thayer

M&B™

**DID YOU PURCHASE THIS BOOK WITHOUT A COVER?**
If you did, you should be aware it is **stolen property** as it was reported *unsold and destroyed* by a retailer. Neither the author nor the publisher has received any payment for this book.




*M&B™ and M&B™ with the Rose Device are trademarks of the publisher.*
*Harlequin Mills & Boon Limited, Eton House,*
*18-24 Paradise Road, Richmond, Surrey TW9 1SR*





*ISBN: 978 0 263 86675 9*

*24-0508*

*Printed and bound in Spain*
*by Litografia Rosés S.A., Barcelona*

# MASTER OF MALLARINKA

Margaret Way

**Margaret Way,** a definite Leo, was born and raised in the sub-tropical river city of Brisbane, capital of the sunshine state of Queensland. A Conservatorium trained pianist, teacher, accompanist and vocal coach, her musical career came to an unexpected end when she took up writing, initially as a fun thing to do. She currently lives in a harbourside apartment at beautiful Raby Bay, a thirty-minute drive from the State capital, where she loves dining *al fresco* on her plant-filled balcony that overlooks a translucent green marina filled with all manner of pleasure craft, from motor cruisers costing millions of dollars and big graceful yachts with carved masts standing tall against the cloudless blue sky to little bay runabouts. No one and nothing is in a mad rush, so she finds the laid-back village atmosphere very conducive to her writing. With well over a hundred books to her credit she still believes her best is yet to come.

**Margaret Way has an exciting new novel, *Wedding at Wangaree Valley*, coming in Mills & Boon® Romance in September 2008.**

Dear Reader,

It's a source of great pride and wonder to me that I've been very much a part of one of the world's most successful and iconic publishing houses, Mills & Boon. As a young mother with an infant son, when I sat down at the kitchen table and wrote my first book (in longhand!), little did I know I was embarking on a career that was to sustain, reward and offer me fulfilment for just about my entire adult life. I could say Mills & Boon has *been* my life.

I would like to pay tribute, too, to the memory of Alan and John Boon, who made the halcyon days so very, very memorable. It should be said Mills & Boon not only offers pleasure to our readership but comfort in times of family grief, turmoil and stress. My own readership has told me this in so many touching ways.

Let us all join together, then, in offering our congratulations to a much-loved icon – Mills & Boon – on its glorious and triumphant centenary.

Long may you reign!

*Margaret Way*

# PROLOGUE

ON HER sixteenth birthday Victoria Rushford, already dubbed "the beautiful Rushford heiress" by a media that appeared to be growing bigger with every passing year, had overreached herself terribly. She had done something so reckless, so utterly *gauche,* that four years later the sheer awfulness of it brought a burning blush to her cheeks and an agonised groan from her throat. The incident, a by-product of her pathetic neediness—she really was the proverbial poor little rich girl—had turned a delirium of expectation into a catastrophe inconceivable only the day before. The Disaster—she always thought of it that way—had divided her and Haddo for ever. Never again could they be natural with one another. Never again would they be friends after a lifetime of bonding.

Overnight she had become disconnected from her moorings. She had gone from hero-worshipping Haddo—perfect in her mind, fantastic, dashing, a thousand times more sexy than any guy she knew or ever expected to know, twenty-five to her sixteen—to actively hating him. That was how deep the wounds went. Hating was a development that often occurred when someone was profoundly humiliated, especially after long being held in the greatest affection.

She had never in her wildest dreams imagined Haddo could turn on her the way he had. It suggested dark depths of feeling she had been totally unaware of. For chilling moments she had feared he was going to fling her bodily out of his room, such had been his shock and apparent aversion. Memories were torture, but there were times one couldn't stop them rolling. It was pretty much like being forced to watch a video that was enormously distressing…

The homestead was in darkness. Haddo's suite of rooms was in the West Wing, which meant that instead of doing it with ease, considering the number of times she had walked it, she had to inch her way along the long baronial-style gallery. It was hung with paintings, and antique chairs were set at intervals, just in case someone got the urge to sit down and study the family heirlooms. Huge Chinese porcelain vases stood on stands—*famille rose, famille verte, famille noir,* you name it. The vases were so valuable they should have been in glass cases, but what the heck? This was the ancestral home, not a museum.

She kept moving in a straight line, hoping to goodness she wouldn't veer off to left or right and knock into something. How unlucky would that be? It would be fatal to wake anyone. Quite a few of the rellies who had turned up for her birthday party were sleeping behind those closed doors. Mercifully a couple of them, septuagenarians, were deaf. She understood many problems arose at that age, but at sixteen, seventy plus was such a long way off it was in a totally separate time zone.

She had timed her move exactly to two-thirty. Anyone would think she had a train to catch. Was three a.m. the witching hour? Or was that midnight? She was reduced to giggles. Either way, two-thirty seemed like a good time. Normal people were fast asleep. She had only just achieved lift-off.

Broad rays of moonlight poured through the tall stained glass windows at the top of the staircase, drenching the landing in radiant white light. That calmed her. She wasn't one of those people who favoured the dark. She always had to have light. Now, with the moonlight, she could very nearly see. She hoped she wouldn't encounter the Rushford ghost. Very likely the ghost was about. She was pretty blasé about the whole thing. Every historic house had a ghost or two. It stood to reason that occasionally paths would cross.

Their particular ghost was Eliza Rushford, who had died in childbirth in the late 1800s at the tender age of eighteen. Way too young to start a family! Heaven must have been full up at the time, because Eliza hung around the gallery to this day, drifting up and down it, beckoning to those who had the ability to see her to come and visit the old nursery. Great-Aunt Philippa—she who had trained Victoria to walk about balancing a book on her head—claimed to have seen Eliza many times, and once even got into an in-depth discussion with her, regarding the high mortality rate in childbirth in those days. Otherwise Great-Aunt Philippa, known as Pip, was a remarkably sensible woman, and a wonderful musician.

"I could have been a concert pianist, Tori dear. I was just that good!"

Anyway, Pip sat on the board of the Rushford Pastoral Company and did an excellent job. She knew a humungous amount of stuff—she could easily have won the top quiz shows—and she was great fun. Unlike her sister, Great-Aunt Bea, spinster by choice, who took the fun out of everything.

Victoria didn't really believe in ghosts herself. She had never seen hide nor hair of her adored departed father, Michael, though she and Pip had once had a shot at summoning him up at a séance—until Bea had put a stop to it.

"You can't leave well alone, can you, Philippa?" Bea had said. "Leave the poor child alone. She's screwed up enough as it is!" Great-Aunt Bea was a fine one to talk.

Stealing on, barefoot—how she wished for a flaming torch—Victoria finally made it to Haddo's bedroom door without mishap. She was amazed she was actually capable of doing this. If things went wrong she could always claim she was sleepwalking. An excessively bitchy girlfriend of Haddo's had once called her a "cheeky little brat!" Jealous, of course.

The door wasn't locked. The brass hinges didn't squeak. Haddo would have had them oiled if they did. She had no trouble easing the door open. He was lying on his back in the huge bed, his breathing deep and quiet. She would have been astounded if he had been snoring. Haddo was just too cool! He didn't even stir at her unauthorised entry, though she swallowed hard herself.

So far so good. Fortune favoured the brave. She loved the idea of that.

Moonlight glittered on the verandah. The French doors were wide open to the desert breeze that carried with it the scent of the beautiful boronia. It billowed the filmy central drops of the curtains, with their rich tapestry drapes to either side. A clock was ticking away—not loudly, but perfectly audible in the silvery dark. She couldn't sleep with a ticking clock in the room herself. She just hoped this one didn't chime the quarter-hour. That would have been too unnerving.

She started forward, feeling as if she was floating. Her dark red hair tumbled down her back—masses of it. Coils of it twined around her throat and her shoulders. She had arranged it that way to hide her elf's ears. For the first time in her life she truly felt beautiful. She wasn't one of those people who found her looks entrancing.

She lifted the cream satin-bound hem of her luxurious nightgown clear of the Persian rug, in case she tripped and fell to the floor. That would totally destroy the romance of her entry. It was a beautiful garment, glamorous and seductive; in fact the first glamorous, seductive nightie she had ever owned. She had secretly bought it in an exclusive little shop that sold the most *amazing* lingerie—very naughty. The nightie was a bit big, but the smallest she'd been able to get. There wasn't a great deal of her—especially in the bosom department. But she did feel very much a woman on the threshhold of life.

Haddo's breathing abruptly changed. The swiftness of it took her by surprise. She shook violently. Then he moved. He kicked back the top sheet, turning his dark head on the pillow in her direction. Maybe he thought she was the ghost of Eliza? Maybe poor Eliza often used his shoulder to cry on? Most women would die to.

His voice when it came was half-drugged with sleep. "Tori, is that you?"

She was transfixed. She didn't answer, *Yes, Haddo, it's me.* Instead she thought, *Oh, my gosh, what have I done?* The whole thing was unreal.

She detoured around a chair, then swam closer to the bed on a wave of euphoria. Her eyes were riveted on Haddo's long lean frame. His splendid torso was naked, but she saw he was wearing a pair of boxer shorts. She gulped. When it came right down to it she wanted to start the seduction *slowly.* The top sheet was now tangled up in his long straight legs.

Haddo—her safe haven! Only tonight was special: an uncharted adventure, a voyage of discovery. She was at the side of his high bed. It had been custom-made for a big man—Haddo was six-three. She clambered onto it—not without difficulty. She would have been far better off with a short nightie, but nothing could detract from her ecstasy of yearning. Oh, to lie down with him, beside him, on top of him, under him—to breathe in the same air. It filled her with so much elation she gave a throbbing little moan. If this wasn't the greatest moment of her life, what was?

*I've done it!* she thought ecstatically, feeling strange to herself, and more than a little wild. She had a definite sense Haddo thought she wasn't real, but that too was part of the extravagant adventure. Desire. Dreaming. He wouldn't be able to resist her. As a bereaved child, looking for love and protection, she had turned to Cousin

Haddo out of everyone in her extended family as the source of comfort. Now she had a craving for something altogether different from him: the fulfilment of the bond that had been long years in the making.

To her unending joy, even triumph, he folded her body into him as though he was about to feast on it. It whipped up a fury of sensation, as if a bonfire had been lit inside her. She was instantly aflame. It was difficult for her not to cheer aloud. Then came the moment of supreme bliss. Her eyelids grew heavy, her coltish limbs languorous. Haddo's handsome dark head descended over hers…

*Kiss me. Touch me. My body is ready for you.*

Her brain had shut down at least an hour ago. Haddo, her wonderful Haddo, started kissing her with his beautiful, sensuous mouth. A line of sparkling stars trailed down her throat to between her breasts. Rapture pierced her. Her long legs were moving restlessly up and down on the sheet, turning out at the knees like the petals of a flower. She couldn't quite catch her breath. Her head was swimming. She had over-estimated her own ability to handle this level of emotion. It was so tumultuous it was an agony. She had a notion she was getting scared. She wanted to grab on to his shoulders, feel the strong bones and polished skin, beg him to give her a moment…

Only he had found her open waiting mouth, and his arousal was so powerful, so apparent, it electrified her, thrilling her out of her mind. She was desperate to lift her restless legs and wrap them around him—but she could hear the silk of her nightgown tearing. She had never remotely been in the grip of such rapture before.

She was right at its epicentre, dizzy with it, maybe a little stupefied it was so immense.

Her body was pinned to the mattress. It came to her in an overwhelming rush that Haddo was experienced. She wasn't. He had gone way beyond puppy love. She hadn't even started. She wasn't interested in sloppy teenage boys. Haddo, however, was a splendid young man who had always had girls queuing in line, each hoping she would be the one. How she had hated that! Hadn't any of them realised Haddo was waiting for *her?* Waiting patiently for a few years to pass?

Beneath her sheer nightgown she was naked, and it really, really felt like it. She was so acutely conscious of her own body he might have already tossed her nightie out onto the Persian rug. That was her small breast he was cupping with his hand, the throbbing nipple as ripe as a berry. It was such raging passion, tears sprang to her eyes. Sex was immense, and they had only just begun. For that matter, was she really *adult* enough for this?

*I can't stand it.*

Did she whimper it aloud? She must have.

The entire world came to a halt. Moments later it started up again, in case everyone got thrown off.

Haddo cried out. There was so much pain and shock in his voice, he might have been skewered, like Macbeth, by a dagger. His hand caught her wrists, pinning her to the bed. He was staring down at her as she lay back against the pillows, her long hair tumbling everywhere, the perfume she had misted all over her—every pulse-point, her navel, even the back of her knees— scenting the air around them.

"Tori?"

He sounded absolutely stunned. From groggy with sleep he was now on trigger alert.

"Oh, God, Tori, are you crazy?"

How ghastly was that? Tears sprang to her eyes. They slid silently down her cheeks. His tone was so accusatory she couldn't understand where he was coming from. It was as though he had started to speak to her in a foreign tongue. Not French, or Italian, or German. Nothing like that. At any rate, *crazy* was the very last word she had expected to hear. Were all men like this? Did every last one of them have tricks up their sleeve? She might have represented an extreme threat to his person. Worse, she might have been putting him in danger of committing a heinous crime. Her skin, so heated a moment before, turned to gooseflesh.

"For heaven's sake, Tori. What are you thinking of?" he groaned. "We can't do this. We can't."

Out the words spilled, while her heart dropped to her feet like a stone. The air around them turned dense and suffocating, filled with a crackling electricity. Her whole body was receiving multiple shocks. She thought she would never forget the horror in his voice, the utter condemnation. Her wonderful birthday had been unimaginably spoiled.

"Tori!"

Why was he sounding as if he was overcome by guilt? Just how old did she have to *be?*

She pushed up, as frantic as he, their faces and bodies all but touching.

"What's happening here?" She heard her own voice, distraught.

He took her by the shoulders, holding her forcibly

away from him. His strong hands trembled, as though he was afraid of her. This was like some weird romance, where the heroine got killed off in the first chapter.

*I can't bear this!*

Her body was pumping adrenalin. His was filled with a spring-loaded tension.

"What's wrong? Tell me? Don't you love me any longer?" God, she would die of abject shame if he said No. Or, worse, *I never did.* Nothing else for it after that but to jump out of the window.

"Tori, how can you ask?"

He sounded split apart. She had never ever seen Haddo agitated. He had always impressed her with his marvellous buoyant self-confidence, but a powerful agitation had clearly overtaken him. Scion of the legendary Rushford pioneering dynasty, Haddo had always used the lightest hand in all his dealings with her. He had smiled on her even when she was at her wildest—he had the best smile in the world—though admittedly she had on occasion been made to stand quietly while he delivered a few succinct words of caution. But all in all Haddo had treated her with such a broad deep affection it had forged what she had always believed was an unbreakable bond.

Who could blame her, then, if she was now utterly devastated by his bizarre reaction. The unbreakable bond that had tethered her to him appeared to be no more than gossamer-thin threads.

"All I wanted was your arms around me." She pressed her hands together in anguish, scalded by the inner knowledge that she had wanted so much more.

"You know you're the one I turn to since Daddy went and left me."

Ironically her father, a renowned yachtsman, had been drowned in a freak accident off Sydney Heads. She had been twelve at the time. Twelve was such a crucial turning point in life—on the cusp of adolescence, when all those core conflicts began to emerge. Any person of heart might find her actions understandable, even forgivable.

Not Haddo.

She had trusted him completely. Now he might as well have pushed her out of the Beech Baron minus her parachute.

"You can't possibly stay here, Tori."

If that wasn't rejection, what was? She was diminished in his eyes, in her own eyes. Beyond consolation. What she had previously thought, she discovered to her great shame, was simply not true.

Except for the odd thing. And there was no getting away from it. Despite how he was acting—as if she had been attempting to rape him—there had been those brief moments when it was *he* who had handled her yielding body like the most ardent of lovers. It was *his* mouth that had covered hers so hungrily, his tongue that had lapped hers, his divine sex that had slammed into the delta of her throbbing body, as though desperate to plunge into her.

*I didn't imagine it!* It had happened. Those were the moments that would be burned into her memory.

And why not? Those moments had shaped her.

* * *

Afterwards, with her name, her fortune, her beauty—which was to prove more problematic than anything else—and her social entrée, her relationship with Haddo had still played the dominant role in her life. And not only because he would control the purse strings until she was twenty-five. Despite how much she told herself she loathed him, everyone and everything paled before Haddo. He was the quintessential magnificent male. She had as good as convinced herself she couldn't stand the sight of him, but her whole being yearned for what had been.

Even when her mind shut down on him, her body remembered. The terrible pity of it *then* was that she had been fool enough to believe she could bring a ravishing pleasure to them both. How could she have been so wrong? Surely what she had so strongly desired Haddo had too? How else was she to interpret the way he had been with her that special day? She'd been sixteen: a grown-up, a child no longer. And she had been lovely. Everyone had told her so. Except her mother, of course, who was never happy with her, no matter how she looked or what she did. But her mother, Livinia, hadn't been there for her birthday.

Liv's hectic social life—Victoria wasn't supposed to call her Mum or Mother—centred around Sydney and Melbourne. Liv was way out of her element on Mallarinka. No one in the extended Rushford family liked her anyway, though for the most part they did their best to hide it. All except Pip, who had a long, measuring stare and could be amazingly direct.

Victoria questioned herself constantly about what had happened. Was she certain of the way Haddo had looked up at her as she'd descended the central staircase in her beautiful emerald-green party dress? It had exactly matched her cat's eyes. Yes, she was. She would even swear to it in a court of law if she had to. Not that anyone would ask her to. She hadn't just invented what she saw in his eyes. They had sizzled over her with the blue intensity of a flame.

So, for the record, she hadn't imagined it. She had been tracking men's glances since she had turned fourteen—maybe since even earlier, when Liv had made the horrendous mistake of remarrying. Men were such lustful creatures. No wonder Great-Aunt Bea had never married—never had a steady relationship, for that matter, according to Pip, who had been very hotly desired herself. And hadn't she, Victoria, been the unfortunate recipient of many obsidian glances from her stepfather, Barry? Barry's slimy manner had impelled her to maintain a strict physical distance between them. Though she'd acted just this side of contemptuous with him, privately she had been fearful of the little dark urges towards her she'd read in his predatory eyes.

So, no use to turn to Livinia for protection and advice. Liv only saw what she wanted to see. Besides, Liv wasn't her friend. Liv was that aberration in nature: a woman who was jealous of her own daughter; her only child. Just to make the derangement more reprehensible, having done it once, Livinia had taken a vow that she would never go through the trauma of pregnancy and childbirth again. In other words, she'd got the maternal instinct right out of her system first time off.

"You were a daddy's girl right from the cradle." It had been a frequent accusation, as if the two of them, mother and daughter, were in fierce competition for Michael's attention. "After you were born he had no time for me."

Not strictly true. But close. Up until the age of twelve she had been the adored only child of a loving and admittedly overly-indulgent father. By then her father had been snatched away by a cruel fate, and a lecherous stepfather installed in his place.

Yes, Victoria knew when a man desired her. Only Haddo, a god to her, had turned on her as though she were a tart off the streets—someone who had somehow gained unlawful entry to his bed, with him, six foot three, superbly fit, lying there helpless.

"You're sixteen, Tori. A child. God, you're still at school!"

"Maybe I'll quit!" she had flung at him, at that point pierced by terrible doubts. "So what have I done, Haddo? Please tell me. Have I broken some sacred code of honour? Some powerful taboo?"

She'd hated getting the tribal treatment. She had argued her innocence, all the while fierce little tears pouring down her cheeks.

"I can't do this, Tori." Haddo, breathing heavily, had put paid to her dreams. "You're my cousin. It's my job to look out for you—though God knows these days you're making it bloody near impossible."

She had been driven to attacking him, pounding the hard wall of his chest. He had let her, as though it was too much trouble to stop her. "We're not first cousins, Haddo. We're not even full second cousins. Great-Uncle Julien and Great-Uncle George were half-brothers with different mothers. Why are you so appalled?" She had reached out to him again, surrendering to one last moment of weakness

He'd held her off. "This can't happen, Victoria. I don't want to hurt you, but I'm going to take you back to your room. You're beautiful—so beautiful! Your powers are staggering. I suspect they will only grow stronger. But I can't—I won't—let you try them out on me. No way could I forgive myself."

"Or forgive me either!"

It was over. She had bitten off far more than she could chew.

Disgraced, she had wrenched herself away from him, half sliding half falling off the high bed, blinded by the long riotous masses of her hair. How had she got such uncontrollable hair anyhow—and why *red?* Liv insisted her hair was just like her aunt Rowena's, whom no one had ever seen.

"You know what you've done, don't you?" She had rounded on Haddo in a sick fury. "You've given me a life sentence."

"Don't be ridiculous" His voice, honed by privilege, had sounded unbearably well bred.

"I hate you—okay?" She, on the other hand, had sounded as grim as she felt. "I've got to go home. I can't be near you for another day."

He had made not the slightest attempt to dissuade her, nor sweetened it in any way. "That might be for the best, Tori," he'd agreed. "I'll organise it."

It wasn't until she was back in her own room that she began to cry her heart out, weeping until there were no more tears left and she fell into an exhausted sleep. The day that had begun with such golden promise had all of a sudden ended in ashes. Contrary to what she had been led to believe, she wasn't even vaguely sexy. She didn't inspire lust at all. At least not in Haddo. She had totally misread the look he had given her when she'd come down the staircase. She might remember it for as long as she lived, but to Haddo she was ridiculous.

Her broken heart she kept secret for the next four years.

# CHAPTER ONE

*The present—Mallarinka Station, Channel Country, South-West Queensland*

SUNSET saw Haddo riding back to the homestead, dog-tired and yearning for an ice-cold beer and a shower, in that order. He couldn't wait for cooling rivulets of water to stream over his stressed, dehydrated body. He had even contemplated falling fully clothed into a billabong along the way, but hadn't thought he'd be able to drag himself out. Even his favourite workhorse, Fleetwood, was bone-weary.

"Only a kilometre to go, boy!" He patted the gelding's long satiny neck, offering encouragement. Fleetwood responded with a nodding motion of his proud, handsome head. Once Fleetwood had run with the wild horses—until he had been captured. He had broken in Fleetwood himself, though "broken" wasn't a term he used. A station rule was that none of the horses was to be treated roughly. Only recently he had to let an otherwise good stockman go because of the man's cruel streak.

Over the years he had developed a very different technique from the "breaking" favoured even in his father's day. No spurs, no whips. He didn't so much "whisper" a wild horse into tameness, though it helped. His method was the rope, while keeping constant eye contact with whatever horse he was working. He'd got that eye contact down to a fine art.

Fleetwood had thoroughbred blood in him. His dam was a runaway station mare, and the sire was probably Warri, a big rogue brumby stallion with an impressive harem.

Wild horses were part of the Outback's unique heritage, though the downside was that they did threaten the delicate ecosystems. But out here man and wild horses lived side by side, with properly schooled brumbies replenishing dwindling station stock. Once most of the cleanskins were in, they would start trapping a mob or two. The mobs were coming in from the hill country, in search of water. There were thousands of wild horses out there—many the progeny of good station bloodstock, but others too small or too scrappy to be put to any use.

Gently he swung Fleetwood away from the line of billabongs and up onto the vast open plain. It was thickly dotted with spinifex, golden as wheat. It had been a day of stifling heat, always a big problem. The heat made men, horses and cattle sluggish, which meant all three got careless and under-performed, but he had decided the cattle from the outer areas of the station had to be brought in without delay. The heat wasn't going to get better. No use hoping or praying for a storm—although some of the storm-like displays of late had been pretty spectacular, blazing Technicolor versions of an atomic bomb. But, for all the pyrotechnics, there was no rain. The rain gods just weren't answering these days, and when they did he was pretty certain drought would give way to flood. That meant the cleanskins that had been enjoying the good life, undisturbed by man, had to be mustered and branded. With vast unfenced stations, and cattle wandering miles into the desert, the duffing of cleanskins went on.

Pretty much most of the day had been spent trying to muster a big mob of seriously psycho cattle out of Ulahrii, one of the least accessible lignum swamps. At least they'd been compensated by a brief visual delight: Ulahrii had been alight with the most beautiful and fragrant water lilies, great creamy yellow ones that lifted their gorgeous heads clear of the dark green water. He had come upon them in all their beauty, and vivid memories had caused him to suck in his breath.

Tori on her sixteenth birthday. He couldn't get a picture of her out of his mind. A group of them had been swimming in Silver Lake, and Tori had balanced a blue lotus water lily on her rosy head. To him, she had been the very picture of an exquisite water sprite, with her long sensuous hair, her extraordinary alabaster skin that never freckled, the beautiful slanting green eyes, even her little pointy ears. He thought if he could paint he would paint her as that—*Nymph of the Lagoon,* watching over the water lilies.

Tori.

She had been so vivid, so totally happy that day—a creature of light from some magical place. One way or another she was always in his mind, though she didn't come willingly to the station any more. Over four years now since their drastic falling out, but in that time he had at least held control over her life. That was until she was twenty-five, when she would come into her inheritance.

He had come into his own inheritance a whole lot earlier than anyone in the family had ever anticipated in their wildest dreams. Two years ago Brandt, his charismatic father, had pole-axed them all by abdicating his role of Master of Mallarinka and the Rushford cattle empire to hare off to South Africa, still very rich, to be with a young South African woman he had met on a visit to Darwin and fallen passionately in love with, literally overnight. This at the age of fifty-five. These days his father and his new wife owned and ran an up-market safari camp that catered to well-heeled international tourists looking for a bit of excitement.

His mother hadn't mourned.

"I gave the best years of my life to your father. Now I'm going to pursue a bit of happiness myself."

The trouble was, the steam had gone out of his parents' largely arranged marriage by the time he had left for boarding school at age ten. His mother, a pragmatic woman, had moved on with a vengeance. She, too, had remarried, in the process acquiring a stepson—a wealthy management stockbroker with an investment bank, like his high-profile father—adding to her own family of himself and his younger sister Kerri. His mother now spent her time between Melbourne and Mallarinka, visiting in Melbourne's cold winter.

His very glamorous sister Kerri's marriage was going through a bad patch. Kerri, like their mother, was a bit of a control freak. She had asked if she could visit, and bring a friend—Marcy Hancock. Of course he had said yes, though he had grave misgivings about letting Marcy come. Sometimes he thought Marcy would still be pursuing him when they were both geriatric, or at the very least middle-aged. It was a mind-set. Nothing more. He'd have to start praying some rich Melbourne guy would whisk her off. He'd need to be rich. Marcy Hancock wasn't cut out for normal life in the suburbs.

He rode on, grateful the home compound was coming closer and closer. From time to time he lifted his head to watch the thousands of birds that had been conserving their energy all day head into the swamps and lagoons. Every species of waterbird was among them—geese, ducks, herons, egrets, ibises, blue cranes—and budgies in their billowing iridescent squadrons. There were literally millions of birds on the station. The birds on Mallarinka were doing it lean, like the rest of the desert fauna, but so far they were sticking to their territory. Mallarinka had permanent water, and a few of the larger billabongs, like Bahloo, were still quite deep.

Even at this hour, with the imperious sun losing its heat, the mirage was still abroad. It shimmered across the infinity of desert landscape, creating the most tantalising illusions of distant oases. He readily understood how early explorers responding to those illusions had come to grief. Aboriginal tribes on walkabout could have communicated to them in some way that the inland sea belonged to the Dreamtime, but the aborigines then had been very wary of the white man—and with good reason. Today only goodwill existed on Mallarinka. It would have been impossible to work the station without aboriginal stockmen. They were marvellous bushmen, uncanny trackers and accomplished cattlemen.

He loved his desert home, but he had to admit there was a wild, dark side to it. Man was never in control. Nature was boss. He could only hope to manage his great inheritance and live in harmony with all that stupendous raw power.

The western sky, one moment all aflame was now turning sullen, silver and black shot with a livid green, and the "rain" clouds banked low over the horizon. It would be dark before he arrived. Pip, his great-aunt, would be there. Philippa had long since retired from academic life, and she was staying with him for a month or two. Whatever she liked. He left it up to her. Pip was always entertaining company and he was very fond of her.

"I'm sorry, my dear, but Lucy's having a bit of trouble in Sydney." Philippa was there to greet him the moment he stepped in the back door.

Instantly his heart and head sprang to Tori. He searched Pip's long, distinguished face for clues. "It's Tori, of course?" he groaned, removing his riding boots and shoving them inside the wet room door. 'Just tell me she's all right?" Muscles of anxiety were knotting in his stomach. He was never free of worry where Tori was concerned. Probably doomed to worry about her for as long as he lived. "She hasn't been involved in any accident?"

"No, dear." Philippa hastened to offer reassurance. "Well, not personally. No one was hurt."

"That's all right, then," he responded, his relief apparent. "Just let me have a quick shower. I'm beat. I can't listen to another thing until then. As long as she's all right. And, oh, I'd love a long cold beer."

Philippa laughed. "No problem. I'll join you in a bath-sized G&T." She wasn't kidding either.

Under ten minutes later, Haddo was downstairs again, visibly refreshed. Despite his back-breaking day, his whole being radiated an enormous energy other people saw but he was largely unaware of. He sank into a comfortable armchair, watching Philippa pour him a beer, before making herself a gin and tonic that would knock a lesser woman out.

"God, you're a handsome man!" Philippa remarked with satisfaction, taking an armchair opposite.

Seeing her great-nephew gave Philippa back something of her wonderful brother Quentin—Haddo's late grandfather. There was the same vitality, and the height, the lean powerful body, the finely sculpted features, the flash of those startlingly blue eyes. And, just to top it off, there was the *smile*—so wonderfully engaging, with fine white teeth contrasting with the dark tan of his skin. Quentin had looked just like Haddo in his youth. Haddo would look like Quentin in old age.

Haddo was smiling crookedly at her. "Let's face it, Pip. We Rushfords are a handsome lot," he joked.

"Yes, isn't it wonderful?" Philippa agreed, then abruptly sobered. "Brandt would still be here if he weren't so handsome and virile."

"He's happy, Pip." Haddo sighed. He missed his larger-than-life father. "Dad's having a whale of a time."

"So he says. I wouldn't be in the least surprised if we get word one of these days that the gel is pregnant."

"I dare say as she's half Dad's age she would want

a child." Haddo's answer was reasonable. "Anyway, good luck to them. My heritage is entailed. The Rushford cattle empire remains in my hands until it passes to my son."

"Then you'd better get a move on, dear," Philippa suggested slyly. She knew who she had in mind for her darling Haddo.

"I've got to find a woman to love before I can make a commitment, Pip," he responded, in an off-hand way. "I don't want to be like Dad. I want my marriage to work."

Philippa frowned. "I'm sure Brandt wanted his marriage to work as well. But that South African hussy had him in her sights the moment she laid eyes on him. Bessie Butler told me that. The trouble was, your parents weren't really in love when they married. Not a grand passion anyway. It was all stitched up between the families—the Rushfords and the Haddons. I suppose you could almost say it was a business deal."

Haddo knew the family history. "No wonder Dad craved a bit of adventure, then," he said laconically. "Anyway, it's Tori I want to hear about. So fire away." He downed half his beer at a gulp.

"Poor old Lucy has finally mastered sending an e-mail," Philippa commented.

"That's nice!"

"There are several on your desk in the study. All saying much the same thing. She must have expected you to hit reply on the spot."

"Well, I suppose I'll be doing that shortly," he answered dryly. "All about Tori, of course?"

Philippa nodded her thickly thatched platinum head. In her late seventies, she was a remarkably well-preserved woman: very active, mentally and physically. A fine horsewoman, she still rode out every day. "How I wish Michael had never died! Probably planned it, with Livinia for a wife," she added waspishly.

"Except it wouldn't have felt right. Nothing in this world would have parted Michael from his only love—his daughter."

Philippa sighed deeply. "I know that, dear. I was just making a sick joke. The proverbial cat would have been a better mother than Livinia."

"Agreed. So, what's Tori done this time?" he asked. "God knows how she's missed out on spending a night in the cells."

"Darling girl!" Philippa murmured fondly.

"Little firebrand," Haddo tacked on tersely.

"She's by no means the wild-child the media like to make out," Philippa spoke up loyally.

"You must be the only one in the family not to agree with them, Pip. I know how protective you are of her—"

"And you're *not?*" Philippa's eyebrows met up with her hairline.

"I have to be—as you well know. Don't—and I mean *don't*—tell me it's anything to do with drugs?"

"Absolutely not, dear." Philippa looked shocked. "Tori swore to me she would never touch them."

"And how true is that?" he asked tersely. "They're all around her. She's out every night of the week. Wild parties at the weekend. Always with a posse of press in hot pursuit. And that boyfriend of hers—Morcombe."

"Ah, but it's Josh Morcombe who spent the night in the cells," Philippa now informed him. "Driving under the influence, I'm afraid," she said ruefully. "Unfortunately Tori happened to be in the car with him. That guaranteed a lot of coverage. A couple of their friends were in the back. They'd all been at some nightclub. Anyway, Josh isn't a proper boyfriend, Haddo. She's broken up with him. I believe her latest boyfriend doesn't have two beans to rub together. Tori has never cared about money."

His laugh was short. "Why would she? She's never been without it. So that's the latest misadventure? She was in a car with Morcombe?"

Philippa took a good swig of her drink. 'Nothing happened to Tori. I suppose the police gave them all a talking-to."

"I should damned well think so," he said shortly. "She can't continue like this."

"No, she can't," Philippa agreed. "She's so ferociously bright, that's the thing!"

"She never finished her degree."

"And she was doing so well."

"She's never held down a job. We know she's clever, but she should be making something of herself—not leading this mindless life that can only get her into big trouble."

"Can I tell you, dear, why she didn't finish her degree?" Philippa interrupted gently.

"Pip, I already know. Tori can't put her perfectly good mind to anything."

"Some of the other students—"

"Not the boys?" he jeered.

"Well, no, not the boys. The male of the species loves her. But some of the girls gave her a hard time. She had her hangers-on, of course, but some of the young women who were jealous of her beauty and brains, spread some pretty nasty rumours behind her back. No substance in them, of course. Envy is one of the deadly sins, after all."

"So she quit uni," Haddo said, his expression still severe, "and probably hasn't read a book since. You still haven't told me what Lucinda expects me to do. Though I'm no stranger to her pleas for help. There was never any hope of a quiet life with Tori. She's on a quest to pour as much questionable experience into her young life as humanly possible."

Philippa sighed. "Lucy loves Tori dearly, I know, but she's an ineffectual sort of person."

"That's because she's always had everything done for her," Haddo replied. "But on the plus side, Lucinda is a good woman—and she *is* Tori's grandmother. Tori wasn't safe with that sleazy Barry around."

Philippa pulled a fastidious face. "Livinia has made a career out of marrying the wrong people. Tori still believes it was her grandmother who brought pressure on Livinia to let her go."

"Let's keep it that way," Haddo said. "I don't want her to know it was me. Does Lucinda want me to go to Sydney to read Tori the Riot Act?"

"Reading between the lines, I'd say Lucy wants you to bring Tori back here. Personally, I think it's a great idea. It will keep her out of harm's way, and allow any adverse publicity to die down. You can give the dear girl a job."

Haddo's laugh was short. "That's the thing missing in Tori's life," he said dryly. "A job."

"So there you are. You're the boss. Give her one. You

were bred for being the boss, Haddo dear. Nothing comes easier."

Haddo's chiselled mouth compressed. "Don't mention *easy* and *Tori* in the same breath. Actually, there is something she could do," he said musingly. But he was not sure it would work. It would certainly help them all out if it did, but he didn't know what Tori would think about becoming schoolmarm to more than a dozen station kids, plus the really little people—the four-year-olds.

"*I* know." Philippa aware of everything that went on at the station, read his mind. "She can take over from Tracey." Mallarinka being so isolated had its own one-teacher school. Tracey Bryant was the teacher in residence, and had been for the past two years.

"That's what I was thinking," Haddo said.

"At least until Tracey is over her morning sickness and the pregnancy is well established." Philippa regarded him with a pleased expression. Tracey was now the wife of Mallarinka's leading hand, Jim Bryant. Hired as a teacher for the station school, she had fallen in love with the very attractive Jim and quickly snaffled him up. Her first pregnancy, sadly, had ended in a miscarriage.

"Tori might have other ideas," Haddo said. "But it'll be a real coup getting her out here."

"Yep—well, you're the man to do it," Philippa replied with conviction.

The study was in darkness. Haddo flicked a switch, flooding a room that was larger than most people's libraries with light. A portrait of his greatly loved grandfather, Quentin, dominated the wall behind the massive partner's desk. This was a man's study, the furnishings and décor very much in the style of a gentleman's club. His grandfather had called it his inner sanctum, but he had always allowed him into it, even as a small child. Floor-to-ceiling glass-fronted mahogany cabinets housed books and trophies of all kinds, countless silver cups, ribbons, awards, photographs of family with famous guests at the station. A magnificent gilded bronze horse stood on a tall plinth in front of a glass panel that had been cut out of the wall. By daylight it gave a view of the garden and two splendid date palms planted by an Afghani trader in the late 1880s.

There were two photographs of Tori on the desk. He had put them there himself. One had been taken when she was about twelve, mounted on a horse much too big for her, the other by a professional photographer on the morning of her sixteenth birthday. Her enchanting smiling face looked out at him, vibrant with life. That was before the day had gone to hell.

Abruptly he picked up the three or four e-mails Lucinda had sent. Pip had printed them off and put them in order, securing them with a paperclip. They all said roughly the same thing: Lucinda was desperately worried about her granddaughter, especially the crowd she was mixing with currently. Most of them were years older. Tori—unfortunately—had moved out of her own age group. Lucinda fully appreciated he was "an extremely busy man", but she wouldn't ask if she didn't believe the situation called for his active intervention. Tori only listened to him anyway.

That was news to him.

It wasn't possible to get away until the end of the week. He would let Lucinda know he would be arriving the coming Saturday. They could have a good talk then.

The beautiful Rushford heiress, of all people, an Outback schoolmarm. The thought gave him a wry laugh.

*Sydney, Capital of New South Wales*

Tori had spent the afternoon at the shelter for which she was a silent patron. She had a few other pet projects—breast cancer research was high up on the list; she had had no idea a woman could contract the disease so *young*—but she always insisted her philanthropy be kept strictly private. So far her requests had been honoured. Whenever she visited the shelter she always wore a dark wig and a headscarf tied pirate fashion. Her long red hair was a dead giveaway. To aid anonymity she dressed Gothic, black from head to toe, with the obligatory black boots on her feet. She thought she looked suitably disguised, but despite the less than flattering gear, her natural beauty shone through.

The mother of one of her girlfriends, Tiffany, had focused her interest on the shelter. Tiffany's million-a-year barrister father—street angel, home devil—regularly beat up on Tiffany's mother. Never in places that showed. Incredibly, Tiffany's mother, a beautiful woman, bore the abuse in silence, full of shame, until her teenage son Luke had, one momentous night, threatened to kill his father if he didn't stop. Right there and then. The threat had come as a rude shock, and mercifully had worked. Luke's father had picked up on the avenging light in his son's eyes—and on the golf iron in his son's strong young hands. So it had been Tiffany's mother who had told her about the women's shelter on Wyndham Street, and the good work they did. Tori had become a patron first day out.

Her visit to the shelter, talking to the women and children there who lived in constant fear, only served to draw attention to the extravagant harbourside party that was now going on all around her. All the bigwigs and the high rollers were there, and the so-called celebrities who always appeared in the society pages—she was one of them—anyone, in fact, on the Rich List. Getting on the bandwagon had to be one of the most stupid things she had ever done. But she had been so caught up in it, it was near impossible to get off.

It was only halfway through the evening, yet already she was fed up. What was wrong with her all of a sudden? The truth was, she wasn't really a party girl—though she didn't expect anyone to believe her. You could say an accident of birth—being an heiress and all—had brought her to a place where she didn't really belong. What she really wanted….*really* wanted…

*Time you grew up, Tori. You ain't gonna get it.*

God, that music was *loud.* She felt like finding her hosts and lodging a complaint. She could feel her head pounding. The evening had been doomed from the start.

She looked towards the spacious entrance hall.

"Vicki—a dance?"

This was an offer she could well refuse. "No, thanks, Tim."

"Come on, babe, I insist!' Tim, the airhead son of one of the state's biggest developers, clicked his fingers energetically.

"Not now." She waved Tim off, ducking and weaving through the crush of people. There had to be at least a thousand!

A moment more and she came to a dead halt. Shock poured into her. At first she thought she might be hallucinating. It wasn't possible. Maybe she was dazed by the events of the day? Before the shelter she had attended a very boring charity breakfast and fashion parade, then she had talked with Trish Harvey, the editor of a top magazine, who was trying to persuade her into a fashion shoot. Hallucinating was ruled out! She kept religiously to her vow never to touch drugs when dope was all around her. She had, however, tossed back a couple of non-lethal cocktails when she'd arrived, just to get in the mood. The rest of the time she had drunk club soda. She felt stone-cold sober, yet she was in the middle of a surreal experience.

She blinked hard. The vision didn't go away. It became even clearer.

Across the jam-packed room, filled with laughing, drinking, gyrating partygoers, was Haddo—in the flesh. It didn't seem possible. How could he possibly be here? Yet there he was, standing head and shoulders above everyone else, a man who instantly commanded attention. Mimi Holland the pop star was trying to hit on him—what girl wouldn't?—but his astonishing blue gaze was moving like a searchlight over the crowd. She knew who he was looking for.

*Her.*

Would you believe it? She nearly lay down and cried. There was only one explanation. Nan must have sent for him. She had to do something. Like scream! Only screaming was too tame an option, considering how agitated she felt. Hastily she tugged at the hem of her silver mini-skirt. Wrong place. Wrong clothes. It would always be that way with Haddo. She tried to lose herself in the swirling crowd, flopping one side of her long hair over her eye. It wasn't a perfect disguise, like her Goth, but it would have to do.

"Come on, Vicki, dance with me?" Another guy surged towards her, looking half stoned, but she briskly waved him off, wedging herself up against a soaring indoor plant. To no avail.

"Tori!"

Instantly she was thrown back to her old weakness. Haddo was there, looking down at her, his blue eyes taking in the hairstyle—she had had her riotous mane straightened for the night—the itsy-bitsy sparkly dress, the silver stilettos. "It wasn't at all hard to spot you," he said dryly, then, as adroitly as if he were cutting out a cute little poddy calf, he manoeuvred her into a relatively quiet nook.

"Haddo!" she retorted with feigned delight, regardless of her gut-churning emotions.

It hurt to see him. Really *hurt.* Once she would have walked on her hands for Haddo. He looked great. Right up there with the all-time hunks, and a very snappy dresser even when casual. His black tee was top quality, so were the black jeans, and the super bomber jacket in sexy, supple bronze Italian leather worn over them must have cost a mint. The breeze off the Harbour had tousled his hair, so a crow-black lock fell onto his tanned forehead. The back of his hair curled up enticingly at his nape. His blazing blue eyes sparkled. Was there ever such a great combination as crow-black hair and intensely blue eyes?

"Had no trouble finding me?" she queried. "You couldn't have, since you're here."

He smiled down at her, in that super self-assured way he had. "Isn't there something dangerous about wearing your hair like that?" he asked with seeming concern. "You could bump into something."

She wanted to stomp off. Instead she tossed back the offending curtain of hair. "How did you get here?"

"The Rolls. What else?" He stared about him with an expression bordering on wonderment.

"Brody bring you?" Brody was her grandmother's long-time major-domo and chauffeur. His wife, Dawn, was the housekeeper and cook—a very good one.

"Having someone else drive me brings me out in a cold sweat," he mocked.

"You could have walked, or even hitch-hiked," she pointed out with sarcasm, still trying to get the dizzies under control. "It's not all that far away."

"I was just too anxious to see you." His glance dipped to her long slender legs. "Where does that dress disappear to when you sit down?" he asked, as if he really wanted to know.

"God, you're so old-fashioned, Haddo!" she said shortly, close to despair. "You should take in the bright lights more often."

He shrugged a careless shoulder. "I wouldn't live in the city for a cool million."

"And this is a guy who's worth—what?" she jeered.

"More than you, anyway. But enough of the repartee. I've come to escort you home, Victoria, if you'd be so kind as to come without making a scene. Your grandmother has become very worried about you of late."

That incensed her. "She has no need to be," she said loftily.

"Not even *you* believe that." He chopped her off. "I had a quick glance through the newspapers Lucinda showed me. They said some pretty mean things about you and your crowd."

"So what?" She flushed hotly. "It's all envy-driven. I found out early that envy is a terrible thing. Just about everyone who writes negative things about me suffers from the sin of envy."

"I must be one who doesn't."

"Well, I always did bring out the best in you."

Their fairly crackling exchange was cut short as a young man wearing round glasses suddenly appeared at Tori's shoulder. "Vicki, sweetheart! How lovely to see you. Kiss, kiss." He moved right in close, planting kisses European style on Tori's cheeks. "You've no idea how I've missed you. I see Josh landed himself in a bit of trouble. I warned you about him, didn't I?"

"All the time," said Tori.

"And this is?" The young man, Peter Weaver, stared up at Haddo, who was dwarfing him, with interest. Peter had never seen the big guy before. Mighty impressive—even if Vicki wasn't looking at him exactly *lovingly.*

"My cousin Haddon—Haddon Rushford," Tori said, curling her fingers around Peter's arm. "Haddo, this is Peter Weaver."

"Now I get it! The cattle baron!" Peter went to slap Haddo on the back, but stopped himself just in time. The cattle baron didn't look the type of guy one slapped on the back. "What brings you to Sydney, Haddon?" Peter asked, slipping an arm around Vicki's tiny waist instead.

"Business, Peter," Haddo answered. "Actually, I'm here to collect Tori. Her grandmother isn't feeling particularly well. She wants Tori home."

"Oh, no!" Peter moaned. "I've just got here. Took me half an hour to get through the door with all these people. Say, Haddon, do you know just how many women are eyeballing you?"

"He's used to it," Tori answered, sounding disgusted.

"Could you make it a half-hour?" Peter pleaded. "Come on, Haddon, relax. I wanna dance with Vicki."

"I'm sure you'll find another dancing partner, Peter," Haddo said pleasantly, taking Tori's slender arm. "Tori always puts her grandmother first. It's one of the reasons we all love her to bits."

Peter realised immediately his pleas would do no good at all. The cattle baron meant what he said. "Night, Vicki!" Peter called mournfully, watching the crowd automatically fall back to make a path for the big guy. There were lots of men in the room multimillionaires—his own dad was one—but none had Rushford's presence. He supposed it was the man-of-action stuff, the hero figure. Peter spent a fortune on fake tan. Rushford's was *real.* Good thing he was Vicki's *cousin.* Honestly, no other guy would be in any race with the cattle baron for a rival.

"Why am I supposed to do what you tell me?" Tori asked wrathfully, aware of Haddo's impact on the room and not liking it one bit.

"Leaving early, Vicki?" Mimi Holland separated herself from the crowd, lamenting. She was unable to take her eyes off the drop-dead gorgeous man with the skinny heiress. Who *was* he? From the expression on Vicki's face, he was no fun at all—gorgeous as he was. Mimi didn't believe that for a moment. This was a seriously sexy guy. God, she should have found out his name.

"That was Mimi Holland," Tori told Haddo sharply.

He nodded. "I believe we met briefly."

"You're not normal at all, are you? Most guys would leap at the chance of hooking up with Mimi."

"Really?" Haddo sounded dubious. "You can't enjoy this sort of thing, surely?" he asked, looking at the couples dancing with single-minded abandon, some of them kissing, others looking as if they urgently needed a private room.

"Again, most people would kill for an invitation."

"Good God!" he exclaimed. "Wouldn't they be better off working out at a gym?"

"Funny," she said tartly. "I have to say goodnight to my hosts."

"Of course you do. Good manners get one smoothly through life. I'll come with you. I just can't imagine how your hosts got to be so notorious, can you?"

They were moving out into the star-spangled night when Haddo suddenly said, "Where's your coat? It's cold with the breeze off the water."

"I don't feel it," she said briskly, trying to sound as tough as nails. She had been driven right up to the door in an air-conditioned Rolls. She hadn't wanted a top coat to spoil her appearance.

"Oh, for God's sake, Tori." He tutted. "You never

used to be so vain." He stripped off his leather jacket and held it cape-like for her to slip on.

"I don't want that," she said, almost fearfully, as though to wear something of his would be dangerous.

"Put it on."

No mistaking that for an order. She did as she was told. His jacket enveloped her, and then some. How foolish she had been to accept it. Instantly the warmth of his body hit her, rocking her to her wounded heart. His male scent was so familiar it gave her the most piercing sensation of intimacy. Her limbs lost their strength. It always happened when she and Haddo were together. Why *was* that? She had the dismal notion she was about to topple over. To counteract the peculiar feeling she slowed her steps, uncharacteristically awkward in her silver stilettos.

He took her arm, steadying her. "You're lost in that."

"I only put it on to make you happy," she replied ungraciously. "So where is it?" She stared about the light-bathed drive.

"The Rolls?"

"What else? Unless you've organised a horse and carriage?"

"It's out in the street. There was no room here." The drive was packed with luxury cars.

"Then you'd better take a peek outside," she advised. "There's bound to be a photographer hanging around."

He glanced down at her. "So you're going to slip the jacket off? Is that it? Strut your stuff?"

"I'm going to do no such thing," she said huffily, trying without success to pull away.

They were out on the tree-lined avenue and, just as

she had predicted, a man with a camera—Tori recognised him as one of the usual gang—began to move swiftly towards them.

Tori snuggled deeper into Haddo's jacket. It had become her igloo, shielding her from the chill wind and from plain sight. "Why is it always a man?" she muttered. "I've never laid eyes on a woman photographer yet. It's all men shoving a camera in your face."

"You can't blame them, though. The public devours this sort of stuff." Haddo's tone lifted a few notches. It was a voice long used to being obeyed. "No photographs, pal." He spoke in an unconfrontational way, yet a stone-deaf man would have got the message.

The photographer gave a conciliatory chuckle. "Who's the little lady you're hiding there? It's not one of the celebs, is it? Or maybe it's our own little home-grown heiress?"

"Just do what I tell you," Haddo returned crisply. "Move out of the way, pal."

"Hey!"

Her head withdrawn like a tortoise, Tori heard the photographer cry out. Agitated, she parted the leather jacket and peered out. The photographer would be no match for Haddo. In fact he was reeling away. Surely Haddo hadn't hit him?

"I don't like cameras being shoved in my face," Haddo was saying, almost pleasantly. "Don't worry. I'm not going to damage it. I'll give it back to you the moment we're on our way."

The photographer didn't answer. He simply followed in their wake.

"It's astonishing how people pay attention when

you're six-feet-three," Tori commented as they drove off. The photographer was now busily snapping away at whatever images he could get: the back of her grandmother's Rolls, the number plate.

Haddo didn't answer for a minute or two. Then, "What the hell is happening to you, Tori?" he asked, in a dead serious voice.

*Here it comes—the lecture!* She averted her head, staring out of the window at the star-spangled night. "Isn't it obvious? I'm being kidnapped. Getting photographed goes with the territory, Haddo. Those guys get paid for their pictures. Sometimes it's quite a lot of money. I don't need to tell you that."

"And it's you they seem to want to see."

She blushed hotly. "Hey, they won't want to see me when I'm old."

"If you *get* to be old," he rasped. "That's one of the reasons I'm here. I told you, your grandmother showed me all those newspaper clippings about Morcombe's driving under the influence. The reason it got so much coverage was *you.* It can't go on like this, Tori. I won't have it. Rushford has been a well-respected name in this country since the early days of settlement."

She positively hated him then. "So what do you want me to do? Sing the National Anthem? Isn't it wonderful the Rushfords are so unquestionably top drawer? You must have hated it when your dad blotted his copybook, running off with that Aleesha, or whatever her name is."

"I don't want or need your opinion about that, Tori," he said shortly. "And it's Shona who is now his wife."

"Shona, then. Pardon me. Of course you don't want

to talk about your dad. You'd rather talk about me, and how totally immature I am."

"Are you trying to tell me you're adult?" he asked scathingly.

It was like a very hard slap. She swallowed hard. "I'll never be adult enough for you, Haddo." Wasn't that the stark truth?

He flicked a glance over her small, mutinous face. "The reason I'm in Sydney, Tori, is because your grandmother asked me to come. We've had a long discussion, and the upshot is I'm going to take you back to Mallarinka with me. Once there, I intend to put you to work."

That piece of news positively galvanised her. She swung her head, aghast. "I'm an heiress," she protested strongly. "I don't *need* to work."

"We're all supposed to work," he said, in a bracing type of voice. "Work won't kill you."

"And you'll be my boss?" The very thought sent jolts of rebellion through her.

"Don't sound so shocked. Who else?"

She clenched her long, beautifully manicured fingers in her lap. "I'd be a lot happier working for some *other* dictator. So what have you got in mind for me?" she asked grimly. "Even supposing I'll go."

"Oh, you'll go, all right." His tone deepened.

"Where does it say I have to obey you?"

He shot her a brief glance, one black eyebrow up. "Actually, there's a file about a hundred pages long. "

"You just wait until I'm twenty-five," she said, gritting her small teeth.

"I can't wait, actually. Until then I'm not quitting on you. I'm the boss. You'll do what I say."

"Beast."

His handsome mouth was amused. "I don't have to be. Just do what I tell you and everything will be okay."

"So what do you have in mind?" she asked, her voice dripping sarcasm. "Housework? General maintenance? Camp cook? I can't make a damper, and I'm rarely invited into a kitchen. Or do you intend to take me on as a jillaroo? I'd need to polish up my skills for that."

He sighed. It sounded quite genuine. "Don't you feel you really should have finished your education? There's still plenty of time. Anyway, I have decided on a job for you." Smoothly he overtook a slow-moving car. The young driver saluted them, obviously in fun.

"To hell with that!" she growled. "This is silly. I'm not going *anywhere* with you. Damned if I am."

"Oh, yes, you are." His striking face in the light of the dash indicated he didn't expect nor would he tolerate disobedience. "Or I'll definitely cut your allowance. Big-time."

She shook her head, infuriated, blinking back hot tears. "And you're just miserable enough to do it. It's all for my own good, of course."

He glanced at her. His jacket all but swallowed her up. "Your well-being is very important to me, Tori."

She snorted in disgust. "You really expect me to believe that?" At the very least he should feel guilty he had broken her heart.

"Well, it's true," he answered quietly. "And you *want* to believe it, I think, deep down."

"No way," she scoffed. "So, what is this little job? And just how long am I supposed to endure detention?"

He flashed her just a glimpse of his marvellous smile. "For as long as it takes, Victoria."

"But that's blackmail!" she gasped. "It's a violation of my human rights. Listen to me, Haddo." She twisted her body in the seat, staring at his chiselled profile. "I need a time-frame here. A month, two, six months, and you'll pay me to go away. Put it this way. I don't much mind going back to Mallarinka. But, unless you've forgotten, I've become addicted to hating you."

"Now, that's just plain childish," he said. "A childish passion. I think what you actually mean is you're addicted to *pretending* you hate me."

"You—are—so—bloody arrogant," she muttered. She couldn't handle Haddo at all. She just wasn't equipped.

"Play it cool, now, Tori," he advised.

"I'm serious."

"So am I."

"God!" she moaned, hugging herself beneath his jacket and toiling away at keeping angry. "Okay—let me have it? What's the job? If you think I'm going to clean all those blasted chandeliers or all that silver you've got another think coming. I wouldn't mind working in the office an hour or so a day. But the rest of the time I want off. I mightn't love you any more, but I do love Mallarinka."

"Well, obviously you'll be given time off. That's only fair. But I expect you to do a fair day's work for a fair day's pay. I *will* pay you."

"If you feel you have to," she said, bittersweet. "Gee,

just think! I had all these parties and functions lined up. Instead, I'll be doing—what? You're being very coy."

"You'll be taking over the station school from Tracey Bryant," Haddo announced.

"You're joking!" she cried, appalled. "You're having me on, aren't you?"

"On the contrary. I'm dead serious."

'So what's wrong with Tracey?" she burst out jerkily. "I thought she loved it?"

"Tracey is pregnant."

"Ah, *lovely!*" She softened at the news. "Better luck this time."

"And not at this stage terribly well."

"Ooh!"

"Will you stop oohing and aahing?" he said crisply. "She's okay. She's going to stay with her sister in Warwick for a while. I had been considering hiring a replacement until Tracey is ready to come back to the job—she will be given adequate maternity leave—but out of the blue you've been delivered to me on a silver platter."

"If you're trying to make me angry, you're succeeding."

"I'm not trying to make you angry at all."

"You only have to look at me to make me angry," she fumed.

"I realise that." There was a slight hardness in his tone. "Anyway, to get back to your job. I won't say you're *perfect* for it—you might be tempted to play hookey with the kids—but I think you can manage. What do you say?"

"Hire that replacement."

"Okay, I can do that. If you don't like the idea of

being schoolmarm to a bunch of kids, there's always the station store. The hours aren't as good. Nine to five as opposed to nine to three."

She looked towards him, a sigh rippling up from her throat. "Haddo, you know perfectly well I have no training whatsoever for teaching kids," she said tightly.

"You completed two years of your arts degree," he pointed out. "You were a straight A student. I think you could manage it if you brushed up a bit."

She groaned. "What about the little kids? The really *little* kids? That's childminding."

"Take it or leave it," he clipped out. "But believe me, you'll be on Mallarinka to do a job of work."

Her emerald eyes flashed. "The fact you can dictate to me like that makes me want to hit you."

He laughed heartlessly.

Ten fraught minutes later they were driving through the massive wrought-iron gates of the Rushford mansion. Inside the six-car garage, the Rolls slid into its parking bay alongside the Mercedes Lucinda used on the occasions when she drove herself, and a silver SUV that "came in handy"—Lucinda's words. Brody and Dawn's private vehicles, little runarounds, were parked to the left.

Immediately the Rolls stopped, Tori threw open the door and jumped out, exhaling a long pent-up breath. Relief? No, not relief. What, then? High tension? She couldn't possibly relax around Haddo. It was a deeply complex thing beyond understanding. She had to pass him to get to the steps that led up to the house. That alone gave her the jitters. How could *any* man be so sexy? Hastily she slipped out of his jacket and held it out to him, shaking it a little, as though if he didn't take it immediately she would drop it on the concrete. Her heart was beating awfully fast. She felt naked now, without its warmth and protection.

"What? No thanks?" he chided. "Where are your manners, Victoria?" His eyes were so brilliant and mocking they unnerved her.

"I put them away when you're around," she responded tartly.

"I haven't failed to notice. Why so jittery?"

She was endeavouring to inch by him, but he caught her arm. "For God's sake, Tori, I'm absolutely harmless."

"Not damned likely!" she shot back. She could feel the electric connection that surged between them. For her it meant intense physical attraction. God knew what it meant to him.

"Look, why don't we get this over?" he suggested.

"Get *what* over?" *Oh, oh, oh!* A gaping abyss opened up. She could feel her heart commence a slow drumroll. "I haven't the slightest idea what you're talking about, Haddo," she told him sharply. Lies, all lies.

"I'm pretty sure you do," he replied. "You've been wondering since you were a kid what it would be like if I kissed you."

Her cheeks flamed. "Surely you've already done it?" she cried, affronted. "You *have* kissed me. Remember?" She lifted her chin.

"Sorry. Actually, I do recall the two of us sharing a pillow for about five seconds," he said, very dryly. "I had no option but to let you go, Tori."

"After lashing me with your tongue." The past was swirling around them like a London fog.

"It was a hellish situation. If I hurt you—"

"Ah, don't give me the *if!*" she cried scornfully. "I'm allergic to ifs."

He kept his sapphire gaze trained on her. "My suggestion is this. If only to prevent you from having a nervous breakdown every time we're thrown together, why don't we get one *last* kiss out of the way? Think of it as closure, if you like. You may well decide you don't love me any more."

"I never loved you in the first place," she said, with furious offended pride. "You're just trying to make a fool of me."

His eyes dazzled. "And you haven't given *me* a rough ride these past four years?"

"So now you're going to take me hostage? Is that it? You want to get square? You want to make me grovel?"

"How can you possibly look at it like that, Tori?" he asked with cool reason. "It's not an end-of-the-world situation. I just want to get a few things settled."

How could he do that, when *she* was becoming more and more unsettled? "Well, that's too bad, because I'm not ready to settle anything. I'm going upstairs." She tried to speak firmly, only the quiver in her voice let her down.

"We'll both go up in a minute," he promised. "This won't take long."

Despite his casual manner, she could see the sizzling intensity in his eyes.

"Haddo, no!" She threw up a hand, bracing herself for the inevitable avalanche of sensation.

He could see the panic in her eyes. "Come here to me," he said gently.

The odd tenderness in his voice played hell with her mixed-up emotions.

*Stick to your agenda!* her inner voice warned her. *Don't let him do this to you. Where's your pride?*

The only trouble was she was in an awful emotional mess. Her brain was telling her one thing, her body another.

Her body won. It was a big lamentation in life how often that happened. Her defences, so carefully constructed over the past four years, imploded.

*Give in. Give in,* her poor weak woman's body cried out in anguish.

Not a peep out of her brain. She could feel the meltdown start up inside her. In one way she hated it. It gave her no peace. The tragic truth was, for all she had previously stated, she *did* love him. Damn him! She had spent sixteen years loving him. It was going to take a heck of a lot more years than four more to flush him right out of her system. No wonder she felt like sobbing. The most humiliating thing was that from his expression he knew all about the fierce battle that was going on inside her. He was right in his element, playing the dominant, irresistible male.

He drew her to him. Nothing hurried, but very sure. He turned her face up to him. "Tell me how many times you've been kissed since then," he said, looking deeply into her eyes.

Suddenly she felt the balance of power had shifted slightly her way. She gave him a look of sparkling malice. "You really want to know?"

"I do." His tone turned edgy.

She threw off a bittersweet laugh. "Hundreds and hundreds of—"

Before she could get out *times* he silenced her. His mouth came down squarely over hers, so warm, so compelling, so utterly perfect to her, it ignited a flame of physical desire. Call her weak, call her a complete fake, she still yearned for him. The bitter truth was, she was a closed case.

Everything was lost in a tide of sensation. It swamped her, carrying her under. It was a mercy he was so much taller, because she desperately needed support. Why did this happen with Haddo and no one else? Why did her legs go so weak and trembly? So, for that matter, were her arms. It was a kind of physical disintegration. She couldn't have pushed him away even if she'd wanted to. Hers was a classic case of obsessive love. Only obsessive love never made anyone happy. She should know. People died for love. Killed for love. Some gave up *everything* for love, only to finish up with nothing but untold grief and unending heartache. Sex *and* love could be a fatal combination.

When he finally released her all she could manage was the single word. "God!"

When you loved someone as she loved Haddo it went on for ever, and there was no way to dislodge it.

Tremors were still racking her. Her voice was so husky she might have been coming down with a cold. "Can I go now?" she found herself near pleading.

"I'm not stopping you."

They were in her grandmother's garage, yet she felt as if they were sealed off from the rest of the world. She couldn't look at him. She couldn't allow him to search her eyes. Her eyes had always betrayed her.

He was standing very still, yet somehow he was giving the powerful impression he was about to swoop on her again and pull her into his arms. She was terrified that this time her arms would go up and lock around his neck, never to let go. Turned out she had no pride at all. The only way she had been able to carry off her role of indifference was in company. When they were alone together it was a vastly different matter.

"So? Are you going to move?" She made a truly Gallic gesture, lifting her shoulders and holding out her hands.

Haddo obliged without haste, giving her just enough room to push past him. He waited until she'd reached the bottom of the stairs before asking, "How long will it take you to pack?"

She felt liberated by the space between them. "Don't you supply a school uniform?" she asked with sharp sarcasm.

"I thought you'd had enough of uniforms? You certainly won't be needing anything like you've got on now. Or dare I say *nearly* got on?"

She swung back to him, her beautiful auburn hair in disarray, green eyes glittering, a flush enhancing her alabaster skin. "*You* mightn't know it, but this is a *great* dress. I'm a trendsetter."

"You mean the less you wear, the trendier you get?"

She laughed hoarsely. "Oh, go to the devil! By the way, I'm going to bring a friend with me." The idea had presented itself to her on the instant. Her attitude defied him to object.

"You're kidding!"

"I couldn't be more serious."

A warning glitter came into his eyes. "I just hope you're not going to tell me your friend is male?"

"Why? Would you put your foot down?" she cooed, pursing her lips provocatively.

"You bet!"

He would too. No idle threat. "My friend is female," she snapped. "And she's desperately in need of a change of scene."

"In trouble with the law, is she?" he asked dryly.

"She's quite respectable. Her name is Chrissy Graham." If anyone at the shelter needed help it was Chrissy, with her broken front tooth and her less visible broken ribs. She might leap at the chance of an Outback holiday. Then again, she mightn't. "She's a couple of years younger than I am. Maybe eighteen months."

"Let's see—that makes her barely out of school. So what's the connection?"

"She's a friend, okay?" Tori answered in some agitation, still feeling threatened.

Her whole body was thrumming with an uncontrollable excitement. She wanted to go back into his arms again. She wanted him to pry open her mouth, let the tip of his tongue slide over her teeth. He had only to touch her for her veins to turn into molten glass.

"Am I allowed to I ask where Chrissy lives?" Haddo's tone was laconic.

"She lives in the inner city," she supplied, purposely vague. "She doesn't have any money. She's young, and she's struggling. She's had a chaotic life."

She didn't tell him that Chrissy, after the death of her

mother, with her father unable to cope, had been put in a home at age eleven. Over the years she had been bounced from one home to the next. Set free at sixteen, in under a week flat she had fallen into the clutches of an abusive boyfriend—hence her periodic retreats to the shelter.

"I want to help her," she told Haddo defiantly. "Are you going to help *me?*" She was straining not to shout at him, but she couldn't seem to control her voice.

"If you think it's going to make your detention any easier, by all means." He lifted an arm to switch off the lights. "What is she? A guest?"

"Why are you asking?" She frowned crossly at him.

"I just thought she might require room service. You, my girl, as I said, are going to *work.*"

"I'm not damned well useless, I'll have you know!" She flounced on up the stairs, beautiful long legs very much on display. "You can find a job for Chrissy too," she threw over her shoulder.

"What can the mysterious Chrissy do? Can she ride?"

She swung about, a considering frown on her face. "I would think so. She was born on a farm."

"Lovely!" Haddo said with exaggerated satisfaction. "I'll put her straight to muster work. Now, I can't be too long away from the station. I'd like to leave the day after tomorrow. It will be an early start. I'd appreciate it if you and Chrissy could get yourselves organised by then."

She shrugged. "I'll never get my punishment over otherwise. Just remember," she warned, "*I'm* the one under house arrest. Not Chrissy."

"No need to shout at me." He began to mount the stairs, tall commanding, insufferably sure of himself. "I can't wait to meet her. Tell me, has she heard terrible things about me?"

"She hasn't heard a damned thing about you," Tori told him fiercely, reaching out to seize the door handle. He beat her to it.

"Well, that's a relief. Allow me." His hand was over hers: a beautiful hand, long-fingered, strong, calluses on the pads. His tone mocked her.

Tori took a deep shaky breath. At times like this it was brought home forcibly that skin was the largest organ in the body. *Skin on skin!*

*Oh, God!* she thought helplessly.

*Try to think of it this way.* Her inner voice unexpectedly came to her aid. *Love is only a four-letter word.*

But it was a magic word. That was the thing. A word so powerful it changed lives.

She burst into the house as if a stalker was close on her heels, not Haddo. "Goodnight," she tossed at him, very fast. "I know I'll sleep soundly knowing that was our *last* kiss."

"How long will it remain the last, I wonder?" Haddo called after her.

She didn't answer, but a fierce flush burned her cheeks.

## CHAPTER TWO

BRODY had the job of driving them to the commercial airstrip, where the Beech Baron awaited them, but first Chrissy had to be picked up from outside the women's shelter. Tori had made a quick dash to the shelter the day before, to issue Chrissy with an invitation, not really sure whether Chrissy would accept or not. The truly bizarre thing she had learned about some of the battered women at the shelter was that husbands or partners only had to say they were sorry, they hadn't meant it, and cite pressures and stresses, for the women to pack up their few possessions and return to the same dreadful situation. Not only that, but take their poor frightened little kids with them. It was heartbreaking! But Chrissy deserved a chance. She had sworn to Tori she was going to break free—"If only he'll let me!"

When Tori had issued the invitation Chrissy had burst into tears. "God, Vicki, I don't believe this," she had sobbed, desperate to take the support offered. "No one has done anythin' for me. Ever! Not since Mum died."

Tori had wiped the mascara streaks from Chrissy's thin cheeks. "You're going to love it, Chrissy," she assured her. "And best of all you'll be safe."

Chrissy's bully of a boyfriend would be in huge trouble if he ever found out where Chrissy was and decided to follow. One could almost wish he would, just so he could be taught a lesson he would never forget. Violence against women and children occurred everywhere in the world, but not on Mallarinka. Chrissy would be safe.

As it happened, the Master of Mallarinka was now asking, "If it's not a rude question, Victoria, where exactly are we going?" Haddo was up front with Brody. Tori was in the back.

"Not far now," she said vaguely, as the Rolls proceeded on its stately progress through one of the least desirable parts of town. Gangs of adolescents at neither school nor work were standing about on street corners. A few turned to make vulgar salutes at the Rolls, accompanied by the usual look of challenge in their eyes.

"I've a feeling you haven't been straight with me," Haddo observed crisply.

"No kidding?"

"Well, if I offend you I don't give a damn. Chrissy isn't a prostitute, is she? One with a heart of gold?"

Brody turned a laugh into a cough, while Tori said sharply. "Of course not! Chrissy is a good kid. She just needs a break."

"It's a women's shelter, isn't it?" Haddo guessed, staring out at a heavily moustachioed bald guy who looked like a movie bank robber.

"You've never seen such sad cases in your whole life," Tori lamented. "Oh, there she is!"

Up ahead Chrissy was waiting in front of the shelter, a suitcase at her feet. Tori had warned her in advance she would most probably be picking her up in a Rolls-

Royce—something that had made Chrissy choke with laughter—so when she saw the Rolls approaching Chrissy began to wave a hanky very energetically.

"And that is Chrissy?" Haddo turned his head over his shoulder to enquire.

"Miss Victoria takes a real interest in the shelter," said Brody, a long time confidante, with considerable approval in his tone. "No one could say Miss Victoria is lacking in heart," he added fondly.

"You dark horse, you, Miss Victoria." Haddo's blue eyes mocked her. "You've been very careful to keep that to yourself, haven't you?"

"That's the way I am!" she retorted breezily. "I notice you don't advertise all *your* numerous acts of philanthropy either, or all your good deeds. It's a family thing. Now, let me do the talking, Haddo," she said, as Brody pulled the big car into the kerb beside Chrissy, who was almost tap dancing in excitement.

"Go right ahead," he invited nonchalantly. "It'll take me a moment to catch my breath anyway."

A beaming Chrissy awaited them, decked out in her finest. Some might have said they were extraordinary garments. Others might have mistaken her for a little bag lady. A red beanie was pulled down over brown corkscrew curls that stuck out at random. Her ears were pierced with several metal rings. She wore a fake diamond stud in her nose. Red stockings to match her beanie clothed her brolga-thin legs. A pair of substantial black boots weighted down her small feet.

The two young women, who couldn't possibly have presented a more dissimilar image, exchanged hugs while a fascinated Haddo took in Chrissy at a glance.

Just what I need, he thought. Someone else to worry about. And as for Tori? Tori was constantly surprising him. Not that she hadn't always had a tender heart. This poor little waif, who showed every sign of having had a tough life, was Tori's friend—though he thought Chrissy could look a whole lot better minus the heavy metal, dressed in decent clothes and with more weight on her. They could take care of that part of it.

It was obvious she was wildly excited, even kissing Brody, who had stepped out of the Rolls to store her small tattered suitcase—she wasn't over-burdened with possessions—in the boot. Brody took the kiss well.

My turn! thought Haddo, detecting from long practice the look of anxiety Tori was trying to hide behind big black Gucci sunglasses.

"This is Haddo," Tori introduced him, rapid fire. *Get it over.*

Chrissy blushed scarlet and gave him a nerve-strangled, "Hello. Pleased to meet you, Haddo. Or should I call you Mr Rushford?" Haddo noticed the broken front tooth.

"Haddo will do," Tori clipped off for him.

He gave Tori a quick glance. "Well, you *did* say you'd do the talking. Nice to have you along, Chrissy," he said. That tooth had to be fixed. He filed it away for future attention. He didn't want to waste any more time, so he began to shepherd both young women into the back seat. "Better get going," he murmured to Brody as he slipped into the passenger seat. "Before someone throws a rock at the Rolls."

"Will do, sir," said Brody, surprised someone hadn't already done so.

* * *

The flight into Mallarinka was the most exciting event of Chrissy's young life. In fact it was the *only* flight Chrissy had ever taken. She had never been anywhere near a plane, much less seated in one, looking out at the white billowy clouds. It was all too fabulous! She had thought she was going to be apprehensive, but Haddo was a great pilot—and what was even more astonishing was that he flew his *own* plane. How cool was that? And so was *he.* Gorgeous, and such a gentleman. He treated her as if she was one of Vicki's *real* friends, instead of someone Vicki had been kind enough to rescue from a women's shelter.

Everyone at the shelter thought of Vicki as their guardian angel. Vicki had blushed when she had first heard it, and held up protesting hands.

"Listen up, ladies! You haven't got enough; I've got too much. It balances out."

Be that as it may, no other heiresses had ever stopped by. Vicki had heart.

They all knew her. Some had formed not terribly complimentary opinions—beautiful, an heiress, little asked of her, less expected, and so forth. They had seen the photographs in the newspapers and magazines. Photographers never seemed to get tired of her. And why not? She was amazingly beautiful, even when she came into the shelter dressed up in the Goth stuff and gave them all a good laugh. Nevertheless, it was just the most unlikely thing that *the* Victoria Rushford had turned up on the doorstep of the shelter wanting to help. Vicki and all of her friends were seriously rich, whereas for most of Chrissy's life she had had to struggle just to stay alive. It gave her an enormous feeling of security to know that just being a visitor on Mallarinka meant she was free of Zack's intimidation, and the periodic beltings when he was drunk. Easy for Zack to belt *her;* she would love to see him try to swing a punch at Haddo. That was if he could even reach Haddo's chin.

They had been flying over Mallarinka for some time. Now they were on their descent, which gave Chrissy a fresh burst of pleasure. For the first time she could see the homestead and all the outbuildings. It looked so exciting, yet bizarre. Who would expect what looked like a small town to be set down smack in the middle of absolutely nowhere? Chrissy had been born on a dairy farm near the lush Queensland/New South Wales border, and it was a fantastic experience to see the *real* Outback—especially from the air.

She was stunned by the vastness, the emptiness, and most of all the riot of dry ochre colours, that flared all over the landscape: the umbers, the yellows and purples, the orange and the dominant red. No wonder this was called the Red Centre. She had never thought of the Outback as full of colour, but more usually as arid, with wide brown land stricken by drought, but there it was beneath her, awe-inspiring. She was glorying in it. The fiery red of the plains that stretched to the horizon contrasted brilliantly with the cobalt blue of the sky and the big golden bushes like giant pincushions. She supposed it was spinifex, yet it made such a gilded splash.

Mallarinka—she loved the name—meant five lagoons. Haddo had told her. To her further astonishment, the station itself looked like a miraculous green sanctuary in a million square miles of shimmering red sand. She could feel the blood tingling in her veins. It was truly breathtaking—and she had to admit frightening too. It would be perilously easy to get lost down there. She knew—every city dweller did—that the Outback was a dangerous place, especially the desert. Poorly schooled, she had nevertheless learned about the early explorers who had perished there on their ill-fated expeditions. And Mallarinka was on the great desert fringe, the legendary Channel Country—a riverine desert and the stronghold of the nation's cattle kings.

It was just so *glamorous!* Like Haddo and Vicki. They were glamorous people. Their life was so very far removed from hers they might have existed on a different planet. Yet they couldn't have been nicer. Glamour in abundance they might have, but they completely lacked what she thought of as airs and graces. It gave her a warm feeling to know she had such friends.

To the west lay a huge area of hilly country that rose from the extraordinary flatness of the plains, making them appear much higher than they were. The peaks had eroded over eons into glowing rounded minarets, rust-red in the blazing sunlight, purple in the shadowy canyons. Beyond the wing-tip she could see a vast ocean of red sand, with towering dunes running in parallel lines for all the world like ocean waves. Closer in to the homestead there were numerous long pools of water, surrounded by trees. Those were the billabongs, and there were also the five lagoons. Excitedly she counted them. One glinted like silver foil, another was an incredible light blue, like aquamarine, two more had an opalescent milky-green sheen.

It was unearthly, unreal!

Chrissy considered herself the luckiest girl in the

world. From the first day they had met and clicked, Vicki had shown her nothing but kindness. She would have to find some way to repay her.

Philippa stood, straight as an arrow, at the front door to greet them. She extended her arms to the full and Tori went into them.

"Darling girl, I've missed you!" Philippa said, placing a gentle hand on Tori's luxuriant mane of hair, including Chrissy in her warm, welcoming smile.

"I've missed you too, Pip." Tori patted and rubbed her great-aunt's thin back, all the while blinking back a few radiant tears. "I expect you know Haddo kidnapped me?"

Philippa's face broke into a smile. "Haddo has always had your best interests at heart, dear. Anyway, it's so lovely to have you."

"This is my friend Chrissy, Pip." Tori turned to introduce them.

Chrissy didn't come unheralded—Philippa had been informed—so Chrissy too got a hug. Neither woman, young or old, faltered at going into an embrace. It was very difficult to resist Philippa who carried with her a natural air of authority that demanded deference, but a bred-in-the-bone kindness too.

"Now, what say I show you to your rooms?" Philippa said. "You can settle in, then we'll have some afternoon tea. Haddo, dear?" she called to Haddo, who was standing on the verandah, pointing to the suitcases—all Tori's with the exception of one—for Bert, the station handyman, to bring in. "Are you going to stay for afternoon tea?"

"Sure," Haddo responded. "But I have to have a word with Archie first." Archie Reed was the station overseer. "Give me about twenty minutes."

"Right, dear. Now, come on, gels." Philippa led the way up an imposing main staircase that had a central landing then branched off to either side. "I've put Chrissy across the hallway from you, Tori, so she won't be lonely," she explained. "It's a big house."

Chrissy turned saucer eyes on Tori. "It's *humungous!*"

"Won't take you long to get used to it," Tori said, companionably taking Chrissy's arm and dismissing the ancestral home of one of the great landed families of Australia.

During that first week Haddo gave both girls time to settle. Chrissy, at first clearly overawed—it was all *too* much—sat silently and very shyly at the dinner table, but gradually began to thaw under the influence of so much ease and kindness. She was getting to know the house, and becoming more used to its splendour, its size, the furnishings, and all those paintings and beautiful things. It literally took her breath away.

Tori was the same as ever, though Chrissy couldn't help being in awe of Haddo and his status—but he was so nice to her—and Philippa was lovely. Not a bit stiff and starchy, even if she did speak like the Queen. Yet still Chrissy felt extraordinarily out of place. She sometimes thought it was like stumbling on to a movie set with beautiful rich people who lived in their own kingdom. But they had their troubles like everyone else.

Tori had confided in her that she didn't much like her life as the Rushford heiress.

"Just an accident of birth, Chrissy. You could have been the Rushford heiress."

"Not darned likely!" Chrissy had choked on laughter.

Aware Chrissy was still feeling like a fish out of water, tactfully Tori had left the idea of supplementing—or to be truthful *changing* Chrissy's wardrobe until the day before Kerri and her friend Marcy were due to arrive. She had seen more than enough of Marcy to know she was a terrible snob, with a gift for the throw-away insult, even among her own moneyed set. One look at Chrissy in her current gear and the knives would be out—even if they were behind Chrissy's back. Still, Chrissy would *know* she was a source of droll disdain.

Philippa listened carefully when Tori explained. "The last thing I want to do is hurt Chrissy's feelings, but I have so many things I can give her to wear. You know what Kerri and that awful Marcy are like."

Philippa sighed to herself. "I certainly do. God forgive me for saying it, but I do wish they weren't coming. Marcy will grab any opportunity to see Haddo. I'm tempted to tell her she's been wasting her time all these years."

"Don't you think Haddo should be the one to tell her?' Tori asked crisply.

"I'm fairly sure Haddo hasn't given Marcy any encouragement, dear," Philippa assured her, veiling her eyes. "Anyway, as regards Chrissy, what harm can it do, showing her what you've got? She's a good bit shorter than you, but you're both very slender. Personally, I don't think you'd know Chrissy with a little bit of a makeover."

"I want her to look her best," Tori said. "And I'm going to get that tooth of hers fixed," she whispered, although Chrissy was a good distance off, with Kate in the kitchen. Chrissy felt at home there, to the extent that Kate, Mallarinka's long-time housekeeper, was giving her cooking lessons. It had been Tori's idea, and it was a good one.

The two girls had fallen into a routine of riding in the afternoon. It hadn't taken Chrissy long to get the hang of riding a horse again, once a nice quiet mare was found for her, and Tori worked out safe rides in advance. That afternoon they had decided on being a bit more adventurous and visiting a stock camp at Cobbi Creek. Tori knew a party of stockmen was scheduled to head off to the rough hill country, to bring back all the cattle they could muster. Haddo had mentioned it at dinner the previous night. The muster was expected to go on for several days, which meant the men had to take along extra horses—at least three or four to a man—so they could rest the others when they were ready to drop from fatigue or, as sometimes happened, when they got injured. Mustering meant physical exhaustion.

When they arrived at the camp, surrounded by a near solid wall of coolibahs, and areas of the creek packed with fragrant pink water lilies, they dismounted and left their horses tethered in the abundant shade. Tori's eyes immediately picked out Haddo's tall, commanding figure. He was standing outside the corral talking to Snowy, their top aboriginal stockman and tracker, who most probably would be in charge. A whole bunch of horses had already been rounded up for the trip. She counted roughly thirty. They were standing quietly inside the corral, almost at attention.

Haddo turned his head and came towards them, emanating that vibrant masculinity that was so much a part of him. He looked stunningly handsome even in his everyday riding gear, with a bright red bandanna knotted around his darkly tanned throat.

"How's it going?" He reached them, smiling. And what a smile he had!

Chrissy responded with her own sweet smile, broken tooth or no. "Great—just great, Haddo. I'm absolutely loving this. I'm finally getting used to being back in the saddle too. My bum doesn't hurt so much. Can you swim in this creek?"

He nodded, with a glance at the glittering water. "You could, but there are much better places to take a swim. Tori can show you." Now his smouldering sapphire gaze slicked over Tori, who stood with a classy white akubra tilted nonchalantly over her eyes. "Hi!"

"Hi!" she responded, momentarily blinded to her surroundings. Haddo did that to her.

"I like the way you call her Tori," Chrissy said. "Everyone else calls her Vicki."

"Well, I've been calling her Tori so long I couldn't possibly change," Haddo explained, glancing back at the camp. 'The men will be taking a break shortly. You're welcome to stay for some billy tea—and some I guess you could call them damper scones."

"That would be lovely!" Chrissy said, looking to Tori for approval.

"Billy tea, yes. I'll pass on the scones," Tori drawled.

"They're better than you think, Chrissy. Don't let Tori put you off." Haddo's eyes narrowed over Tori's small, vivid face. She had plaited her dark red hair into a silky rope that hung down her back. Her cream shirt was silk, her skintight jodhpurs a darker cream. Her riding boots, very expensive, were dark tan with a high gloss. She looked perfect for a fashion shoot, her very slim, attenuated body falling naturally into elegant lines that could have been poses, but were not. Tori had always been marvellously graceful.

"What's with you?" he asked.

"Nothing," she retorted, with heightened crispness.

"You're not usually a woman of few words."

"Why is it your voice always has that thread of mockery?"

He shrugged. "I don't plan it. But come along. Everybody knows you, but I can introduce Chrissy." Haddo moved off, leaving the girls to follow.

Chrissy's big brown eyes sparkled. Most of the men were middle-aged, but there was one young blond guy, in a check shirt and tight jeans, with a black akubra shoved back on his head. He looked kinda cute…

"Who's the blond guy?" she whispered urgently, taking Tori's arm. "He looks a bit like one of those western movie stars, don't you think?"

"As a matter of fact, no," Tori answered truthfully.

"Come on—he *does!*" Chrissy insisted, as if she had big plans.

"Well, maybe just a teeny-weeny bit," Tori relented. The jackeroo, Shane McGuire, looked *nothing* like a movie star in her opinion, but he *was* nice-looking, with blue eyes and blond curly hair. Better yet, everyone liked him. But there was the fact Chrissy had lived through a couple of very harrowing years with an abusive partner. Shouldn't she be more cautious?

"What's his name?" was Chrissy's follow-up question.

"Behave yourself, Chrissy," Tori admonished. So much for Zack, she thought—and good riddance. "Okay, it's Shane McGuire. He's the jackeroo."

"He's not married?" Chrissy queried. "If you say he is, I think I'll cry."

"Save your tears." Tori laughed. "Haddo doesn't hire married jackeroos. They have to learn the ropes before they can think of settling down. Anyway, Shane's only about twenty, twenty-one. Life hasn't properly begun at that age." Hadn't she made a total fool of herself at sixteen?

"It began for me when Mum died," Chrissy said, shrugging off some pretty horrendous times.

"I know. I'm sorry." Tori, who had suffered her own bad times and because of them was empathetic, hugged Chrissy's thin shoulders.

"That's okay. I've found a pal like you." Chrissy smiled. "Am I allowed to speak to him?"

"Of course you are."

"I mean when you aren't around." Chrissy watched in delight as a big flock of yellow-crested cockatoos came to rest in the coolabahs on the opposite bank, looking for all the world like giant white flowers.

"You don't have to consult me about whom you want to speak to, Chrissy. But just take it easy, okay?"

"Yeah, sure!" Chrissy gave her saviour a great big hug.

*So what have we here?* Tori was left to wonder. *Love*

*at first sight?* Her biggest regret was there hadn't yet been time to get Chrissy's front tooth fixed, but maybe someone like Shane would see past that to the sweetest of expressions and those big brown eyes?

Chrissy had already confessed she would love to stay on Mallarinka if Haddo would only give her a job. She was willing to do anything—domestic work, or she could learn stock work. She would die to become a jillaroo, but that wasn't on the cards. Mallarinka was a man's world. School-teaching wasn't in her repertoire either. Chrissy had paid little or no interest in school-work at the various homes she had been shunted around, and consequently her three Rs were pretty sketchy.

That was something else Tori was set to fix. School would start up again tomorrow morning at nine o'clock sharp—a time Tori had come to think of as more or less daybreak.

In the end Tori didn't have the heart to refuse a damper scone smothered in lashings of wild plum jam. Wild plums grew in abundance right across the desert fringe, and they did make good jam—deliciously tart. The scone however, stuck in her chest. Maybe another mug of billy tea—which *was* good—would wash it down.

She rose from the fallen log she and Chrissy were sitting on—Chrissy was tucking into the scones with gusto—to walk towards Lliam, the half-Irish, half-Chinese camp cook. She should have put her sunglasses back on. The sun was dazzling, making her squint. She put up a hand to protect her eyes, then in the next breath she was caught in a one-armed grab from behind, and swung aside so powerfully she thought she might crack a rib. As it was, she fell to her knees, her face white with shock.

"Let go, yah bastard!"

It was Snowy, the stockman, roaring a whole chain of obscenities, ladies present or not. At about the same time she heard Haddo let out a harsh rattle of pain.

*Oh, no!* Instantly she realised what had happened. Like a fool, she had walked too close to the rear of the pack donkeys. They were standing together, four of them—bad-tempered at the best of times, not an affectionate one between them. These donkeys would just as soon greet you with a bite or a swift kick than with brays, snorts or snuffles, but they were intelligent, and could carry food and gear across the roughest terrain. Haddo must have seen she was in danger and come instantly to her rescue. The mule hadn't taken a bite out of *her,* but it had certainly got a grip on Haddo's arm.

How could she have been so careless? she upbraided herself, wanting to sink through the bright red earth. Haddo was paying the price. To make it worse, she knew all about these mules—their stubbornness, their cleverness, and their disconcerting habit of trying to sink their big teeth and jaws into anyone who just so happened to annoy them. These weren't animals suitable to be kept as pets. They weren't at all calm, and they didn't particularly like people. One always needed some protective weapon to hand just in case they played up.

She bent over, gulping for air, aware that everyone was crowding around her.

"Jeepers, Vicki!" Chrissy was crouching beside her, aghast at what had happened with such lightning speed. Not familiar with donkeys, Chrissy had imagined they would be very mild-tempered animals—not to say exceptionally docile.

"Tori? You're okay?" Haddo demanded brusquely. He too went down on his haunches, his burning blue gaze moving steadily over her.

For an instant she couldn't speak. All the silly bravado had been knocked out of her. Then slowly she lifted her head. "I'm so sorry, Haddo," she said, in a small, subdued voice. "So ashamed. I should have realised. Did the blighter bite you?"

"It certainly had a go," Haddo confirmed wryly, ignoring his left arm, where the donkey's teeth had made quite a dental impression.

"I'm just so sorry," she repeated, tears springing into her eyes.

"Forget it." He drew her to her feet, noticing how she gave a little involuntary wince. "Did I hurt you?" He knew he had grabbed her hard and fast, but there had been no help for it.

"You could have cracked a couple of my ribs," she tried to joke.

"Don't worry. We'll get you checked out."

He was serious. She knew that, so she shook her head. "I'm okay—*really.* Why didn't you just let the damned thing bite me?"

He suddenly smiled, his good humour utterly convincing. "Because I need you to teach the kids."

"Brilliant!" She found herself smiling back into his face. Something she hadn't done for a long, long time. "You have every right to be angry with me."

"Well, I'm not,' he clipped off, powerfully affected by that smile.

"You've had all your shots, haven't you?" she asked solicitously.

"Of course. Everything's okay, Tori. End of story."

"You need something to put on that, Haddo," Chrissy broke in, sounding as subdued as Tori.

"Yes, you do," Tori agreed, staring at Haddo's strong arm. The donkey's teeth had barely punctured the skin, but there would be a lot of deep bruising.

"Snowy will find me something." Haddo shrugged it off. Snowy was a medicine man of some renown, with a host of bush remedies many qualified doctors would like to get their hands on.

Snowy, in fact, was grinning happily. "Lucky I had a stout stick, eh, boss?"

Snowy—so called because of his fine head of snow-white curls, which contrasted with his shiny black skin—was still holding it, after having given the still glaring pack donkey a few telling whacks before it could be persuaded to let Haddo's arm go.

"Not the first time you've come to my rescue, Snowy," Haddo said, with real affection.

Snowy, a wry sixty, pointed a thumb at his own chest. "Snowy will never let anyone or anythin' hurt yah, boss. Now, I'm gonna look around and mix you up somethin' to put on that."

"Thank you so much, Snowy," Tori broke in gratefully. "Haddo can't afford to overlook any injury—battery of shots or not."

After dinner Philippa had fallen into the habit of playing the piano—which just happened to be a Steinway concert grand—to entertain them. The whole family loved the fact Philippa was so talented, and she had been greatly blessed in that she had miraculously escaped any form of arthritis in her pianist's hands. Haddo and Tori were well used to her wonderful musicianship, but Chrissy, who had only heard some truly woeful strumming in her short and troubled life, was enthralled. While Philippa played she had a captive audience in Chrissy, who was soaking up her various experiences like a desert claypan soaked up rain.

At one stage that evening Haddo left the drawing room. Tori gave it a few minutes, then quietly went after him. Man-like, Haddo was totally discounting his injury, but she knew his arm had to be hurting badly. Kerri and Marcy would be arriving in the morning—they stuck together like sisters—so she would get fewer and fewer opportunities to talk to Haddo alone. Despite the lack of encouragement, Marcy still thought she had a chance with Haddo, and Kerri, as her friend, was going to do her best to help Marcy out. Tori wasn't about to wish Marcy luck. She wanted someone altogether different for Haddo.

*Like who, young lady?* It was hard to get away from her inner voice.

Haddo wasn't in his study. The library was in darkness. He must have gone upstairs. She debated following, but she still thought she would never get over being so carelessly negligent that day. She wasn't ignorant of the bush and bush life. She knew as well as anyone how ill-tempered donkeys could be, and she had practically walked right into the pack, upsetting the leader. It had seemed to her that over dinner—she had watched him very closely—Haddo had had a faint pallor beneath his tan, something that made her feel very guilty. She didn't like to speculate on what might have happened if the donkey had got its jaw around her own slender arm. The reason it hadn't was Haddo.

"Haddo?" she called as she walked along the upstairs gallery. If he was in his rooms she wanted to warn him in advance she was coming.

*Not like the last time, dear!* The voice volunteered another scathing little comment.

"Haddo?" She slowed her steps as she approached the bedroom door. It was open, and the lights were on. That did nothing to soothe her nerves. When he suddenly appeared in the open doorway she actually jumped. "You startled me," she croaked.

"Now, how could I startle you, Tori?" he asked. "You were looking for me. Here I am. Do you want to come in?" He stood away from the door, the soft, long-sleeved blue shirt he had been wearing at dinner unbuttoned and pulled free of trousers threaded with a belt.

"You mean I'm *allowed?*"

He just smiled—a smile that made every other guy's look washed out. "Come in, Elf. I was just going to put some of Snowy's concoction on my arm."

"I *knew* it was hurting," she said worriedly, her eyes travelling around the large room, with its twelve-foot ceilings. The suite comprised an adjoining dressing room, a bathroom beyond, and a sitting room on the opposite side. There was nothing even mildly rustic about it, given the Outback setting. It was very grand, very comfortable, very masculine, with a big bold aboriginal painting hung above the huge bed she had once managed to negotiate. She had never worn that nightgown again.

"Just a bit," he conceded. "Could have been worse. The brute could have taken a piece out of *you.* Now, that would have been a catastrophe. That particular donkey has been playing up of late. When the muster is over we'll set it free."

As he was speaking he was stripping off his shirt, intending to replace it with a short sleeved tee. For all he knew Snowy's green ointment could stain.

Tori stood transfixed, her throat suddenly dry and her heartbeats picking up erratically. God, he had a superb body! She found herself blushing hotly. What the heck was she doing here?

*Ask a silly question, you get a silly answer, dear. You can't keep away.*

She tried to ignore the taunt. "Can I do that for you?" she offered, watching him pick up a small painted pot of ointment from the bedside table.

"You'd like to try your hand at playing nurse?" He searched her small, fine boned face, his smile faintly wry. She was wearing a very pretty short dress with a silver, blue and green pattern. As usual, she looked like an exquisite pool nymph. The deep green of the silk exactly matched her tilted eyes. The way she had arranged her long mane fascinated him. She had any number of ways: up, down, plaits, coils, ponytails that fell down the back or to one side. Tonight she had left her hair loose and curly, just the way he liked it. It sprang away from her face, framing it in a rich rosy cloud.

"Why not a nurse when I'm going to be a schoolmarm?" she parried, advancing several steps across the Persian rug towards him.

"You're not nervous about it, are you? You'll be fine."

"Of course!" She threw up her chin. "I'm going to barricade the door so no one can get out. Some kids really hate school. They want to be outside communing with nature. You know they do."

"They might get hysterical if you tried to lock them in," he commented dryly.

"You know perfectly well I was only joking. Leave it to me. I can handle a bunch of children." *I think.* "Chrissy has asked to sit in on some of the classes."

"Poor Chrissy." He sighed. "I guess she missed out on a bunch of stuff. That's a good idea."

"Pip wants to help her as well."

"Another good idea," he replied. "Now, are you going to come over here, or do you intend to work your magic from there?"

He sounded both casual and mocking, his brilliant blue eyes alight with some sort of devilment. "Shut up, Haddo," she said sweetly.

His skin was the colour of polished bronze. There was a fine mat of dark hair on his strongly muscled chest. Talk about a six-pack! She could search the world and she would never find a man she wanted more. His upper left arm, to her shame, was already turning into a spectrum of livid colours—black, blue, yellow, purple.

"Oh, dear, dear, dear," she sighed, taking the little pot of ointment from him. "This is all my fault."

"Yes, it is," he agreed, straight-faced.

"No need to rub it in."

"What else can I say?" He relented, and laughed. "That's what you're supposed to do, by the way, Tori. Rub it in. *Gently,* please."

"A good thing I don't want to hurt you," she said meaningfully.

"You mean there's a chance we might start over?"

"*No* chance," she retorted. She took a small amount of the dark green unguent onto her index finger, then began to apply it very tenderly to his badly bruised arm. "This has coloured up very quickly, wouldn't you say?"

"It's doing what Snowy intended it to do," he answered, thinking that under her ministrations he was bound to lose his phenomenal control. "The ointment brings out the bruising"

"It smells lovely," she said, in some surprise, having expected a strong medicinal smell. She lightly sniffed the fragrant substance—what was it? Could it be good for the skin?—then gently eased him down onto the side of the bed with a little pressure on his shoulder. "You can't tower over me."

He put his arm around her waist, drawing her closer. "Unlike the donkey, I don't bite."

"So, tell me, have you *changed,* then?" she asked crisply, hiding her searing reaction. Why didn't she just collapse into his lap, like she'd used to when she was a kid?

"Can't you tell a changed man when you see one? This has to be the best night of my life, Victoria. You have the most exquisitely gentle fingers."

Those same fingers gave a little tremble. "Being nice to me *now* won't win me over," she warned. "I'm treating you like I'd treat any other casualty."

"I don't think so," he drawled.

"You'll just have to believe me." She continued on for a moment in silence, drenched in sensuality. "I think that does it," she said briskly. "I'll just wash the ointment off my hands, if I may? Though it smells lovely—like a mix of wildflowers. I wonder what's in it?"

"I'll ask Snowy to tell you when he gets back. Grab a fresh handtowel off the stack."

"Will do."

She was back in a moment, watching him shrug into a navy T-shirt that clung to his splendid physique. Michelangelo would have *adored* him.

"Feel any better?" she asked expectantly.

"I don't deserve you," he said, pinning her gaze. 'I'm pretty sure you'll have to keep doing this."

She saw the mischief. Blood came to her cheeks. "Have your fun."

"*Seriously,* sweet, penitent Tori—how I love you this way—I appreciate your concern."

"No problem!" she replied, turning on her heel so he wouldn't see the expression in her eyes. "Are you coming downstairs again?"

"Sure!" He caught her up at the door, giving her a challenging look. "Do you mind if I give you a thank-you kiss?"

"We've had our last kiss—remember?" She felt duty-bound to remind him.

"A *cousinly* kiss is what I mean," he corrected her, his beautiful smile twisting a little.

"If you must!" She presented her alabaster cheek, thinking how very difficult it was going to be to discourage such a practice.

"Oh, I *must!*" he assured her, his voice deep and dark, and turned her into his arms.

It was intolerable. And at the same time it was what

in her heart of hearts she so fervently longed for. Haddo was the best and the worst of her. A dyed-in-the-wool feminist would have been scandalised.

"You're so sure of yourself, aren't you?" she accused him, hostile little sparks flaring in her green eyes.

They stood inches apart, staring at one another.

"Yes, of course I am," he retorted. "And you wouldn't have me any other way." He took her wrists and raised them, kissing the delicate inner network of blue veins one after the other.

She shivered, every nerve leaping beneath the thin sheath of skin. "I've never met a man with more ego."

His blue eyes glittered. "Come on," he scoffed. "I'm in a unique position to know what goes on inside that ruby head of yours."

"Are you now?" Rebellion hit her bloodstream. Incongruously, it was mixed in with a wildly rampaging excitement. She fixed him with an intense stare. "Okay, so what am I thinking now, Svengali?"

"You want to open your mouth for me," he said, in that dark, seductive voice that rocked her to the core.

As a kiss it was fabulous. Instantaneously marvellously familiar—she hadn't forgotten the first time—like the meeting of predestined soul-mates and at the same time powerfully and wondrously *new.* Such kisses were surely the most fantastic gift.

As a lover he would be flawless. For the last four years she had fantasised about those moments out of time when he had had her in his bed—kissing her, cupping her breast, her nipples on fire, his sex against hers for all their brief coverings. Fleeting heaven! And she had to be neurotic, because she had never recovered.

People looked at her, read about her, and immediately jumped to the conclusion she couldn't be a virgin. Not with her lifestyle, her perceived sophistication. In the third millennium too.

Well, she *was.* How was that for fidelity, however angst-ridden? Why else would she be letting him do this to her? It was like diving into an unknown crater lake without a second thought. She had sworn she would never again let him see how much she loved him. He couldn't be getting the message.

When he stopped kissing her she was breathless, bubbles in her blood. "That's your little thank-you kiss, is it?" she gasped.

"You're nearly twenty-one, aren't you?"

"So what happens *then?*" She eyed him sharply.

"You'll have to wait to find out."

"You mean we might end up in your bed again?" Her voice dripped sarcasm.

"You were *sixteen,* Tori, for God's sake," he groaned.

"Do I have to be twenty-one?"

"Well, twenty-one's not *that* young," he pointed out bluntly. "A heck of a lot better than sixteen."

"Put the whole thing out of your mind," she said. "I'm not going to be staying long enough. I'm going to take my punishment—for that's what it is—and then I'm zooming back to Sydney. If your dear old friend Marcy, who's arriving tomorrow, knew about this, and about the sorts of things you're saying to me, she'd kick up a big fuss."

His answer was to take her face gently between his hands. “Who’s Marcy?” he asked, then dropped another kiss on her small, straight nose.

## CHAPTER THREE

TORI was fast asleep when a pounding came on her bedroom door.

*Oh, my gosh!*

She turned on her back with a start. This was a big day for her. The most important day of her life if one considered this was the very first job for which she would be paid. The night before she had been full of good intentions—full of confidence, for that matter. There were only about a dozen or so kids she would have in front of her. From a couple of little pre-schoolies to the eldest, Charlie Worangi, who apparently was stuck on Grade Five. In her efforts to impress Haddo—she pretended she didn't care, but she cared desperately—she had even gone so far as to set the alarm on her bedside clock for seven a.m.

Seven a.m. had well and truly come and gone. The digital reading was now 8:10. Frantically she tried to kick her legs free of the top sheet that somehow during the night had begun to wind round her like a mummy.

"Tori?"

She could have sobbed with frustration. "Go away!" she yelled furiously, finally fighting free of the sheet.

"I'm coming in."

"What for? A quick chat?" Hurriedly she looked about for something non-valuable to pitch. "Try it and I'll call the police."

"I *am* the police, by the way." Haddo was standing in the now open doorway, flaunting his signature blazing energy and the Great Outdoors. "Surely you could make an effort on your first day?" he said, making no attempt to disguise his disgust.

"I set the alarm!" she cried.

"No!"

"I did too!" She picked up the small clock and aimed it at him.

He caught it deftly, not even glancing at it. "School starts at precisely nine o'clock. Tracey was always there well beforehand."

"Very commendable," she said briskly. "Now, are you going to get out of here and let me get dressed?"

His blue eyes ran all the way over her. She looked absolutely enchanting, his Elf, but he wasn't going to tell her that. "Whatever happened to the fancy nighties?"

She tugged at the short hem of her girlish pink cotton and white lace number. "I find it very strange you remember that nightie."

"It was lovely!" he said. "Though it didn't give you much cover." He started to turn away, all dynamic male. "I'll organise some breakfast for you."

"I don't *want* breakfast." She wrapped both her slender arms around her, radiating irritation.

"As I said, I'll organise breakfast for you. I don't want you falling asleep on the kids. Then I'll take you down to the schoolhouse and introduce you properly.

They know who you are, of course, but not as their schoolmarm. It might be an idea to dress the part."

"I've never had the pleasure of wearing a corset," she said sharply. "So, how many at the last count?" she asked, busy unwinding her long plait.

"Wait and see," he said.

"What happened to Chrissy?" she exploded. "Couldn't Chrissy have come to wake me up? I thought she was my friend."

"Don't take it out on Chrissy." He shrugged. "Chrissy couldn't come because the last time I saw her she was out riding, about two miles from home. That was around sevenish."

"Oh!" Chrissy had taken to Outback life like a brolga to water. "Chrissy is used to waking up early. I'm *not.* Now, get out of here, Haddo."

His sapphire eyes glittered. "Technically, Victoria, I'm your *boss.*"

"Sorry!" She didn't sound in the least sorry. "I've known you so long I forget these things. Try again. Could you *please* get out of here, *sir?*"

Haddo and Tori were greeted with big beaming smiles, rippling giggles and clapping hands. It was obvious this was an *event.* Tori did a rough head-count. Fifteen pairs of eyes were staring back at her. The two of them stood at the front of a large airy classroom, furnished with four long desks to each side of the room, and divided by a wide centre aisle—for me to do the walking, Tori thought, charmed by the reception. Each desk could easily accommodate four to five students, although three sets of four and one of three had spread themselves out at the desks now. Fitted into the wall behind them was a monster blackboard for the teacher to write on. At the centre of the dais was the teacher's large comfortable desk and chair, with a couple of trays on it and a whole selection of chalks, pens and pencils, whatever. Someone had placed four perfect yellow liliums in a small dark blue ceramic vase.

The schoolhouse had only one double doorway but several side windows, and looked out onto the main tree-lined driveway up to the home compound, so Tori thought she would know exactly who was coming and going. The small white-painted timber building was protected from the hot desert sun by a broad verandah, and big white ceiling fans whirred overhead. Haddo, who appeared to be idolised by the children, introduced her as "Miss Victoria".

"Good morning, Miss Victoria." Young voices drawled her name in unison.

"Good morning, children." Best not call them kids.

"So far so good," Haddo murmured a few moments later, giving Tori a quick smile just as Chrissy slipped into the classroom and collapsed at the back desk. "Ah, there you are, Chrissy," he said.

"I'm so sorry I'm late." Chrissy went pink.

"Barely a minute." He smiled. Chrissy could come and go as she pleased. Not so Miss Victoria. "Children, this is Miss Chrissy, who will be helping Miss Victoria out and sitting in on the lessons."

"Morning, Miss Chrissy!"

The children shifted in their seats, heads swivelled. Not one, but two teachers. Miss Victoria had the most amazing long curling dark red hair, pulled back in a pony-tail, and eyes as green as a deep lagoon with the sun on it. Miss Chrissy had short corkscrew dark curls that went everywhere, and big brown eyes. Miss Victoria was dressed the part in a blouse and skirt. Miss Chrissy was in jeans with a blue T-shirt. The children were fascinated.

"I'm off," Haddo told Tori crisply. "You can tell me all about it at dinner. Kerri and Marcy will be arriving early afternoon, don't forget."

"No way to put a stop to it?" she asked sweetly.

For a minute it looked as if he was about to drop a careless kiss on her cheek, but instead he laughed, waved a hand and strode off down the aisle, calling, "Goodbye, kids! I'll be hearing about how you behave. That goes for you too, Charlie!" He directed a finger in Charlie's direction.

Eleven-year-old Charlie, whose greatest ambition was to become a stockman on the station, gave a whoop of laughter. Why anyone would want to go to school was a mystery to Charlie, but to run off or go walkabout would be to jeopardise his chances with the big boss—Mister Haddo. Charlie stopped lolling and sat forward, looking as if he was going to make an effort to pay attention. Of course it wouldn't help him one bit to become a good stockman, much less a tracker, but the teachers were so pretty—especially Miss Victoria—so he guessed it was cool.

By the time Tori rang the bell for "little" lunch, sent down for the children from the homestead—no junk food, just sandwiches, fruit, muffins—she had formed a few ideas of her own. First of all she had made each child come up to the blackboard to write their name, age and class. Next she had decided she wanted one brightly painted feature wall, where the children could display their artwork. She wondered what talent she might discover. She had also decided the schoolroom needed a small upright piano, so there could be singing. She rather fancied forming a junior choir. She wasn't a highly accomplished pianist, like Pip, but she had some talent, and had managed to gain an Associate Diploma by the time she left school.

By three o'clock, the end of the day—though it was two o'clock for the two little four-year-olds, who took a nap anyway—she was bursting with ideas. The children had not only to be taught, they had to be entertained. Music, the universal language, would be a good start. She didn't need Haddo to supply the piano—though she had better talk to him about it first—she could buy it herself and have it trucked out.

"I didn't know I was such an idiot!" Chrissy said, folding her skinny arms over her head. "Even Charlie knows some of his tables. And that little kid, Leila, writes better than I do. Just look at her name and mine." Chrissy, a virtual orphan, who had regularly been beaten up at her various homes, pointed to the board.

"Some of the best-educated people in the country have terrible writing," Tori laughingly pointed out. "There's no such thing as a copybook, like in the olden days. You should see Pip's writing. It's beautiful. Haddo has a good hand. And mine's not too bad."

"It's beautiful!" Chrissy said strongly. "And you're so *smart!* The kids really enjoyed their lessons. The way you put things and explain. I did too."

Tori's tender heart broke a little. "Don't worry, you'll catch up to where you want to be in no time, Chrissy," she promised. "All you have to do is *want* to."

* * *

In the time she had been on Mallarinka Chrissy had been protected and cushioned by the kindness of the household—Tori, Philippa, Haddo, motherly Kate in the kitchen, with whom she got on extremely well—and had an uncomplicated friendship with the house girls Kate had trained so well. But now, within days of the arrival of Haddo's sister Kerri—tall, bone-thin, very glamorous, unhappy and because of it on the caustic side—and her friend Marcy—by way of contrast, a short, very pretty brunette, carrying a few extra pounds, but shapely with it—the atmosphere took on an abrupt sea change. Marcy, who was remarkably skittish around Haddo, was given to passing snappy, loud comments when he wasn't around, and Chrissy was the butt of many of Marcy's wisecracks. Sometimes they were funny, but they had a core of ridicule that came perilously close to insult.

Tori came in for her share too. The only difference being that Tori had no difficulty firing off a quick retort, while Chrissy couldn't handle repartee, and she had no confidence whatever around "posh" women like Kerri and Marcy—the social elite. As far as Chrissy was concerned they came under the label of "rich bitches". Women who had never had to fend for themselves and were way out of touch with what Tori sardonically called "the lower orders". And the first and last time Marcy had smilingly interrogated Chrissy about what had happened to her front tooth—feigning fascination—Tori had told her if she didn't ease off Chrissy she might be missing a front tooth herself.

"Oh, sorry—sorry, Victoria!" Marcy, dressed in a white linen shirt and matching trousers, performed an exaggerated salaam. "You're such a firecracker, aren't you? You've done so many wild things since you were a kid—and your *friend,* Chrissy!" She rolled her eyes. "You found her in a shelter? What next? Is that a wig she's wearing, or her own hair? And what's she doing down at the school? Not helping you *teach,* I bet! She's got no verbal skills. I try to engage her in conversation but she can't even string two words together. Even when I say hello she's pushed for an answer."

"Whereas you more or less don't let up," Tori retorted bluntly, stung on Chrissy's behalf. "Chrissy is having difficulty responding because you go out of your way to make her nervous. To my mind, that's cruel."

Marcy's bosom heaved with the level of affront. "I can't begin to imagine why Haddo is so fond of you," she muttered grimly.

"That's something even I'm not capable of answering," Tori quipped. "But then, you're no closer to Haddo than you were six or seven years ago. That's *sad,* Marcy. Maybe it's time you asked yourself the Big Question: *could I be wasting my time?*"

Marcy threw back her shiny head, cut in the latest style, "Terribly amusing, my dear." She glared. "But then you always were obnoxious."

"Charming!" Tori murmured. For some reason Marcy, several years older, had always been afraid of her. Why, exactly?

"And you're heading for a cropper." Marcy's crystal tones sharpened. "Don't think I don't know why you've been sent out here. The family are worried about the sort of people you hang out with."

"*Your* sort, Marcy," Tori reminded her dryly. "You

know—the so called shakers and movers. The *in* crowd."

Marcy all but choked. "The only difference being *I* know how to behave. You simply *don't.*"

"So why is it you always look envious?" Tori smiled. "What you don't take into account is that I'm smart, and I recognise it in you. Anyway, I'm doing great! Not that it's any of your business. And, yes—I do believe *I'm* family, while you're just a visitor here. So don't try telling me off. Or Chrissy."

"Oh, my goodness!" Marcy made a face, as if she had never encountered such rudeness. "A visitor? Everyone knows I'm much *more* than that. Kerri and I forged our friendship in school, and Haddo and I have always been close, as it so happens. Why else would he have me here?" She gave a thin, knowing, smile. "We all have our little secrets, dear. What would *you* know about what's gone on in the past few years? And what about what *you* have to deal with? You don't fool me one little bit with that smart aleck manner you've adopted with Haddo. It's just an act. Haddo is *far* more to you than you're letting on."

"Of course he is!" Tori flashed a breezy smile. "I won't lie. He's *Cousin* Haddo, and I just adore him. But to get back to Chrissy. She was really enjoying being here until you arrived. It's important to me we keep it that way."

"Right you are!" Marcy gave an unkind laugh. "But how could a little street person like Chrissy be at home *here?* As the old saying goes, you can't make a silk purse out of a sow's ear. If she feels bad it's because she recognises that fact. She's totally out of place when you consider what her natural habitat has to be. She could have been doing drugs, for all you know. Or prostitution. Lovely! Her feeling bad has nothing to do with me, Victoria. Actually, I've made attempts to be kind to her."

The redhead in Tori got the upper hand. "I don't regard barely disguised ridicule as kindness," she said, very sharply indeed. "And, for the record, Chrissy is totally drug-free and she was never into prostitution. You think you're so superior to the Chrissys of this world, don't you, Marcy?"

Marcy gave a throaty laugh, placing a hand on her curvy hip. "Don't think so, I *know* so, dear."

"Such is arrogance." Tori sighed. "Shouldn't you remember it was just an accident of birth? Chrissy, through no fault of her own, was dealt a really bad hand. Don't we, with so much more, have a responsibility to help out? If you spent some time checking out how the less fortunate live, it might make you a better person."

"Please don't lecture me, dear," Marcy said, with a curl of her lip.

"And you can quit calling me *dear* in return," Tori replied sharply. "You consider yourself pretty classy, but a *real* lady would never torment anyone less fortunate than herself. Would you try to remember that for the duration of your stay?"

"Can't promise anything." Marcy glanced pointedly at her designer watch. "Better get cracking, then. Haddo wants me to join him for the day."

Tori, who'd been about to turn away, stopped short. "Now, there's a howler if ever I've heard one. Pip is taking morning classes for me while Haddo flies Chrissy and me into Koomera Crossing. We'll be taking the chopper. Chrissy has a dentist appointment. We want to get things started on fixing that tooth. She'll need a porcelain crown."

"Ugh!" Marcy shuddered, as though Chrissy was in desperate need of a full set of false teeth. "Makes you happy, does it, *dear?* This dispensing largesse to the poor and the needy?"

"Yes, it does, actually," Tori answered quietly. "I've come to realise that's what makes being an heiress worthwhile." She turned on her heel before her disgust grew too much for her. "See you this evening, Marcy," she called over her shoulder. "Kerri is a wonderful horsewoman. Why don't you get her to help you brush up on your many lessons?"

Marcy started with indignation. "Why the hell would I want to ride a *horse?*" she asked haughtily, and strode away in the opposite direction.

While Chrissy was bravely coping with her dental appointment—the second of her life, the first having been bad enough to make her think of it ever after as torture—Haddo and Tori took a walk around the prosperous Outback town, which had its own bush hospital, with visiting medical and dental specialists. At the well-stocked pharmacy Tori bought a few toiletries Pip wanted, then they headed towards a good coffee shop.

Once inside, they were shown to a quiet banquette that looked out on the broad sunlit main street. Four-wheel drives and utilities were parked practically bumper to bumper to either side. "How are you going to go about convincing Marcy she's not the love of your life?" Tori asked by way of conversation, after their order for coffee and sandwiches had been taken.

"Why are you so desperate to get me to?" Haddo asked, equally casual. "Are you jealous?"

"Hell! I hate you," she said flippantly. "Haven't you found that out yet?"

"I'm okay with your hating me." He shrugged. "It makes you heaven to kiss."

She flushed. "The kissing has to go! It's not in my best interests. I can't worry about you."

He gave a half-laugh. "You should. I'm getting on. Damn nearly thirty, and I have a compelling need to marry and have kids."

"Marcy can't help?"

"Ah, don't be ridiculous,' he said, shaking his crow-black head. "There have been women in my life other than Marcy."

Her mind immediately darted back to a few. "Yes, that's right. There was Georgina Thomas—and whatever happened to Rosie Armitage? I always liked Rosie. She was very sweet to me when people like Marcy were never nice. Marcy's not good around Chrissy either."

He nodded, looking directly at her. "It hasn't escaped me. I'll have a word with her."

"That might be helpful. Is Kerri's marriage falling apart? She won't speak to me."

"She's jealous of you, Elf. Don't you realise that?"

"Oh, come on, Haddo," she said quietly. "Why would Kerri be jealous of *me?*"

"You actually *know* the answer to that question," he said bluntly.

Colour flooded into her flawless skin. "So Kerri's resented me right from the beginning? Is that what you're saying? She was your sister—your only sibling. She wanted all your love and attention. Instead you made a little pet out of me."

His smile was crooked. "I promise you, you were the most enchanting little girl that ever drew breath. You had so much life in you, even after you lost your father and were in so much pain. I couldn't *not* love you, Tori."

She drew a tortured breath. "So why did you treat me the way you did?"

He groaned and put a tanned, elegantly shaped hand to his temple. "Not again! Because you were a *child,* my little *Elf,* with your cute little pointy ears. I absolutely adored them."

She swallowed down a rush of emotion at the use of his old nickname for her. It was part of him—and her. The halcyon days. "Let me remind you I've grown into my ears," she said sharply. She hadn't *really.*

He appraised her with indulgent eyes. "Your ears are fit for a faerie princess, Tori," he consoled her. "As for the myth of my cruel treatment of you. I would have thought I'd made the reason for that abundantly clear. Surely in retrospect you can understand?"

Maybe some part of her did. Only her emotions weren't keeping pace with her head. "I wasn't there for an *orgy,*" she told him heatedly.

"You never thought you might have *got* one?" He pinned her emerald-green gaze.

She blinked at the bluntness of his tone, then drew back. "You would never hurt me, Haddo. Anyway, I wasn't wrong about the way you looked at me. You looked at me in a way no one else ever has, and I've had more than my share of attention. Don't deny it. That look led me astray."

"So I made a mistake." He sighed very deeply. "You were just so beautiful. Everything about you cried out, *Haddo, look at me!*"

"So it's still my fault, is it?" she flared.

"It's *always* the woman's fault." He smiled, his blue eyes so intense they made her feel disorientated. "You don't know your own power."

"Nor you *yours,*" she said sharply. "If I had to lose my virginity—"

"Have you?" He caught the tips of her fingers, holding them in a tight grip.

"That's none of your business!" She attempted to wrench her fingers away.

He allowed her to, lounging back, intense one moment, nonchalant the next. "Well, we've been friends for so long I thought you might want to tell me. I've already heard about the hundreds and hundreds of kisses."

She gave a little involuntary shudder. "I couldn't wait to lose it after *you.*" She gave in to the deeply entrenched desire to hurt him as he had once had hurt her.

"So what held you back?"

She fixed him with spirited eyes. "Who said anything did?"

His expression gentled, and that tender smile played about his lips. "You're sort of my girl—aren't you, Tori?"

All the fight went out of her. Just like that. Emotions waxing and waning. "Yes," she said. "Isn't that too damned odd? Especially since you turned me into a juvenile delinquent. All I wanted was for you to love me. Instead you made me so unhappy."

"I'm sorry." His brilliant eyes reflected all the sincerity in the world.

It shook her, yet perversely pricked her into giving a *who-would-care* flick of her hand. "Anyway, I—" She stopped short as she saw the young waitress fast approaching. "Here comes the coffee."

"Forget that for a moment," Haddo said in a deep, quiet voice. "I promise I'll do everything in my power never to hurt you again as long as I live."

She was touched that he should say such a thing. How could she ever distance herself from this man? "So help me God. You *must* say it."

"So help me God," he solemnly intoned.

It was such a strangely moving moment her eyes filled with brilliant, unshed tears.

The smiling waitress arrived at their table, then set down their order. Black coffee for Haddo, cappuccino for her, and a plate of delicious-looking club sandwiches, artfully decorated with a few little salad items to the side, for them to share.

It was Haddo who restored the mood to something like normality. "To answer your question about Kerri—she's having trouble conceiving. It's making her very edgy, and I have to say bitterly sarcastic."

"I bet her husband's copping it," Tori remarked ruefully. "I wouldn't wish Kerri being bitterly sarcastic on my worst enemy. Why doesn't she get off that strict diet she's on? She's so thin, and you must have noticed she doesn't eat! Perhaps if she were eating properly, and took a course in meditation or something, they might have more luck?"

"I sort of suggested that." Haddo's expression was wry. "And maybe a long, relaxing trip together. She needs to unwind."

"If there's one thing I've learned about Kerri, it's that she finds it very difficult to relax." Tori shrugged. "I truly hope she follows your advice. Heck, she could make you an uncle. That's fabulous!" Her face lit up.

"Here's hoping!" He took a test mouthful of the coffee and found it very good. "I wonder how Chrissy is going on? No gain without pain, I guess." He pushed the plate of sandwiches nearer her. "Who's paying? You or me?"

"I'm paying for the porcelain crown. You're paying for this. Another thing. I have an idea Chrissy is falling for your jackeroo, Shane."

Haddo's expression turned deeply sardonic. "She's only known him for about two weeks."

"Maybe it was love at first sight?"

"So what are you suggesting? I have them followed on those early-morning rides?" he asked dryly, picking up a sandwich and casually examining the filling.

"What do you think?" She wanted his opinion.

"They do seem to be attracted to one another," he conceded. "But seriously. Chrissy from all accounts has had a chaotic life. She needs to give herself time before she can chart the right course."

"We've got her on the right course," Tori exclaimed, judging it the right moment to approach him. "What Chrissy really needs is a job."

"I was wondering when you were going to get around to that," he returned smartly.

"Jillaroo?" She tried out Chrissy's number-one ambition, not at all sure Haddo could be persuaded. Chrissy had a natural affinity with horses and animals, and she had experience of farm life—but that bore little resemblance to the rigours and isolation of Outback life.

His handsome mouth tightened. "Tori, you know as well as I do it's a tough life. Generally speaking women aren't mentally strong enough, let alone physically, to handle the hard work involved or the lonely environment. A woman wouldn't have any problem on Mallarinka because I wouldn't tolerate it. But men leading a man's life tend to become very macho. They like to keep the women out."

"But our guys are just great!' she protested.

"That's because you're Victoria Rushford," he told her dryly. "Chrissy could expect to come in for a lot of ribbing."

"It'll be a piece of cake after what Chrissy's lived through," Tori said. "She's been through hell. She desperately needs a safe place, security, a helping hand."

"I thought we were giving her that?" Haddo commented mildly, blue eyes resting on her highly animated face. "Okay, we can start her off doing some time in the store. Then she can graduate to a few minor chores. We'll see how she handles herself and whether she's accepted. She's a nice woman. I like her. But she's not altogether in her comfort zone at the house, is she?" Haddo met her eyes directly.

Tori couldn't deny it. Chrissy remained intimidated by her surroundings. "Especially since Kerri and Marcy arrived," she said. "She's lost all confidence around them." She could have said a lot more, but didn't.

"I suppose if Chrissy genuinely wants a job—"

"Oh, she does!" Her heart bucked up. "She loves being here. She really does."

Haddo held up his hand. "Listen, I really approve of your efforts to help Chrissy, and others like her, but we'll take it a step at a time, if you don't mind. I'd have to think about providing suitable accommodation. We rarely take on jillaroos—for the reasons I stated. Women are trouble just by virtue of the fact they're women. Obviously Chrissy can't bunk in with the men."

"What about the teacher's bungalow behind the schoolhouse?" Tori suggested eagerly, having thought it all through. The bungalow hadn't been in use since Tracey and Jim had married and been allotted more spacious married quarters. "It's set up. All it needs is a lick of paint and a bit of sprucing up. I think she might like that. It would make her feel independent. *Please,* Haddo." She stretched out a hand to him, emerald eyes imploring, the colour in her cheeks emphasising her gleaming white skin.

He took it, giving her an ironic smile. "So, you leave Chrissy here, and you go back to Sydney? Is that it?"

Gently she withdrew her hand, acutely conscious of their electric connection. Haddo would always be able to penetrate her defences. To give herself time she looked out of the bay window. Today she had arranged her hair very artfully, with lots of lustrous stray tendrils. It created a rosy nimbus about her face. She started to finger one of those tendrils. Just the thought of being away from Haddo pierced her with a fresh pain that bordered on agony.

After a while she glanced back, managing blithely, “There’s no rush. I haven’t quit my job *yet.* I intend to get a choir going. Music. Painting. Pip thought it a great idea. Oh, and I want the kids to get involved in making a garden around the front of the schoolhouse.”

“Anything else?” he enquired politely. “I have a lot of free time on my hands, as you know.”

She tapped his hand sharply. “Just give me your okay. I’ll do the rest. We could consider putting up a flagpole for them. They’d like that. Flags too—the Aussie flag and Mallarinka’s logo. And what about an adventure playground out the back, fenced in because of the little ones? They *need* me, Haddo, at least until Tracey comes back.” *And I need them.* “Why are you laughing?” She broke off to challenge him, at the same time revelling in the irresistible tenderness of his smile. All right, he had a sensational smile—but he didn’t smile at *everyone* like that, did he?

He shrugged a wide shoulder that pointed up the leanness of waist and hip. “I’m just thinking that deep inside you there was a dedicated schoolmarm fighting to get out. Who would ever have thought it of the Rushford heiress?”

# CHAPTER FOUR

FOUR hectic weeks followed, during which time Tori managed to fit in all the things she had intended to do—but only just. The children spent many afternoons after school preparing and then planting out their new garden, with the help of Mallarinka's head groundsman Vince, a station employee for over thirty years. It was Vince's job to keep the homestead's extensive grounds in order, but he was having a lot of fun helping the kids.

"This was a great idea of yours, Miz Victoria," he told her enthusiastically, noting how much the children were enjoying having their hands in the soil. "You'll find all the plants will thrive. They thrive up at the house. They're all adapted to the dry conditions, and all the little lilies and violets are native, as you know."

"I wish you'd help me with the adventure playground, Vince," Tori cajoled.

Vince's weather-worn face crinkled into a thousand lines. "The boss told me you were bound to ask and yes, it's okay."

If the children were delighted with making a garden, it was nothing to the fever of anticipation on the afternoon the piano arrived. Pip was there, of course, to witness the arrival, and later to play for the children, who thought everything was wonderful—even Charlie, who had done a lot of work helping Vince, and was making unprecedented progress at school.

Every time Tori passed him she lightly patted his shoulder, with a "Well done, Charlie!"

Archie, the overseer, took time out to chopper Chrissy into Koomera Crossing, where she was at last fitted with a porcelain crown that did wonders not only for her smile, but her confidence. Later she told Tori she felt as if she was walking on air. Chrissy didn't hesitate, either, to have her over-permed corkscrew curls cut off by a male barber, who gave her a really chic short crop that suited her features to a T. Chrissy now spent her mornings catching up with her studies and her afternoons working, under supervision, in the station store. She was on the payroll, and she couldn't have been happier. The store stocked all manner of work gear, and jeans, wind jackets, shirts, belts, bandannas, a range of riding boots and akubras, socks, underwear—you name it. Everything was supplied and sold to the staff at a good discount. As stocks went down they had to be replenished. Accounts had to be kept. Three staffed the store—four with Chrissy, who slotted in with no problem. No wonder she seemed to be walking on air.

"I've never been so happy," she told Tori, giving her a big hug.

Tori returned the hug with a lump in her throat.

What really put Chrissy over the moon was moving into her own little bungalow. Tori had gone to a lot of trouble to make it tranquil and welcoming.

"My own home!" Chrissy said, starting to cry. "I'm sorry." She swiped the tears away with the back of her hand.

"Don't be sorry about tears of joy. Be excited!"

"I *am* excited." Chrissy stood framed in the doorway, staring rapturously around the open-plan living/dining area that was so bright and cheerful, and the well-equipped galley kitchen with a refrigerator beyond. The bedroom—there was only one—and the bathroom led off a corridor, with a laundry at the rear. "I'll never, never be able to thank you enough, Vicki."

Tori swept an arm around her, letting it enclose her friend's thin shoulders. "Wait and see." She laughed.

Kerri and Marcy were leaving first thing Monday morning. Haddo was to fly them to Longreach, where they would pick up a domestic flight.

"That's good!" Pip murmured, the night before, when she heard, having suffered through the stay. "Kerri was never such a wet week before. I've told her she has to buck up. She's got everything going for her, when she thinks of that poor child Chrissy and what she's survived. If Kerri's not falling pregnant it's because she's forgotten what it's like to eat. I've no patience at all with her fad diet. All she ever seems to do is push food around her plate. Just how thin does she want to be anyway? Moderation is the answer, and daily exercise. Marcy, on the other hand, loves her food. And drink," she added dryly. "But Haddo must have spoken to her, because I've noticed she's laid off Chrissy."

"And I promised I'd give her a broken tooth if she didn't," Tori confided.

Pip shook with laughter. "Oh, I do love you, Tori."

"That's good, because I love you too." Tori put out a hand, helping Pip rise to her feet.

Pip had already said she was ready to turn in. Both Kerri and Marcy had gone upstairs a short time before. Tori was feeling a little tired herself, but she wanted to finish off the last couple of chapters of her new book. She had visited Venice twice, so she was finding the book—set in that fabled city—doubly engrossing.

Some time later she closed it with a satisfied sigh, then went in search of Haddo to say goodnight. Haddo was always the last to turn in and the first to get up, more often than not pre-dawn. She would never see him as anything else but a dynamo.

She'd thought he would have been in his study, but although the lights were on there was no one there. A horse-lover, her eyes were irresistibly drawn to the magnificent gilded bronze horse that stood on a tall plinth in front of a feature glass panel. She moved over to give it a pat goodnight, aware that the exterior lights were spilling all over the huge date palms in the garden. She glanced out, thinking she could hear voices…

The voices seemed to be mocking her.

Her expression changed, became alert.

She heard them before she saw them. Now they came into sight. Haddo and Marcy, out in the garden. Hadn't she somehow anticipated this? Urgently she moved to one side of the glass panel, blocking herself from their sight. She could feel her face burning with blood. Hope all but abandoned her. Marcy had changed out of the pretty flirty dress she had worn at dinner into a tangerine caftan, decorated all around the neck and halfway down the front with lots of glitter.

*It's got to be what it seems to be,* her inner voice warned her.

Yet she held fast. Haddo appeared to be frowning—maybe even protesting? Marcy, as usual, her glossy head tilted up to him, was talking a hundred to the dozen.

Tori's stomach began to churn with nausea. She shut her eyes.

*Don't look. Don't!*

When she opened them again they were locked in a passionate embrace. Even the dark shadows that surrounded them had turned molten. Marcy's arms were fully stretched to encircle Haddo's neck, and his hands were grasping her rounded hips, pulling her to him.

Oh, my God! Oh, my God! Inside she was moaning.

Another of her illusions: she actually thought she could hear her heart breaking. She didn't hate him. She loved him. It would always be that way. Another thing she had to accept, like the loss of her father. Haddo was a sensual man. She knew that. Not everyone was given sexual radiance. She could think of a few people who had it—none of them with conventional good-looks. Sexual radiance was something quite apart. Haddo had been given too much.

She felt a sob stick in her throat. She didn't realise it but tears were running from her eyes. He and Marcy could have been lovers over the years. Why not? Haddo had had plenty of girlfriends. Women literally threw themselves at him. From the look of it he was still involved with Marcy. Or getting his kicks where he could. Most men would find Marcy a luscious armful. The sheer humiliation of it had her bending over double, like a woman in agony.

*Oh, Haddo!*

*You deserve better, she told herself. He can't kiss you the way he's taken to doing and have maybe another half-dozen women on the go. Marcy among them.*

It was her own fault. In the last four years she had tried to ease him out of her life. In a matter of six or seven weeks he had drawn her back inexorably into his force field.

She peered out again, grasping at the edge of the plinth to prevent herself from falling. She hadn't the faintest idea how to handle this new situation, but one thing was certain. It made her position untenable. Just as she had come to love life, she was back on the awful merry-go-round.

*To hell with you, Haddo. To hell with you both.*

The tableau had changed. Marcy was now clutching Haddo around the waist, her head buried against his chest. Haddo appeared to be intensely moved, his hand lost in her thick shiny hair.

*Get going,* Tori's inner voice whispered hoarsely. *Get out of here.*

Trembling hard, she moved stealthily around the bookcases, banging her knee against the big burgundy chesterfield before her shaking fingers found the light switch. She turned the lights in the study off, so she couldn't be seen fleeing, but even flooded with anger had the sense to leave the exterior lights on.

*Caught them. Caught them,* that inner voice gloated.

But hadn't Marcy warned her in a fashion about her little secrets?

She had never felt so empty in her life.

They must have moved with bewildering speed, because the two of them were suddenly in the entrance hall.

God, where to hide?

She heard them talking together, but they hadn't kicked in to full voice. Probably a continuation of murmured sweet nothings.

Behind the chesterfield?

Adrenalin blew in. *Why hide?*

*I'm going to kill him if he comes in here.*

It wasn't in her nature to stay calm.

Probably the two of them would continue up the staircase. *And so to bed!* No, Haddo would turn off all the downstairs lights first, while Marcy tippy-toed along to his bedroom. With so much else on his mind he might think he had already turned off the study lights.

No such luck! He was coming her way.

She straightened up, ready to confront him.

With his hand on the light switch, the study still in darkness, he questioned, "Tori?"

She had stopped crying by then, but her eyes glittered fiercely. "Hi," she said, as the lights came on. "How did you know I was in here?"

"I always seem to know where you are," he answered quietly, immediately sensing her agitation. "It's like radar."

"So you *wanted* me to see you out in the garden, did you?" Her arms went tightly around herself lest she run at him, arms flailing.

"My God!" he groaned, and dipped his sleek dark head away.

*Guilty as charged.*

"Is that all you've got to say?" she demanded wrathfully. "You know I have to go home now, don't you?"

"This *is* your home," he said, making a move towards her.

He looked so big and formidable she sprang back behind the massive desk. "I'm going home and I'm not coming back. *Ever!*"

"Would you please listen?" he said, slipping into the voice she had heard him use so often when he was taming his wild horses.

"I'm through listening," she stated. "I knew how dangerous this was for me, coming out here. You've just been playing with me, roping me in, you son of a bitch."

At that designation his eyes flashed blue fire and his jaw muscles clenched. "Tori, you're the *only* person I know who's oblivious to the fact *I'm* the boss. *Your* boss. I don't know what you think you saw—"

"Ah, don't give me that." She chopped him off fiercely. "You were kissing the damned woman. You were running your hands all over her *big* hips."

A commanding stranger looked back at her. "So that's what you thought you saw," he rasped. "Give it a rethink."

"Are you going to tell me you were just saying a fond farewell?"

"I don't know about *fond,*" he said, in a perfectly hard voice. "You're going to have to trust me, instead of rushing to judgement. You're like a rocket that can fire off at any given moment."

"And then plummet back to earth? Is that what you're saying?" She was nearly dancing with rage, hot tears pricking behind her eyes.

"I'm saying I've taken all the punishment from you I'm going to take," he informed her harshly.

"Would you listen to him?" She threw up her hands in a wildly theatrical gesture.

"I think you'd better stop, Tori." Haddo was trying to control his own sudden rage. She looked so beautiful, so fiery, incandescent with outrage. And she was so *wrong.* Poor Marcy had come on to him. Her last bid. "Because I swear if you don't—!"

She came around the desk at a run, filled with a deep primal urge to lock horns. "You'll do *what?* Not even you would consider three in a bed."

"Hell!" Haddo's own temper burst out of bounds. He didn't speak. He reached for her.

"Don't you dare!" She defied him frantically, aware of his immense physicality.

He ignored her totally, catching her and pinning her slender, attenuated body hard against him. He had loved her too much for too long. There had to be an end to this.

"You're hurting me. *You're hurting me.*" Her breath was coming short. She struggled wildly, but it was no use. She was no possible match for him. No wonder women feared men. They were so strong.

"I don't care," he said, his mouth against her hair. "I've been far too kind to you up to date. No way am I in love with Marcy. I never have been. The pity of it is, she couldn't seem to take it in."

"She just forced herself on you, did she?" She threw

up her head, emerald eyes glittering with misery and contempt, the breath labouring in her chest.

"Pretty much," he said tersely, capturing her face between his strong hands. Never in his life had he felt so close to the edge. Not even that night when as a schoolgirl she had come to him. "I love *you,* you little wildcat."

She stopped struggling for a moment. "Oh, God, Haddo, stop it!" Tears welled.

"Grow up!" he ground out.

She couldn't think straight. She couldn't *think.* He didn't give her time. Completely routed, she just stood there, her fists clenched against his chest, while he kissed her into broken submission.

Somehow they were on the chesterfield. She was lying across him…his hand was caressing her naked breast. She tried to suppress the moans but she couldn't. She was growing weaker and weaker, her body melting against him. The fingers of his one hand brushed along her leg, up her thigh, sliding down over the faint curve of her stomach and under the line of her briefs, a trifle of amethyst satin and lace.

There were brilliant shards of light behind her tightly closed eyes, then his voice. "Tori…." He sounded like Samson, brought to his knees by a mere woman.

Her heart was pounding so fast she thought it would never slow down. Her throbbing sex *ached.* She let him do what he wanted, surrendering herself to this exquisite pain. Oh, the powerful seductiveness of him! She was a beat away from screaming that she loved him. No matter if he was going to ruin her. *She loved him.* That was her fate.

Haddo too was getting pushed past his limits, his passion for her volcanic.

"My God, what am I doing?"

Abruptly his hand stilled as he tried to hold on to that remaining frail thread of control. His Tori! His little virgin. He knew that for a certainty now. It thrilled him. At the same time it gave him pause. His agonised body was screaming out for release and no one could blame him. He was desperate to take her, to undress her, to hold her naked body astride him. He knew he could do what he so powerfully wished, but the consequences would be swift. This wasn't what he wanted for her. For either of them. She meant far too much to him. He would die for her.

He drew back, looking down at her bewitching, willowy body, sprawled in utter abandon across him. Her eyes were closed, high colour was in her cheeks, her long curling ruby hair trailed everywhere. Her beautiful, delicate dress, patterned with roses like an impressionist painting, was bunched at her narrow waist, exposing her long slender legs and lower body. Even that little lick of fire at her delta was exquisite. He was wild for her, yet perversely he was all about protecting her. It would never change.

Tenderly he adjusted her clothing and drew her up into his arms, cradling her as if she had morphed into the child she had once been. It was his only hope. He half expected his urgent hunger for her to win out, but slowly she opened her eyes. She looked like a young girl, hypnotised by sensation.

He had to let go of her. He knew he had to.

Her voice was just a whisper. "You couldn't lie to me,

Haddo, could you?" she implored, in those brief seconds pitifully vulnerable.

"I'll never lie to you," he said. "I thought I'd sworn that." He reached behind her back to pull up the zipper of her dress.

"Then you meant what you said?' She began to rake her fingers through her tumbled hair.

"What do *you* think?" He couldn't risk even the lightest kiss on her mouth. "You'll never be rid of me, Tori." Decisively he lifted her up in his arms, then slowly set her on her feet. "Go upstairs now. Go to bed. It's late, and you're all eyes. We'll talk again tomorrow, I promise. First I have to drop Kerri and Marcy off."

She stared back at him intently. "You want me?" Despite everything, she couldn't rid herself of the old grief.

"God, girl, how can you ask?" His striking features were set in stone.

It was an extremely fraught moment. "Then why don't you take me?" She had to hold her fingers against her thrashing heart, lest it leapt out of her body.

He moved away from her to the drinks cabinet, pouring himself a good shot of bourbon. "Because it isn't the time or the place," he said, believing it to be the truth.

She gave a soft keening laugh. "Do you think that time will ever come?"

Haddo tossed the bourbon back in a single swallow, then turned to face her, bluer than blue eyes blazing. "Yes, Tori." He spoke with absolute authority, as if in his mind he had already set the date.

* * *

No one was overly concerned when Haddo didn't fly back on time. He might be catching up with the many people he knew in Longreach. He was an experienced pilot, who knew the vast semi-desert area like the back of his hand. Besides, life on the station was very hectic. Cattle trains were coming in and out, dam sinkers were on the job, itinerant stockmen were looking for work, there were visiting vets, freight planes landing on the strip. There was hardly any time for sitting around or watching the clock, so the hours flew.

Mallarinka's head stockman had come upon a couple of stressed and stranded English tourists who had strayed onto the station. They had been taken up to the house for a shower, a change of clothes and a full meal, and a station mechanic had been detailed to service their four-wheel drive. When they had recovered sufficiently they would be pointed in the right direction.

"We were having the most marvellous time too," the wife told them wryly. "But the Outback is so *vast!* One has to see it to believe it!"

It was also very unforgiving to the unwary.

By two p.m. station people found themselves casting frequent glances towards the sky, willing the Beech Baron to appear, with the boss at the controls. Pip had contacted the domestic airline, to be told Kerri and Marcy had boarded their flight, which had already landed safely in Sydney. Another call confirmed the Beech Baron had departed the commercial airstrip at the time designated on Mr Rushford's flight plan. Was it possible he had put down on another station?

"Haddo would have told us, surely?" Pip said, trying very hard not to let her sick panic show.

School was out, and she and Tori were sitting together, close to the phone and radio. Tori was becoming very distressed, biting her lip and twisting her hands. Pip was perfectly aware that, for all the estrangement that had gone on, Haddo was the love of Tori's life—and as far as she was concerned Tori was the love of Haddo's life. No one could tell her any differently. But love could also mean a terrible fear of loss.

There had been many dreadful light aircraft crashes in the Outback over the years. These crashes were very traumatic for all station people, where flying was a way of life. Had Haddo encountered a mechanical problem? Had he made a forced landing? They had found out he hadn't cancelled his search and rescue time in accordance with his detailed flight plan which accurately profiled his flight path, but he couldn't be reached by radio. Maybe the radio had packed in? It didn't seem likely, when the faithful Beech Baron was regularly serviced, though radio problems weren't all that unusual. It was too early to call a full-scale air search, though their overseer had come up to the homestead to tell them that in another hour or so he might take the chopper up.

"I'll come with you, Archie!" Tori leapt to her feet. She couldn't sit around doing nothing, with fear rioting through her mind. Though she was making a valiant effort to keep her emotions under control, she knew she was becoming distraught. And why not? What would life be without Haddo? Suffering was made to be borne, but she didn't think she could cope. She hadn't even told him how much she loved him. Instead she had wallowed for four long years in silly, misplaced pride. Haddo always did the right thing. It was she who didn't.

But Archie refused to take her and had scarcely left when a radio message came in from Sovereign Downs. Haddo was on his way home. His radio was out.

"I hope none of you has been worrying," Jack Jensen from Sovereign said, using the usual bush logic that problems with aircraft and choppers weren't unusual, so folk would understand. "Haddo kindly dropped off a spare part I urgently needed. His radio was playing up, so he asked me to give you a call. Have to confess it took a while. We had a bit of an emergency. You should see him shortly, I'd say."

Tori raced out onto the verandah, dragging in a lungful of warm, bush-scented air. A great wedge-tailed eagle sailed overhead. A good omen. Like lightning the news travelled all over the home compound. All was well! The boss was on his way in!

Stockmen way out in the bush, unaware of the home drama, casually noted the Beech Baron flying over.

"I can honestly say I haven't felt so panicky in all my life," Pip finally admitted. "We won't tell him, will we?" She held Tori's eyes. "It would only worry him. Besides, we women of the west are supposed to be stoic."

Haddo landed to a royal welcome. As he taxied into the hangar he could see Tori standing beside one of the station Jeeps. She was waving both her arms in the air. It was a habit she had picked up, starting years back. He thought there was a certain measure of desperation mixed in with the enthusiasm of the wave. He hoped he hadn't worried her with his delayed arrival. Jack

Jensen's wife, Meryl, had insisted he stay for lunch. He had wanted to keep going, but found it difficult to refuse. Of course they'd all got talking. Both Jensens were missing their young son, their only child, away at boarding school for the first time.

Tori ran at him, her whole being radiant. "Haddo!"

He heard it for what it was. A great cry of love and relief. He caught her up, swinging her off her feet and holding her there above him. "Poor baby—you've been worrying."

"A little," she said, contradicting that by dropping frantic kisses all over his face. Then she stopped, looking down at him with most beatific smile. "I love you. Love you. *Love you.*"

"I know." He gave a triumphant laugh, lowering her gently to the tarmac. He held her at the waist, staring down into eyes glittering like emerald lakes.

"There couldn't be anyone else in the world for me but you, Haddo," she said, with deep emotion.

"I know that too." His voice exquisitely tender, he bent to kiss her. "I know because that's exactly the way I feel about you."

"Oh, God—oh, thank you! Then why don't you marry me?" she challenged. "I don't want to end up an old lady, knowing you always loved me but never got around to marrying me."

He laughed, slinging an arm around her shoulders and leading her to the Jeep. "What about when you turn twenty-one, in a few months' time?" he suggested. "I couldn't bear to wait any longer than that. Besides, we'll need all of that time to do the planning. There are an awful lot of people we'll have to ask. And most importantly there's your dress."

"My dress?" She burst out laughing as joy poured over her.

"Is a man crazy to want to hold a picture of his beautiful bride in her wedding dress for the rest of his life?" His blue eyes were smiling, but there was seriousness in his expression.

"Why, not crazy at all," she said, unbearably moved. "I think I can promise you won't be disappointed."

"I like that." He hugged her to him, before opening the Jeep door. "Let's head home. Pip will be the first to know—though I don't think she'll be at all surprised."

Pip was out on the verandah waiting for them as they swept up the drive. She watched them walking towards her, their arms locked around one another. Two young people she loved dearly. Their body language confirmed everything she needed to know.

An enormous lightness of spirit seized her. *Isn't love grand!* Her mind filled with her own poignant memories. Nothing in this world, *nothing at all,* could match it.

* * * * *

# HIRED: HIS PERSONAL ASSISTANT

Jessica Steele

**Jessica Steele** lives in the county of Worcestershire with her super husband, Peter, and their gorgeous Staffordshire bull terrier, Florence.

Any spare time is spent enjoying her three main hobbies; reading espionage novels, gardening (she has a great love of flowers) and playing golf. Any time left over is celebrated with her fourth hobby, shopping.

Jessica has a sister and two brothers and they all, with their spouses, often go on golfing holidays together. Having travelled to various places on the globe researching backgrounds for her stories, there are many countries that she would like to revisit. Her most recent trip abroad was to Portugal, where she stayed in a lovely hotel, close to her all-time favourite golf course.

Jessica had no idea of being a writer until one day Peter suggested she write a book. So she did. She has now written over eighty novels.

Dear Reader,

I have had a long and happy association with Mills & Boon. It began with a first lunch with Frances and Pat, the then chief editor and chief copy editor of the company. This was after I had entered several stories in a short story competition Mills & Boon were running at the time.

Later, on acceptance of my first novel, I had lunch with Alan Boon, a man of great charm. There were many trips to London for lunch after that, all splendid and most joyful affairs.

Apart from leaving home to journey to London, I have made many other trips in relation to my writing. Trips overseas to places as diverse as Italy, China, Siberia, Japan and Peru. I had a splendid time in Mexico and thought Egypt and its antiquities absolutely breath-taking.

I have just returned from Switzerland where I have been doing a little research for my next book – my eighty-seventh for Mills & Boon. Normally I do my research trips on my own, but for the Swiss visit my husband was able to come with me, so it was an especially enjoyable trip, and such a pleasure – as is being an author for such a wonderful company.

*Jessica Steele*

# CHAPTER ONE

IT WAS early when Sorrel left the apartment she shared with her flatmate, non-blood sister and best friend, Donnie. With her mind set on getting in and out of the offices of Brown and Johns before the start of business that day, Sorrel barely noticed the car that slid into her parking space as she pulled away. She was vaguely aware of the two suited men who vacated the car, but she had other more important things on her mind.

She was not at all enthusiastic about the errand she was executing on Donnie's behalf, and had, in fact, argued against her friend's pleading. But last night when Donnie had phoned—on her boyfriend's phone because, naturally, she had accidentally left her own phone behind—she had sounded quite desperate and, perhaps as Sorrel had known all along that she would, she had given in.

The thing was that Donnie, the same twenty-three years old as Sorrel, seemed to have an awful time of keeping any PA job for very long. Prior to being taken on by Brown and Johns, Marine Engineers—a firm acquired not so long ago by the mammoth Ward Maritime International—

Donnie's career path had been littered with 'I'm sorry, we're going to have to let you go' speeches.

But, since working for Trevor Simms at Brown and Johns—still for the moment run as a separate entity from Ward Maritime—Donnie really seemed to have found her niche. 'I love it there!' Donnie had enthused of her job as PA to the finance controller. 'I never want to leave. Trevor is so lovely! Even when I sometimes get things a bit mixed up he's so kind and tells me not to worry.'

Sorrel had worked for a finance director herself, and had often been able to clarify matters for Donnie when she'd brought home paperwork that appeared to totally fox her. It was a fact that Donnie was frequently bewildered when it came to anything academic. While she was the loveliest person—kind-hearted, generous, and with a passion for all dumb creatures—Sorrel had wondered many times during their training if her friend was truly meant to work in an office.

To keep her thoughts from straying to the task before her—a task which she did not want to perform but which, because of Donnie's impassioned, 'Oh, Sorrel, I'll just about die if I lose this job!' she was—Sorrel made herself concentrate on other matters.

She thought back to how it seemed she and Donnie had always been friends. She had actually been staying with Donnie and Donnie's divorced mother when the awful news had come through that Sorrel's parents had been killed in an accident. She had been ten, and her mother and Donnie's mother, 'Aunt' Helen, had been the very best of friends. Helen Pargetter had put aside her own grief at the news and had fiercely hugged Sorrel to her.

She had continued to look after her in those first few days of Sorrel losing both her parents until, about a week later, after much telephone discussion, Lionel Hastings, a relative on Sorrel's father's side and her legally appointed guardian, had come to claim her.

He'd been a newly retired barrister, and a wonderful guardian. He'd been understanding, and had done his very best, but, after a couple of months of watching the child withdraw more and more into herself, he had contacted Helen Pargetter.

What had passed between them had later been explained to Sorrel by her uncle Lionel. Mrs Pargetter would very much like to have Sorrel live with her. Would Sorrel like to go and live with her and her daughter Donalda? Sorrel had felt that she would, but she had learned to love her uncle, and hadn't wanted to hurt his feelings.

'Would you mind if I did?' she remembered asking tentatively.

'Not if you promise to come and stay with me at least four times a year,' he had answered.

Gradually Sorrel had come to terms with losing her parents. Helen Pargetter had been unfailingly kind to her, and Donnie had been the sweetest of children. But it was perhaps Donnie who had played the greatest part in bringing Sorrel out of herself. Because Donnie had always been getting into some scrape or other, many had been the times Sorrel had pulled away from a grief-stricken moment to go to Donnie's aid.

So they had grown up together, and they had changed

schools together—Donnie quickly earning the nickname Dizzy Donnie. While Sorrel had helped Donnie with her homework, Donnie, who could swim like a fish, had taught Sorrel to dive, and to laugh again. And four times a year, as promised, Sorrel—sometimes with Donnie, but more often on her own—would visit her guardian. He had grown to be very dear to her—and she to him.

She was far more academic than Donnie, and when she had decided to go to secretarial college, Donnie had decided she would go too. Sorrel had left college with top marks. Donnie, coached nightly by Sorrel when coming bottom of the class, had at least succeeded in scraping through her exams.

After college Sorrel had got a job with the high-powered firm Blake Logistics. Donnie had got a job there too—she'd lasted two weeks. While Sorrel had regularly got promoted until, with her flair for figures and business, she had been made PA to the finance director himself, Donnie had drifted from job to job.

Mostly they had been happy. Socially they had gone out together—sometimes in a foursome, sometimes on a date without the other. But nothing very serious. They had both still been waiting for the big 'love of their life'.

Surprisingly, it had not been they who'd found the love of their lives, but Helen Pargetter! 'Mummy!' Donnie had squealed when, about a year ago, Helen had announced that the American she had been seeing, Mike Gilbert, had proposed and she had accepted.

And all at once everything had changed. The lease on the property they'd been renting had ended just as

Helen had married Mike and gone to live with him in Florida. Sorrel had funds from the sale of her parents' property that Lionel Hastings had put into trust for her until she was twenty-one, and she had thought about purchasing a property. But she hadn't been sure where she wanted to live, so she and Donnie had rented a flat in Surrey—and had been happy there.

Then Lionel Hastings had been diagnosed with a terminal illness, and Sorrel had dropped everything and dashed to Little Bossington on the east coast to be with him. A month or two later a nurse had been in regular attendance, but Sorrel hadn't been able to bear to think that the man who was so dear to her should not have someone of his own near.

Her work came easily to her, and she had been thinking of looking for PA work that was more of a challenge. Edmund Apsley, her boss, had been more than good about the time off she had taken, to make frequent trips to Little Bossington, and had said he did not want her to leave—which had all been very flattering. But Lionel Hastings had been a fantastic guardian, and in her view it had been time to put him first.

'My guardian's prognosis is not good, and I want to be with him for as long as I can,' she had replied. And, knowing that she could not expect him to keep her job open for her in the weeks or months it might be, she'd quit her job.

With occasional trips back to Surrey, Sorrel had made her temporary home in Little Bossington. Uncle Lionel had been well looked after, and there had been little she could do but be there, to sit with him, to read the newspaper to him, or a book she thought he might like. But he'd seemed comforted that she was there.

It was as she had been shopping in nearby Shoeburyness one day, while one of her uncle's friends was visiting him, and taking time out to have a quick cup of coffee before she went back, that Sorrel had found herself sharing a table with Guy Fletcher.

'Mind if I sit here?' he'd enquired. 'The place is a wee bit crowded.'

'Not at all,' she'd replied. She'd liked the look of him. It had seemed he felt the same way; his glance had been admiring on her red-brown hair and her beautiful wide green eyes.

'I haven't seen you in here before,' he'd remarked charmingly, adding, 'I would have remembered.'

With anyone else it would have seemed like some corny kind of practised remark. But it hadn't seemed so then. She had explained that she was living in Little Bossington. And before long she had learned he was Guy Fletcher, who worked for a boat design company and was hoping to one day have his own business.

On her part she had explained that she was between jobs and was staying with her guardian at The Gables.

'The Gables!' he had exclaimed. 'I know it. Well, not that I've been there. I pass by it sometimes.'

It had been a pleasant interlude, and she had made her way back to The Gables. Then, out of the blue a couple of days later, the telephone had rung—and it had been Guy Fletcher. He had apparently asked around, discovered that the owner of The Gables was a Mr Lionel Hastings, and had looked him up in the phone book.

But she didn't want to think of Guy Fletcher—the

man, the *worthless* man, she reminded herself, to whom she had given her heart. And it still hurt to think of Little Bossington now that Uncle Lionel was no longer there. Instead she made herself concentrate on Donnie and her plea of last night. 'Do this for me, Sorrel, and I'll never ask you to do another thing for me—honestly!'

It was not enough that—often better able to decipher Donnie's shorthand than Donnie herself—Sorrel had typed the wretched report for her. Now she had to jolly well go and deliver it too!

But, as always, Sorrel could not stay cross at her friend for long. Donnie too had fallen in love, and Sorrel knew full well how jumbled-up inside that could make you feel.

Donnie had met Adrian Caswell while Sorrel had been away in Little Bossington. He was a zoologist, a kind and untidy man, with hair that always seemed to need a trim. But he seemed to dote on Donnie—and for Sorrel, who was used to watching out for her, that was all that mattered.

It was with Adrian that Donnie had gone off tracking in Africa 'in places wild'. Sorrel found the fact that Trevor Simms had sanctioned Donnie taking six weeks off so soon after starting to work for him at Brown and Johns little short of amazing. But, as Donnie had said, Trevor was a wonderful boss. And when Donnie was in pleading mode, her big blue eyes moist with unshed tears, she was extremely difficult to resist.

Which Sorrel, pulling up onto the forecourt of Brown and Johns and recalling that plaintive telephone call of last night, knew only too well.

The report should have been locked away in Trevor Simms' office desk last Friday. Only Donnie had been very busy with matters pertaining to the start of her holiday the following day. Apparently Trevor was going into hospital on Wednesday, for surgery of such a personal nature that Donnie had not liked to ask more. But he would be in work on Monday and Tuesday, clearing up all loose ends—and this report was a vital part of his getting all work 'done and dusted' before his hospital incarceration.

'Type it for me—there's a love,' Donnie had requested on Friday evening. And had added sunnily, all wonderful with her world, 'You said you were going to look for another job—it'll help you keep up your typing speeds.'

'You could charm the leg from a chair,' Sorrel had replied, and had got busy typing.

It was true she did intend to look for another job—though first there were frequent trips to be made back and forth to The Gables in Little Bossington. As her guardian's heir, it was up to her to clear the house and make it ready to be put on the property market.

But she was not going to think about The Gables in Little Bossington—or anything to do with Shoeburyness either. She must concentrate solely on getting this delivery job done.

Taking hold of her briefcase, she left her car, musing that she could positively murder Donnie sometimes. If her job was so vitally important to her, why on earth couldn't she remember she had been supposed to drop the report in at her office on her way to the airport last Saturday? Feather-brained didn't come into it—though love did. The poor besotted creature couldn't think past this wonderful opportunity of spending six whole weeks with Adrian Caswell!

Realising she had an indulgent smile on her mouth, Sorrel headed for the entrance of Brown and Johns, reminding herself that this was deadly serious.

At first she had refused point-blank when Donnie had asked that she go to her boss's office and put the report in his desk drawer, for him to find when he came in.

'Why can't I just hand it in at Reception?' she had asked, determined not to weaken.

'Because it's supposed to be in his desk drawer!'

'But you said it had to be locked away. I might just as well hand it in at Reception as leave it on top of his desk!'

*'Don't do that!'* Donnie had squealed, shocked. 'You know how much my job means to me! As nice as he is, he'd have grounds to dismiss me if...'

At the rising panic in her friend's voice, Sorrel had felt herself starting to weaken. 'Calm down,' she'd instructed, in all honesty not feeling all that calm herself. 'We'll keep your job for you somehow,' she had promised.

'I knew you would. You're lovely,' Donnie had said breathlessly. 'I left the office keys on top of the report in the top drawer of my chest of drawers.' It amazed Sorrel that Donnie—who was, it had to be admitted, as dizzy as some said—could on the one hand be so careless of the report that she had forgotten to take it with her on Saturday, and yet the night before had hidden it away in her chest of drawers. In case of what—burglars?

Shaking her head slightly, Sorrel pushed her way

through the swing doors of the building—and came to a momentary halt. She had thought there would be no one around at his hour, but she was sadly mistaken!

With her insides churning, she recognised the uniform of a security guard. But it was the other man who caused her to stop dead. He was tall, tanned and fit—and he was looking straight at her!

His glance held hers for about two seconds at the most, but in that briefest of times she felt as if she had been stripped down, taken apart and put back together again. And that was all before, without acknowledging her presence in the slightest, he turned his back on her—as if she were a person of no possible interest—and carried on his conversation with the security man.

It was a truth that she was not used to being so dismissively looked over and ignored. She had often been called beautiful and, without vanity, was grateful for her fine features and pretty spectacular complexion. So she didn't like him for a start—whoever he was.

But, all that aside, her insides were still creating a merry dance within her. For one weak moment she half turned back to make her escape. But with Donnie's 'You know how much this job means to me' haunting her, Sorrel checked the movement. For all she did not think what she was doing was illegal, it just the same did not seem right. But against that, Donnie was of the view that she stood to lose her job if that report was not in Trevor Simms' desk when he arrived at nine. And Donnie, dear dopey Donnie, had never done anyone the smallest harm.

The two men, both now with their backs towards her, were not the smallest bit interested in what she was doing there. But they might well be if she did not get a move on.

The decision was made for her. She knew where Donnie's office lay. Donnie had come out to proudly show her around one evening when Donnie's car had been playing up and Sorrel had called to collect her after she had finished work at her own office.

Though as she hurried along the corridor, trying not to break out into a run, her nerves were starting to fray. She tried telling herself that inside the next five minutes it would be all over—but that did not make her feel any less agitated.

She made it successfully to Donnie's office, and went quickly into the next-door office. Going straight over to Trevor Simms' desk, she placed her briefcase on it while she got out the keys. Fumbling with the keys, she opened the drawer Donnie had indicated at her third bungled attempt, and took the report she had typed with her usual meticulous care from her briefcase. She was halfway to putting it into the drawer when it all went wrong!

'What are you doing?' asked a firm, well-modulated voice—and she nearly passed out with fright!

Sorrel jerked a startled and guilty look at the man who had so silently come in—the man who, in fact, must have wasted no time in following her, she quickly realised. Because *she* had not hung about.

Her first thought was that he might be Trevor Simms, come in early in order to get everything completed before he left on Tuesday after business. But, according to Donnie, Trevor Simms was fifty—this man was somewhere in his mid-thirties. He was the tall, tanned man she had seen a minute or so earlier. She had thought he was not the least bit interested in what she was doing in the building. But was that the impression he had wanted to give? Had he deliberately let her think she was of no concern to him? Sorrel suddenly felt sure she was right—and it did not make her like him any better.

With a sinking feeling in her stomach, she recalled he had been with the security guard. Was he Security too?

'Who are you?' she asked, playing for time. So, okay, the report was confidential—but she had typed far more confidential reports when she had worked for Edmund Apsley.

But her question had not gone down well, it seemed. 'You've got a bloody nerve!' he retorted sharply. 'You're obviously in cahoots with Simms! Where is he?' he demanded curtly.

In cahoots with Simms! What was he talking about? 'I've never met Mr Simms,' she replied without thinking. But, getting over her shock a little, she realised she was in something of a pickle—though she knew above all else that she had to say nothing that might lead to Donnie losing her beloved job.

'You've never met him!' the tall man snarled, clearly not believing her for a second. 'So how come you know your way about his office and have a key to his desk drawer?'

Ah! 'It's—er—quite simple, really,' she replied, her voice very much cooler than she felt. She was still playing for time when, having been floored a few minutes earlier, her fighting spirit was revived. 'But before I say another word, I insist on knowing who you are.' His eyes narrowed—she felt nervous again, but was not waiting for a repeat of what he thought of her nerve. 'Are you Security?' she asked—and guessed then that if all else failed she was going to have to come clean.

He neither agreed nor denied that he was Security, and Sorrel was conscious the whole of the time of how important Donnie's job was to her. Not that they would dismiss her for this one little lapse surely?

'The name is Caleb Masterson.' He yielded that much, but was unrelenting as he demanded, 'And you are?'

Stubbornly, she did not want to tell him. But she supposed if he were Security—though she had never come across any security guard like him, or one with such an arrogance of manner—that he was entitled to such information.

'Sorrel Oliphant,' she conceded reluctantly.

'Is that your proper name, or an alias?'

'*Alias?* What on earth are you talking about?' she erupted.

He ignored her question, just as he ignored her flare of temper. 'Where's Donalda Pargetter?' he wanted to know.

Well, that was no secret. 'Somewhere in Africa by now, I should imagine.'

'With Simms?' he fired back, before she could blink.

'*No!*' Sorrel exclaimed. 'She's on holiday with her boyfriend!' But as instinct prodded that there might be something more serious going on here than the fact that she had been caught by Security in a place she should not have been, 'What's going on?' Sorrel demanded.

'You tell me!' he countered.

'Nothing's going on, as far as I know!' she retorted.

'So what are you doing in the finance controller's office, taking papers from his drawer that have been locked away for the weekend?'

'I wasn't taking them out—I was—er—putting them in,' she confessed, her face flaming in spite of her efforts to stay cool.

'Why?' Just that one short, clipped word.

Sorrel sighed heavily. So much for her wanting to be in and out in five minutes! 'Because Mr Simms will expect to find them in his desk drawer when he comes in at nine.' She glanced at her watch—ten past eight. This was starting to be a nightmare!

'Let me see.' Caleb Masterson approached her. Sorrel pulled the folder out of his reach. He had cold grey eyes, she noticed.

'It's confidential.'

'Nothing in this office is confidential from me,' he rapped.

She stared at him, and suddenly started to feel weak at the knees. 'You're a big cheese from Ward Maritime International?' She brought out her only logical conclusion. He did not answer, and she still held the folder away from him. 'Mr Simms will be here himself soon. He—'

'I very much doubt it.'

'He's gone into hospital earlier than he expected?' she asked, surprised.

'Hospital?'

Sorrel was beginning to have doubts about this man. Surely word would have got through to Ward Maritime

International—basically Brown and Johns' head office—that the finance controller was going to be off sick for quite some while?

'You *do* know he is going into hospital on Wednesday?'

Caleb Masterson considered what she had said. 'For what reason?'

'I don't know. I've never met him. It was—um—something very private, I believe.'

'I'll bet! Folder!' he demanded, stretching out his hand for the folder she was withholding.

'I told you—it's confidential.'

He let go an exasperated breath. 'How do you know it's confidential?' he grunted.

*Mainly because I typed it!* Her fighting spirit was starting to rear up again. 'I've had enough of this!' she said snappily, closing her briefcase. She was hampered by not knowing what to do with the file, but preparing to march out of there.

'Go if you want to.' Caleb Masterson read her mind before she could take so much as one step. 'But you won't get very far before the police stop you.'

Her eyes shot wide. 'Police!' she exclaimed, and only then did the seriousness of this situation start to hit home. 'What on earth has happened?' she asked faintly.

'You—a non-employee—come waltzing in here, *keys in hand,* and expect me to believe you *don't know!*'

She shook her head in bewilderment. 'Tell me.'

'You say you don't know Simms. Are you saying you don't know Donalda Pargetter either—his partner in crime?'

'Yes, I know Donnie... *Partner in crime?*' she questioned, disbelieving her ears. 'Donnie's as straight as a die… What crime?'

Caleb Masterson surveyed her sceptically. 'This is the first you've heard that Trevor Simms and Donalda Pargetter, having electronically relieved the company of over a million pounds, have floated off into the sunset somewhere?'

There was a chair a step away. Stunned, Sorrel collapsed on to it. 'Not Donnie,' she denied croakily, as Caleb Masterson came closer and took the folder she was holding out of her numbed fingers.

He did not straight away open it, but grated, 'Yes, Donalda Pargetter. Yes, Trevor Simms. My one query is—what's the involvement of Sorrel Oliphant?'

Sorrel was still too stunned to answer or to defend herself.

'We know you met Donalda Pargetter here on Friday.'

Sorrel made a small spasm of movement, and started to come to. 'How do you know?''

'We have CCTV footage of you pulling up and getting out of a car to go and help her with her many parcels; presumably goodies for her new life.'

With so much whirling around in her brain—over a million pounds, good heavens!—Sorrel found that she was asking a totally irrelevant question—probably from shock. 'You knew I knew Donnie before you asked if I knew her?'

He did not bat an eyelid. She supposed she had not expected him to. But, drawing up a chair close to hers, he looked sternly into her disturbed green eyes and bluntly stated, 'What I need to establish here is the extent of your lies.'

'Well, I passed that one, didn't I?' she exclaimed, referring to her acknowledgment that she knew Donalda Pargetter. 'A million pounds! How?' she asked. 'How was it done?'

'Very cleverly,' he returned, his grey eyes watchful.

'Over the weekend?' she asked, her stunned brain coming to life. 'How did you find out so quickly? The day's business hasn't even started yet! Trevor Simms might yet come in…'

'He's quit his flat—clothes and baggage.'

Sorrel stared at him, dumbfounded. 'There was no hospital operation, was there?' she realised faintly.

Caleb Masterson did not answer, and Sorrel continued to work it out.

'Trevor Simms—he set it up—his embarrassing illness—so Donnie wouldn't ask questions—as cover…' Feeling winded, Sorrel just sat for long moments, letting it sink in. She knew that this man Caleb Masterson was observing her, though. 'I had nothing to do with it,' she said after some seconds. 'And neither did Donnie.'

'You seem sure—or are you just trying to cover up her crimes?'

'She isn't a criminal! Donnie's had no hand in this, I promise you.'

'Even though I've traced a document with Donalda Pargetter as counter-signatory?'

Sorrel stared at him, startled—but was ready to defend her friend to the death. 'I don't care what evidence you have. Donnie wouldn't do such a thing!' she flared heatedly.

'How well do you know her?'

His question had been sharp. But if he was trying to trap her into some sort of admission, Sorrel did not care. Donnie was not the crook this man had accused her of being, and there was only one way to deal with this—that was honestly.

'We're like sisters,' she told him up-front—if Donnie was in trouble, she'd be in trouble with her. 'We were brought up together.'

'Why?'

*'Why?'*

'That was my question,' he slammed back.

Sorrel let go another heartfelt sigh—the man was a brute. 'Donnie's mother and my mother were great friends. When I was orphaned my guardian felt I would be happier living with my friend Donnie and her mother than living with him. I was lucky—Donnie's mother thought so too.'

'How old were you?'

What had that got to do with anything? 'Ten,' she mumbled.

'I wouldn't call that lucky,' he commented coolly—unsympathetically. Not that she had been looking for sympathy, more answering his question. Without another word he opened the folder and began reading its contents.

'I brought that in for Donnie,' Sorrel explained quickly, past caring about the confidentiality of the matter, and wanting to do what she could to help Donnie keep this job that she loved so much, she went in to bat for her. 'Donnie has a great sense of responsibility. She phoned last night to say she had forgotten about the work she'd brought home…'

'She phoned—from Africa?' he pulled his head out of the paperwork to enquire.

'Yes. She wanted to ask me to bring the file in for her, so that it would be locked in Trevor Simms' drawer for when he arrived.'

'You have her phone number? Perhaps I should give her a call.'

Sarcastic hound. He seemed to know in advance that by no chance was he going to be able to have a nice interrogatory chat with Donalda Pargetter.

'She was using her boyfriend's phone. She—um—forgot to take her own.'

He did not seem surprised. 'What's the boyfriend's name?' he questioned, obviously still believing she was in cahoots with Trevor Simms.

'Adrian Caswell,' Sorrel replied, without the smallest hesitation. 'He's a zoologist.'

Masterson took that in without a change of expression. Flicking a glance back to the contents of the folder in his hands, he demanded crisply, 'Who typed this?'

Sorrel's lips parted in surprise. 'What's wrong with it?' she asked, getting herself back together.

'Nothing. Absolutely nothing. Which is why I know that your friend Pargetter had nothing to do with it.'

He was smart—too smart. 'Donnie loves her job,' was the best she could do for her. 'I promise you she had absolutely nothing to do with this—er—crime. I know her. I've lived with her. She wouldn't touch a penny of anybody else's money. I've offered her money, but she wouldn't take it.' Sorrel warmed to her theme.

'Why, she even sold her car last week, so she would have her own money and not be a drain on her boyfriend.'

'Very commendable,' Masterson returned cynically. 'So, answer my question. Who typed this report?'

There was no time for Sorrel to dream up an answer that would cover Donnie, but she tried just the same. 'Donnie had such a lot to do, getting ready for a six-week holiday and…' She faltered when he raised an eyebrow at the revelation that the PA to the finance controller had been given six weeks off—and had not suspected a thing. Only now was Sorrel herself seeing something more than Trevor Simms just being extraordinarily kind. It would suit his book very well if Donnie disappeared out of the office for a while and would not be around to answer questions that might unknowingly give some clue to what he had been up to. 'Er—Donnie—um—she didn't want to let Trevor Simms down. So, because she was so frantically busy, I offered to—um—type it for her. I used to work in finance too,' she quickly qualified, so he should know that Donnie was conscientious enough not to farm out work to just anybody.

'You typed this?' Caleb Masterson questioned toughly.

She was beginning to go off him—had in truth never been much *on* him. 'Donnie was extremely busy,' she said shortly.

'You still live with her and her mother? Or has the airhead moved in with her boyfriend?'

Airhead! Sorrel compressed her lips. Frustratingly, she recognised that she was in not position to do what she wanted to do and storm out of there. A million or more pounds had gone missing—ye gods!

'Donnie's mother has remarried. Donnie and I share a flat in Surrey.'

She guessed he already knew Donnie's address when he turned his questioning away from that theme and went back to the previous one. 'Given that this paper-work should never have left this office—' he indicated the folder he was holding '—do you often clear up work Miss Pargetter is too busy to complete in her nine-to-five slot?'

Sorrel was unsure how to answer. 'Donnie only brought work home when she was exceptionally busy,' she replied quietly. Aware—as she didn't doubt that he was—that she had not answered his question, she left it there.

To her surprise, he let her get away with it. Though she rather thought from the shrewd look of him that he knew the answer anyway as cold grey eyes bored into her and he tried another tack.

'Where do you work?' He continued his interrogation.

'I don't.'

A glint appeared in those cold grey eyes, and he looked about to go for her jugular if she was playing games with him.

'I'm between jobs at the moment,' she explained hurriedly.

'How long have you been unemployed?' he challenged.

'About four or five months.'

'Where did you work before you decided on a life of idleness?'

'There's no need to be unpleasant!' she fired.

'You think I should *pleasantly* accept that one million or more has been taken from a firm my family have strong connections with?' he fired straight back.

'Well, I didn't take it. And neither did Donnie,' she added, before he could say anything. 'And if you must know I used to work at Blake Logistics.'

'Where?'

'Where?'

'Which section?' he barked impatiently.

'I told you!' Her impatience matched his. 'Finance.'

Caleb Masterson leaned back in his chair. 'You worked for Ed Apsley?' he enquired slowly.

Trust him to know him—though most people called him Edmund. 'I was his PA,' she revealed belligerently.

'The devil you were.' He seemed surprised. 'Why did he sack you?'

'I didn't have my fingers in the till!' she flew. 'And he didn't sack me! I left of my own accord.'

'Why?' was the next challenge.

It irked her terribly that she had to sit there and take this. But, given that Brown and Johns—and ultimately Ward Maritime International—were out of pocket to the tune of over a million, and taking into account she had taken a liberty by waltzing in here in the first place, she realised that she was just going to have to sit it out. Sit there and take it.

'If you must know,' she began—his look said she had very little option. 'I handed in my resignation when my guardian became ill and I started taking more and more time off.'

'You nursed him—your guardian?'

She shook her head, her anger fading. 'He had nursing care. I just wanted to be near him, and I felt that it was a bit of a comfort to him to have me around.'

'I take it he's no longer with us?'

'He died a month ago.'

'Humph!'

Thanks for the condolences! She was starting to get uptight again, but began to wonder what was going on *now* when Caleb Masterson got up and went into the adjoining office. She watched through the open doorway as he switched on the computer.

She was in the middle of wondering if he had finished with his questions when he called her in. She picked up her briefcase and took it in with her. 'Sit down here,' he instructed, indicating the computer chair. Past wondering what was happening, she was nevertheless little short of amazed when he ordered, 'Let me see how good a typist you are.'

'What?' she exclaimed, starting to feel she had drifted into someone else's night-time terror.

'When you're ready I'll dictate a—'

'You want me to type?'

'From what you've said, I've gathered your friend and flatmate wants to keep her job here. You sound just about desperate enough to want to help her keep it.'

Sorrel stared up at him. Confusion did not cover it. But banging away in her head was what he had just said. That she might be in a position to help keep Donnie's job for her. And, remembering Donnie's 'You know how much my job means to me!' and her own reply of, 'Calm down,' and, 'We'll keep your job for you somehow,' she knew that she had to try.

'You're saying I *can* help her keep it?'

'Might,' he answered briefly. And at that Sorrel went into PA mode.

Ten minutes later and at his speedy dictation she had typed back a perfect piece of work. She printed it and handed it to him.

'I'm impressed,' he remarked, on reading it through.

So you should be! She had felt a complete bundle of nerves, typing while he stood over her. Another two minutes and she wasn't sure she would not have started making mistakes.

Caleb Masterson put the work from him. 'Thank you, Miss Oliphant,' he said politely, though his tone was no warmer. 'I'll be in touch.'

That made it certain for Sorrel that he knew where she and Donnie lived. But he had said that she might be able to help Donnie keep her job. 'You…' Sorrel began. But suddenly she realised that she would get no more out of him until he had assured himself that Donnie was in no way involved with this awful crime. 'You're saying I'm free to go?' she questioned.

He nodded. Sorrel left her chair and, with her honest head in the air, briefcase in hand, she went to the door.

'Miss Oliphant?' He stayed her as she opened it.

She halted and then turned. She wasn't going back into the room, whatever he said. 'I know,' she said coolly. 'Don't leave town.'

Incredibly, his mouth twitched. She, it seemed, had amused him. 'Got it in one,' he replied.

She went, and went quickly. Oddly, though, it was not the crime, nor Donnie and how she must do all she could to see that she had the job she loved to come back to, that occupied Sorrel as she left the building.

All she could think of as she went over to her car was what a difference that half-smile had made to that cold, unfeeling brute Caleb Masterson. Why, he was quite good-looking—and almost human!

# CHAPTER TWO

HER head was in a whirl as Sorrel drove home and recalled her conversation with Caleb Masterson. Though to her mind what had taken place had been more of an interrogation than a conversation.

Over a million pounds! Oh, heavens! She was still reeling with the shock of it when, letting herself into the small apartment block where she and Donnie lived, she was waylaid by Mrs Eales, their chatterbox neighbour who lived down the hall.

'Is everything all right, Sorrel?' she asked, sounding concerned.

Sorrel wondered if she was as pale as she felt. 'Everything's fine, Mrs Eales, thank you,' she answered brightly. 'How—?' She did not get to finish asking their neighbour how she was, because Mrs Eales was butting in to relate that two serious-looking men had called before eight, looking for Donnie.

'I was wondering if perhaps her mother had had an accident, or something of that nature?'

Sorrel immediately remembered the two men she had barely taken any notice of as she'd driven away.

'Donnie's in Africa, on holiday,' she answered cheerfully. 'They didn't say who they were or what they wanted?' she enquired, instinctively knowing that they must have been part of Caleb Masterson's security team.

Assured by Mrs Eales that the men had revealed nothing of who they were, or why they had wanted to see Donnie, Sorrel parted from her with the light comment that she supposed if it was important they would be back.

She let herself into their flat, knowing that the fact that the men had turned up at their address could only mean one thing: Caleb Masterson, who seemed to be in charge of this investigation, must have sent them to Donnie's home.

It took Sorrel the rest of that day to come to terms with all that had been revealed—and the horrendous shock of it. While at the same time her nerves were on edge as she waited for a ring at her doorbell, telling her that the two security men were back.

She half wished Donnie would phone again, but barely knew how to begin telling her what had happened if she did ring.

By the time she went to bed that night, with neither a visit from Ward Maritime International security nor a telephone call from Donnie, Sorrel had established several factors in her head.

While there was absolutely no question in her mind that Donnie was totally innocent, other small incidentals had started to jump out at her as obvious clues now that she knew. Hindsight, as ever, being a wonderful thing.

She knew full well that Donnie, while having the

loveliest nature, had struggled, to put it politely, to make the grade as a PA. And yet, even knowing that, she had been so pleased for her when Donnie had landed this job—and had lasted more than a couple of months. She herself, Sorrel mused, had not been in the least suspicious of Donnie's easygoing boss.

Many had been the times Donnie had come home and confessed about some slip-up she had made—and how Trevor had been marvellous about it.

No wonder! Feeling very disloyal to her friend, Sorrel began to see that to have spirited away over a million pounds must mean that Trevor Simms had been planning it for months. Donnie, with her sweet and trusting ways, not to mention her lack of experience working for a head of finance, must have been a godsend when she had applied for the job. Donnie would not have noticed he was up to no good even had he waved a banner at her saying 'I'm a crook'. She would most likely have asked him where he would like her to file it!

Sorrel felt that she might be a little to blame herself, in that perhaps she should have spotted some sort of irregularity in the work she had completed for Donnie. But maybe Trevor Simms had been more subtle than that. He wouldn't have wanted any evidence of his intended crime to be put down on paper for anyone passing to glance at.

Which meant someone would have to physically work alongside him in that office to be able to pick up vibes of anything slightly untoward.

But, anyway, hadn't Caleb Masterson said that the

theft had been perpetrated cleverly—electronically. Which in turn must mean by means of a computer.

Sorrel got up the next morning with her head immediately spinning round with the same thoughts with which she had gone to sleep. No wonder Trevor Simms had made doubly sure Donnie would be leaving the country on Saturday; no wonder he had been quite happy for her to take six weeks off. Had she asked for six *months* off he would probably have said yes.

He no doubt intended to electronically steal that money late on Saturday or early on Sunday—no one any the wiser. They would all have been running around like headless chickens come Monday, and he wouldn't be there. Perhaps no one would even have known that the money had gone for some hours—days, even.

Sorrel was making herself a cup of coffee when two things struck her. One was to realise that somebody must have been well and truly on their toes to have noticed *before* the start of business on Monday that a vast amount of money had disappeared. The other, with total surprise, was to realise that she had not thought of Guy Fletcher since she had entered the Brown and Johns building yesterday. Not once!

She supposed, on reflection, that with yesterday's happenings being so momentous it was hardly surprising that she'd had little else on her mind. Though up until yesterday Guy Fletcher and his treachery had always seemed to have an insidious way of pushing into her thoughts, no matter how much she did not want them to.

Guy went from her head again, pushed out by a memory of her reaching Caleb Masterson's 'amusement button' with her comment about not leaving town. The man had come very close to smiling a full smile.

In her opinion he was an arrogant man, nevertheless, and tough with it. Though she supposed with the job he had to do he had to be tough until he had established if she was telling the truth.

Did he believe her? She did not know. Though he hadn't set the police on her, had he? Something she felt sure he would not hesitate to do should there be the smallest doubt.

But, about that 'not leaving town'—she had matters to attend to. And, for all she did not want to go back to Little Bossington, things over there would not clear up by themselves. Perhaps she had better leave it a day or two, though.

By Friday Sorrel had had enough of waiting around for Caleb Masterson to honour his 'I'll be in touch'. Her phone had stayed silent, with no call from him—she didn't doubt he had her phone number—and no call from Donnie either.

Sorrel had just decided she was going to spend the weekend at Little Bossington when suddenly her doorbell pealed for attention. She went over to the intercom. 'Hello?' she queried.

'Masterson.'

That was all he said, but it was enough to bring warm colour flooding to her face. Without a word she buzzed the outer door to unlock it, and had about a minute to get herself together before he was in the hall outside her flat. That minute was not long enough.

With her insides churning—she had not expected him to come in person—she went to let him in. Her mouth went dry as she opened the door, half expecting he would not be alone but would have some official from the law with him.

He was alone. And, for all she was entirely innocent of any crime, a huge surge of relief washed over her that it did not look as if she were about to be arrested.

'Come in,' she invited. If this interview was going to get nasty, then she did not want the ubiquitous Mrs Eales to happen along the hall and witness it.

Unspeaking, his cold grey eyes assessing her in her jeans and white tee shirt, Caleb Masterson stepped over the threshold. She led the way into the sitting room.

But, on turning, he seemed too close. She was five feet nine herself, but he seemed to tower over her. 'Take a seat,' she invited—and immediately wished that she hadn't. She did not want him to stay long. Just long enough to say what he had to and then be off.

She took a couple of steps away from him. He remained standing. 'If you haven't come to arrest me—would you like coffee?' she asked—and could have bitten out her tongue.

'Coffee would be good,' he accepted. She headed for the kitchen.

Needing a few minutes to get herself more of one piece, while realising that through her own stupidity she was now stuck with him for another ten minutes, Sorrel busied herself making coffee.

She was on the point of carrying the tray into the sitting room when it only then struck her that Caleb Masterson would not, presumably, have accepted her offer of coffee had he intended to make some kind of an arrest.

Although that did not cause her to like him any better, she did feel a little less tense as she walked into the sitting room and set down the tray.

'Have you lived here long?' he asked as she poured his coffee. She glanced at him suspiciously, starting to get uptight again. Then she realised that whatever question he asked she was going to see a double meaning—as he must have noticed, she realised, when he added, 'I'm not trying to trip you up.'

She handed him his coffee, leaving him to add milk and sugar if he wanted it.

'Not long,' she answered, and, deciding to take the question at face value, volunteered, 'When Donnie's mother remarried and moved to the States with her American husband, Donnie and I moved here.'

'You've heard from your friend since Monday?'

Now, that one was *not* an innocent question! Though Sorrel all at once saw no point in treating him like the enemy. He had a job to do, and she should be helping him to do it. And, since there was no question in her mind that Donnie had not the smallest involvement in the crime—and bearing in mind that Donnie would not thank her for losing her her job if there was the smallest chance of saving it for her—Sorrel decided to be as open as she could.

'No,' she answered, aware that, though he had seemed an impatient man on Monday, he had waited remarkably patiently for her reply. 'And I don't know whether I'm glad or sorry about that,' she added honestly.

'Why?' he asked—she was beginning to think it was his favourite word.

'Oh, I don't know. Donnie truly loves her job. She thought the world of Trevor Simms—thought she had never had a boss like him. Which, of course, we now know she hadn't. How do I tell her he's a crook? She was so blissfully happy when she left last Saturday. She—'

'Even though she was a counter-signatory to several large withdrawals a few days prior to the electronic theft, you're still certain she had nothing to do with the embezzlement?' he cut in sharply.

That hit her like a bucketful of ice water. They had obviously found out further misappropriation of funds in the finance office. But Sorrel was not concerned with Trevor Simms, and hotly defended, 'I *know* Donnie had nothing to do with it!' To blazes with being honest—Masterson was not a friend she could talk to honestly; he was an interrogator. 'Surely you've found out for yourself by now that Donnie hasn't a dishonest bone in her body?' Sorrel added snappily. Oh, heavens, this got worse! Donnie had trusted Trevor Simms so implicitly she would have signed 'D. Pargetter' to any piece of paper he put in front of her.

Caleb Masterson studied the fire in her flashing green eyes impassively. 'I'm working on it,' he answered, calm in the face of her aggressiveness.

'Have you found Trevor Simms yet?' Sorrel followed up.

'Brazil's a big country. But we'll get him.'

'He went to Brazil?'

Caleb Masterson nodded. 'All being well, he'll be back here before too long.'

That sounded quite ominous. By the look of it, Trevor Simms was not going to be allowed to get off lightly.

'Donnie didn't know anything about it!' Sorrel blurted out suddenly, starting to panic that her dear friend was being tarred with the same dishonest brush as Trevor Simms. Then all at once it hit her that *she* might be being tarred with that same brush too. 'Why are you here?' she demanded abruptly, only just keeping her feelings of panic down.

Caleb Masterson continued to survey her coolly. 'Did I not say I'd be in touch?' he reminded her.

'You still think I had something to do with it, don't you?' she challenged hostilely.

He shrugged. 'Whether your friend is up to her neck in this, or whether she isn't, I'd say it's highly unlikely—in the event you're in this too—that she would ask you to trot along to Simms' office the way you did last Monday, wouldn't you?'

Sorrel tried to keep up with him. 'Because…?' she faltered.

'Because, Miss Oliphant, as dim as your flatmate appears to be, I cannot see even her—should you be as crooked—putting you somewhere where you're at risk of being caught and having to tell us all there is to tell.'

Sorrel chewed that over for a moment or two. She didn't like the words 'dim' or 'crooked' when appended to her friend, but knew by then that further protest on her behalf would be useless.

'So—I'm in the clear?' she asked. But before she could breathe a sigh of relief about that, something else suddenly struck her. 'You've had me checked out, haven't you?' she accused.

'With my company losing out to the tune of over a million—did you think I wouldn't?' he countered.

Put like that, she supposed not—even though she did not feel very comfortable at having some investigator prying into her life. She glanced over and noted his coffee cup was empty. Good. She didn't think she would breathe freely until he had gone.

'Thank you for dropping by,' she said, by way of telling him he had delighted her with his presence for long enough.

'You're between jobs, I think you said?' He refused to take the hint.

She blinked. What had that got to do with anything? 'I intend to have a look round when I've—' She broke off. He wouldn't be interested in her trips to Little Bossington. 'That's right,' she replied, and would have left it at that.

'You can afford not to work?'

'I'm not using your money to keep afloat!' she flared. 'I've ample funds from my parents' estate!'

He nodded, and she had the sudden feeling that he'd already known that, and had been baiting some kind of trap for her. 'So, just how keen are you to try and keep Donalda Pargetter's job for her?' he asked.

Sorrel did not merely blink, she stared. 'You're saying, after all this hullabaloo—not to mention you still haven't established that Donnie is as innocent as I keep repeating that she is—that there's a chance her job will still be there for her when she comes home?' She did not believe it.

He seemed unconcerned with what she believed, but did allow, 'On balance, with what I've discovered so far, I'd say that, while culpable through ignorance, Donnie

Pargetter did not have a clue what was going on, and is therefore most probably innocent.'

Sorrel continued to stare at the dark-haired, grey-eyed man. She wanted to warm to him because it looked as though he was ready to consider Donnie not guilty, but she was wary—not sure she was yet ready to trust him or his motives.

'I'll do what I can to save her job, naturally,' she answered, ready as ever to do what she could for Donnie, the same way that Donnie would pull out all the stops for her. 'What exactly are you suggesting?' she asked, having no clue.

And was left staring at him stunned when, without pause, he replied, 'I would like you to come and work in her office. To—'

Sorrel did not even have to think about it. 'Oh, no!' she exclaimed. He wanted her to go and work where everyone would know she was there under dubious circumstances!

He glanced back at her, as if to say *suit yourself,* but stated silkily, 'You're giving notice on Miss Pargetter's behalf?'

That shook her rigid! 'I'm not doing anything of the kind!' she erupted.

'That's what it sounds like.'

'How can you expect me to work there?' she protested. 'Everyone will know that I'm working there under a cloud—that Donnie is under suspicion!'

'No, they won't. While it will all come at out Simms' trial, I want, for the moment, to keep this whole business as quiet as possible.'

Sorrel stared at him mutinously. His firm was internationally known for its expertise in marine engineering, both above and under water. 'Ward Maritime International don't want the whole wide world to know that they've been ripped off?'

'Exactly. As for you, you'll be there as a temporary PA while Donalda Pargetter is away—which will afford you every opportunity of giving her a good press.'

Sorrel thought about it and knew that, for Donnie, she would do what she could. But… 'I don't get it,' she confessed. 'With Trevor Simms gone there isn't a finance controller for me to work for. So what am I supposed to be doing all day?'

'To be frank,' he answered, 'the finance office is a shambles. Everything I've looked through—all the in-house stuff—is littered with mistakes. It needs straightening up—' He broke off, and then stated, 'From what I've heard, you are the very person to do it.'

Sorrel looked at him, sorely wanting to take up cudgels on Donnie's behalf, but aware that, since she knew only the tiniest amount of what Donnie did in her office day, she was unable to speak up for her from a work point of view.

Which left her challenging him on another point. 'You've been in touch with my former employers, haven't you?'

'Ed Apsley speaks very highly of you.'

'You didn't…?'

'He knows nothing of the circumstances at Brown and Johns.' Caleb Masterson read her mind. 'I told him I was thinking of asking you to come and work for me.'

*After* the 'speaks very highly' reference, not before, she did not doubt. She thought of something else.

'Presumably you haven't chosen a suitable replacement for Trevor Simms yet?'

'We're taking our time over that one.'

'But you'll have a new finance controller by the time Donnie returns in five weeks' time?'

'At the moment auditors are going through that office with the proverbial fine-tooth comb, checking to see if there are any other funds Simms has secreted away.'

'I'm to work with them? The auditors?'

'Give them every assistance, should they ask. But they'll know by Monday that you're as much in the dark as they are. That is,' he stated smoothly, 'if you truly are prepared to do what you can to ensure Miss Pargetter holds on to the job you have stated she loves so much.' He paused for a moment, and then went on, 'I suggest you come in on Monday and work through the remainder of her holiday.'

Five weeks! He was 'suggesting' that she spend the next five weeks working at Brown and Johns—on the chance of saving Donnie's job for her. Sorrel looked at him crossly. Of course she was willing to do everything she could to secure Donnie's job. It went without saying. But from the way he had spoken of her friend—'dim' and 'airhead', not to mention he thought Donnie deserving of blame, albeit through ignorance—she thought it most doubtful that Donnie would be welcomed back.

'You are telling me that, should I come and work for you, Donnie's job will be secure, even though you describe her office as a shambles?'

Caleb Masterson was silent for a few moments, and then quietly he replied, 'It is my belief that Donnie Pargetter was vastly misdirected by Trevor Simms. His replacement will be a man of our choosing, of our standard—that is Ward Maritime's and not Brown and Johns'. We will make sure he is of a calibre to know how to direct staff. Meantime, all accounting staff will carry on as normal.'

'With me sorting out the shambles Trevor Simms allowed the office to become?' Sorrel stated, trying to draw any blame away from Donnie and wondering at the same time where exactly she was supposed to start, going in blind like that.

'I have every confidence in you, Sorrel,' he answered, using her first name and all at once seeming to her to be less imperious than he had.

She felt her own attitude softening, but she was quite aware that Donnie's job was far from safe yet, and knew she could not allow herself to go soft. 'But why me?' she challenged. 'Surely you could get someone el—?'

'You did hear me say I wanted to keep this as quiet as possible? You already know what is going on,' he reminded her.

Didn't she just! Yet still she wasn't ready to just submit. 'You haven't just invented this job purely so you can keep an eye on me?'

'Wait until Monday; I'm sure you'll see that your expertise is very much required.'

There wasn't any answer to that, except, 'This will be a job for five weeks only? I'll be able to leave when Donnie comes back?'

Caleb Masterson looked at her as if he was surprised she should think that there was any doubt about that. Feeling uncomfortable under his gaze, she said, 'I mean, I've a lot of other—um—stuff to do besides.'

'You've applied for a job elsewhere?'

'I'm taking my time about that. But I've been trying to sort out my guardian's home. He was a barrister before he retired and—' She broke off, suddenly realising that this man opposite would not do any kind of a half-investigatory job and would already know that. When this embezzlement investigation landed on his desk, he would see it through and would leave nothing to chance, she felt sure. 'But you know all about Lionel Hastings. Where he lives—lived—the size of his house, and possibly what's in his papers that I'm wading through.'

'It must be quite a task, making sure you're not throwing out papers that might be important,' he replied.

Caleb Masterson might not have directly answered her question about knowing where her guardian lived and all the rest of it, but she just knew that he did. It gave her an uncomfortable feeling, knowing she had been so thoroughly investigated, and suddenly she wanted to be by herself.

She stood up. 'Will nine o'clock on Monday be all right?' she asked, knowing that she would be pleasantly relieved if he said that no it wouldn't.

But he was on his feet too. 'Quite all right,' he replied, and added, 'Thanks for the coffee.' He didn't wait for her to say she would show him out—but went.

Sorrel followed through her intention to spend the weekend in Little Bossington, but her thoughts kept returning again and again to Caleb Masterson. She still could not quite believe that, somehow or other, she was starting work for him next week.

He was not in the building when she presented herself at Brown and Johns on Monday. She went straight to the office she knew as Donnie's, and had barely had time to wonder where on earth did she begin, than a man of average build, a few years older than her twenty-three years, walked in.

'You must be Sorrel Oliphant,' he greeted her with a warm smile. 'James Tew,' he introduced himself, holding out his right hand. 'I'm with the audit team. Would you like me to show you around?'

And so the day began. By eleven o'clock Sorrel had been able to form her own opinion that 'shambles' didn't cover it. Everything she touched seemed to be in total disorder.

Both she and Donnie had trained at the same college, but since then Donnie appeared to have adopted her own peculiar and quite unfathomable filing system.

Hoping that the system was one which Trevor Simms had developed and instructed, as a way of covering up his sins, Sorrel saw that the only way round it was to re-file everything. That way, rather than spend wasted half-hours searching every time the auditors wanted something, she would know exactly where to look.

The day sped by, and it was close to five when the phone on Donnie's desk rang. Sorrel picked it up, realised she could not state *Mr Simms' office,* so instead answered with a pleasant, 'Finance.'

'How's your day gone?' enquired a voice she knew straight away.

No way was she going to say a word about Donnie's bizarre filing system. 'I've managed to keep busy,' she replied pleasantly.

'It hasn't been too tedious for you, I hope?'

She had a feeling he knew jolly well she would say nothing but good about her day—certainly nothing detrimental about Donnie's work. 'It's been most interesting, Mr Masterson,' she answered politely.

'Cale,' he replied.

'Pardon?'

'Most of my business colleagues call me Cale.'

'Oh, I see.' Grief! 'Call me Cale' was a bit of a change from the acid way he had been with her the previous Monday! And—*colleagues?*

'The auditors aren't getting under your feet too much?' he enquired.

Good heavens. This was a charm offensive and then some. 'They're all extremely pleasant,' she answered as evenly as she could. They were too. James had brought her a coffee that morning, and William had brought her tea that afternoon. 'Er—we're working well together, I think.'

'Good,' he commented. 'Sing out if you need anything.'

That was it. He was gone. Sorrel replaced her phone and started to clear her desk for the day. Then realised she was smiling. Good Lord! No need to go overboard just because that brute of a man had just shown her he had a pleasanter side to him.

She was on her way home when she began to wonder if that invitation to call him by his first name, and his implication that they were now colleagues, was his way of saying that, after such a bad start, he now trusted her.

She supposed to a certain extent he must trust her—or no way would he allow her to set foot over the threshold of the Brown and Johns building, much less allow her to spend her day working freely with their financial paperwork.

Sorrel went to bed that night, having got over her surprise at Caleb Masterson's phone call, and by then feeling fairly certain that the next time she saw him he would be back to being his blunt, brutish self.

The next time she saw him turned out to be late on Thursday afternoon. By then she was feeling quite comfortable with the work she was doing. While some of the audit work was done off the premises at the audit company's offices, some of it was being done in the next-door office, which had been Trevor Simms' before his abrupt departure.

Which, in turn, meant that both James and William were constant visitors. James had, in fact, just been to see her—to ask her for a date. As nicely as she could, she had turned him down.

'I shall keep on trying,' he was saying, undeterred, and just then the door opened, and Caleb Masterson came in.

He nodded a curt kind of greeting, and James went back to the other office. Cale went and closed the communicating door. 'Does he spend much time in here?' he enquired coolly.

She guessed he was Mr Masterson today. 'No more than he should.'

'He's just asked you out.' It was a statement, not a question.

She shrugged. 'It happens.'

Caleb Masterson studied her, his glance taking in her long red-brown hair, gorgeous green eyes, and her slender figure in her dark trouser suit. 'Often, I shouldn't wonder,' he remarked finally, not a smile about him. 'Going?'

She shook her head—not that it was any business of his. 'I'm off men at the moment,' she informed him shortly.

Cale looked at her steadily, then all of a sudden his lips twitched. 'And that includes present company?'

He didn't expect an answer. 'You said it,' she replied.

'What happened?'

'Who said anything happened?'

Cale eyed her shrewdly. 'You're a beautiful woman, Sorrel,' he commented, without making it sound like a compliment. 'Men are going to want to date you. And have in the past, I'm sure. So what has happened that has caused you to be between boyfriends just now, and not wanting to do anything about it?'

'Funnily enough, going out with some male or other is not the be all and end all of my existence,' Sorrel told him snappily. He might, for the moment, be her boss, but that didn't entitle him to— She broke off that thought as another thought sped in. 'Is this third degree on account of your thinking I'm in league with some man with regard to that missing money?'

'Not at all,' Cale replied, seeming surprised that she had seen it that way. 'I was merely concerned that something had happened with your last boyfriend that might have brought about your present attitude.'

Stubbornly, she wouldn't give him the satisfaction of knowing just how right he had got it. 'It's none of your business,' she told him stonily.

'Was it so bad?' he asked. But when—boss or no boss, colleague or no—she was quite prepared to tell him to go and take a running jump, suddenly Caleb Masterson smiled the most wonderful gentle smile and asked, while her insides did a ridiculous kind of flip, 'Who was your last boyfriend, Sorrel?'

And she found she was answering. 'Just one of your normal run-of-the-mill sharks!'

'Sharks?' He seemed intrigued—she wished she had not said anything.

She was starting to be angry. Though just then she was unsure if it was Caleb Masterson she was angry with, or Guy Fletcher. 'He led me on for just one thing!' she snapped shortly.

'Sex?' Caleb Masterson misunderstood. 'That's a given, surely?' he added, though did qualify, 'After a matter of time.'

'Not with me, it isn't!' she erupted. 'And that wasn't what I meant!'

She was aware of him looking at her sharply. And when she was wishing that he would just clear off somewhere, still he persisted, 'So, if it wasn't sex, what was this particular shark after?'

By that time Sorrel was beginning to wonder how on earth this kind of conversation had got started. But, perhaps, still uncertain about her because of the embezzlement, this man was trying to make her fall into a trap of some kind. 'Not an "in" with this company through my friendship with Donnie!' she retorted.

'Did I suggest anything of the kind?'

'You might not be saying it, but I'm sure you were thinking it.' He shook his head slightly, but she flared on just the same. 'For your information, it was not this company's money he was after, but *mine!*'

She'd had enough. There were still twenty minutes to go before going home time, but she picked up her bag and marched straight out of there.

Cale Masterson did nothing to stop her, but watched her leave, the light of something quite unfathomable in his eyes.

## CHAPTER THREE

SORREL was still feeling a shade upset when she went to work on Friday. Thankfully she did not see Cale Masterson that day.

She did not thank him that because of his probing questions she had last night relived that dreadful time at Little Bossington, when Guy Fletcher's live-in girl-friend had sought her out.

Had Emma Gray been bold, brassy and strident, perhaps Sorrel would not have felt so wretched. But Emma Gray was the total opposite of that. She was sweet, pretty, and a gentle type of person. She had come to the house a few days after Lionel Hastings' funeral and had stood at the door and asked, 'Is it possible for me to have a word with you?'

'Yes, of course,' Sorrel had agreed, having no idea that, at the end of that twenty-minute 'word', she would feel totally shattered, her dreams in ruins about her.

Guy, according to Emma, had been spending more and more time away from home—the home they shared! She had asked him if anything was wrong. He had been buoyant when he'd replied that matters could not be more right. He had been hoping to go into business on his own. All he needed was some quite substantial investment. Very soon, he was quite confident, that investment would be to hand.

Sorrel had been stunned. She had actually given serious thought to helping Guy start his own boat-designing business! More than that, she had actually decided to let him have the investment he had 'reluctantly' admitted he needed.

Only then had she started to see a different slant on his delicate probing and questioning. Questioning that had resulted in her confiding that she had always known that she was her guardian's heir.

An hour after Emma Gray had left, Sorrel had started to disbelieve her first impression that Emma had told her the truth. Sorrell had recalled how Guy had declared that he *loved* her, for goodness' sake. How could any man do that while living with someone else?

He'd been due to call that evening, and she'd wondered if he would keep their arrangement. She'd been convinced when she saw him leave his car and come bounding over to the front door that Emma Gray must be an ex-girlfriend whom he hadn't seen in a very long while. And who possibly wanted him back again.

Her first question to him, though, and his reaction to it, had told Sorrel that Emma Gray had been speaking the truth.

'Emma Gray and I had a chat today,' she'd stated, pulling back when he would have greeted her with a kiss.

He'd gone a fiery red. 'Emma's been here?' he'd exclaimed, and, as something furtive came to his expression, 'How the hell did she find out?' he'd asked, clearly shaken.

'You're living with her?' Sorrel had questioned, for some reason needing to hear him confirm it.

'Look, I—er—I can explain,' he'd begun to bluster.

And Sorrel had known at that moment what a sham of a man he was. 'Goodbye, Guy,' she'd bade him coldly.

'Let me explain,' he'd tried again. 'Emma and me—well, I've—um—been trying to break with her. But—well, she loves me, and...and...' He'd floundered—and Sorrel hadn't needed to hear any more.

'It's a good job somebody does,' she'd told him—and, closing the door on him, had known herself a liar. She loved him. Loved him still, despite his treachery.

Friday at Brown and Johns seemed to pass tediously slowly, with no sign of Cale Masterson. James Tew asked her out again. Again she refused.

Sorrel spent another weekend at Little Bossington. Her guardian had been a tidy man, but had never seemed to throw anything away. She worked diligently on disposing and keeping, and designating more and more ready for the charity shops.

She did not feel at all rested when she went into the offices of Brown and Johns on Monday. But she worked hard.

As the week progressed, she felt extremely restless, but was able to find many reasons for that. She had relived Guy Fletcher's two-timing courtship, she was missing Donnie, and she found Caleb Masterson most disturbing.

Though the reason for the latter was pretty obvious—

she was trying to hang on to Donnie's job for her, and he—Masterson—had the yea or nay on that, she suspected.

Funnily enough she found that of late she was thinking of him more frequently that she thought of Guy.

She wondered if Cale was any nearer to finding Trevor Simms. Wondered, if he had, if Britain had an extradition treaty with Brazil. Whether they had or hadn't, Cale had sounded pretty emphatic when he'd said, 'He'll be back here before too long.'

Having not heard from Cale Masterson all that week, Sorrel discovered she was rather pleased to hear him when he phoned on Friday afternoon.

'Busy?' he asked.

'Nose to the grindstone,' she replied cheerfully.

And she actually heard a smile in his voice when he said, 'I know you've been doing a splendid job.'

She did not know from that if he meant he guessed she was doing a good job, or if he meant he had enquired of James, William or perhaps Lawrence, a senior auditor who floated in from time to time.

'You busy?' she asked, to prevent herself from attempting to fish for the answer. She was sure it was of no concern of hers from where he gleaned his information as to her usefulness.

'Just flown in,' he replied. She would not ask from where, but it explained why she had not heard a peep from him since last Friday. 'Did you want to see me?' he asked, and she realised she had prompted his question with her question of 'You busy?'.

'Not particularly,' she answered, feeling oddly flustered, but added truthfully, 'Though in all honesty there's not enough work here now to keep me busy until Donnie returns.'

'You're not thinking of leaving before then, I hope?' he said shortly—his way, she felt, of reminding her that she was honour-bound to work the full five weeks she had agreed to.

'Not if you don't mind me bringing my knitting in!' she flew—and actually heard him laugh.

'Leave it with me, Sorrel,' he said, his tone amused. 'I'll see what I can do.'

'Welcome home,' she said, and, believing their conversation was at an end, put down her phone. Oddly, she realised that she was smiling.

When she arrived home that night she found there was a card from Donnie. A breathless kind of card, on which she'd scribbled everything down in a rush. Africa was wonderful. The sky was endless. The animals they had seen were simply stunning. Adrian was in his element. Adrian knew so much, was so clever. She had never, ever met anyone so absolutely fantastic as Adrian before. Adrian was unbelievable, and—more unbelievable—Adrian didn't think she was half bad either. 'Love you lots, Donnie.'

Sorrel so missed her. She wished Donnie would phone—but then again, as she had told Cale, she didn't know whether she was glad or sorry not to speak to her. Donnie sounded so ecstatically happy—how could she think to put a blight on her happiness? Sorrel sighed. Time enough for Donnie to know all about the unpleasant situation she had left when she returned.

Sorrel spent the weekend at Little Bossington, and felt that she was at last making headway. She went into work on Monday, but with no one there to give her instruction, and James, William and Lawrence working off the premises, she found the day hanging heavily.

By then she was acquainted with one or two in the general office. But, since she was unsure if Cale would want her to work anywhere other than where he'd put her, she didn't think she could go and ask if anyone wanted a hand with anything.

It was just after two on Tuesday afternoon, and, even though James and William were back, she was seriously contemplating taking up knitting or bringing in a book to read. She was in the middle of thinking, So much for Caleb Masterson and his 'I'll see what I can do', in response to her saying she did not have enough work, when he rang.

'You've decided there's no need for me to stay on here?' she suggested, before he could say why he had called.

'It's so bad?'

'Having little to do makes it a long day.'

There was a pause before, 'You're still anxious to keep Donalda Pargetter's job for her?'

'That was a low blow.' She retorted, yet had to admit that the only reason she was there was because of Donnie. 'I've cleared up most of the outstanding stuff. Everything is up to date for when the new man comes in,' she rattled off. 'Yet you still want me to sit here, nine to five, bored out of my skull.'

'Actually,' he cut in, when she paused for breath, 'I had intended giving you a call yesterday, but the day got away from me.'

She calmed down a trifle. He had been away from his

office last week, so must have been busy yesterday catching up. 'You've got some work for me?' she guessed—why else would he intend to give her a call?

'There is something you can help me out with,' he agreed, adding, 'I'm still tied up here. Can you find time to come over, do you think?'

My, wasn't he being polite? He could have just ordered her to go and see him, and for Donnie she would have gone. 'You're over at Ward Maritime?' she asked, wondering why he couldn't tell her what he wanted done over the telephone.

'I should be free around four-thirty. But, in case I can find a spare ten minutes before then, perhaps you wouldn't mind coming earlier?'

He really was being exceedingly pleasant. 'No problem,' she replied and, knowing how busy he was, she put her phone down.

Shortly after that she tidied her desk and went along to the cloakroom to tidy herself. For no special reason she was glad she had chosen to wear a newish suit of pale green that particularly suited her.

She went back to her desk and then decided that, since there appeared there might be a chance Cale could fit her in before four-thirty, she might as well go over to Ward Maritime now. Wishing she had thought to bring her briefcase—though if Cale had any paperwork he wanted her to bring back he could find a folder to put it in—Sorrel went to tell James and William that she was off to head office.

She found the offices of Ward Maritime International without too much trouble, and, expected, it seemed, was directed up to Cale's PA's office.

Victoria Ross was a pleasant woman, somewhere in her mid-twenties. And Sorrel, who had once been a busy PA herself, recognised the signs of somebody who was snowed under. She was half minded to ask if there was anything she could help with, but knew she herself would have refused such an offer.

'Can I get you some tea or coffee?' Victoria enquired, when Sorrel had introduced herself. 'I'm afraid Cale is likely to be in a meeting for another hour.'

'Oh, no, thanks.' Sorrel refused the offer of refreshment, and, knowing that the PA would much rather get on with her work than have to sit and socialise, was saying, 'I'll come back later,' when the door opened and a man of average height, about thirty, came in.

'There's a chance he may be free sooner,' Victoria Ross stated—and Sorrel was unsure what to do for the best.

'I'll—er—go and wait in Reception,' she said with a smile, starting to feel very much in the way—the PA must be wanting quite urgently to get on with her work. No doubt Cale had brought back loads for her to deal with.

'Can I help at all?'

Both women turned to look at the new arrival.

'Miss Oliphant is from Brown and Johns—part of the audit team,' the PA explained.

'Ah,' he said, and, a wolfish kind of gleam in his eyes, he extended his right hand. 'Rex Dunne,' he introduced himself. 'I'm head of the PR team.' He beamed a smile and Sorrel found herself shaking hands with him. He addressed Victoria. 'Cale not free?'

'You're second in the queue,' she informed him.

'Then why don't we both go and wait in my office?' he suggested to Sorrel.

Of the two, she would have preferred to wait with the PA. But, against that, she did not want to keep the woman from her work or hold her up in any way.

'My office is on this floor, and Victoria can tell Cale where to find you,' Rex Dunne assured her, with his ever-present smile.

They were going along the corridor before Sorrel had time to say that she didn't want to be an imposition on Rex Dunne either. 'I can quite easily wait in Reception,' she offered.

'Wouldn't dream of letting you,' he responded cheerfully, and stopped at a door. 'Here we are,' he said, and ushered her into a large airy office. He cleared some sort of a display off one of the chairs. 'Come and take a seat.'

'Thank you,' Sorrel answered politely.

'I can't keep calling you Miss Oliphant,' he said smoothly.

'Sorrel,' she replied.

'Would you like some tea?'

'No, thank you. I don't want to keep you from your work,' she commented apologetically.

'Trust me. I worked in overdrive this morning—I'm due a little relaxation. Now, tell me what goes on over at Brown and Johns?'

*Wouldn't dream of it!* 'How much do you know?' she hedged.

'I wouldn't have known anything except I had to be warned in case the newspapers somehow get a whisper of it and I get contacted to give some sort of press release. I know only the bare basics—the rest they're keeping it very much under wraps. But they don't recall chaps like Cale Masterson without some very good reason.'

'He was away at the time?'

'He was on holiday in sunny climes. Though it's true in his role as chief troubleshooter for the firm—not just in finance—he travels all over the world. So—what happened?'

She smiled, realising she liked Rex Dunne. He was obvious, but open with it. 'We're keeping it under wraps,' she bounced back at him.

'Now, that is *mean!*' he complained, but he was laughing. And then he revealed, 'Thank goodness we'd got a team in updating their computer system that Sunday.'

'It—couldn't have been better,' she murmured, having not a clue what he was talking about, but playing along.

'I'll say. I don't know what was discovered—other than that, fortunately, while the computer specialists were updating and linking the system to ours, one of those geeky kind of kids on the payroll was messing about with things computer brilliant—way above my head—when all of a sudden he's yelling, "Hey—where did that go?" or something along those lines. A passing supervisor overhears, and the next you know Cale is jetting back—leaving languishing whichever lovely he's with—and straight into harness here.'

Sorrel had been hooked on the fact that, were it not for some computer geek playing around in the system at the very moment Trevor Simms had robbed the firm of a million-plus pounds, the theft might not have shown for some while. But suddenly she discovered that her interest was elsewhere.

'Cale didn't—er—take his wife on holiday, then?' she asked.

'He's not married,' Rex informed her. 'No female's been lucky enough to catch him.'

Sorrel was sure, belatedly, that she was not that interested. Though, 'Why lucky?' she found herself asking.

'You've seen him,' Rex obliged. 'And, apart from everything else he's got going for him, his family own half of this company.'

'He mentioned a family connection,' she recalled.

'The firm was started by his grandfather Ward. His uncle is the present chairman. Quite a few of the family work here,' he added. 'Our Cale is wealthy in his own right—but proving much too fleet-footed in the romance stakes to get caught. Are you married or attached?' He abruptly changed the subject to her.

'No—and not interested,' she replied, hoping to stop him before he went further. No chance.

'I'm not suggesting marriage, so you're quite safe there—I tried it once, didn't like it.' Rex beamed her a smile. 'But we could have a pleasant time if you'd like to join me for dinner one evening?'

'Thanks, but no thanks,' she replied.

'Lunch, then?' he suggested. She shook her head. 'A picnic in the park? Strawberries at Wimbledon? A trolley dash round the supermarket?' he fired in quick succession.

She burst out laughing—just as the door opened and Cale Masterson came in. He glanced from one to the other, his glance returning to Sorrel and her upturned mouth.

'I trust Rex has been able to keep you entertained?' he enquired dryly.

Sorrel suspected a touch of the 'acid' factor. 'You're free for a few minutes?' she asked, refusing to apologise for something she had thought funny.

'Come with me,' he instructed, and, with a nod to Rex Dunne, Cale help the door open for her.

'Lovely day.' She commented on the weather as he escorted her along the corridor.

'Did Rex Dunne ask you out?'

'I was thinking of bringing my raincoat this morning, but it doesn't look as if I shall need it.'

Cale gave her a wry look and halted by a door that was next to the door of his PA's office. He opened it and led the way into what she presumed was his own office, which, besides the usual office furniture, housed a couple of sofas with an occasional table in between.

He invited her to take a seat on one of them, and when she was seated he took the other. 'Are you going?' he enquired.

Presumably out with Rex Dunne. 'Do you think I should?'

Cale shook his head. 'He eats little girls like you for breakfast.'

She had to laugh. While she thought he had a nerve, poking his nose into what might be her private life, she thought their exchange funny. 'You take your job as investigator much too seriously,' she replied.

'Dunne told you I was an investigator?' Cale asked, his glance on her upturned mouth.

'He wasn't talking out of turn—and I didn't either,' she added hurriedly. 'I mean, I never told him anything about the—er—problems over at Brown and Johns. Um—he thinks I'm part of the audit team.'

'That's what I've told Victoria,' Cale remarked—and Sorrel warmed to him because it seemed he had given neither her nor Donnie a bad press.

'Er—Rex didn't actually say you were an investigator, more a chief troubleshooter,' she found she was explaining.

Cale studied her for some moments, and then said, 'Good.'

'Good?'

He smiled then, that smile that peculiarly did dizzying things to her heart region. 'It's part of why I asked you here.'

Sorrel's spirits dipped and she surveyed him solemnly. She'd been asked there, she had thought, because she did not have sufficient work to keep her busy and because he was going to find her some. 'You've found out something about—?'

'I'm still working on it,' he cut in.

'You want me to—troubleshoot in some way?' It was the best she could come up with.

'I think you can leave that side of it to me.' He let her know she had got that part wrong. And, when she looked puzzled as to what she was doing there, 'What I need you for, more specifically, is to act as my occasional personal PA,' he enlightened her.

Her eyes shot wide. 'PA?' she echoed. 'Your *personal...* personal assistant?' She did not like the sound of that one little bit.

'Don't get alarmed.' He attempted to calm her before her imagination took off. 'You're not my type,' he added. *Thank you very much!* 'By "personal" I mean that very occasionally I would like you to accompany me when I entertain clients and perhaps their womenfolk.'

Her eyes widened in surprise. Good heavens, she had never imagined anything like this! 'Surely one of your women-friends would be better suited?' she protested, realising even as she said it that she did not like the idea of that either—though she could not fathom why on earth she didn't.

But Cale was already shaking his head. 'The present situation I'm thinking of will be a semi-business dinner, one where conversation might stray into areas I would want to keep highly confidential.'

As in one of his women-friends might blab? Sorrel supposed she was flattered, in a way. Yet she still didn't like the sound of it. 'What's wrong with your own PA? Your full-time PA?' She refused to yield. 'Surely Victoria…?'

'Victoria would by far prefer to go home at night and dine with her new husband than dine with clients. Besides which, her day working for me is pretty full without the poor woman having to put up with me after office hours as well.'

Charmingly put! Sorrel felt a mixture of confusion and—yes—pleasure. Yet… 'You trust me?' she questioned.

'It would appear so. Even without Ed Apsley's glowing reference, I've my own sighting of the work you produce, the competent way you run an office.'

It warmed her to hear him say that. But—hold on a minute, here—it was not so long ago that he'd been accusing her of being a crook. Or at least of being in league with crooks. And don't forget Guy Fletcher—was she gullible or was she gullible? Never again!

She got up from the sofa. 'Get someone else,' she stated coolly.

Cale was on his feet too. 'Why?' he demanded. 'When you would be so ideal…'

'I…I…' She was stumped for a minute. But, feeling backed into a corner, she suddenly erupted, 'I'm nobody's plaything!'

His answer was to smile a warm and genuine smile. 'Given that I've not asked that of you—or am ever likely to,' he assured her nicely. She went a tinge pink—well, how was she supposed to see it? 'Have you ever been?' he enquired, with not a blush about *him.*

'Of course,' she promptly answered; she wasn't having him thinking she hadn't a clue what went on.

But apparently he thought that anyway when, his tone gentle, 'Liar,' he becalled her.

'How can you tell?' she asked, mystified.

And was on the receiving end of a most superb grin. 'I can't tell,' he replied, his lips twitching. 'You just told me.'

'Swine!' she becalled her boss.

'So I'll pick you up at seven tonight,' he informed her, and half turned from her—too confident, to her mind, that that was the end of the argument. She was about to tell him differently when, 'When are you seeing Rex Dunne again?' he threw over his shoulder.

'I'm not!' she snapped, before she could think. He

half turned again, and she saw his lips twitch. He had got from her what he had always intended to find out. She gave him a furious look before turning smartly about and marching out of there.

That man! *My stars, was he in the right job.* What he didn't know, he made sure to find out.

Sorrel was so annoyed she found she had absent-mindedly driven home, instead of back to Brown and Johns. She was unrepentant—blow the lot of them. If she was going to a business dinner on her own time tonight… If?

By the time she had been in her flat and made a pot of tea Sorrel had calmed down considerably. She supposed—apart from Cale Masterson getting from her that which she had not wanted to tell him—what lay behind her fury was the fact that she liked to make her own decisions about which male she went out with. Which male she dated.

Though that gave her pause for thought. This wasn't what you could call a proper 'date', was it? It was business. And she supposed, if anything, she should be rather pleased that after such a dreadful introduction Cale Masterson had observed sufficient of her to know that she would safeguard anything she might overhear that was in the tiniest bit confidential.

Suddenly she was feeling a whole lot better. Suddenly she was of the opinion that, since she had been going to have a meal of some kind, tonight she might as well be an occasional *personal,* personal assistant.

Not, she realised when she had showered and changed, that while this sword of Damocles was hanging over Donnie's head she had very much choice but to jump when Caleb Masterson said jump.

He was on time, and seemed to approve of her in her warm red silk two-piece. 'I didn't go back to the office,' she confessed as they drove along.

'I don't blame you,' he replied good-humouredly.

'It wasn't intentional—I just found myself back home.' She wished she hadn't started; she felt foolish.

'Don't worry about it,' he answered smoothingly. And, straight on the heels of that, 'You're looking rather gorgeous,' he commented.

She did not take it personally. He was more trying to make her feel at ease than piling on the flattery. 'Are you troubleshooting tonight?' She decided to treat the occasion as strictly business.

'If I need to. But tonight is more about socialising and listening for any sign of problems I should know about—being ready to answer any queries that might crop up with regard to future business.'

'How many…?'

'Just the four of us this evening. Philip Kirk and his wife Penny.'

'You've met them both before?'

'You'll like them,' he replied.

'Is there anything in particular I have to do?'

He half turned, a hint of a smile on his quite superb, she realised, mouth. 'Just be yourself,' he answered, and made it sound so intimate that her heart gave a fluttering kind of beat.

She turned swiftly to look out of the side window. Grief, she was being totally ridiculous! This was business—nothing, positively nothing, more. Well, she knew that already—and had to wonder why she'd had to remind herself.

'So—um…' She turned to face the front again. 'So how did you come to be a troubleshooter?' She put the conversation where it belonged—strictly business. 'I mean—do you have a degree in it or something?'

'My degree's in oceanography,' he revealed. Then added, 'In my student vacations and in my first five years with the firm I worked in most sections of the business.' He shrugged. 'It was noticed that I appear to have a natural bent for problem-solving and sorting out trouble. More and more of that kind of work was put my way.'

'You enjoy it?'

'I prefer being sent far and wide to sort out some tricky situation much more than I do being stuck at a desk week in and week out.'

'But you do have a desk—*and* a PA.'

'A necessary evil. Not Victoria—she's great. But you can't have caviar the whole time.'

Sorrel could feel herself warming to him. He need not have told her what he had. Could, for that matter, have ignored her question altogether. But, maybe in an endeavour to make the evening flow, he was prepared to share something of himself with her.

And the evening did flow. Sorrel took to Philip and Penny Kirk straight away. Philip was somewhere in his early forties, Penny a few years younger.

They dined well and comfortably in a busy but not overcrowded restaurant. Conversation was fairly general, and business was lightly touched upon from time to time.

Though work did crop up again at the dessert stage

of their meal, but not the 'big business' side of it, when Penny enquired, 'Are you a lady of leisure, Sorrel, or do you have a job?'

'One way and another Sorrel is kept pretty busy,' Cale answered for her. 'Sorrel's guardian died recently and, as well as attending to his effects, Sorrel is doing me a favour by helping out at Brown and Johns while we have a staffing shortage.'

Favour! That was one way of describing the way she had been press-ganged into working for him. But tonight was not about her fighting her own corner, it was about being nice, was about her 'just being herself', so Sorrel swallowed on that 'favour' and commented that she liked to be busy.

'I'm sorry about your guardian,' Penny said sympathetically, seeming to appreciate that to have had a guardian must mean that she had lost her parents too. 'Perhaps when you're less busy we could meet for coffee or lunch?' she suggested.

Cale was driving Sorrel home when she gave in to the impulse to remark, 'What a lovely couple Philip and Penny are.'

'They are,' he agreed. And asked, 'Will you meet up with Penny when she rings?'

Sorrel thought about it. 'I'd quite like to. But how do you feel about it—business-wise?'

'It wouldn't be a problem,' he answered. 'Business-wise, I'm sure I can rely on your absolute discretion.'

Sorrel felt a warm glow. Cale really *did* trust her. She was still feeling most congenial towards him when they arrived at her apartment building.

She turned to say goodnight to him, but discovered

that he was getting out of the car. Sorrel found her house keys from her handbag and turned to open the passenger door. Cale was there, already opening it.

'I'll say goodnight,' she said as he escorted her to the pavement.

'I'll see you to your door,' he replied, and before she could protest that that was unnecessary he was taking her keys from her hand and unerringly selecting the correct one.

He held on to her keys as he went with her up the stairs. They stopped at her door and she began to feel just a little on edge. As unerringly as before, Cale unlocked the door of her apartment. Then, opening the door, he stood back.

She looked at him. She hoped he was not expecting to be invited in for coffee. 'Goodnight,' she said.

'It wasn't so bad?' he enquired as he handed her keys back to her.

'This evening? I enjoyed it,' she replied openly.

'Good,' he replied, and, his steady grey eyes holding hers, 'Thank you, Sorrel,' he said—and held out his right hand.

They shook hands—her skin felt all warm and tingly—and he took another step back. 'Er—goodnight,' she said again, and went through her doorway.

'Goodnight,' he said, but waited until she was inside, then closed the door for her. Having seen her safely inside, he went on his way.

But, inside her flat, Sorrel had not moved. She had been wrong to tense up the way she had, she realised—and quite unexpectedly became aware that there was a curve of a smile on her mouth.

In all honesty it suddenly came to her that she much preferred Cale's company to quite a few of the frogs she had dated!

# CHAPTER FOUR

SORREL awoke early and immediately began to relive the events of the previous evening. When she considered the awful way in which she had first become acquainted with Cale Masterson, she could only wonder anew that she had enjoyed her evening with him so much.

Not that it had been just she and Cale, of course, but he had treated her as an equal—and she had felt like an equal. But she got out of bed knowing that, for all his sophisticated courtesy of the previous evening, she must never forget that Donnie's job still hung in the balance here. Nor forget that one Caleb Masterson was in a position to tip the scales very much out of Donnie's favour.

Sorrel drove to the offices of Brown and Johns, wondering again at the tension that had gripped her at her door when she had briefly thought that Cale might expect to be invited in. Why would he have wanted to be invited in, for goodness' sake? It had been a business arrangement and nothing more. And why tense? Had she panicked because he might attempt to kiss her?

Oh, good grief! Don't go down that road! Had she

not established quite firmly that it was not a 'date' date, but merely an occasion when Cale had thought it more fitting to even up the numbers with a confidential partner.

And, yes, she knew all of that, but as she parked her car and went into the Brown and Johns building Sorrel still could not understand why she had felt just a little emotionally out of sorts when she'd gone to bed. Nor why that mixed-up emotional feeling was still with her that morning.

Whether Cale had been in touch with the auditors or not, she did not know, but happily, if a little tentatively, both William and James asked for her assistance that day.

'If you're not too busy?' William asked diffidently.

'Not busy at all,' Sorrel replied, warming to William, a new father, with traces of ejected baby milk showing on the right shoulder of his jacket.

The day brightened. She was busy. The phone rang. It was Cale. Funnily enough, she felt suddenly all sort of fluttery inside. 'Behaving yourself?' he asked lightly.

'Keeping out of mischief,' she replied.

'Good,' he said, and paused briefly. That was it. 'Is William around?'

He must have forgotten the auditors had a direct line, she mused as she put the call through to the next-door office. Realising that she was feeling a little flustered inside, she thought it about time she had a cup of coffee.

Cale's was not the only telephone call that day. Rex Dunne, the head of the PR team whom she had met yesterday, rang during the afternoon. 'I forgot to mention yesterday that I make a most fabulous curry,' he greeted her.

'Oh, I'm so sorry—I'm allergic to curry,' she lied.

'Damn!' he exclaimed. She had to laugh.

The phone on her desk, which was for the most part usually silent, rang again the following morning. Sorrel was deep into spreadsheets at the time, but, recognising that it was almost exactly the same time Cale had phoned yesterday, her insides took an instant leap. She found she had to swallow hard before she could answer it!

'Finance,' she said into the instrument.

'Sorrel!'

Her jaw dropped. *It couldn't be?* 'Yes,' she replied.

'Guy,' he supplied. 'Guy Fletcher.'

Half a dozen or more questions flooded her mind. Guy was a boat designer. Brown and Johns did marine engineering work. Was Guy ringing about work? And if not how had he discovered she was working there? And why would he ring her anyway?

'What can we do for you?' she asked efficiently. She had left him in no doubt, she had thought, that she had no interest in going out with him while he was seeing someone else.

'Emma and I have split up,' he lost no time in informing her.

'I'm sorry to hear that.' The words came automatically.

'Oh, don't be like that. It's you I love. I was a fool, I soon realised that, but…'

Sorrel was unsure at that precise moment how she was feeling, other than all churned up inside. But when at that exact second the door to her office opened and Cale Masterson came in, hot colour warmed her skin. 'H-how did you find out I worked here?' she asked. Somehow, with Cale standing there, her head seemed all of a flutter.

'By a stroke of luck, actually. I never did get your home number, much less your Surrey address.' There had been no need for him to know either detail. She had spent more time in Uncle Lionel's home than her own—had been right there whenever Guy had wanted to phone or call. 'I tried Blake Logistics—I remembered you said you used to work there. But they wouldn't give me your address.'

'You rang Blake Logistics?' she questioned incredulously, wishing Cale would go through to the auditors' office, instead of just standing there taking in every word.

'It was important to me that I got in touch with you,' he answered, causing her to bite down the words *You're still not getting a penny.*

She gave Cale a look that should have told him she wouldn't mind if he disappeared. But he, it seemed, appeared to be intent on staying.

'So then I remembered your friend telling me when I told her I was a boat designer that she worked in marine engineering at Brown and Johns. I rang asking for her—called her Bonnie not Donnie, but they knew who I meant—and they said she was on holiday. On the off-chance I asked if they knew her friend Sorrel—and here you are!'

'Yes, well, I'm very busy just now.'

'Oh, don't be like that,' he protested, sounding hurt—

after the way he had hurt *her!* 'Look, I'm in London for a couple of days next week. My firm are having an exhibition. I'd love it if you'd join me at the party afterwards—a week tomorrow?'

'I'm sorry, Guy,' she responded, still on autopilot, 'I can't meet you.'

'Why on earth not?' he asked, and, all cajoling, 'You loved me once, Sorrel. I can't believe you've changed so suddenly. We love each other, and—'

For the moment she forgot that Cale was in the room, listening to every word she said. Painful memories stabbed at her. She had given Guy her whole trust and he had betrayed her—and now he was talking of them loving each other, as though nothing had happened.

'Actually, Guy—' she interrupted his amorous entreaties '—I'm going out with someone else.' And with that, perhaps fearful that she might yet weaken, she put down her phone.

For how many seconds or minutes she stayed staring blindly at the phone she had no idea. She was not even sure what she was thinking, or if she was thinking at all.

But then, into the silence, 'Are you?' Cale asked, and, taking up a chair, he brought it over to her desk and sat down.

'What?' she asked witlessly.

Cale studied her now pale face. '*Do* you have some man in tow?' he asked.

As if it had got anything to do with him! 'No!' she retorted shortly, wishing he would go so she could sort her head out.

Still Cale continued to study her. 'You seem—upset,' he commented quietly. 'Who is Guy?'

She gave him an impatient look. '"He was my man—but he did me wrong",' she quoted acidly.

Cale was undaunted. 'The shark?' he probed. And, stern suddenly, 'You still love him?' he questioned abruptly.

'Yes,' she answered, without thinking. But then, as Cale appeared to frown darkly, 'I—don't know,' she corrected honestly. 'I did—I—do. I don't know. I feel too churned-up to think.'

Cale surveyed her for long moments, and then pronounced, 'I don't think you do.'

'And what would *you* know about it?' she flared. This wasn't about work, it was personal, and she didn't need Cale Masterson sticking in his two pennyworth!

He was unabashed. 'You'll have to see him,' he asserted decidedly.

'No, I won't!' she fired back. But found she was asking, 'Why will I have to see him?'

'To find out.'

'Find out?'

'You need to move on, Sorrel,' Cale answered quietly. 'Before you can do that, you need to find out if you still have feelings for him. Only then will you know where you're going.'

'I thought I was doing very well the way I was,' she replied, still a shade belligerently.

'From what I know of you, I'd say you're brave enough to face up to it,' Cale stated.

'It's all right for you,' she retorted snappily.

He had no idea of the gut-wrenching time she had endured. He with his self-assured 'You'll have to see him'! Suddenly, though, as she looked at Cale, an idea came to her that was so outrageous she almost didn't voice it. Had he not made her so cross with his statement that she'd have to see Guy again—just as if it was that simple—she probably would not have voiced it. But she was cross—annoyed.

So she stared solemnly at him for a few further seconds and then, in all seriousness, stated, 'I've heard that you're quite wealthy.'

Cale stared back at her, his look as serious as hers as he appeared to be trying to work out this new element in their conversation. 'I get by,' he admitted at length, and asked, as perhaps she'd known he would, 'Why the interest?'

Sorrel supposed she must be pleased he was asking rather than assuming she had some financial ulterior motive. 'Guy wants me to go to his firm's post-exhibition party. I need a boyfriend—one who isn't after my inheritance,' she replied. Cale's expression remained bland, and, thinking of the temporary job she was doing for him, she felt obliged to continue, 'Temporary capacity only.'

A look of something she could not define came to his eyes. But, instead of telling her in no uncertain terms *No way,* he ignored part of what she had said to enquire, '*You're* wealthy?'

She shook her head. 'Not by your standards, I suppose.'

'You inherited a tidy sum from your guardian.' It was more of a statement than a question.

'How did you know that?' she exclaimed. She knew she had told him of her guardian's death, but she would swear she had not said a word about being his sole heir!

Cale Masterson shrugged, and did not look in the least shame-faced as he replied, 'It's my job to know these things.'

That shook her. She stared at him faintly disbelieving. 'You really did do a thorough investigatory job on me, didn't you?' He did not answer, and she realised he had no need to. When that money had disappeared it had been his job to check her out to the nth degree. 'Is that when you started to believe me? When you knew I had no need to steal?'

His mouth curved upwards. 'Who could look into those beautiful honest green eyes and not believe you?' he replied charmingly.

'Pfff!' she scorned. 'You must have forgotten our very first meeting.' But, not wanting particularly to remember that herself, she went quickly on. 'Anyway, Guy knows that, apart from the money from my parents—and I expect you know all about that too, down to the last penny—my guardian has left me "well provided for". The estate won't be settled for some while, I expect, but Guy was—and still is, I suspect—after some of it to start his own business.'

'You hadn't thought about backing him?' Cale enquired.

'Of course I had!' she replied snappily. 'I was all set to ask how much. But—but…' She stumbled. It still hurt. That betrayal still hurt.

'But?' Cale prompted.

'But then a woman—very pretty, very gentle—came to Uncle Lionel's door and to my complete astonishment explained that she and Guy were living together. During our twenty minute chat she told me of Guy's ambitions, and of how he'd confided that the substantial investment he needed would very soon be in his bank.'

Cale stayed looking at her, his expression serious as he enquired evenly, 'And what was his response when you asked him about it? I presume that you did ask him about it?'

Sorrel nodded. 'I knew she had been speaking the truth the moment I mentioned her name to him.'

'And he still had the nerve to seek you out today!'

'He's just told me they have split up.'

'He's not good enough for you, Sorrel,' Cale stated forthrightly.

She sighed heavily. She had been feeling emotionally out of sorts these last few days.

But suddenly Cale's tone had changed, and was sympathetic, gentle somehow, as he asked, 'So where do I come in?' and she knew that he must be referring to her statement earlier that she needed a boyfriend.

She felt a smile coming on, but didn't know if it was Cale's gentle tone that had provoked it or the fact that she was about to astound him somewhat—she knew in advance he would say no. 'I need a man,' she began sweetly.

'Always happy to oblige,' he replied wickedly, his lips twitching.

Sorrel gave him a speaking look, but pressed on, 'You heard me tell Guy that I was going out with someone else—and it *was* you who said I needed to see him to find out what my feelings for him are. So I need a male escort to—'

As anticipated, Cale wasn't up for it. 'I'm not sure I'm free then.'

'You don't know when it is yet!' she immediately batted back. She had known in advance that it wasn't on—did not even want to go to the wretched party herself, for that matter. But for some peculiar reason she felt a touch miffed that quite obviously he did not wish to be her escort. 'Oh, forget it!' she snapped hostilely, and would have turned to immerse herself in her interesting work on spreadsheets. But then she noticed that Cale was looking remarkably affable.

And could not believe her ears when he said, 'Sweet Sorrel, I wouldn't dream of allowing you to go off to meet your ex without me.'

She stared at him, thunderstruck. She had never intended he should go with her—she hadn't even been going to go herself! 'You'll come?' she gasped.

'Since it was my idea, not to mention you did me a favour last Tuesday when you accompanied me, I don't see how I can refuse.'

Good heavens! 'I'm—er—not certain I want to go myself.' She tried to back out.

'Sure you do,' Cale countered. 'When is it?'

She was floundering, and knew it. 'Friday,' she said. 'A week tomorrow.'

'Where?'

'I've no idea,' she answered.

'Who does he work for?'

'A firm called Fleet Design. He's a boat designer,' she explained.

Cale stood up and put his chair back where he'd got it. 'I'll find out,' he said, and went on his way.

Feeling stunned, Sorrel forgot all about spreadsheets for a while. Cale—Cale was taking her to the party.

Cale had said he would find out where the party was—and he would too. She did not doubt it.

Her head was abuzz, not only with the fact that Guy had been in touch again after all this while, but also her astonishing conversation with Cale just now. She was at last spreadsheet-minded—or thought that she was—when it dawned on her that Cale had not said what he had come into her office to see her about.

She heard not a word from him the next day, and spent the weekend in Little Bossington, feeling lonely and wishing Uncle Lionel was there—she missed him.

She returned to the flat she shared with Donnie and missed her, and wished she were there too. Donnie could invariably make her laugh in her down moments. In truth, Sorrel admitted, she had never felt so unsettled.

She wandered restlessly around the flat, half hoping Donnie would phone—and half glad when she didn't. She would have to tell her about Trevor Simms treachery, but did not want to.

She found a little relief from her loneliness of spirit when, late on Sunday evening, Donnie's mother rang from Florida. Aunt Helen had been like a second mother to her, and Sorrel loved her dearly.

'How lovely to hear you!' she exclaimed. Helen—Gilbert, as she was now—had been away on a motoring holiday with her husband, and had not been in touch since before Donnie had gone away.

'Lovely to hear you too, darling,' Helen replied.

'How's Mike?'

'Fine. We're both in what you might call rude health,' Helen answered. 'But I'm a bit worried about Donnie.'

'Why? What's wrong?' Sorrel asked immediately,

anxiety starting to nip that Aunt Helen had heard something she had not.

'Oh, nothing, exactly—other than there was a card from her waiting for me. We've only just got in. Who's this Adrian she's raving about? Have you met him?'

Sorrel's anxiety started to fall away. Aunt Helen's concern was nothing more than a parent's natural concern—Donnie had never before raved about anyone the way she raved about Adrian.

'I've met him. He's a zoologist, and he's lovely,' she answered.

'Is he right for her? You know she needs someone special. You both do, for that matter.'

'Oh, Aunt Helen…' Sorrel was touched. 'Yes,' she replied, 'from what I've seen of him, of the two of them together, I would say, yes, he is right for her.'

Able to quiet any fears Helen Gilbert might have about the man who had stolen her daughter's heart, Sorrel chatted to her for a little while longer. But, within five minutes of the call ending, Sorrel's spirits were back down again.

She had not been able to tell Donnie's mother about the cloud of suspicion that had hung over her daughter's head. And might still hang over her head for all Sorrel knew. Aunt Helen had been worried by the fact that her daughter might have fallen in love with someone unworthy of her. How on earth would she be if she knew the smallest part of how Donnie had been duped into putting her signature on any piece of paper her crooked boss had put in front of her? That she'd worked for and, unknowingly, had aided and abetted an embezzler?

Sorrel shuddered, just thinking about it, and decided

she would ask Cale Masterson about it the next time she saw him. Surely by now he must know that Donnie was totally in the clear?

She did not, however, get to see him for a while. He telephoned, though. 'I'll pick you up on Friday around eight,' he instructed more than said—he was obviously busy, with no time for a chat.

'If you're sure?' She offered him a let-out, having had second and third thoughts about the whole idea.

But she was speaking to herself. Swine! She had to smile, though—why was she getting upset? In actual fact, she rather liked him. Quite plainly he had already discovered where Fleet Design were holding their after-exhibition party.

Someone else she quite liked telephoned her on Tuesday. 'I almost forgot to tell you about my steak and ale pie,' Rex Dunne invited.

She laughed. 'I almost forgot to tell you I'm a vegetarian.'

There was another card from Donnie waiting for Sorrel when she arrived home on Wednesday. In a breathless rush, pretty much the same as her last card, Donnie wrote of everything being so 'utterly sublime'. Adrian was 'more fantastic than ever', the scenery was 'heart-stoppingly wonderful'. She left just enough room at the bottom to write 'Donnie'.

Sorrel smiled affectionately. Donnie would be home two weeks next Saturday—she really had to have something positive to tell her before then. Sorrel went to bed with visions of Cale Masterson—and perhaps members of the police fraud squad—meeting Donnie off her plane. Very definitely something was going to have to be sorted out before then.

Most peculiarly, all thoughts of Donnie and her possible predicament went out of Sorrel's head when Cale called for her on Friday. He was wearing an immaculately tailored suit, and as she opened her door to him for one breathless moment her heart seemed to stand still. Tall, broad-shouldered and good-looking with it—and he was her boyfriend for the evening!

He stood there, his grey eyes travelling the length of her in her green silk dress, its mini length showing off her superb long legs admirably.

Neither of them spoke, and for a few seconds they just stood and looked at each other. Then Sorrel got her breath back, to tell him in a rush, 'We don't have to go. You needn't—'

'Stop trying to chicken out of it, Sorrel Oliphant,' Cale drawled, and, with a hint of a smile, 'Just try and remember that you are going to be the most beautiful woman in that room.'

'Oh,' she said on a gasp of breath—and knew she was all over the place. She didn't want to see Guy. She just didn't. And yet she was too mixed up suddenly to know if it was because she feared she might still love him or, hopefully, because of the way he had led her on.

Cale drove through London to a quite pleasant hotel. 'Want to hold my hand?' he asked as they went in and followed the easel that said 'Fleet Designs'.

'Shut up,' she said. But found, as they went through the door into what must be some ballroom or other, that she did place her hand through his arm.

She might have pulled away as they stood there,

looking around, but Cale's other hand came to hold her hand through his sleeve. 'Tell me pretty things and smile,' he instructed pleasantly.

Sorrel had just started to smile—and not because Cale had told her to—when out of nowhere, coming towards them, was Guy Fletcher.

'Sorrel,' he said, as he reached them, his tone uncertain as he eyed the well-to-do-looking man she was with.

'Hello, G-Guy,' she answered, and felt the pressure of Cale's hand on hers increase. She turned to smile at Cale. 'This is Cale. Cale—Guy—um—Fletcher,' she introduced them.

'We're on our way elsewhere,' Cale said evenly, not bothering to let go her hand to shake hands with the other man. 'But we were so close we thought we'd stop by to say hello. I hope your exhibition went well?'

It was the shortest party Sorrel had ever been to. A few minutes' chat with Guy Fletcher, a drink refused on the grounds that they would be drinking later, and then Cale, clearly of the view she had had sufficient time to discover if she still loved her ex-boyfriend, was looking down at her.

'Ready to go, darling?' he asked.

She was incapable of speech, and just nodded.

A second or two later she was able to find sufficient of her voice to utter a pleasant, 'Goodbye, Guy. It was kind of you to invite us.' Then, all in next to no time, Cale was escorting her back to his car.

'Was it so bad?' he asked as he started up the engine.

'You were a bit wonderful.' She felt she owed him.

'It's a gift,' he replied wryly. 'Do you feel up to eating?'

The last thing she wanted him to think was that seeing Guy again had wrecked her appetite. 'You don't have to extend the evening,' she answered. 'You've done more than enough.'

'I've got to eat—and that frock's wasted on beans on toast for one in your flat.'

'You certainly know how to charm a girl.'

Cale took her to a smart restaurant where he appeared to be quite well known. They sat in a lounge off the dining area, and were reading through the menus when Sorrel imagined that Cale's eyes were on her.

She raised her glance from her menu—and felt the most peculiar thump in her heart region when she found that Cale's steady glance *was* on her, and that it was not her imagination. For no reason she could think of she did not want him asking questions about Guy—she somehow seemed to know that that was in his mind.

'I told Rex Dunne I was a vegetarian!' she blurted out—probably because she had just scanned the nut roast option on the menu.

'Not a bad way to evade a discussion,' Cale commented, still with that apparent uncanny ability to read her mind. And he was smart in other areas too. 'Presumably you lied because you were turning down one of his dinner invitations?'

'I think he was going to cook, actually,' she replied lightly, realising that Cale had recalled she hadn't been a vegetarian when she had dined with him and Philip and Penny Kirk.

But Cale was not taking her reply as lightly, and

Sorrel saw shades of their first meeting when, his expression stern, he ordered bluntly, 'Don't even *think* of going to his place with him.'

As if she would! Like Rex she might, but she knew a rake when she saw one. But she disliked being ordered about—even if Cale had done her one enormous favour that evening. So she fluttered her long dark lashes at him. 'Any particular reason why I shouldn't?' she asked sweetly.

Cale had the grace to grin, probably realising that he had come on a little bit heavy. 'You go.' He shrugged. 'Get your fingers burned—see if I care.'

She laughed. She didn't see that she could do anything else. But, most ridiculously, she felt a pang of something that seemed oddly like regret that Cale did not care and never would!

'I think I'll have the salmon,' she said.

Cale was driving her home when it all at once came to her that, for an evening she had not been looking forward to, it had turned out to be one of the most enjoyable evenings she could remember. Not the first part; she had felt a bundle of nerves going into that party. But from the minute they had left, given that small scratchy hiccup when Cale had more or less warned her against going out—or staying in—with Rex Dunne, it had been pretty good.

Cale had been attentive, witty, charming. He had invited her opinion on all manner of subjects. In fact it seemed to her that they had chattered away unconstrained all through dinner.

Which was why when, as before, he escorted her up to her door and opened up the door to her apartment, expecting to shake hands with him like the last time, she found herself commenting, 'You don't want to come in for coffee?'

'Since you're not offering, no,' he replied. And, looking down into her faintly bemused green eyes, 'But, rather than have a discussion out in the hall and possibly disturb your neighbours, I wouldn't mind coming in for a few minutes.'

They had been talking all evening! 'What's to discuss?' she asked—and immediately knew what the subject was: Donnie. 'Come in,' she invited, and led the way into the sitting room, offering him seat.

'I won't stay that long,' he refused. 'I just want to know—did I do wrong to suggest you see Fletcher again?'

Sorrel later supposed that her surprise that Donnie and the embezzlement was not the subject matter must be responsible for her friend going clean from her mind. 'I—er…' she faltered. But because he had done her one huge favour—she would never have known how she felt about Guy had she not seen him again—'You didn't do wrong,' she said at last.

'You still have—feelings for him?' Cale pressed.

Sorrel shook her head. 'I think I knew it the moment I saw him. Looking at him, I couldn't help wondering if I ever did love him. If—' She wasn't used to opening up like this, and stopped.

But Cale, it seemed, wasn't ready to leave it there. 'If?' he prompted.

'I—um—think now that it must have been something of an emotional thing. What I mean is, I was more or less permanently living with my guardian in his last few months. I knew he was not going to get better, that he was going to die—I suppose my emotions were pretty raw. While at the same time I was having to hide from Uncle Lionel that the thought of losing him was breaking me up inside.'

Cale nodded sympathetically. 'You seriously needed someone to hold on to—and along came Fletcher.'

'That seems awfully shallow of me,' she mumbled. 'I truly thought I loved him.'

'Your emotions were all over the place at that time,' Cale excused her. 'You must have known every day that the time was coming ever nearer to when you would have to say goodbye to your guardian.'

Each day had torn her apart—which was perhaps why Guy Fletcher's sickening behaviour had had such a crushing effect on her. But she did not want to dwell on it. Not now. Not ever again.

'Well, thanks to you, Guy Fletcher can't hurt me any more,' she said lightly. And, knowing that the evening was over, she held out her right hand. 'Thank you, Cale,' she said.

His right hand came out to meet hers. 'My pleasure,' he murmured, but held on to her hand to draw near and to bend—and to lay his wonderful mouth against her cheek.

'Oh!' she exclaimed, letting go his hand and touching her own hand to the cheek he had just kissed—to find she was staring up into a pair of warm grey eyes.

'Oh, indeed,' Cale said softly—and, before she was fully aware of what was happening, and just as if his mouth liked the feel of her skin, he had gathered her into his arms and his mouth was covering hers.

For all of two seconds Sorrel gave in to the fantastic feel of Cale's strong arms about her. For all of two seconds she gave in to the feel of his superb mouth on hers. For all of two seconds she felt a need to respond—and actually did stretch out her hands to his waist.

But this was utter madness. Had she not only just recovered from months of emotional turmoil? Had she not only just got her emotions back on an even keel?

Forcefully she pushed him away from her, and, on a gasp of angry breath, ordered, 'Cut that out!' in no uncertain terms—even if her voice was a little shaky.

His answer, not at all abashed, was to grin a lop-sided grin at her. 'Nearly had you going then, didn't I?' he remarked good-humouredly.

He could say that again! She had no defence, so did the only thing she could do. 'Clear off,' she told him.

Cale seemed to think that amusing too. 'Did anyone ever tell you you have a most kissable mouth?' he enquired politely.

Oh, heavens. The way he was looking at her was turning her legs to water. 'I think, Mr Masterson, that it's time you left,' she told him, while she still could.

His glance went down to the mouth he had just called most kissable. But when he looked upwards into her wide green eyes, all sign of humour had gone from him. 'I think, Miss Oliphant, that you may be right,' he responded.

He did not stay any longer and, securing the door after he had gone, Sorrel saw that her hands were shaking. She was not surprised. What did surprise her was the realisation that she was more than a little attracted to him!

# CHAPTER FIVE

IT TOOK Sorrel the whole of the weekend to get herself back together after Cale Masterson's kiss. It had not been a passionate kiss, but a warm and giving kiss, and she had wanted more.

She did not go to Little Bossington that weekend, but knew that she should. She knew she should keep busy. But she did not go, and felt more restless than ever.

Sorrel did not feel very much better when she went in to work on Monday. She felt jumpy, oddly, and her nerves tensed every time the door to her office opened.

She was not liking Caleb Masterson because for some unknown reason *he* could do this to her. She knew it was his fault. She had not felt jumpy like this last week—before he had kissed her. Grief, she had been kissed before, many times, and more passionately, so why…?

It was around mid-morning when her office door opened again. Sorrel glanced up from what she was doing—and felt colour burn her skin. Which was ridiculous; she never blushed! Well, hardly ever—and only since knowing him!

Cale glanced back at her—noting her blush, she was certain—but said not a word. And Sorrel couldn't take it. Without saying a word she collected up a document that required filing, left her seat and, turning her back on him, went to the filing cabinet.

'You're finding enough to do?' he addressed her back coolly.

'Ample,' she replied, her tone equally cool. 'Not that it matters. My stint here will be finished on Friday,' she added, turning to face him.

'You're leaving?' he questioned sharply.

'Donnie will be home on Saturday—my job here was never permanent,' she retorted. 'I'm only here because…' Suddenly his attitude was just too much. 'I had *nothing* to do with that money disappearing!' she erupted furiously.

Cale stared at her in surprise. 'I know you didn't,' he replied.

That mollified her, but only slightly. 'And neither did Donnie!' she went on for good measure. 'When you catch up with Trevor Simms he'll tell you…'

'I've already caught up with him.' Cale stopped her in her tracks.

'You have?' she exclaimed. 'You've seen him?'

'I've seen him.'

'You've managed to get him back here?'

Cale shook his head. 'He's still in Brazil.'

Her green eyes shot wide. 'You've been to Brazil!'

'Last week,' he confirmed.

Feeling faintly staggered, Sorrel questioned, 'He confessed?'

'He didn't have much option.' Oh, dear—she wouldn't

like to get on the wrong side of Cale when he got tough. 'The evidence against him is somewhat damning.'

'But—but—he cleared Donnie?'

Cale was silent for a few moments. 'She'll have questions to answer too, but on the face of it she looks to be in the clear.'

Sorrel felt a weight lift from her. But then, as it dawned on her that he had been to Brazil and back again by last Friday, she started to grow annoyed. 'You might have told me that on Friday!' she erupted suddenly.

But, having brought up the subject of Friday evening, the reason for Cale's cool attitude all at once struck her. And, recalling how on Friday he had been warm and giving—totally different from the way he was now...

'That's it, isn't it?' she exploded. And, ignoring his look that suggested he hadn't a clue what she was talking about, 'Look here, Caleb Masterson.' She went into orbit. 'You kissed me—not the other way around!' She had just about had it with him. 'I'm not after you!' she told him forthrightly.

Tall and straight, he sent her a quizzical look. 'You're—not?'

How could he think such a thing? 'I am not.' she flared.

'You're not interested in me?' he persisted—she thought he actually looked pleased at the notion.

Her pride was instantly up in arms. 'Strange though it may seem,' she began loftily, 'I have other fish to fry.' She hadn't, but he need not know that.

His expression darkened—she was pleased to see that *he* looked annoyed. 'Not the shark?' he rapped.

And suddenly her sense of humour received a prod, and she just had to laugh. He knew darn well she had finished with Guy. 'Wash your mouth!' she told him—but her spurt of fury was over.

So too, it seemed, was Cale's annoyance with her. At any rate the air between them seemed to have been cleared when, with a mock sigh, he declared, 'Our romance, Miss Oliphant, is over.'

'One must be thankful for small mercies,' she replied, and suddenly they were both laughing.

Then he took a glance to his watch. 'I'm out of here,' he said.

And that was it—he went, never knowing the trauma he had left behind.

With her heart racing, and the memory of Cale's laugh echoing in her head, Sorrel stared at the door he had just gone through and closed. No—*no.* She tried to deny it. It couldn't be. She could not—could *not*—be in love with Cale Masterson.

Sorrel collapsed onto her chair, her head spinning. Only on Friday she had worried that she might still love Guy. Now today, Monday, with her heart hammering just to hear Cale laugh, she was in love with him?

She tried to deny it. It was still there. She had thought she loved Guy—but loving Guy had never felt like this. She loved and was in love with Cale; quite simply there was no comparison between the emotion she had thought she had for Guy and this utter blown-away feeling that she had only just realised she had for Cale.

Feeling winded, her concentration shot, Sorrel just wasn't ready to get stuck into work. But somehow the long day ended—as soon, she knew, the week, her last with Brown and Johns, would end. What would she do then?

Sorrel drove home knowing that when the week ended, when Friday came, she would leave Brown and Johns for the last time—and in leaving would immediately lose any chance of seeing Cale again.

Her head was a quagmire as thoughts many and varied chased through her mind. Where at one time she had kicked against being made to go to that office to preserve Donnie's job for her—for that had been the agreement, that she work in Donnie's stead for a full five weeks—Sorrel now wanted to continue to be where she might stand some remote chance of seeing Cale at some time.

Knowing she was being pathetic, but seeming unable to do anything about it—never had she experienced an emotion so debilitating as this—Sorrel attempted to think of something else.

She pinned her thoughts on her dear friend. But it brought her no pleasure to know that at some time between the moment when Donnie walked in through the door on Saturday and left for Brown and Johns on Monday she was going to have to sit her down and tell her what a conman Trevor Simms, the man she had so looked up to, really was. And not only that, she would have to make Donnie aware that she would also have some pretty tough questions to answer.

Sorrel only hoped that if Cale was the questioner—and she rather thought he would be—he would go gently with Donnie. She herself had seen a gentler side to him…

It was hopeless. Cale was back in her head again.

Cale was still in her head when she went to work the next day. Again she tensed whenever somebody opened the door. She now understood the reason why she did that. But it was never Cale.

That did not prevent her from feeling fluttery whenever the phone rang, though. It rang twice. The first time it was Penny Kirk. 'Sorry I haven't been in touch. Philip and I have been away for a few days,' she explained. 'I wondered how you were fixed for lunch one day this week?'

Sorrel felt good that Penny had remembered, and that her parting suggestion of them meeting up for coffee or lunch had been genuine. 'Next week would be better,' Sorrel answered, a smile there in her voice. 'My stint here finishes on Friday. I'll be a free agent from then on.'

They made arrangements to meet the following Wednesday, and, armed with Penny's phone number, just in case something unforeseen cropped up, Sorrel turned her attention back to work.

Less than five minutes later the phone on her desk rang again. Sorrel swallowed, took a calming breath, and hoped she was ready. 'Finance,' she stated.

'Did anyone tell you you have a lovely voice?'

'Hello, Rex,' she responded cheerfully—it wasn't his fault that she should experience a feeling of anticlimax.

'I was thinking, if you don't care for the idea of my splendid home cooking, why don't I come to your place for a meal?'

'Goodbye, Rex.'

She felt brighter for that small exchange, but was still feeling lost and fidgety when she arrived home that night.

Donnie's room was immaculately tidy, but, needing something to do—anything to try and counter this restlessness of spirit—Sorrel got out the vacuum cleaner, deciding to spruce up her room before Saturday.

Inevitably, it seemed, her thoughts drifted to Cale Masterson. She hadn't even liked him when she had first met him. What had there been to like? He had been cold, blunt, suspicious—but, yes, her heart prodded her, she had reached his sense of humour that day. As she'd been leaving, a sort of half-smile had made it. Had she started to fall in love with him then?

It seemed crazy to think so, yet this tremendous feeling she had for him must have begun at some time. Her thoughts drifted to her conversation with him yesterday. By the sound of it he must know that Donnie had had nothing to do with that embezzlement.

Suddenly half a dozen questions were fighting for precedence in her head. If he knew Donnie had nothing to do with the embezzlement then her job was safe—wasn't it? They couldn't dismiss her—could they? Or could they? Donnie hadn't been with the firm terribly long, and to be brutally honest, though Sorrel would bite out her tongue before she would tell Donnie so, she just did not seem up to the job.

Though hadn't Cale said that Donnie had been very badly misdirected, and that the new finance controller—when he was appointed—would know how to direct staff properly?

With relief, Sorrel knew from that statement alone that Donnie's job would be secure. Of course it would, Sorrel realised. Otherwise why in creation had she been going to Brown and Johns this last five weeks? Her whole purpose, as Cale had suggested, was that she should try and keep Donnie's job for her.

Fairly certain that with a new head of finance, who would surely soon pick up on Donnie's lovely and willing nature, Donnie would fare better, even if initially she might be in for a tough time of questioning, Sorrel's head was again taken up with thoughts of Cale.

She had not seen him at all that day, nor heard his voice over the telephone. What if she did not see or hear from him again tomorrow? For all she knew he could be out of the country—she'd had no idea he had paid a visit to Brazil last week, had she? What if she did not see nor hear from him again before she left Brown and Johns for the last time on Friday? What if she never, ever saw him again?

Feeling dreadfully desolate, Sorrel took herself off to bed.

She got up on Wednesday feeling pretty much the same, and knew she could not go on like this. Being in love was supposed to be exhilarating, exciting, wasn't it? Not in her experience!

When in the early afternoon Rex Dunne telephoned and asked her out to dinner, Sorrel was feeling pretty much at rock bottom. And she didn't know which one of them was more surprised when she answered, 'I think I'd like that.'

'You do? You will?'

Already she was regretting it—but a night out with Rex had to be better than another night in on her own, like last night. Even so… 'I can't manage tonight,' she started to backtrack hastily.

'Tomorrow will suit me fine,' Rex said quickly, and, before she could say that tomorrow was not convenient either, 'You'd better let me have your address.'

Sorrel was still feeling winded ten minutes later. Prior to that morning, had she been asked, she would have said no way would she go out with Rex Dunne. Yet here she was… *It's all your fault Cale Masterson.* She laid the blame squarely at his door.

Then to her hidden delight the door opened—and there was Cale. She looked at him, and then quickly down at her work, lest her joy at seeing him was there in her face—it had more than once crossed her mind that she had seen the last of him on Monday.

'I can see you're busy,' he commented.

She made herself appear calm—her heart was going like some demented pneumatic drill. 'I'm just checking a few things for James,' she replied, and was suddenly feeling so overwhelmed by him and her feelings for him that she had to search for something normal-sounding to say. 'Um—I had a chat to Penny Kirk. You've nothing against me having lunch with her next week?' *Idiot.* She had already cleared with him that she might have contact with Penny again. Hadn't he said he was sure he could rely on her absolute discretion?

'You look a touch pink,' he observed—for which she did not thank him. But he was, as ever, as sharp as a tack. 'Who are you lunching with *this* week?' he questioned, his expression serious.

Oh, help. Guiltily, she recalled Cale's warning that Rex Dunne ate little girls like her for breakfast. She had either hesitated too long or Cale had read that touch of guilt in her eyes—though why she should feel guilty she hadn't a clue.

'Not Fletcher?' he demanded. 'He's been in touch?'

And suddenly it annoyed her that he was poking his nose in; that he, when she had done nothing wrong, was making her feel guilty.

'No, he hasn't!' she answered shortly.

'Who? James?' he guessed.

Good grief! No wonder he was doing the job he was doing. Even when it did not concern him he couldn't leave off being an investigator.

'If you must know, Rex Dunne!' she fired back.

'You're having lunch with Rex Dunne?' He did not seem best pleased.

Tough! 'Dinner, actually,' she snapped.

Cale eyed her uncompromisingly. Then, as if having warned her once he did not intend to waste his breath a second time, he shrugged. 'They're your fingers.' And she hated him that he should rub it in that he didn't care a button if she got her fingers burned or what she did. 'Tonight?' he queried absently.

'Tomorrow night,' Sorrel answered, and, starting to feel really down, looked pointedly at the work she was checking, then back up to the man who could somehow make her love him and hate him at one and the same time. The hate side gave him a broad hint that she would rather have his room than his company. 'Is there something I can do for you?' she enquired coolly.

His glance went to her red-brown hair, where a shaft

of sunlight from outside lit it to more of a shining red. He transferred his gaze to her face, and for long seconds he studied her. Then, to her complete surprise, he collected a chair, the way he had before, and brought it over to her desk and sat down. Her heart picked up a giddy beat at this evidence that Cale was not rushing off.

'I do have a job for you, as a matter of fact,' he replied.

'I can shelve this, if you want some work finished today,' she volunteered, all bad feeling evaporating. She was in love with him again. He had a wonderful firm chin, a strong jaw, and his… She caught herself up short—grief, she'd be drooling in a minute!

'It's not work for today,' he corrected her. 'I have a job for you for next week.'

'Next week?' she exclaimed. 'You've forgotten I leave Brown and Johns on Friday?'

'I've forgotten nothing,' Cale assured her. 'And you wouldn't be working for Brown and Johns. You'd be working for me.'

By 'me' she knew he meant Ward Maritime International. 'I don't know that I want a job,' she replied, amazed at the way her tongue was running away with her just lately. First she had accepted a date with Rex Dunne, and now here she was denying herself a first-class opportunity of further contact with Cale after this week.

'Of course you do,' he countered, to her relief. 'I know you're still sorting out your guardian's goods and effects, but with an organised brain like yours, not to mention your qualifications—'

'Is there nothing you haven't found out about me?' she butted in—*my goodness, had he been thorough!*

He smiled. She melted. He went on. 'The thing is, Sorrel, that I occasionally need a peripatetic PA. Most often when I go abroad. Victoria does a splendid job when I'm home.'

Peripatetic PA. Abroad! Oh, heavens—oh, heaven!

'It occurred to me that, while you are not yet looking for a full-time job, you might well alternate your visits to Little Bossington with this kind of trip for me.'

'You want me to be your occasional travelling PA?' she repeated quietly, somehow managing to hold back from grabbing at this wonderful opportunity.

Cale looked into her wide green eyes. 'You're quite an asset to the company,' he complimented her.

It was no good. She had absolutely no chance of holding down the smile that rushed up from the heart of her. 'You're only saying that,' she murmured.

He seemed taken for a moment by her upturned mouth. But then pressed, 'You'll accept? You'll come with me on Monday?'

Oh, somebody help her—she was having a hard job to not start dancing around the room. She made herself hang back. 'Where to? The Bahamas?' she queried, only just preventing herself from beaming from ear to ear.

'How does Norway sound?'

With him? Absolutely brilliant. 'How long would we be away?'

'I've a bit of business to clear up that will probably take until Friday—perhaps Saturday. Are you all right to work on Saturday if need be?'

'Yes, of course,' she answered—and realised then, as he from his grin had already realised, that she had just accepted the assignment. 'Er—what exactly will I have to do?' she asked.

'Be with me most of the time.' It couldn't get any better! Her heart was racing. 'Take notes, type them back. We'll need to do a quite extensive report on our findings.'

*Our* findings! He would be doing all the work, but the fact he had teamed the two of them as a pair sounded utterly fantastic in her ears. 'Right,' she acknowledged. She knew she was good. She only hoped she got the chance to prove it. She'd never forgive herself if she let him down.

But, as ever a busy man, Cale had got up and returned his chair to its proper place. 'I'll be in touch with the details of our flight,' he said, then bade her a pleasant farewell and went through to have a word with the auditors.

When Sorrel left her office at the end of her working day she was still trying to adjust. She had thought that after Friday she would have left behind all chance of ever seeing Cale again. Yet here she was, actually going to Norway with him on Monday!

She was still catching her breath as she made herself a meal that night. She was doubly lucky, she realised, because now that Cale's investigation into the Trevor Simms affair must be more or less coming to an end—all but tying up any loose ends—she knew she could assume that his visits to Brown and Johns would cease. Which meant that she would have had no chance of

Donnie bringing home so much as a snippet of what Cale was doing.

Sorrel left her bed on Thursday, knowing that she did not want to have dinner with Rex Dunne that night. Though she quickly realised that she could not use having to get ready for her impending Norwegian trip as an excuse. So much of Cale's work was highly confidential—which meant that she should not give anyone a hint of where she was going. Nevertheless, she did try to contact Rex and put him off, but discovered that he was out of the office for the day.

As it happened, though flirty, Rex proved good company that evening. He did not go in for in-depth discussions, and that was quite all right with Sorrel. He was bright and clever, and happy to answer anything she asked.

Though at the end of a pleasant evening Sorrel felt that crunch time had arrived when, as he drove her home, he enquired warmly—hopefully—'Since I've behaved impeccably all evening, am I going to get to come in for coffee?'

'I don't do coffee on a first date,' she replied with a smile.

'There has to be an answer to that,' he replied.

He still searching for one when, at her flat, he walked to the outer entrance with her. Sorrel made sure to hang on to her keys. 'Thank you for a very pleasant evening,' she said, as they halted outside the entrance to her apartment block.

'I was thinking,' he answered, 'that since I offered you tea once, this just has to be construed as our second date.'

She laughed. He might be obvious, but he was amusing. 'Goodnight, Rex,' she replied prettily.

'Don't I even get a goodnight kiss?' he asked, his hands coming to her waist.

*Here we go!* 'Where are my manners?' she said lightly. 'Close your eyes and say prunes.'

He closed his eyes. 'Prunes,' he obliged, and stayed with his mouth puckered. She inserted her key in the lock, turned about and bent forward—and kissed his cheek.

'Night,' she said again, and, while he was still complaining that the night was yet young, she quickly unlocked the outer door and slipped inside.

It *was* early too, she saw as she took off her watch prior to taking a shower and cleaning her teeth. Only just gone ten.

Having taken a shower earlier that evening, Sorrel made her shower a quick in-and-out affair. But she was in her nightdress, her hair still pinned up in a knot on the top of her head, contemplating getting into bed, when the outer door buzzer sounded.

She was surprised! She had thought Rex halfway home by now. She did not want to prolong what had been an agreeable evening, and was in two minds whether or not to answer it. But it *had* been an amiable evening, and at least Rex had taken her thoughts off Cale for some of the time.

The buzzer sounded again. She went over to it. 'We've said goodnight,' she reminded him—and nearly dropped with shock when the voice that answered was not that of her escort!

'Masterson,' was the reply. 'I've something for you.'

Cale! Her heart rejoiced even as she tried to flatten it. 'I'm ready for bed!' she protested.

'Well, I'm here now—you might as well let me up.'

Without a word she activated the outer door release, then stood stunned, indecisive about whether she had time to rush and get dressed. She did not have time. Cale was at her door before she'd got herself together.

Feeling flustered, she hurried to get a wrap. Tying it as she went, her heart was sprinting as she reached the door—gladness in her heart, caution in her soul.

'How did you know I was in?' she queried as she opened the door and was pierced by the direct gaze of the man she loved.

'I was in the area—I thought I'd chance it,' he replied smoothly. 'Any chance of a coffee?'

Sorrel stared at him, her brain numb. Common sense said no—but it was roundly defeated by the wonder of having him near, by this wonderful chance to spend some time with him. 'It will have to be a quick one,' she responded primly. She stood back from the door and Cale came in, following her to the sitting room. 'I'll—er—just put the coffee on and then go and get dressed,' she said a trifle jerkily.

'No need for that,' Cale responded. And even while she was guessing that he was quite at home seeing women in their night attire—or without it, for that matter—he was holding out the case in his hand and explaining, 'I only stopped by to drop off this laptop—you'll need to bring it with you on Monday.'

Monday. Norway with him. Her spine threatened to turn liquid. 'I'll—um…' She left it there and hurried to the kitchen.

Had she hoped, however, to have five minutes by herself, in which to get herself more of one piece, she very soon knew that it was not to be. 'I've just remembered,' Cale began, following her into the kitchen, 'you were supposed to be going out with Rex Dunne tonight.'

Sorrel turned to look at the man who held her heart. She would have said that there was very little Cale Masterson failed to remember. So from that she could only deduce that either he was lying, or the fact that she'd had a date with one of their fellow workers was too insignificant for him to slot into his memory bank.

'I did go out with him,' she responded, starting to feel a little scratchy with Cale, even if she did love him.

'You're home early.'

'Rex had to wash his hair.'

Cale's lips twitched, but his voice was serious as he asked, 'Did he behave himself?'

'Impeccably,' she replied.

'Before or after you slapped him down?'

'He was fun,' Sorrel volunteered.

Cale grunted, but was not put off from asking that which he wanted to know. 'Are you going to see him again?'

Sorrel hesitated, as though considering his question. 'Well, not next week—I'm otherwise engaged,' she replied. And, on a sudden thought, 'I didn't mention or discuss the Norway trip with him, by the way.'

Cale smiled then. 'I never thought you would,' he replied and, his tone somehow softening, 'I'm not sure that you're not even more beautiful without make-up on as with it.'

Her breath caught. 'You think I'm beautiful?' she asked faintly.

He looked at her for long moments. 'Didn't you know?' he asked softly.

'I—er…' she began, and could feel her colour rising. But all at once Cale was taking a step back.

'I think I'd better go,' he announced.

'Just when you're starting to sound interesting?' queried a mischievous, teasing and unknown part of her that seemed to be getting out of control.

Cale's glance raked her face. 'You're asking for trouble, Miss Oliphant,' he warned her.

She turned from him and began fiddling about with the coffee percolator, striving to get back in charge of this until now unknown wayward part of her that was trying to surface. She felt on very shaky ground here, but could not help it. She did not want him to go. 'The coffee won't be long,' she mumbled as she gained control. 'But if you want to go…' It was as far as she got.

All at once Cale's hands descended on her shoulders—she hadn't heard him move. 'It's better I go,' he murmured. But, as if the nape of her neck was too fascinating to resist, he bent his head and laid a tender, unhurried kiss on the back of her neck.

A dart of electricity shot through Sorrel—and made complete and utter nonsense of any control she had been able to resurrect. She just had to turn about and face him. Perhaps she had expected he might take a step back. She did not know. But he did not step back, and she was overwhelmingly aware that with the work unit behind her, and Cale in front, she was sort of hemmed in.

'Cale,' she whispered helplessly, discovering that she quite liked him this close.

He looked down at her, not moving, and it seemed to her then, in her heightened sense of awareness of him, that he appeared incapable of moving away—of breaking some kind of spell. 'Don't worry,' he said at length, 'you're not in any danger.'

Sorrel stared up at him, something inside her taking over from good sense, 'Unless I—w-want to be?' she stammered.

A warm look entered Cale's eyes and he seemed to take a shaky breath. 'You shouldn't say things like that unless you mean them,' he stated quietly.

Just then Sorrel was unsure what she meant, other than that she would quite like to feel Cale's arms around her.

'Er—just now I wouldn't mind a hug,' voiced that part of her over which she appeared to have little control.

She felt disappointed when Cale did not immediately respond, but instead warned, 'You're on dangerous ground here, Sorrel.'

She smiled at him, gave a small swallow, and that imp of mischief was there again as she replied, 'I'm prepared to risk it if you are.'

He eyed her solemnly, and was solemn still as he instructed, 'Come here.' He did not touch her until, swaying towards him, Sorrel leaned against his chest.

His chest was warm and wonderful. But more wonderful still was the way gently, tenderly, his arms came around her. She sighed in pure bliss, and felt she had reached home when Cale laid a light kiss on the top of her head.

Slowly she raised her head to look at him. She wanted to kiss him, wanted him to kiss her, and realised that he had read the message in her eyes when he lowered his head to hers. His lips touched hers and she thought she might faint from the utter beauty of that contact.

He smiled into her eyes as the kiss ended. 'You're not going to tell me to "cut that out"?' he queried, reminding her of that other time he had kissed her.

'Actually, a phrase from *Oliver Twist* springs to mind,' she replied shyly—and loved him, loved him, *loved him* when she did not have to explain further.

Cale's head was coming down again. 'You want more?' he murmured.

And there was more. One kiss was never sufficient. They seemed to be clinging to each other as they shared kiss after wonderful exploring kiss. Cale's hands were warm through her thin covering, and Sorrel delighted in his touch as he stroked her spine.

*Oh, Cale.* She wanted to sigh his name, but he was kissing her again. Then he was trailing kisses down her throat, pulling her to him. She adored the feel of his firm body against her, and she pressed into him.

'Darling…' He broke off to halt her. 'Do you know what you're doing?'

That 'darling' transported her. 'Um—I'm not very experienced. Hmm—or experienced at all, really,' she whispered. 'But I do know what—er—what's happening.'

Cale kissed her again, long and lingeringly, his hands caressing until they found the full swollen globes of her breasts. She gave a muted cry of pure ecstasy, and Cale broke his kiss and dropped his hands to her waist.

'Do you want it to happen?' he asked quietly. A simple question, no pressure.

Sorrel did not have to think about it. 'Yes,' she answered shyly, huskily, and knew as Cale buried his head in her throat that she had just agreed that she wanted to make love with him.

Cale kissed her again, then pulled back to look into her shining green eyes. 'Perhaps we'll be more comfortable…'

'…in my bedroom?' she finished for him, with barely a blush.

She was aware they were moving, kissing and holding, holding and kissing, but whether she guided him to her bedroom or whether he instinctively knew where it lay she had no idea. She opened her eyes to find she was standing with him by her bed, and that he was tenderly removing her wrap.

'There's still time to change your mind,' he offered, though he made no move to stop.

'What sort of a girl do you think I am?' she teased, and loved him, loved his body, when, his shirt gone, she felt the heat of him through her thin nightdress.

She was still pressed up against him when he slipped her nightdress from her shoulders. Sorrel clutched on to him, in uncharted waters, wanting him with all her being but suddenly shy.

'It's all right.' He gentled her, his eyes on her face as he raised his hands to her hair and released it from its confining pins.

It *was* all right too. She smiled up at him. He held

her face in his hands and tenderly kissed her eyes, her mouth, and she sighed in rapture, her heart thundering. Then, as Cale looked down at her, one of his hands came to where the thin material of her nightdress was caught between them. Unhurriedly he removed the material, away from her breasts, and her nightdress fell to the floor.

'Sweet darling,' he breathed, his eyes on the fullness of her pink-tipped breasts. 'You are exquisite,' he murmured, and bent and took the hardened tip of her right breast into his mouth.

'Cale!' she whispered shakily, the sensations he was creating in her causing havoc.

He must have picked up that shaky note in her voice, because he immediately raised his head. 'You want to change your mind?' he queried quietly.

She shook her head, feeling too full to speak. 'No,' she managed, and he smiled, and the next she knew he had divested himself of his footwear and trousers, and she, as naked as the day she was born, was lying on her bed with him. She was no longer thinking—in fact had not been thinking for some while, only feeling.

Cale lay half over her, trailing gentle kisses down her body, caressing her left breast with the same unimaginable tenderness with which he had kissed her right breast.

Her hands strayed to his chest, stroking the fine hair there, giving in to a sudden urge to explore his nipples. An urgent fire was starting to go out of control within her.

'I want you so,' she whispered, on an upsurge of her need for him.

'Slowly, my darling.' Cale held back, his hands on her naked buttocks, moulding her into him. 'I want this first time to be right for you.'

'Oh, Cale,' she sighed, enchanted by his consideration for her, in raptures over his tenderness, his thoughtfulness with her, as she marvelled at his precious tenderness with her innocence. 'When did I ever think you a brute?' she whispered.

'Me?' he teased, with a warm, giving smile.

Her heart turned over. She smiled at him as—in an effort to, for the moment, hold down her urgent need for him to make her his—she dreamily reminded him, 'When we first met and you were accusing me as well as Donnie—' Sorrel broke off when, on the instant of her mentioning Donnie's name, something seemed to hit Cale four-square, and with a strangled kind of groan he wrenched his hands from her and rolled to the other side of the bed.

'Sorrel, I—' he began. He sat up, his legs over the side of the bed, his body half turned away from her.

'What…?' she gasped, her brain too far gone for her to make any sense of what was happening now. 'Did I do something wrong?' she asked, struggling to sit up.

Cale turned to look at her and took hold of her hand, but he remained on the edge of the bed—away from her. 'No. No—not you,' he said heavily. 'Me.'

'You?' she queried witlessly, suddenly very much aware of her nakedness when a minute before she had been mindless of his gaze on her. With trembling fingers she pulled to get part of the duvet that was free to cover her.

'I can't make love with you, sweet Sorrel,' he began, as if choosing his words carefully, 'only for you to discover very shortly that your friend—your sister-friend—is going to be dismissed the moment she sets foot inside Brown and Johns on Monday.'

Stunned by what he had said, Sorrel stared at him. Donnie was being *dismissed!* Bereft of speech, Sorrel was open-mouthed. Had Cale hit her with a sledgehammer she could not have felt more stupefied. She couldn't be hearing this! Why, the only reason she had been working at the firm had been to ensure that Donnie *kept* her job! She had thought that Donnie's job *was* safe! The more the weeks had gone by, the more secure she had felt that Donnie's job was!

Yet still it wasn't going in. She loved Cale. He couldn't, wouldn't do this to her. 'This—this is a recent decision?' She at last found her voice—about the best her brain could come up with just then. But he was already shaking his head.

'I've known from day one that we would not be keeping her on,' Cale admitted.

'But—but…' Sorrel was staggered. 'But the only reason I've been working for you is because…'

'I know, and I've misled you.'

Just like that! Sorrel was starting to get to grips with what Cale was saying—and as she did, so she began to grow angry. And never had she been more glad of that anger—otherwise she would have been in pieces. 'I'll say you misled me!' she erupted, throwing his hand away from her.

'Sorrel—' Cale tried.

*'No!'* she exploded. No to whatever it was.

'Look at it logically,' he tried again. 'Try to—'

'*Logically?*' she cut in, all at once more conscious than ever of her lack of clothing—he at least did have the advantage of his undershorts.

'Yes, logically,' he stated evenly. 'Think logically, and you'll see that there is no way I can avoid sacking her.'

'You're obviously going to do it personally—presumably before *your* plane takes off for Norway on Monday?' It was for sure she wasn't going to go with him!

He heard her emphasis on *'your'* plane—and did not appear to like it. But he went determinedly on. 'Think about it—you've worked in finance. You must be able to see that had she been on her toes she would have been unable to avoid seeing that something fishy was going on.'

'It wasn't Donnie's responsibility to check her boss!' Sorrel flared, starting to become incensed.

'It was her responsibility to check what she was signing, and not to sign documents without having the least idea of what she was putting her signature to. Her responsibility to not put her name to anything with nothing but a muddle-headed notion of what it was all about—with no comprehension at all of contents and effects. Apart from the utter shambles she left that office in—there is no way I can save her job for her.'

'You surprise me that you may have tried!' Sorrel tossed at him acidly. Her heart might be fracturing within her, but pride refused to allow her to break down in tears with him there.

Cale did not care very much for her acid. She could

tell from the tough look he gave her before, in a few summing-up sentences, he totally froze her heart. 'The new finance controller would not wear her for more than ten minutes,' he said, adding, 'In all fairness I would not expect him to,' and went on. 'She is just not up to the job. There was nothing I could do but recommend she be dismissed.'

Barely believing her ears—she had worked for him for five weeks, for goodness' sake, and he had *recommended* that Donnie be dismissed! On the understanding that she was safeguarding Donnie's job, she had spent five weeks going backwards and forwards… She was still having trouble taking it in. For *five weeks!* And Cale had known before she had so much as set a foot inside Brown and Johns—he had known that there would be no job for Donnie to come back to. Worse—he had *actually* recommended that Donnie be dismissed. All this while she…

Sorrel stared at him, icy fingers shrivelling her heart. That ice transferred to her eyes, and it was there in her every look, impenetrable frost there in her voice, as cuttingly she told Cale, 'I don't think I need to hear any more. Close the door on your way out.'

'Sorrel…'

She deliberately turned from him, her back rigid; it was the end.

She was glad when a minute later, as if he knew that obdurate just did not begin to cover her mood, and that he would be wasting his breath and his time in staying and trying to talk to her, Sorrel heard movement that indicated he was getting dressed.

A minute after that she heard the outer door quietly close. Only then, as the pain of his cruel deception engulfed her, did she break down in tears.

# CHAPTER SIX

SORREL supposed she must have fallen asleep at some time during that long night after Cale had gone, but it did not feel like it. It was still early when she left her bed.

Her thoughts were instantly on Cale and his unspeakable duplicity. She felt haunted by him, by what he had done—and by his tender lovemaking!

But she did not want to think about that! She had been so vulnerable, he so ardent—although with crippling honesty she had to admit that it was she who had been the instigator. She, not Cale. He must have sensed what had been in the air—he with his, 'I'd better go.' He had tried to warn her. 'You're asking for trouble.' She had ignored that. All she had been able to think of was the joy of having him near. Again he had said, 'I'd better go,' repeating what he'd known was the right thing to do.

Yes, but she hadn't asked him to lay that kiss on the back of her neck—she supposed she had been pretty much out of control after that. She had certainly not heeded his controlled, 'You're not in any danger.' Her face flamed as she recalled inviting 'Unless I want to be'—and she had even pretty much asked him for a hug!

Oh, grief, what was the poor man supposed to have done? *Poor man?* After what *he* had done!

With nothing to do and all day to do it in—all day to crucify herself with thoughts of her forwardness—where in creation had her pride been?—Sorrel knew that she had to keep busy.

But busy at what? It was for sure she was never setting foot inside Brown and Johns ever again. How Cale could ever have been so underhand about her working there in the first place defeated her. He had *known*—all along he had *known*—that Donnie would be dismissed the moment she entered her office. In all probability Cale would be there to do the job at first hand—before he went to Norway on Monday.

Sorrel felt heart-sore that Cale had deceived her all along. Even while he'd been fully aware of his disgraceful behaviour he had actually had the nerve to ask her to go to Norway with him on Monday!

Sorrel just couldn't get over that! He had *known* that Donnie's job was gone. He had *personally recommended* her dismissal. And yet all this time…

If he'd known Donnie was going to be sacked, why the blazes had he wanted her best friend to go and sort out the shambles of her office? Under those circumstances Sorrel would have thought he would not have wanted any close friend of Donnie's within five hundred yards of the place—shambles or no shambles.

Trying to outrun the mammoth tangle of her thoughts, Sorrel scurried around, doing what few chores she had. But it was no good. Cale and his mendacity were with her the whole while.

She needed to get away—but where to? She couldn't

go anywhere, she all at once realised. Donnie would be home tomorrow afternoon. She had to be there for her. No way could she leave everything that had to be said in a note for her to find.

Sorrel started to feel agitated suddenly. She couldn't settle, and knew that she would not settle. On impulse she took out an overnight bag. She could come back in the morning and be here well before Donnie was due.

Twenty minutes later she was on her way out. She met Mrs Eales, collecting her mail. 'It's the early postman this week,' she announced. Sorrell collected her own mail, recognised a letter from Donnie, and popped it in a pouch in her overnight bag. 'Going away, Sorrel?' Mrs Eales enquired.

'Only overnight. Donnie's back tomorrow.'

'Oh, she'll have such tales to tell, I'm sure.'

Sorrel was in her car, heading for Little Bossington, her thoughts only briefly on how, typically Donnie, when she would be home tomorrow she had left it until now to write of her doings.

The house where she had spent so many happy holidays seemed cold and cheerless when Sorrel let herself in. She felt weepy suddenly, but knew that it was not all on account of Uncle Lionel no longer being there.

She wandered restlessly around the house, noting furniture that would have to be removed before the house was sold, and making a mental note of the various chores she must attend to. But her heart was not truly in it.

Sorrel was upstairs when she belatedly remembered Donnie's letter. At any other time she would have been impatient to read its contents. She blamed Cale Masterson that, because of what he had done to her head, to her heart, she had all but forgotten her good friend's letter.

Realising that, such was her mood, she was ready to lay all the sins of the world at his door, Sorrel retrieved the letter from her overnight bag in her bedroom, and, thinking to make a cup of coffee, went down the stairs to read it.

She did not get to make the coffee, but read the letter first—and then didn't know whether to laugh or cry. All that had happened in her attempt to keep the job for Donnie that she had been so desperate to hold on to—and now Donnie was writing to say, among other things, that she no longer wanted the job!

Sorrel read through the letter again. Adrian was the most absolutely everything. Adrian had been offered a management job in the animal world—in Africa. Unbelievably, he would only take it if she, Donnie, would stay in Africa too! They were getting married—wasn't that utterly sublime? They were going to Florida, so Donnie could introduce Adrian to her mother. They would then make a flying visit home. And—all in the same breath—Donnie would write to Trevor Simms and tell him she wasn't coming back. If Sorrel was still intending looking for a job, perhaps she could have Donnie's. Sorrel would simply love Trevor.

Sorrel slipped the letter back in its envelope, feeling stunned. But it was not long before Cale Masterson and his lying, underhand, despicable actions were back in her head. She choked down a dry sob—the worst of it was, she still loved him.

She did not thank him that his conscience had suddenly got to him at the very last moment. *Very last moment! I'll say!* She blushed just to think of it. She—

The doorbell shrilled, cutting off her thoughts. She was in two minds about answering it. Then she remembered that her car was parked out on the drive. Although the way she was feeling she was not particularly bothered who knew that she was there and declining to answer the door.

The bell sounded again—strident and longer this time. She sighed and went out into the hall. She supposed it could well be some meter reader about his business—and pulled back the door, only for her face to go scarlet. Cale Masterson!

'Perhaps you didn't see the "No hawkers. No lying, untrustworthy, cheating investigators or troubleshooters" sign on the gate?' she jumped in furiously before he could say a word. She did not wonder how he knew where she would be—Caleb Masterson seemed to know everything. She hated him, and would be quite happy to tell him so.

He ignored her outraged comment. 'I need to talk to you,' he said evenly.

'Tough!' she erupted, and went to slam the door shut in his face. Moving swiftly, his foot was in the way—she hoped it hurt.

He might want to talk to her, but she had nothing she wanted to say to him. She turned her back on him and marched along the hall to the drawing room. Cale followed—she supposed she had known he would, for all she had not invited him in.

Taking a deep and angry breath, Sorrel turned in the

middle of the drawing room and icily faced him. It was an effort, but she somehow managed to push back her love for him, which was threatening to defeat her.

'Presumably you've some reason for coming here and forcing your way in?' she enquired—not very nicely, she had to admit. But she loved the swine, and just to have him there—tall, dark-haired, his grey eyes steady on hers—was battering at the wall of indifference she was attempting to erect.

'One of your neighbours said you'd be back tomorrow,' he commented, his eyes fixed on her.

Thank you, Mrs Eales. 'From that you deduced I'd be away from home overnight?' she replied shortly. And, as the thought struck, 'You've been to my flat?' she asked.

'When you didn't show at the office, it seemed the best place to start looking.'

She determined not to say another word, but then found that she was asking, 'You've been to Brown and Johns this morning?' It was still relatively early. He must have gone there before he'd gone to his own office! He really must want this conversation!

'As I said, I need to talk to you. There are things I need to—'

She was shaking her head before he went any further. 'I don't think so. I think I've heard more than enough from you, thank you very much.'

Cale continued to observe her with that steady gaze. Then, quite gently, he asked, 'Have I hurt you so very much, Sorrel?'

'Not at all!' she exclaimed rapidly. Just his gentle tone was starting to thaw the ice she needed to get through this. 'I thoroughly enjoy being lied to, being deceived. It was the thrill of a lifetime, working for a firm I had never planned or wanted to work for. I don't know when I was more delighted than to discover that I'd done that job for five weeks under the totally pathetic illusion that my good and dear friend would still have the job she loves when she came home. I can still hardly believe that you had me working there under the false pretence—'

'You've every right to be angry,' Cale cut in. 'I *have* deceived you and allowed you to think that everything would come right for your friend—even though you must know now that she no longer wants that job.'

That took the wind well and truly out of Sorrel's sails. 'How do *you* know that?' she demanded. 'I had a letter from Donnie this morning, but…'

'Your neighbour's a chatty soul. When I commented that your flatmate would be home soon, she said that she'd noticed you received a letter this morning with a foreign stamp on it.'

'It comes naturally to you, doesn't it—to poke and pry?'

'I swear, apart from that, all I said to her was that I was most anxious to get in touch with you—and your neighbour was ready to chat the day away.'

'Phwph!' Sorrel scoffed, but was intrigued despite herself. 'So, if you weren't nosing around… And how do you know that Donnie no longer wants her job anyway?' she challenged.

'I know she'll be visiting Florida before she returns to Surrey, and that it will only be a brief visit, during which time she intends to pop into the office to say hello to Trevor Simms—but meantime would he mind very much taking her letter as her resignation?'

'She wrote to him—at the office?' Sorrel guessed.

Cale nodded. 'I was there before nine. When you hadn't shown by ten past, I knew you wouldn't be coming. I was about to leave when the post girl brought the letter in.'

'And you opened it?'

He shrugged. 'There was no way I was going to forward it on.'

'I should have guessed.' Her sarcasm was lost on him. He didn't even flinch. 'Donnie's getting married.'

'And setting up home in Africa,' Cale completed. 'There was enough information in her letter—not least her sincere hope that Simms' surgery had been one hundred per cent successful—to confirm what I'd already established. That she had absolutely no idea of the fraud that was going on and that, in that regard, she is totally blameless. But that's not why I'm here, Sorrel,' he went on. 'You and I have some unfinished business.'

She stared at him. Unfinished? Could he go whistle!

'Personal business,' he added succinctly.

'If you think I'm coming to Norway with you next week, you have another think coming!' she retorted.

Cale looked at her long and levelly. Then, taking a long-drawn breath, 'You're not going to make this easy for me, I can tell,' he said. And, when she looked ready to flare up, 'And no one would blame you,' he quickly assured her. 'But—' he paused '—there *are* extenuating circumstances.'

'I'm still not Norway-bound!' she butted in, though unsure that he still wanted her on that trip. Her heart was behaving erratically, as it had since she had first opened the door to him.

'Look, this may take a little while. Would you mind if we sat down?'

He obviously thought that to be seated would calm her and, although she had no intention of agreeing with anything he said, she was weak where he was concerned—she knew she was—and found she was stating, 'Provided you aren't intending to bamboozle me with more of your specialised underhandedness.'

He took that on the chin, and answered, 'I swear to you—no more lies, no more deception.'

Idiotic though she knew she was being, Sorrel wanted to believe him.

'Take a seat,' she invited. She went over to one of the well-padded chairs; he took the sofa nearby. 'So, what's so very important that you decided to neglect your job and drive over to Little Bossington?' she asked coolly.

'You are,' he replied, without a moment's hesitation. And, while she stared at him, slightly open-mouthed, 'I've hurt you, Sorrel, and I can't say how sorry I am about that. But when we were making love last—'

'There's no need to go into all that!' she interrupted in a rush, knowing her colour was high.

'I think we do,' he replied, his eyes on her flushed face, gentleness there in his voice again. 'Lord knows how I managed to tear myself away from you. But you speaking your friend's name brought me up short. And I was being thumped with the memory of how I'd warned you against Rex Dunne, and had actually told you that the deceiver Fletcher was not good enough for you—and I was being hammered by the thought—was I any better?'

Sorrel continued to stare at him. Then she mentally shook herself. She was getting all soft and squashy about him—and that would never do. 'So that's it, then?' she said stonily. 'You came to apologise. Well, you've done that.' She got to her feet, only to find that Cale was on his feet too—and was closer to her than she wanted. 'I'll see you to the door,' she said woodenly, but had managed barely a step before Cale caught hold of her arm and held her there.

She looked pointedly down at his hand on her arm. He followed her cutting look, but chose to ignore it. 'I've come about more than that,' he stated, continuing to hold her there. 'There's more than that between us, between you and me, Sorrel Oliphant, and you know it.'

She did. But she hadn't thought that he knew it. Unless he went around kissing all the females he came into work-day contact with—and whatever she thought of him she did not think he did that—then their relationship *was* more than that of simply thrown together work acquaintances.

But he was making her nervous. She made to move back to her chair—but found he had somehow manoeuvred her over to the sofa and was sitting down beside her. He half turned to look at her.

'We met, you and I, under some of the worst circumstances,' Cale opened.

Sorrel cleared her suddenly choky throat with a nervous kind of cough. 'They could hardly have been worse,' she had to agree, and he gave her half a smile.

'Try to understand, my darling,' he said—and that

'my darling' knocked her sideways—'that money had disappeared, nobody had ever heard of you—and yet there you were, keys in hand, messing about in a drawer that was kept locked. At that early stage I was just doing my job.'

'Lying and deceiving.'

'I had to be sure about you.'

'Pfff!' she scorned, finding a touch of backbone from somewhere. 'That must have taken quite some while—or why else continue to let me believe—?'

'It took no time at all,' Cale cut in seriously. 'But even in that short time I knew that I did not want to lose contact with you.'

Her heart did a giddy flip. But he was sharp, was Caleb Masterson, clear thinking, and an expert at leading her in a false direction. 'Because I was your route to Donnie!' she challenged snappily.

Cale studied her hostile expression. 'Partly that, to begin with,' he conceded, and then paused, looking into her eyes. 'But I very soon discovered that I had an overwhelming compulsion to have some sort of communication with you that had nothing at all to do with your friend.'

'Oh,' she murmured, feeling on shaky ground suddenly. Then she realised that Cale had drawn encouragement from her murmured exclamation, because he all at once caught hold of one of her hands. She tried to jerk her hand away, but he would not let her.

'Whatever else I've said, whatever other way I have deceived you, trust me in this, Sorrel?' he asked. 'Trust that I was very soon sure about you.'

Her throat felt dry. 'Be-because your enquiries about me showed…?' she attempted.

'I had you investigated,' he agreed. 'There was little I didn't know about you in a very short while.'

'You knew about this house, my guardian…'

'All of that, sweetheart,' he said gently, turning her bones to water. 'And I knew about your relationship with Fletcher—the fact he'd been two-timing you. The—'

'You *knew* about *him?*' she exclaimed, with another angry tug at her hand in his. His grip stayed firm. 'You pretended not to. You said…' She was so stunned she could not remember what he had said. 'You already knew his job, where he worked, before I told you!' she accused.

'It's my job,' Cale said quietly.

'You're a treacherous rat!' she exploded. 'You've pretended to—'

'I've pretended quite a bit with you,' he openly admitted. And again very nearly floored her when he further admitted, 'Even to the extent of pretending to be pleased when you as good as told me you weren't interested in me.'

Her thinking went hazy. 'That was when you went all anti-Sorrel Oliphant—when I saw you again after you'd kissed me,' she recalled.

'I wasn't anti-you, Sorrel,' he said softly. 'I'd come into your office purely because I was bereft without a sight of you.' She swallowed hard, her eyes fixed on his face. 'You blushed so delightfully as you remembered our kiss—and I, sweet love, was so absolutely besotted with you I had to take some kind of evasive action.'

Her green eyes went wide. 'You were—um—besotted—with me?' She picked the most important bit out of all he had said.

'I still am, my darling,' he confirmed tenderly.

'Oh,' she whispered. And, as her heart galloped inside of her, 'And—er—you've finished deceiving me?'

'Honesty only from now on,' he promised.

'But you had to pretend otherwise?' She decided to take it step by tiny step. Just one hint of a lie and she was throwing him out on his ear. But, for the moment, she loved him enough to want to hear more.

'Male pride,' he owned. 'You'd said you no longer loved Fletcher. Did I believe that? Did I want to be yours on the rebound? Add to that, you were pretty aloof with me too—though I confess I did draw comfort that you might have been protesting a little too much when you were making sure I knew you were not interested in me.'

Sorrel sent him a disgusted look. 'You know too much about women!'

'But not enough about you. Not nearly enough.'

'I'd have said your investigation of me left little out!' she retorted sniffily.

'When it came to you and your background, your friends and acquaintances, I had the lot,' he owned, and she had to give him top marks there for his honesty. 'But what I didn't know,' he went on, 'was what was in your heart. And that, Sorrel my love, is what is more important to me than anything.'

*Oh*—her breath caught in her throat. He was looking at her as if he cared. But hadn't she been fooled before? She wasn't in the business of risking it again.

'Could you try to be a bit more specific?' Where had that cool note come from? Sometimes she surprised even herself.

Yet Cale did not look surprised. In fact he looked encouraged by her cool tone, by her question. 'You're nervous. I'm nervous,' he admitted. 'I'm hoping it's because you love me as I love you.'

'I—er…' She seemed to be having difficulty in breathing. 'You—l-love me?'

He smiled gently into her eyes. 'With everything that's in me, Sorrel,' he answered softly.

'Oh,' she managed. 'And—you're not lying?'

He shook his head. 'I didn't know at first why I felt this tremendous pull to have you near. All I knew was that there was no way I was going to lose sight of you.'

She was still struggling for breath when something quite startling hit her. 'W-was that why you—er—proposed I should work at Brown and Johns to try and keep Donnie's job for her?' she gasped.

Cale looked at her tenderly. 'All I knew at first was that I wanted to see you again. Yet it went without saying that you would have rejected me out of hand had I asked you out on a date.'

Feeling little short of amazed, Sorrel stared at him. 'So—you made me an offer you knew I wouldn't refuse?'

He smiled. 'It seemed then to be the only sure-fire way I was going to be able to keep in touch with you. In my defence, I hadn't at that stage cleared Donnie.'

Donnie, love her though Sorrel did, was somehow now a side issue. 'You did—what you did—because you were—um—attracted to me?'

'In a big way,' he agreed. 'I had to have you where I could see or hear you. You were in my head, my love. Looking back, it seems to me now that there have been few moments since I have known you when you were *not* in my head. I fell in love with you even before I'd found out everything about Fletcher.'

'When?' she asked.

'When did I fall in love with you? Almost at once. Certainly within two weeks of knowing you,' he answered, without having to think about it. 'It knocked me all of a heap. There am I, knowing I have got to keep a cool head. And there are you, clearly not yet over some other male—and there's that green-eyed monster jealousy saying take that for your trouble.'

'You were jealous?'

'Of any man who asked you out.'

'Oh, Cale,' she said softly, without thought.

His lips formed a smile. 'But it will all have been worth it if you can bring yourself to tell me I haven't been wasting my time dreaming of a future with you.'

'Whoo…' A rush of breath escaped her.

'I'm going too fast?' Cale asked urgently.

'No—no,' she replied quickly.

'Then—you love me?' he queried, as sharp as ever, deducing from her answer that she was not stopping him.

'You know I do,' she answered.

'I thought—I hoped. When you were the way you were with me last night, I was sure. But I had to go. I was only making you more upset by staying. But the minute I was on the wrong side of your door I was being belaboured by doubt. And, after the longest sleepless night of my life, I knew I'd have to have something settled with you today—or go completely off my head.' He smiled then. 'Is it safe to take you in my arms?' he asked, with sinking charm.

Sorrel's heart was full to overflowing. His arms came about her, and for long, long moments Cale held her close up to him. Sorrel put her arms around him and gently, tenderly, adoringly, he kissed her.

'Oh, Cale,' she sighed, when he pulled back to look into her face.

'Are you feeling all nerve-ends, yet rapturous too?' he asked softly.

'I never, ever felt like this about Guy Fletcher,' she said shyly.

'You're sure?'

'I know it.' She smiled at him. 'What I feel for you makes what I felt for him pale into insignificance.'

Cale kissed her tenderly again. 'I'm glad to hear it,' he said, and there was a smile there, in his voice and on his mouth, as he looked at her. 'When?' he asked, and she knew what he meant.

'I've been asking myself the same question. You gave a sort of a half-smile when we parted that day we met, so I suppose it must have slotted into my brain that you were not a total ogre. Then I started to get jumpy on the few occasions my desk phone rang…'

'In case it was me?'

'True.' She could admit it now.

'You do realise that I phoned you just because I needed to hear your voice—only for my brain to desert me when I heard it. And like some youth with a first crush, I either asked for one of the auditors or rang off.'

'You?' she gasped. 'But you're always so sophisticated, so sure…'

'See what falling in love with you has done to me?' he teased. 'I've had to remind myself to keep a cool head. I was in love with you, but clearly you were in love with somebody else. There were plainly issues you had to resolve. Yet I wanted you near the whole time—if I couldn't see you, I wanted to phone you. Sweetheart, I've been tormented that you might still be in love with…'

'I was never *in* love with him,' she inserted gently. And, with a smile, 'It was you who suggested we went to his firm's party—brief though that visit was.'

'Little love, it's not in me to just do nothing. I had to find out one way or another how you truly felt about him.'

Sorrel stretched up and kissed him—purely because she had to. 'I love *you,*' she said. 'Am *in love* with *you.*' And she was held warmly up against him, and tenderly and lingeringly kissed.

'You are so beautiful,' Cale breathed as he drew back to look at her. And, with that warm smile again, 'You opened your door to me that party night and my breath caught. I was in fear when I made myself take you to see your ex-love.'

'You kissed me,' she reminded him dreamily.

'My heart was full as we stood there—I just couldn't resist you, even as I knew it was too soon.' His smile was all loving as he confessed, 'I decided, madam, that I'd keep away from you, that—'

'You came to the office the next working day!' she exclaimed.

'So I couldn't keep away?' He grinned. 'Though you have to admit I did a valiant job in pretending I was glad our "romance" was over.'

Sorrel laughed. She just had to. And, to her delight, Cale joined in. But she sobered suddenly and just had to ask, 'Donnie?'

She had no need to say more because Cale straight away understood.

'If she's living in Africa we may be able to use her written evidence without the need for her to appear in court. But she'll have to be told, darling.' And, when Sorrel looked a shade troubled, 'We'll break it to her together, shall we? As gently as possible?'

Sorrel looked lovingly at him. From the company point of view Donnie had messed up badly. Yet here was Cale, when he had every right to take Donnie apart, talking of breaking the news of the consequences of her ineptitude to her gently.

'You know something, Cale Masterson?' she said softly. 'You are one very special kind of person.'

He grinned as though he'd really needed to hear her say that. 'And, despite what you said, you'll come to Norway with me on Monday?'

'Wonderful,' she confirmed. 'I've still got the laptop.'

His grin became a touch shamefaced. 'Strictly speaking, you won't really need that. I only brought it over to your place because, while I felt fairly confident you wouldn't go back to Rex Dunne's place with him last night, I needed an excuse to butt in, had he cajoled you into giving him an end-of-the-evening coffee.'

Her eyes shot wide. 'Truly?'

'Truly jealous,' he responded.

'But…' Memory triggered. 'But you made out—inside my flat—that you'd only just remembered I was seeing Rex last night.'

'See what loving you has done to me?' he said lightly, and confessed, 'I'd been lurking around outside your building for quite some time.'

'You saw me come home?' she asked, shaken.

'And saw you kiss him,' Cale replied.

'On his cheek,' she said, and smiled. She just had to love him. 'Anything else I should know?' she asked.

Cale shook his head, though did own, 'Well, since I'm being totally honest with you here, and from now on, I suppose I should mention that I don't in actual fact *need* to take you with me as a peripatetic PA on Monday. It's just that, my sweet, lovely darling, I love you so very much that just the thought of spending five whole days away from you next week seemed like an eternity.'

Sorrel stared huge-eyed at him. 'You—invented the job?' she gasped.

'I love you,' he answered.

He loved her that much! Though, come to think about it, a week without seeing him was for her not to be borne. 'I love *you,*' she told him.

Cale kissed her, and she loved him so. 'And you'll come with me?'

'I don't think I could bear to be left behind—not now I know you—um—care for me.'

'Love you, sweet Sorrel. *Love you.*' Again he kissed her. But, pulling back, he began, 'Ideally we'd be married before we went—' As her eyes went saucer-wide, 'But I believe we have to give the authorities a couple of weeks' or so notice of our intent, so we just haven't the time—' He broke off, noticing that her beautiful green eyes were wide and shocked. 'It *is* all right with you if we marry when we get back?' he asked urgently.

'You—w-want to marry me?' she stammered.

Cale looked stunned for a moment, then spoke speedily, 'Oh, please, Sorrel—don't tell me you're refusing me, that you're saying no!'

He looked quite shattered by the thought, and Sorrel could not bear it. 'I wouldn't dream of it,' she assured him quickly.

'That's a yes?' he insisted.

'Yes,' she willingly replied. 'The happiest yes of my life.'

Cale smiled in relief. 'Sweet Sorrel,' he breathed, and drew her to him.

* * * * *

# THE TYCOON'S MARRIAGE BID

Patricia Thayer

**Patricia Thayer** has been writing for over twenty years and has published thirty novels. Her books have been twice nominated for the National Readers' Choice Award and a prestigious RITA® Award. In 1997, *Nothing Short of a Miracle* won the *Romantic Times* BOOK Club Reviewers' Choice Award for Best Special Edition.

Thanks to the understanding men in her life – her husband of over thirty-five years, Steve, and her three grown sons and three grandsons – Pat has been able to fulfil her dream of writing. Besides writing romance, she loves to travel, especially in the west where she researches her books first hand. You might find her on a ranch in Texas, or on a train to an old mining town in Colorado, and this year you'll find her on an adventure in Scotland. Just so long as she can share it all with her favourite hero, Steve. She loves to hear from readers. You can write to her at PO Box 6251, Anaheim, CA 92816-0251, USA or check her website at www.patriciathayer.com for forthcoming books.

**Look for Patricia Thayer's next new novel, *Texas Ranger Takes a Bride*, in September 2008 from Mills & Boon® Romance.**

Dear Reader,

It's such an honour for me to be included in the 100th year celebration for Mills & Boon. And for my story to be grouped in an anthology with Margaret Way and Jessica Steele is incredible.

I've been published for sixteen years, and an avid reader most of my life. Romance novels have always been my favourites. Growing up in a large family, I used reading to escape into my own private world. I still believe it helps all of us to relax and get away. And I hope my stories help you…

THE TYCOON'S MARRIAGE BID takes place in the wine country outside of Medford, Oregon. For over a hundred years, Ellie Flanagan's family roots have been buried deep in the rich, fertile soil. Now with only herself and her grandfather, she's determined to follow her dream and build a winery for their Irish Rogue label. Instead, she ends up in a fight just to keep from losing it all.

Businessman Hugh McCutcheon's job is to buy up failing companies and downsize them so they'll make a profit. He's become very wealthy in his own right. It isn't until he comes to Emerald Vale Vineyard and meets Ellie that he realises how empty his life has been…and suddenly, it's not about business any more.

Enjoy,

*Patricia Thayer*

# CHAPTER ONE

"YOU'VE got four weeks...but I want this deal wrapped up in two."

Hugh McCutcheon held the cellphone to his ear, listening to his father's orders as he drove his rental car along Interstate 5, just outside Medford, Oregon.

Why should he be surprised at the request? Whatever he'd done for the company, Richard "Mac" McCutcheon wanted more. "I thought Flanagan hadn't decided to sell...yet."

"And since when has that mattered to you?" his father asked. "I'm expecting you to come through for me. We need the orchard to control the area. More importantly, we need the vineyard."

Hugh should be used to getting this treatment from his father. *If the job's tough, give it to the kid. He'll do anything the old man dangles in front of his face.*

"I can't make any promises, Mac." It had been agreed he wouldn't call him Dad during working hours...that meant all the time.

"I don't need promises," he growled. "I need results. There's a lot riding on this, Hugh. Including the regional director's job."

Hugh sighed. *Yeah, right.* He'd been promised the position for the last year. "I'll do what I can. I need to go; my turn-off is coming up. I'll check in later." He shut the phone and tossed it on the passenger seat, next to the proposal for this project: Emerald Vale Orchard and Irish Rogue Vineyard.

On his flight from San Francisco to Medford he'd been able to scan it over, but not much more. His father wanted a lot, but he always had. Problem was the family patriarch, Cullan Flanagan, wasn't eager to sell his family business. The one positive thing was that the owner was giving the McCutcheon Corporation the opportunity to come and talk with him.

Hugh rubbed his hand over his face. He hated not being prepared for a job. In most cases he was always organized. But he'd just finished a six-week stay in Atlanta, where he'd downsized a recently purchased electronic parts plant. By the time he'd left the company was running efficiently, with a twenty percent reduction in personnel. That was sure to raise the next quarterly profit. It was important that he increase his value at the McCutcheon Corporation, too.

Hugh wanted that promotion…and he had that much of his father in him to ensure that he went after it. He'd gotten used to his lavish lifestyle. More than that, he enjoyed the thrill of his job.

*So bring on the next challenge.* He looked up to see the sign overhead: "Emerald Vale Orchard, est. by the Flanagan family in 1908. Home to the Irish Rogue Vineyard, est. 2002." He drove through the archway to see neat rows of pear trees along the hillside. On the other side were the ribbons of trellised vines.

Hugh continued on about a quarter of a mile and spotted a large barn, painted white with burgundy trim. In the front was a general store. He pulled up in the parking area next to picnic tables shaded by colorful shade umbrellas.

After climbing out of the car, he slipped on his suit coat. He glanced further up a grassy knoll to see a huge house with a flagstone façade that peeked out through the trees. A wraparound porch held baskets of summer flowers along the gingerbread trim. The manicured lawn was edged with more pink and purple plants.

Then suddenly the colors seemed to fade as a young woman stepped out onto the porch. What he noticed first was her rich auburn hair. The thick tresses went well past her shoulders and were clipped back from her face. She had a slender build. His gaze moved over her figure. A cream-colored blouse was knotted at her tiny waist, and her long legs were nearly covered by a gauzy peach-hued skirt. She moved gracefully as she lovingly attended to each plant.

He found his breathing suddenly labored, but his gaze didn't waver from the sight.

"The lass is easy on the eye, that's for sure."

Hugh jerked around to see a smiling older man in his seventies. He had a head full of thick white hair, and his face was weathered from years in the sun. Cullan Flanagan.

"I apologize for staring, sir," Hugh said.

The man's smile widened. "No need to apologize for appreciating a beautiful woman." He nodded in her direction. "I did the same thing the day I first saw her grandmother. And I felt the same way for the next fifty-three years." He sighed and blinked his eyes rapidly. "Sorry, I still miss her. And seeing Ellie every day brings back so many memories." He stuck out his hand. "I'm Cullan Flanagan. Welcome to Emerald Vale."

"Hello, Mr. Flanagan. I'm Hugh McCutcheon from the McCutcheon Corporation."

"Ah, Mr. McCutcheon, I've been expecting you." He looked him over. "So you think you can convince me to sell my land?"

Hugh gave him his best smile. "I plan to give it a try."

"It's going to have to be over my dead body," a woman's voice said.

Hugh swung around to see the redhead standing there, with her hands on her hips, glaring at him with large green eyes. She was even more beautiful close up. And he couldn't seem to find his voice.

Ellie wasn't going to let some big-city corporate guy come in here and take away her home. Not as long as she had any fight left in her.

"At a loss for words, Mr. McCutcheon?"

He shook his head, then smiled. "I assure you, Ms. Flanagan, I do not want any dead bodies."

"Oh, really?" She managed to look away from his dark chocolate eyes. "That's not what your reputation states. Don't they call you the Hatchet Man?"

He grimaced. "This business can be tough, especially when the companies we acquire are in financial trouble."

"Well, I guess you aren't needed here, since there isn't anything wrong with our orchard or our vineyard."

Hugh McCutcheon seemed to relax a little as he

folded his arms across his massive chest, looking comfortable in his suit coat even when the temperature was in the high eighties.

Ellie didn't like that.

She didn't like men who walked in and acted as if they owned the place already. Well, no matter how handsome or well-built the man was, he wasn't going to take Flanagan land.

"Studies show there's always room for improvement."

"We're not a study, Mr. McCutcheon. We're a family and this is our livelihood. So go buy up someone else's place. We're not for sale."

"Eleanor Anne…" Her grandfather's voice broke in. "That's no way to talk to a guest."

Ellie turned to her sole grandparent. "It's true, Papa. Word has spread throughout the valley." She nodded to the stranger. "His company is buying up all the family orchards in the area."

"They were all willing to sell," Hugh added. "We didn't coerce anyone. We gave fair market value for all the properties."

Ellie made a huffing sound. "I doubt that," she said. "No one gets paid for all the years they've worked the land." She pointed toward the orchard. "Their blood, sweat and tears are out there. You can't put a price on that."

"I agree. But the owners who sold to us were ready to get out."

Silently, Ellie glared at him. She wasn't getting anywhere with the man, but she was more worried about her grandfather. Since the death of his wife Eleanor, two years ago, he'd been so unhappy. Nothing gave him joy anymore. Not even the winemaking. Something they'd planned and worked on together. The Irish Rogue label had been their collaborative dream. Now he was thinking about selling out.

Hugh knew Ellie Flanagan was going to do everything in her power to stop this sale. And his job was to do whatever it took to stop her. From what he'd read about the orchard, Cullan Flanagan was the sole owner of the land...and Ellie was his only heir. But she didn't have any control until after her grandfather's death.

"Maybe your grandfather is ready, too."

This time she couldn't hide her disdain. "He is not." She turned to the older man. "Papa, you can't be serious?"

"Can't hurt to hear what the man has to say."

Before Ellie could speak, Cullan raised his hand. "We'll discuss this later, lass. Please show Mr. McCutcheon to the Sunset Cottage."

She blinked those big emerald eyes, but quickly masked her anger once again. "Fine."

Cullan kissed his granddaughter, then looked at Hugh. "Please, make yourself comfortable, and I'll see you at dinner."

"Thank you, sir."

With a nod, the older man, his back bent slightly, his steps slow, walked across the gravel road toward the orchard.

"Just because he's invited you to stay doesn't mean he's going to sell you...all this," Ellie said, and she spread her arms, taking in the acres of lush green vines that led all the way up the hillside. On the other side were the rows of pear trees, dotted with the dozen workers who cared for them.

Hugh sighed. "I have to say, it's pretty impressive."

She drew a breath, too. "And it belongs to the Flanagan family. And I will make sure it always belongs to us."

"You have a big job ahead of you. Especially since there aren't many Flanagans left."

She straightened. "You don't need to worry about us, Mr. McCutcheon. Besides, who's to say I don't have a would-be husband around?" she tossed out. "Now, take your car down the road to the turn-off with the sign that says 'Cottages'. I'll meet you there." She took off toward the house.

Hugh enjoyed watching her walk away…too much. He wondered if there *was* a man in her life. She was beautiful enough to have several.

He quickly shook away the thought, and knew he'd better be able to handle a spitfire. "*Damn.* Keep your head on business. This trip is all about the business," he chanted, but the nudge of attraction didn't go away.

Ellie waited at the oak door to the studio cottage. The bungalow was usually rented by newlyweds, or couples who wanted the seclusion the peaceful orchard offered them. Not businessmen who wanted to rip her life apart.

The luxury rental car pulled up under the tree in front, and McCutcheon climbed out. He'd removed his suit jacket, revealing a crisp white shirt that showed off his broad shoulders and well-developed chest. Her gaze lowered to his trim waist, then, when he turned to walk to the car's trunk, she got a glimpse at his tight rear end.

She quickly glanced away, angry that she could find anything to appreciate about the man.

With a dark leather suitcase in hand, Hugh McCutcheon walked toward her. Without comment, she opened the door and went inside. The combined scents of roses and peaches teased her nose as she stepped into the large room. As expected, there were fresh-cut flowers on the table. On the kitchen counter was a large bowl of fruit, along with several bottles of Irish Rogue wine. Soft music filtered into the space from strategically placed speakers.

There was a cozy seating area in front of the fireplace, and across the large room was a king-size bed covered in ivory satin, with miles of sheer fabric draped overhead, creating a canopy.

Definitely a place for lovers.

She looked at Hugh McCutcheon and noted his amused look. "I guess you don't have many singles, huh?" He loosened his tie as if he were too warm. She watched as he undid the top two buttons of his shirt, revealing dark chest hair.

She swallowed and turned to the phone on the table. "Sorry, we don't have the rooms equipped for Internet use."

This time he turned a wicked grin toward her. "I doubt that anyone staying here is thinking about business."

"No, not usually. Most of our guests have other things on their minds."

His gaze never left hers. "There are a lot of nice things to distract you here."

Silence hung between them as the music changed to

an enchanting love song. The singer's sultry voice created an even more intimate feeling in the room.

Ellie froze under the man's gaze. She felt a sudden stirring low in her stomach. She swallowed, finding her mouth bone-dry. She blinked and finally broke the hold.

"If you need anything, Mr. McCutcheon, just call the office." She backed up, but came in contact with the coffee table and began to stumble.

Hugh reached out and grabbed her, pulling her upright. His hands gripped her arms, holding her firmly.

"You should be more careful," he said, his voice low and husky. "You could hurt yourself."

She nodded, not trusting her voice as her gaze locked with his once again. His brown eyes were incredible. Close up, they were the color of aged whiskey.

She glanced away, silently berating herself for her crazy behavior. This man was the enemy. He was here to take away her hopes and dreams. Straightening, she pulled away from his hold.

"I'm always careful, Mr. McCutcheon. I know what I want, and I'll do everything I can to keep what's mine."

He smiled. "Is that a threat, Ms Flanagan?"

"No. Just the truth. This land has been in our family for a hundred years, and I'm not about to let someone come in and take it away."

Hugh stood back and looked her over. Man, she was a powerhouse. Under other circumstances he would love to get to know her better. He pushed aside any thoughts of what might have been a passionate relationship. This was business—and business always came first.

"Times change, Ms Flanagan. It takes money to run an operation like this."

"We've been running it just fine for years."

"But at a profit?"

Hugh saw a flash of sadness in those mesmerizing eyes, but she quickly masked it. "Not everything is measured in dollars. And just because my grandfather and I are the only ones with the Flanagan name, it doesn't mean we don't have plenty of family around."

She gave him a once-over look that made him feel as if she could see inside his dark soul.

"I doubt you could say the same thing, Mr. McCutcheon." She swung around and walked to the door.

Hugh was just a bit quicker as he went after her. She reached for the knob, but he stopped her from making a grand exit.

"You know nothing about me, Ellie Flanagan…or my family." He spoke softly into her ear. "So don't go making assumptions. I'm not doing anything illegal, but I will do what it takes to get end results."

She turned around and flashed those big eyes at him. His gaze moved to her hair, already teasing his nose with a fresh lemony scent. He itched to run his fingers through the silky auburn strands.

"Then be warned, Mr. McCutcheon. I can fight dirty, too."

He couldn't help but smile as he stepped back. "I'll look forward to it."

She nodded, then pulled open the door and stalked out.

Hugh stood in the doorway and watched as she walked down the hill toward the house. With her head held high, her natural grace drew his interest more than it should. He wanted to blame it on a lack of female attention due to his heavy work schedule, but he knew the sassy redhead intrigued him all on her own.

If he allowed it, Ellie Flanagan could make him forget every other woman he'd ever known. She could also make him forget the reason he was here.

He frowned. No, he couldn't let that happen.

# CHAPTER TWO

Two hours later, Hugh leaned back in his chair in the Flanagans' dining room. He glanced at the sage-green walls with a honey oak trim, and at the teardrop chandelier hung overhead. He took a sip of his wine, savoring the fruity taste.

"The meal was delicious, Ellie," he told her.

"Thank you," she answered, although she didn't look too happy with his compliment.

Cullan Flanagan smiled. "My granddaughter has many talents. She manages the vineyard and schedules all Eleanor's Special Events, then at the end of the day serves up a tasty meal."

"Papa, throwing together a stew isn't a difficult task."

"And homemade biscuits," he added.

"Well, it sure was a treat for me," Hugh said, meaning it. "I usually eat in restaurants while I'm on business trips."

"You travel a lot?" Cullan asked.

"More than I'd like," he conceded, wondering when he had ever loved it. He'd been supposed to get some time off now, but Mac had other plans.

"So your home is in San Francisco?"

He nodded. "But I'm sorry to say I don't have much time to enjoy the city."

Cullan sighed. "That has to be hard on your family, you being away so much."

"Then I guess it's a good thing I'm single."

"It can be a lonely existence."

"Maybe some people like the single life," Ellie added as she got up from the table and retrieved the coffeepot from the antique sideboard. She leaned close to Hugh to refill his cup and he inhaled her fresh scent. The sudden feeling of awareness caught him off guard.

He quickly looked back at Cullan. "There is my father, but he works just as much as I do."

The older man smiled. "I've talked with…Mac. He speaks highly of you. You must have a close relationship."

Hugh stole a glance at Ellie. She sat quietly, drinking her coffee. Suddenly he felt like a kid again, making excuses for his father's lack of attention. "Like I said, I don't have much personal time."

"That's a shame," Cullan said. "I don't know what I'd do if I didn't have my Ellie here with me."

"And I love living here, Papa." She reached over and gripped a gnarled hand that showed his years of working the earth. The love they shared was obvious.

Her grandfather looked sad. "Sometimes I wonder what kind of life it's been for you, lass."

Ellie smiled at him. "Papa, you've given me everything." She glanced at Hugh. "This land is important to me…I love managing the vineyard."

"It's been her life since she came home from

college," Cullan said, then turned to his granddaughter. "You don't even think about a husband?"

A soft blush rose over her cheeks. "Why should I go looking for someone when you've never approved of anyone I've brought home?"

Hugh suddenly felt jealous of every one of those men.

Cullan waved his hand. "None of those fellows were worth your time. None of them loved the vines…not as you do. You need someone strong, someone who will let you follow your heart."

"My heart is just fine, Papa."

Cullan grinned as he looked at Hugh. "She is stubborn. All I want is to see her happy and to have a chance to play with a great-grandchild before I leave this earth. Is that too much to ask?"

Hugh raised a hand as he looked at the beautiful woman…who no doubt would give a man beautiful babies. "I think I should stay out of this."

"Good idea," Ellie agreed, then eyed her grandfather. "Papa, it will be a long time before you go anywhere. So stop talking foolish."

Ellie hated that her grandfather had brought up this issue, especially in front of a stranger. Had that been the reason he'd been entertaining the idea of selling the orchard and vineyard?

"See, she puts me in my place," her grandfather said. "Is it any wonder that men go running?"

"She hasn't scared me off," Hugh said.

That brought a big grin from Cullan Flanagan. "I knew I liked you. Now, I'm going to retire for the night."

He stood and went to kiss Ellie. "I hope your accommodation is satisfactory, Hugh."

"Yes, it is. The cottage is very comfortable."

Flanagan nodded. "Then I will see you both in the morning." He walked out of the room.

The last thing Ellie wanted was to be left alone with Hugh McCutcheon, but she saw her grandfather's fatigue and knew he needed sleep. She turned back to Hugh and began to stack plates. "You should probably turn in, too."

"It's early yet." He, too, gathered up some dishes, followed her into the oversized country kitchen, then placed them on the counter.

"Thank you," she said.

When he returned to the dining room for more dishes, she spoke up. "You really should turn in. We get up at dawn around here."

"I will. After I help you clean up."

"You're a guest here."

"I'm a businessman, and your grandfather was nice enough to invite me to supper." He leaned against the counter and after a while said, "I know you don't want me here…"

"How observant of you, Mr. McCutcheon."

"Please, could you at least call me Hugh?"

"Maybe." She began placing the plates in the dishwasher. "But then why would I want to get too friendly with someone who wants to take away my business?"

"I'm not taking away anything. I'm making an offer. Your grandfather is the one who decides to sell or not."

The last of the dishes were put in and she shut the door. "Okay, it's done. Thank you. I'll say goodnight now." She started to walk away. Anything to get far from this man.

He reached for her hand and stopped her. "Please, it's early yet," he told her. "Why not give me a tour through the vineyard?"

She tried not to be distracted by the warm tingle caused by his touch, but couldn't hide her surprise at his request. "And why would I want to do that?"

"To show me why this place is so important to you. I've read a lot, but my knowledge is limited when it comes to orchards…or growing grapes."

The last thing Ellie wanted to do was help in any way to promote this possible sale, but Hugh McCutcheon wasn't going away anytime soon. Not until he was ready. So what would it hurt?

"Fine, I'll take you." She headed for the back door. Grabbing a sweater off the hook, she went out to the porch, not waiting to see if he was following.

"Hey, wait up. I didn't know this was a race."

Ellie stopped and swung around, only to collide with him. Immediately she raised her hands to regain her balance, and felt his hard body beneath his starched shirt. But when his hands gripped her arms she felt gentleness, too.

In the moonlight, she saw the shadow of his handsome face. She couldn't see his eyes, but felt his piercing gaze.

"You should be more careful," he said, his voice husky. "There isn't much light out here."

His warm breath brushed against her face, causing her heart to pound in her chest. She needed to step back, but couldn't seem to move. "I've been running through this orchard day and night since I was a child."

As much as he hated to, Hugh let her go. "You must have had quite a childhood."

They walked across the narrow farm road and through an open gate to the vineyard, and started down an aisle of grapevines woven along trellises. "To my parents' dismay," she began, "Papa and Nana spoiled me. It made it difficult when we all lived here together."

He couldn't hide his surprise. "All in the same house?"

She shook her head, and that glorious, wild hair caressed her shoulders. "No. We lived in a smaller house on the other side of the hill." She pointed past the vineyard. "It was my father Daniel's dream to become a winemaker. He planted the first Chardonnay grapes here fifteen years ago."

Moonlight guided their journey through the neat rows of vines. The night was silent, with just the quiet sound of their footsteps against the packed earth. He felt peace come over him and he began to relax.

"Later, my father expanded the vineyard and planted Pinot Noir and Riesling grapes. He had planned to build his own winery…"

"What happened to those plans?"

She kept her head down. "He and my mother, Marianne, were killed in a private plane crash. It had been their first vacation in years…a second honeymoon."

"I'm sorry, Ellie."

She nodded and didn't say anything as they walked

on. "I want to carry on my father's dream and build up the Irish Rogue Vineyard."

"And your grandfather has other ideas?"

She shrugged. "I wouldn't say that… It's just since Nana died two years ago, he hasn't been enthusiastic about much of anything."

"He seems happy enough now."

She stopped, then turned back down another aisle. "You wouldn't say that if you'd ever seen him with my grandmother. They had a special relationship. She'd walk into a room, and Papa's gaze would follow her everywhere. He was always touching her, making her feel special. Every day of their marriage he'd leave the orchard to come to the house for lunch. They shared everything, every decision…every hope and dream. Then she got sick and he couldn't help her…" She stopped, and he heard her swallow before she continued. "All Papa could do was stay with her until the end…then he had to let her go."

Hugh couldn't say anything. He'd never known anyone who'd had a good marriage. His father had had two, and his mother had become bitter over the divorce.

Ellie stopped and looked at him. "Nana asked me to watch out for him. I've tried, but he misses her so…" He could hear the tears in her voice. "That's why I wasn't surprised that he let you come here."

Hugh knew better than to get emotionally involved with a potential client. But Ellie made it hard to stay impartial. "Maybe Cullan is just tired of all the work?"

"He doesn't have to do a thing. I'm here. I'm handling the vineyard. And Grandfather has a manager,

Ben Harrington, for the orchard." She paused. "But you already know this, don't you, Mr. McCutcheon?"

"Most of it was in the report."

She straightened. "So you needed me to fill in the rest? You wanted to find our weak points? Well, you're not going to get any more information from me." She stepped closer. "You can write this down, Mr. Hugh McCutcheon. I don't give up. Not when something this important is at stake."

"I wasn't trying to gather information, Ellie. I was just enjoying a relaxing walk and some conversation."

"Who are you kidding? You're not the type to relax… unless it's to your advantage. And if you think I'm going to make this easy on you, you're crazy. So if you want to take this land, be prepared for a fight. Just remember there's a hundred years of Flanagans who have been in this area. And I plan to carry on that tradition."

Hugh hadn't envisioned any of this, especially this beautiful adversary. "There's got to be a way to compromise," he suggested, but he knew his father had too much invested in this project already to back down.

"As far as I'm concerned there's only one way to do that. Get off my land. It's not for sale." She swung around and marched down the aisle toward the house.

Hugh sighed as he started back at a slower pace. This wasn't going to be easy to pull off, but he wasn't giving up either. That wasn't his style. He thought of his fiery-haired opponent with those sparkling green eyes.

*It's not over, Ellie Flanagan. I'll win you over one way or the other.* But he wondered if his thoughts had anything to do with business.

* * *

"How is it going, Hugh?" his father asked the next day.

Hugh wasn't ready to take a phone call from Mac, but he wasn't left any choice. "Cullan Flanagan has been agreeable, and is willing to show me around, but he could just be playing me. His granddaughter wants me off the property."

Mac made a snorting sound. "I expect you to handle *her* without any problem. Just charm her. It won't be the first time."

Hugh walked to the window of the cottage and looked over the vineyard, seeing workers tending the fields. He wasn't proud of it, but he had in the past used a little gentle persuasion on the ladies.

"Ellie Flanagan doesn't want me here," he emphasized again. "Maybe you should reconsider and bring in Matt Hudson. It was his project originally."

"No, I want you to do this. Now, you can't let me down on this one, Hugh. You know what's at stake."

Of course he did. The regional director's position he had wanted for the past year. "I'll try, but if not, isn't there any way we can work around this section of land?"

"Whether there is or not isn't the question. I've already put in place a potential deal with a chain of discount stores who want to buy large quantities of Irish Rogue wine."

Hugh felt a twinge of regret, knowing that when his father wanted something, he found a way to get it. "I can't guarantee anything, Mac."

"Come on, son. Work some of your magic." With that, the phone connection was cut off.

He tossed the cellphone on the bed with a curse. Son. He'd called him son. Why hadn't the endearment meant more? Maybe because there were always strings attached to it.

How could he let this happen? How could he be talked into something that would possibly destroy a family? Of course he had personal experience of how much his father cared about family. All those years ago Richard McCutcheon had walked out on his wife and ten-year-old son without a backward glance.

In the years that had followed he'd given generously of his money, but had rarely had time to spend with his child. It hadn't been until Hugh had graduated from college that his father had finally acknowledged him. He had asked him to come and work for the company. Now he still seemed to be looking for the old man's acceptance. The way it looked, it was never going to happen.

A knock on the door brought him back from his daydreaming. He went to answer it and found Ellie Flanagan standing in the doorway. She had on snug-fitting jeans and a print blouse. A single braid hung down her back. Those green eyes twinkled with mischief.

A warm shiver went through him. "Good morning, Ms Flanagan. What can I do for you?"

"How would you like to take another trip through the vineyard, this time in the daylight?"

He could only manage a nod. She could lead him around and he'd follow her anywhere.

## CHAPTER THREE

"THE lack of rain has actually been good for the grapes," Ellie said as she stood beside the Riesling vines. "Too much water and the grapes aren't concentrated enough, but too little and the fruit flavor suffers."

Hugh could see her enthusiasm and pride as she did her job as a vintner. She was definitely qualified, having studied Viticulture and Enology at the University Of California.

Ellie plucked a cluster of pale-green grapes, then walked back to the battered Jeep, where Hugh was leaning against the side. Surprising him, she held up a plump grape. Her eyes danced with mischief and challenge.

Suddenly he felt like Adam with Eve, and he couldn't deny her. He leaned forward and took the grape with his teeth, taking a teasing nibble from her finger. As the warm juices filled his mouth she pulled her hand back, a surprised look on her face, but she didn't move away from him.

He made a sound in his throat, but couldn't decide if it was because of the tart fruit, or because of the desire she stirred in him.

"It's very good," he managed, wondering if she was doing this on purpose. He shook away the thought and tried to concentrate on business.

Hugh glanced around the acres of vines that were less than a month from harvest. "Why doesn't Irish Rogue vineyard have its own winery?"

Ellie popped a grape into her mouth and sat on the bumper, not far from him. "Like I said last night, it was my father's dream…and now it's mine. After I came home from college, I presented the idea to my grandfather. He liked my plans, but then my grandmother took ill. Of course we both turned our full attention to her."

She sighed. "Nana was sick for nearly three years. And by the time she passed away it had turned out to be a costly illness. Worse, it took a lot out of my grandfather. He hasn't had the same joy from his work as he always had before…"

Hugh didn't say anything. He glanced at the woman next to him. Her hair was tied back, but still the summer breeze blew at some wayward strands. He caught her near-perfect profile, the long lashes, her delicate jawline. Her flawless skin was dusted with light freckles, and she had a full mouth that was so tempting he had to fight to keep from reaching out to touch her.

Damn, when had he gotten so soft? He looked away. "So you've pretty much handled everything?"

She nodded. "I manage the vineyard, and even though we use an outside winery—the Blackford Winery—I still oversee the process of our label, Irish Rogue. The Blackford family have been friends and neighbors for years. Henry and my father planned to build a winery together, but it never happened…" She paused. "I'm lucky enough to get to work with Henry, so you can say I have my hand in everything, from beginning to end."

Ellie knew she'd already revealed a lot to this stranger. What would it hurt to tell him what was already public knowledge? She got up, walked away, then turned back around.

"But you've already investigated all that, haven't you? I also know that your company tried and failed to buy out the Blackford Winery." She smiled. "You can't always get what you want."

He folded his arms over his chest. "You have no idea what I want."

"So it's not true that your father is trying to buy up all the small vineyards to gain control of the valley?" She felt the anger building. "He'll probably just ignore that every grower's grapes have an individual, unique taste. Does he also plan to throw all the grapes together, and change their labels?"

"Please, give us some credit."

She didn't let up. "I bet you already have new buyers lined up. And they all want to buy in bulk."

"What's wrong with that?"

"You can't rush perfection. Wine takes time. It also takes time to enjoy…to savor."

"Is that why they say women are like fine wines?"

His voice had a husky quality, sending a warm shiver through her. This man was going to be the death of her…if she let him, standing there in his fitted jeans and boots, and a starched blue shirt. She had to fight to resist her attraction to him.

"Maybe you should answer that one," she told him.

"I'm just a simple country girl. My only concern is producing the best wine," she said, knowing she had to change the direction of their conversation. "Would you like to see the orchard?"

"I would rather talk to you about staying on to work for the McCutcheon Corporation."

Her mouth gapped open. "Whoa…you act as though it's already a done deal." She glared at him. "It's not. Besides, why would I want to come and work for your company?"

"To make fine wines, of course."

"I don't believe your managers and I would have the same point of view on how to run things."

"I'm surprised you wouldn't jump at the chance to change our minds."

Ellie wished that were true. "Why? Have I changed yours?"

"In all fairness, Ellie, I haven't seen or heard anything from you to convince me that buying up the small wineries will ruin the quality of the product."

Hugh could see Ellie's anger when she climbed into the driver's seat. "I've told you, it's not a race. I guess that would clash with the big business mantra of 'time is money'?" She started the engine. "I can't picture you sitting around and watching the grapes grow or age in oak barrels."

He grinned. "And that's the reason we need you. To teach us…to direct us." He grabbed the roll bar and climbed into the seat. She started the engine, jerked the vehicle into gear and took off.

Once out of the vineyard and on the dirt road, she picked up speed. They rode along in silence. He was about to start up a conversation, but thought better of it. He squinted into the sunlight. In the last twenty-four hours since he'd met her, Ellie Flanagan hadn't been any other way but straightforward and truthful. She was also beautiful, stubborn, and most of all protective of her family.

Oh, yes, she had to have the last word.

Just past the vineyard, she turned off again and drove along the bare strips of tire tracks in the grass. It was rough going as they rode through a grove of trees and along a rocky creek. She turned toward a shady spot under a large oak and parked. She jumped out of the vehicle and walked to the water, restlessly pacing back and forth.

"Okay, let's say my grandfather does sell this land to your company," she called out. "What responsibility will you take for our employees?"

He frowned, knowing he couldn't make any promises. "What do you mean?"

"The Flanagan family has employed a lot of workers over the years…sometimes entire families. They depend on the work. Will your company guarantee them jobs?"

He climbed out. "Ellie, you know I can't do that."

Her frown deepened. "That's what I thought. So your job is to cut the number of employees. We pick grapes by hand, but you'll probably change to machines."

Last night, Hugh had been reading up on the pros and cons of machine harvesting. "If it's more efficient, we would consider it."

She bit down on her lower lip and glanced at the creek, as if trying to come up with the right words.

"Look, Ellie. I know this possible change will be

hard for you. But have you thought you could have everything you want without the headache? Your label, Irish Rogue, would still exist."

She gave him an incredulous look. "You still don't get it. This is our land. Flanagans have survived here for generations. My grandfather was born in that house," she said, pointing at the structure on the hill. "And my grandmother died here. She's buried here, alongside my father and mother."

Hugh could see her pain. "One of the stipulations your grandfather made was to keep the original small orchard and the house," he rushed to say. "So you wouldn't lose your home."

"Great. I'd have to watch someone else take over. It's not the same." She blinked rapidly.

Having lived in several places growing up, and his so-called family ties having been severed long ago, Hugh didn't understand the connection. But he wanted to, and maybe he was a little jealous she had such deep roots here.

He went to her. "Ellie…why don't you and I sit down with your grandfather—?"

She shook her head, then shot off up the hill. He went after her. When he reached the top of the rise, he found her in a fenced-off area surrounded by black wrought iron. He approached and saw several headstones. The family graveyard.

He stopped behind her. He didn't want to disturb her, but knew just his presence angered her. It had never bothered him before…he was just doing his job. But with Ellie it did.

They both looked down at the headstone for Eleanor

Kathryn Flanagan. "She was more than my grandmother," she said, then drew a breath. "Nana stepped in when my parents died. She didn't even have time to grieve after losing her only son…because she had to deal with a teenager."

There were tears in her eyes as she turned and looked at Hugh. His chest tightened, seeing her pain. He wanted so much to take her in his arms.

"It's a good thing she wasn't here when you arrived. She'd have run you off with a shotgun." Ellie managed a smile.

"I wish I could have met her."

"Oh, I don't know if you'd have liked that. Ask Papa. He'll tell you that Nana is who I inherited my temper and stubbornness from."

"At least you come with a warning." He reached out a tugged on her braid. "Your fiery red hair."

She tensed, but didn't pull away. "When I feel threatened…or think my family is…I fight back."

Hugh couldn't let go of the soft strands of hair. "You have nothing to fear from me, Ellie."

Her lips twitched. "Said the spider to the fly."

His heart raced. She was so beautiful, he didn't want to let her go. "Isn't it the female Black Widow that kills and eats the male?"

She continued to stand there. "You're the one who's not to be trusted."

"I've known a lot of females who can't be trusted also."

"I just bet you have."

"See, there you go, making assumptions. With all the

traveling I do, I don't have time to meet many people… unless it's related to business."

"That's sad," she said. "You have no friends?"

"I didn't say that. I have friends, but I don't have much time to spend with them lately." He couldn't help but be curious about any man in her life. "What about you? Is your life consumed with the vineyard?"

She brushed a strand from her face as a warm breeze blew. "No, I have friends, too, and Papa…" She paused. "He doesn't go many places these days."

"He misses her, doesn't he?" Hugh nodded toward the headstone.

"Yes. I know that's the reason he talks about selling the vineyard."

"You ever think he also wants to secure a future for you, too, especially since you're single?"

"That's crazy." She stepped back. "I don't need a man to support me. I can go to work for any winery and make a good living." She was agitated now. "But I want this vineyard, the grapes that my father planted right here on Flanagan land. And soon I'll build our own winery," she stressed. "I know I can make it work."

Hugh believed her. Ellie Flanagan could do anything.

Two hours later, Hugh was back at the cottage. He was exhausted, and happy to get away from Ellie. He was starting to care about her…and Cullan Flanagan.

Mac's number one rule was: Don't get personally involved with people you do business with.

He was trying, but Ellie Flanagan had distracted him from the moment he'd laid eyes on her yesterday, and the last twenty-four hours hadn't diminished that.

His cellphone rang, and he knew who it was. Mac. He didn't like it when Hugh didn't call to report in.

He answered it. "Hello?"

"Well, it's about time you answered your phone. Where have you been all day?"

"Working."

"Are you making any headway?"

Hugh blew out a breath. "I've only been here a day."

There was a long pause. "At least tell me that you've been spending time with the old man."

*No, his grand-daughter.* Hugh walked to the large window and looked out at the vineyard, to spot Ellie talking with a worker. He wasn't close enough to see her face, but her body language revealed her enthusiasm. When she'd finished, she hurried off toward another destination, greeting other workers along her journey. She smiled and tossed her head, and laughed at something.

Hugh turned away. "No, Mac. I spent the day touring the land. It's quite an impressive operation. Did you know that his granddaughter has been planning to build a winery?"

"I've heard rumors, but it's not my concern. Your job is to get us this property."

"Maybe it should be your concern, Mac. The Flanagans aren't going to sell to us or to anyone. We're wasting time here."

"I wouldn't be too sure of that. I've done some research… Cullan Flanagan is in debt. Big debt."

Hugh had suspected as much. "So? A lot of businessmen take out loans."

"Flanagan had to take out a mortgage when his wife

got sick. Her long illness was expensive, much of which wasn't covered by insurance. Cullan gave his wife anything and everything she needed, but none of it cured her."

Hugh was furious at his father's lack of compassion. "Some men love their wives enough to put them first."

"Okay, let's not stir up the past. What happened between your mother and me was a long time ago. It's water under the bridge."

Maybe for Mac it was, but Hugh could still hear his mother's sobs, and knew the pain his father had caused her. The pain that had transferred to the young boy who'd been abandoned, too. "So you're going to pounce when Flanagan's down and take advantage?"

"No, *you* are. Show me what kind of man you are. Make this deal happen."

# CHAPTER FOUR

*MAKE this deal happen.*

Those words were still in Hugh's head the next morning, when he took off for a quick run to clear away his problems. If for just a little while.

Thanks to the help of the corporate secretary, Rita Copeland, he had plenty of information on the Flanagans, and he'd been awake half the night reading. Most of it was pretty boring. They'd had a few black sheep in the family over the last hundred years, but overall the Flanagans had been an asset to the community of Medford, Oregon.

If Mac had anything to do with it, they wouldn't be landowners much longer.

He turned his attention to the running path and took off toward the vineyard. The firm ground helped with traction as he made his way up the slight rise along the dirt road. There was a gray mist over the land, reminding him of mornings in the San Francisco area.

Here, the big difference was the wonderful silence. Even with workers tending the fields, there wasn't the sound of car horns or police sirens to disrupt his peace.

He'd covered about a half-mile when he spotted someone. With a second look, he discovered another runner. Picking up speed, he got close enough to see a woman in a tank top and shorts, exposing a lovely pair of long legs. His gaze moved up over the firm curve of her rounded bottom to the thick auburn braid bouncing against her back. Suddenly his breathing wasn't so controlled.

Great. So much for putting the woman out of his head.

As if she'd realized she wasn't alone, she turned around and tossed a frown.

It bothered him. "Funny to see you here," he said, pausing next to her.

"It's not funny at all," she told him. "Why are you following me?"

He tried to ignore the slight sheen on her skin, and her chest moving rapidly. He quickly looked away from temptation.

"I'm not following you," he stated. "I run all the time. I had no idea that you did, too."

She studied him for a moment. Her appraisal bothered him, causing his body to stir. Something he didn't need at the moment.

She stopped. "I think I'll head back."

"Wait, there isn't any need for that. Why can't we run together?"

"Oh, yeah. That'll be relaxing," she argued. "You with your endless questions."

He raised his hands in defense. "I don't talk when I run. I put all my energy into what I'm doing."

She rested her hands on her hips. "So you can't talk and walk at the same time?"

He chanced a smile, but didn't say anything.

When she began to walk again, he stepped in next to her. "How about we call a truce for now?" he suggested. "I'll only talk business during business hours." He glanced toward the east to see the sun just barely peeking over the horizon. "It's too early for business."

With her nod, Hugh let her pick the pace. Surprisingly, she was pretty fast. He liked that. He glanced at his running partner. Although she looked delicate, he suspected Ellie could hold her own in a lot of areas, or at least be stubborn enough to try.

"This is my favorite time of day," she said. "The cooling mist…the clean smell of the earth and the air… I can almost feel the life in each vine…each cluster of fruit." Her arms pumped as she glanced at him. "Welcome to my world."

He was touched by her words. "Thanks for sharing it with me, Ellie." They continued on their run, not speaking again…but there was no need to.

That day, Ellie put all her energy into work, and stayed far away from Hugh McCutcheon. After he'd invaded her run, she had decided to avoid him. She didn't like how he'd managed to get her to forget why he was here, but somehow he had.

The next day she learned it hadn't been necessary, since Hugh had been holed up in the cottage for the past twenty-four hours.

No one had seen him.

And, as much as Ellie tried to concentrate on vineyard business, she couldn't stop wondering what the man was up to. Last night at supper, Papa hadn't given her any clues as to what he was planning to do, either. Not even a hint about selling the family business had been brought up during the conversation. Even if they'd talked about it many times before, she knew she couldn't change her grandfather's mind. Not if he truly wanted to take the McCutcheon offer. She knew her grandmother's illness and death had taken its toll on her grandfather. It was as if he'd given up.

Ellie walked through the vines toward the general store, recalling just weeks ago, when Papa had first come to her with the prospective deal. Even though the house and the original tiny orchard were held out of the deal, he was selling her heart…the vineyard.

She felt that was as much a part of her heritage as the house. If only she could buy the vineyard herself. But it would be impossible to get hold of that kind of money. Anger and sadness swept through her. She hated that there was a stranger here who could possibly take over. Why not someone local? Someone Papa respected and trusted?

Ellie stepped up onto the wood-planked porch and walked inside the general store. She smiled when she recognized some of the familiar customers mingling around. Many were locals from town.

"Hello, Ellie," one of the older ladies from the group greeted her.

Ellie recognized a customer, and shook her hand. "It's nice to see you again, Mrs. Powell."

The woman smiled. "We wouldn't miss the concert… and the wine, of course. And that nice man of yours said it should be a lovely night for it."

Suddenly Ellie remembered tonight was the weekly

summer concert in the rose garden, *Good Wine and Good Music.*

"What man?"

"Hugh…Hugh McCutcheon." Mrs. Powell pointed toward the back of the store. "We were visiting the tasting room when he asked us some questions about the wine." Her smile widened. "He's a very polite young man…and handsome, too."

Ellie cursed Hugh silently. She hated the fact that he'd invaded all parts of her life. She kept her smile in place. "I should go make some preparations for tonight."

She excused herself and headed through the doorway in back that led into the tasting room. She glanced around the space, with its comfortable high counter and several stools. A huge built-in wine rack covered the wall behind, where several dozen bottles were laid on their sides.

Summertime usually brought in the tourists, and the weekly concerts increased that volume even more. Along with wine sales.

Ellie spotted Hugh at the counter, along with several other women. Why didn't that surprise her? Dressed in jeans and another starched oxford shirt, he was sampling wine. The young server, Jillian, was behind the counter, holding a bottle of reserve Irish Rogue Chardonnay, vintage 2004.

Ellie tensed. They usually didn't open the expensive wine unless the buyer was a serious one. She needed to put a stop to this. The McCutcheon Corporation hadn't taken over yet.

Laughter rang out as she approached the group. Hugh

turned to her, and his smile widened. "Ellie. We were wondering if you were going to be here."

"Since I run the place, it's a pretty good guess I would eventually show up."

Hugh could tell that Ellie was not pleased with him. What else was new? She hadn't liked him on first sight. He was curious to know if it was just because he was bidding on her property, or if it was more personal.

Funny thing was that he was beginning to care about this woman who'd run beside him yesterday at dawn. She'd shared her beloved land with him…along with a special part of herself.

"I've decided to take your advice and learn more about wine," he told her. "And I hear there's going to be a concert tonight."

Ellie glanced at Jillian, an attractive blond. She was a college student, home for the summer—and, according to her…available.

Hugh wasn't interested in anything more than sharing a conversation. He looked back at Ellie. Not with Jillian anyway.

"There's one every week during the summer," Ellie told him, flashing those incredible green eyes. "It was one of my grandmother's ideas."

"Well, it's a good one."

She seemed surprised at his compliment. "It's probably nothing compared to the concerts you have in San Francisco."

He stood. "If the music and company are good, you can't ask for anything more." He wouldn't have a problem sitting with her in the moonlight.

"You can't forget good wine," she added.

He smiled, and, surprisingly, she returned it. His pulse-rate sped up and he held up his glass. "And this is an excellent vintage," he told her. "But I should let you get back to work. I'll see you tonight."

With his wine purchase, Hugh walked out of the tasting room and back to the deck at his cottage. He didn't want to go inside yet. He'd been locked inside for the past twenty-four hours.

He placed his wine on the deck table outside the cottage and sat down. He needed to do some more cramming to catch up on this project—to learn about the Flanagans and the vineyard. The history of the place had fascinated him. There had been lean years and prosperous years over the decades for the family, and things right now looked bleak again.

And of course Mac McCutcheon had jumped at the opportunity. He'd stepped in and offered Cullan Flanagan several thousand dollars below market value for his land and his business.

Four years ago Cullan Flanagan had borrowed money to help offset the cost of his wife's illness. He'd never given a second thought to the consequences. Who would, when your wife needed treatment to stay alive? Even if it had only given Eleanor Flanagan another two years with her family.

Now it was going to cost Cullan. Everything. There was a balloon loan payment coming due in just a little over a month. Hugh seriously doubted Flanagan had the money to pay it. He'd already gotten one extension on the loan, and there wasn't going to be another. That was the reason Cullan had agreed to have a company representative come here.

Trouble was, Hugh doubted that Ellie knew all the facts about the deal he had come to offer. Did she have any idea that her grandfather was in over his head? Worse…that there was only one way out. To sell to the highest bidder. Right now that was the McCutcheon Corporation.

At dusk, Hugh's thoughts were still on Ellie as he made his way toward the back of the main house and the rose garden, where the concert was being held. Despite all warnings to stay clear of her, he looked forward to seeing her tonight.

He admitted he was drawn to her. He was quickly learning they weren't all that different, just because she lived in the country and he in the city. They had both grown up without the advantage of a traditional family. His parents had divorced, hers had died. They had both excelled in school and come back to work in the family business.

The bad side was, she saw him as the enemy. And she should. He was here to take her beloved vineyard.

"Why, Mac?" he breathed. "Why me?"

Hugh had done exceptionally well at his job of downsizing companies, but usually they were manufacturing businesses. It was all impersonal. But Emerald Vale wasn't just a building and machinery…or overpaid executives. It was a family. The employees were flesh-and-blood people.

Hugh strolled over the rise to see the stack-stone walls. A wrought-iron gate hung open, revealing a huge yard. He walked inside and found a beautiful haven. The stone walls were lined with rows of colorful tea roses.

Slate stepping-stones were woven through the many floral bushes, along with several benches scattered around decorative water fountains.

On the lush green lawn were small round tables with chairs. Hurricane lanterns were lit, illuminating the intimate area. A jazz quartet were tuning their instruments from the platform.

Hugh had heard from some of the guests that the Flanagans' garden had been the backdrop for many weddings and parties over the past few years.

He searched the crowd of people taking their seats, hoping to find Ellie. Surely she would attend? Suddenly, he froze as she walked through the gate. She'd changed into a long print skirt and a fitted T-shirt, covered with a sheer cream blouse and a wide belt around her waist. Her hair was down, dancing around her face.

Smiling, she wove through the tables, stopping to talk with the guests. Taking a bottle of wine from a server, she began to fill glasses. He listened as she spoke about the vintage with knowledge…and pride. She was something. He'd never seen anyone have such passion about their work as Ellie Flanagan.

When the music started, Ellie moved back into the rose garden and stood as soft sounds filled the night air. She felt someone's presence and turned to find Hugh, holding out an empty glass.

"Haven't you had enough?" she whispered.

He grinned at her. "Not nearly enough…"

She felt a warm shiver race through her body. Somehow she managed to fill the glass.

He held up another glass. "Join me…please?"

She glanced at his face in the dimming light. She saw a look in his eyes that was both sexy…and dangerous.

She nodded, and, with his hand pressed against the small of her back, he guided her toward a vacant bench. Once they sat down the roses acted as a curtain, and the other guests were facing away from them.

The rhythm of the music was soft and sultry. Hugh sat next to her, but didn't talk. He seemed to relax as they listened to the quartet.

Ellie, on the other hand, was very aware of the man beside her. She closed her eyes and pushed everything out of her head as she tried to concentrate on the jazz. Instead she felt Hugh's heat, inhaled his musky scent… It was like a pheromone that seemed to heighten her awareness of the good-looking man. She moved restlessly in her seat.

Then there was a warm touch. Just the graze of his hand across hers. She should move it away, away from temptation, but she couldn't. Then his fingers laced through hers, and more heat spread through her.

The music swelled, as if cocooning them in their own private place…and time. She stopped breathing when Hugh raised her hand to his mouth and placed a kiss against the back. Another tingle rushed though her, and she jumped at the sensation.

"Ellie…it's okay."

She finally opened her eyes to see him leaning in. Her throat went bone-dry. "Hugh…" she managed his name.

He touched a finger against her mouth. "Don't talk. Let's just enjoy this," he whispered.

She drew a breath and recognized the raw hunger in those dark eyes. Not wanting to break the spell, she couldn't look away…or speak. But the decision was out of her hands as the music ended and the audience broke into applause.

Embarrassed that he'd managed to mesmerize her, she handed him her glass and picked up the bottle. "I need to get back to the guests." When he didn't stop her, she turned and walked away, wondering if he'd call her back.

The bigger question was, would she stay if he did?

"Is this your best offer?" Cullan asked Hugh two days later. They sat at the dining room table with the McCutcheon bid spread out in front of them.

Hugh wasn't sure what to say. There might be other bids, but he doubted it. "It's a fair offer…considering."

Cullan's gaze met his. His face was expressionless, but not his clear blue eyes. "If you got something to say, lad, you'd better say it."

Hugh sighed, wishing he was in a cold boardroom, with an overpaid executive. Not a man whose lined face revealed his years in the sun, whose hands were rough and crippled from hard, physical work. "I know you mortgaged the land…heavily."

"I figured your father probably knew that when he approached me a year ago about selling. Back then I told him thanks, but no thanks." The old man sighed. "I guess he just sat back and waited me out, figuring I wouldn't be able to make the loan payment."

Hugh tried to stay detached, but it wasn't working. "So you're going to sell the land?"

"Like you said, it's more valuable than the house

and the old orchard." The man suddenly looked years older. "Ellie's vineyard..."

"You'd better tell her. She already suspects something, but she needs to hear it from you."

"It's going to be hard to tell her I failed her."

"You didn't fail her, Cullan. Circumstances made it impossible for you to do anything else but take a loan against your property. You used the money for your wife, didn't you?"

Cullan just nodded.

"Ellie will understand when she knows the reason."

"I'm not so sure. I'm taking away her vineyard...her dream."

Hugh closed his eyes momentarily. "I can't make you sell to me, but you better do something fast—because you'll lose everything if you don't."

"Papa..."

They both looked up to find Ellie standing in the doorway of the dining room.

"Ellie," Cullan said as he got up and went to her. "I thought you went to the winery."

"I just got back." She glared at Hugh. "And it looks like not a moment too soon. Is this how you work, McCutcheon? Divide and conquer?"

"Ellie, please," her grandfather began. "We were talking business."

"Sounded more like coercion to me."

# CHAPTER FIVE

ELLIE had returned from the winery and learned that Hugh and Papa had toured the orchard, then gone to the house. She'd hoped that it was just for coffee. The evidence on the table now, a contract for Emerald Vale, said otherwise.

"Papa…what's going on?"

Her grandfather glanced nervously at Hugh, then back to her. "Sit down, lass. I need to talk to you."

On stiff legs, she moved closer to the table. She didn't want to hear anymore…but she already knew what was coming. And it was going to be life-changing.

"I think I'll stand."

He stood slowly, using the table for support. "I'm going to sell to the McCutcheon Corporation."

She gasped. "No! You can't do that."

"I'd give anything if I had a choice…but I don't. I mortgaged the land when Nana was sick." She saw the pain etched on his face. "I can't pay it back."

The words echoed in her head over and over again. Still she didn't want to believe it.

"I'm sorry, Ellie. I wish it wasn't so, but there's no

choice." A tear ran down her cheek as he came to her. "Please forgive me..."

Ellie wrapped her arms around the man who had loved and cherished her all her life. Who had tried to protect her from every bad thing.

"Oh, Papa. It's okay. You had to do it...for Nana. I just wish you had told me... I wish I could have carried part of the burden. Maybe I could have helped."

"It's too late..."

She forced a smile. "We have so much. We have each other. That's all that's important." She hugged him again.

Hugh walked out through the kitchen, not wanting to disturb them. It was a lot for Ellie to take in. Funny thing was, he wanted to comfort her, too. He wanted to make everything right. But there wasn't any way that could happen. His company was taking over her life. And if the Flanagans remained in their house Ellie would see it everyday... For awhile he would be here, too, supervising things. He would see her...see her anger...her disdain for what he'd done to her family.

Before he reached the back door, Hugh heard his name called, and he turned to find Ellie coming through the doorway.

"Ellie, I want to tell you I'm sorry—"

"I don't want to hear it, McCutcheon." She glared at him. "What I want you to do is listen to what I have to say."

He nodded.

"You might have gotten my grandfather to agree to your way of thinking, but not me. I'm not giving up... yet." She took a step closer, revealing fire and determination in her green eyes. "I told you there's a hundred years of Flanagan history here. This isn't the first time we've had trouble…and it probably won't be the last."

"I know that, Ellie, and I want to help. I truly do. But my father is serious about this deal."

"Then go back and tell him I'm not giving away this land."

Suddenly there was a loud crash from the dining room.

"Papa," Ellie cried as she shot off.

Hugh was right behind her.

Once in the room, they found Cullan collapsed on the floor.

"Oh, Papa."

They both rushed to his side.

"Sorry, Ellie…" Cullan said, pain etched on his face.

"Don't try to talk," Hugh said as he pulled out his cellphone and called an ambulance, praying that nothing else bad would happen to this family.

Two hours later, Ellie paced the hospital emergency room. She glanced across the seating area to find Hugh leaning against the wall.

She owed him a lot. He'd been right there with her grandfather until the paramedics arrived at the house. He'd followed the ambulance in so she wouldn't be alone.

His concerned gaze caught hers and he walked across the room to her. "You should sit down."

She shook her head and bit her lip to keep from crying. "I can't. If something happens to Papa…"

"Shh." He reached for her and pulled her into a comforting embrace. "He's going to be okay, Ellie. He was awake and alert when they brought him here. And, remember, he wants to hang around to see a couple of great-grandkids."

Ellie felt a tear fall…then another. She wasn't anywhere close to giving him that wish. "I'm a rotten granddaughter. All I think about is having a winery. I never realized how much Papa must have been going through. I'm his only family…and I know he'd love babies to spoil. He would never hurt me unless he had no choice."

Hugh placed his hand across her shoulders and walked her to a private corner to continue their conversation. "Of course you want a winery. That doesn't mean you can't have a family to go with it."

She kept her head lowered. She didn't want him to see her tears. "It does when you can't find time in your life for anything else."

"I know the feeling," he answered with a sigh. "I work too many hours and travel too much."

She finally raised her head. "Do you ever meet anyone on those travels?" Good Lord, she had no business asking him that.

Hugh wanted to wipe away her tears. "No…" he told her, but added, "Not until I met you."

Those rich green eyes widened, but before she could speak a nurse called her name. She jumped up and hurried across the room. Hugh followed her.

"The doctor will see you now."

Hugh stood still as she started to go, but she turned back. "Will you go with me?"

His heart leaped in his chest. "Of course."

They walked down the hall and met the doctor. "Hello, Ms Flanagan, I'm Dr. Perkins."

She shook his hand. "Nice to meet you, Doctor. This is Hugh McCutcheon…a friend."

He nodded a greeting, then turned to business. "Your grandfather was lucky tonight. With his heart history—"

"What heart history?" Ellie asked. "You mean he's had trouble before?"

"Yes. At his last check-up we talked about him having an angioplasty procedure done. That was three months ago."

"Three months…" she repeated. "He never said anything to me." She seemed to come out of her trance and asked, "Can you still do the Angioplasty?"

"Not without Cullan's permission. See if you can talk some sense into him."

"Consider it done. How soon can you do this procedure?"

"Right away. I don't want him to leave here, so I can schedule it for tomorrow."

"Okay. May I see him?"

He nodded. "I've sedated him, but he'll know you're here."

The nurse took her to a room down the hall. Her grandfather was in a hospital gown and tucked into bed. The machine monitoring his heart was beeping in a steady rhythm. She went to his side and Hugh made his way to the side of the room.

"Papa… It's me—Ellie."

No response.

She leaned over and kissed his cheek. When she

pulled back a little, his eyes opened. He looked pale and tired, but he smiled at her.

"My Ellie. I love you, lass." He raised his hand and she grabbed hold.

"I love you, too, Papa. Everything is going to be okay. But the doctor said you need a procedure to help your heart."

"I wanted to wait until later…after the harvest. And I didn't want you to worry about anything more…"

Tears filled her eyes. She couldn't lose him. "Don't you know nothing is more important than you are? Please…Papa, no more arguing. You need this procedure."

"Okay, lass." He swallowed. "Hugh…?" His faint voice called out.

Hugh walked to the man's side. "What is it, Cullan?"

"Will you watch out for Ellie?"

Hugh nodded. "Consider it done."

An hour later, Hugh drove Ellie back to the house. Soft music on the radio was the only sound. Hugh glanced across the car to see Ellie staring out the window into the night.

"He's going to be okay. This procedure is done all the time." He turned the car off the main highway onto the road leading to Emerald Vale.

"I know. I just wish I could have known sooner. So many times I argued with him about a winery. I didn't know how much anxiety he was having about paying back the loan."

"It's not your fault, Ellie. It was his choice not to tell you. He didn't want you to worry."

"So he was destroying his own health to pacify me and my dreams."

"That's because he loves you. And that alone means more to him than any business deal."

Hugh couldn't understand that kind of love. His father wouldn't lift a hand to help him with anything. Mac didn't have any idea what his son dreamed of. He had to face it, the man wasn't capable of loving him.

Ellie straightened as they pulled up to the house. "Well, Papa doesn't have to worry alone any more. And I'm still not about to let you railroad us into selling." She climbed out of the car.

Hugh got out, too, and caught up to her. "Do you always have to think of me as the enemy?"

"I have to protect myself and my family, Hugh." She pushed open the door, but he reached for her hand.

"I'm not my father," he told her. "I care about what happens here."

She shook her head. "How can I trust you when you go in and destroy companies?"

"I don't destroy companies," he argued. "I go in and try to save them, make them productive again."

"We don't *need* to be any more productive." She glared. "We only need to be left alone."

That hurt. "Fine." Hugh held up his hands. "I'll leave you alone."

Hugh turned and went down the steps, made his way though the yard, along the lighted pathway and into the cottage. He slammed the door shut and began to pace. He wasn't about to sit and relax.

He hadn't done anything wrong. None of this was his fault. He was only the messenger for his father. Usually harsh words didn't hurt him—business was business… But those other words hadn't come from Ellie Flanagan.

An hour later, Ellie knew she owed Hugh an apology. It was late, but she couldn't let it go until morning. She walked up to the cottage, and had started to knock when the door opened and Hugh appeared.

"Is something wrong with Cullan?"

"No. I called the hospital; he's fine."

He gave her the once-over. "Then what is it, Ellie? Did you forget to accuse me of something else?" He leaned against the doorjamb, folding his arms across his chest, looking very unapproachable. "Or did you just want to call me another name?"

"This was a mistake. I'm sorry I bothered you."

She'd turned to leave when her grabbed her arm and pulled her around. "No, I'm the one who's sorry. I know you're under a lot of stress with Cullan."

He didn't release her, and she felt his warmth against her skin. "Without your help…" She couldn't think of any words as she looked up into his eyes. "I don't know what would have happened."

Hugh couldn't let Ellie go. She looked so lost. "I'm glad I was there." Her chin trembled. "Oh, babe, don't…" He pulled her into his arms.

"I can't lose him, Hugh. He's all I have in the world," she sobbed against his shirt.

He held on to her. "I don't want you to be alone, Ellie." He brushed a kiss against her soft hair, inhaling her lemony scent. "I'm here for you."

She pulled back and stared up at him with those wide cat eyes. With his heart pounding, he lowered his head and brushed his lips over hers. She gasped, and he came back again. Another soft touch, brushing her lips. Another nibble…then he drew back.

"Hugh…"

His gaze roamed her face. "You are so beautiful, you take my breath away."

With a shaky smile, she reached up and touched his face. "You're not so bad yourself."

Hugh grinned, then lowered his head again, and this time it wasn't playful. He wanted her to know how she affected him. His mouth slanted over hers in a hungry kiss. He pulled her close against his body, letting her feel all the hard lines while he enjoyed her softness.

He ran his tongue over the seam of her lips until she parted them to allow him in. He groaned as his tongue danced with hers, tasting her sweetness.

Finally he pulled away, and they were both breathless. "Whoa, you pack quite a wallop," he told her as he continued to give her teasing kisses. "And you're tempting me to my limit."

Ellie reached up and placed her mouth against his in another searing kiss. Her hands were at work, parting his shirt.

When her fingertips caressed his skin, he groaned again. Even though he knew this was disastrous, he couldn't stop wanting her. Without breaking the kiss, he swung her up into his arms, kicked the door shut and carried her to the bed in the dimly lit room. He laid her down on the mattress and stretched out beside her.

Okay, this was what he called heaven. He grew serious. "I've wanted you since the moment I first saw you."

Ellie didn't smile as she touched his jaw. "I don't want to be alone, Hugh. I want to stay with you tonight."

"I'm here for you, Ellie." He leaned down and kissed her, moving his hand under her blouse, touching her skin, her breasts. She murmured his name in breathless want as he caressed her.

"Hugh... Please...?" she asked. "Make me forget everything."

*Forget.* He froze. He couldn't forget his job. Even he couldn't go so low as to seduce Ellie, then go back to business in the morning. Besides, when he made love to Ellie, he wanted her to remember everything that happened between them.

He placed one last kiss on her lips, then pulled back. "Ellie, we can't do this. Not tonight, anyway."

She blinked at him, and desire turned to hurt in her eyes. "Fine. If you don't want me..." She sat up, but Hugh reached for her and pulled her close.

"Wanting is definitely not the problem," he growled. "I want you very much. But you're not ready for this, Ellie. I would just be a distraction for you...and you'd regret what happened between us by morning. I don't want to be just a convenient guy." He pulled her closer. "I want to be here for you...to share your pain, your fears...but when we make love...it has to be because you want me, not because you're hurting."

She buried her face against his chest. "You're right."

He tipped her head up so she'd look at him. "Hey, I'm flattered that you came to me."

"I should go..." She started to sit up, but Hugh couldn't let her go and pulled her back to him. "I don't want you to leave, and I don't think you want to either. Can I just hold you?"

"Maybe…for a little while," she whispered. "I can't seem to sleep, anyway," she said as she went back into his arms.

With Ellie's head resting against his chest, her body snuggled close to his, Hugh fought the feelings she aroused in him. He knew better than to let someone get this close. Besides, it would never work out. He had a job to do. That always came first. It was the safe route for him. He'd watched his own parents' marriage disintegrate, and vowed that he never wanted to chance any commitment.

Not until he'd met Ellie Flanagan. She made him feel things…things he'd never felt before…never allowed himself to feel.

He felt Ellie's body relax and her breathing slow. She was asleep.

He smiled. Yeah, maybe he was a lovesick fool.

# CHAPTER SIX

THE first thing Ellie noticed as she began to wake up was the feeling of strong arms wrapped around her. She snuggled deeper, unwilling to leave the protective place. Then a bright glare caused her to blink. Sunlight… Morning… She was in Hugh's bed. Suddenly last night flashed into her head.

She sat up with a jerk. *Papa.*

Hugh groaned and woke up. "Hey, good morning."

She turned around to find his hair mussed, his shirt open, revealing a muscular chest. Something unexpected stirred in her.

"Morning," she said as she scooted off the bed, looking for her sandals. "I need to go to the house and call the hospital…then get to work."

Hugh got up and came around the other side to meet her. "Slow down. Take time for breakfast."

She glanced at the clock. "I can't. I'm usually out in the vineyard by now. I need to talk to the orchard manager, Ben. He wasn't around last night, and they're harvesting the Bartlett pears today."

She slipped on her shoes and headed for the door.

He followed her. "I can help."

She frowned, watching the man who'd been there for her last night. Could she trust him? She had no choice. "Fine. Meet me in the orchard and wear old clothes." She started to leave again, but he grabbed her and pulled her into his arms.

Hugh's mouth came down on hers and immediately turned on the heat between them. When he released her she was slightly dizzy.

He grinned. "I needed a little spark to get me going. Give me ten minutes so I can shower, and I'll catch up to you." He winked. "Unless you want to join me?"

He was enjoying her discomfort too much. Ellie shook her head. "No, I'm fine. See you later." She managed to get out the door. What was wrong with her? She didn't act on impulse—not over a man anyway. And she'd be crazy if she allowed this man to get to her.

She made her way down the back path to the kitchen door, where she saw Ben standing on the stoop.

"Ellie? I can't find Cullan."

She smiled at the fifty-something man who'd worked for the Flanagans for over twenty years. "It's okay, Ben. Papa isn't here. We had to take him to the hospital last night."

"What happened? Was it his heart?"

Ellie paused. Had Ben known about his condition? "Yes, it's his heart, and he was lucky. But he needs to have a procedure done today, so he'll be in the hospital for a few days. If you'll give me a few minutes, I can help with the crew. You know Papa. He'll want a report when I visit him tonight."

The orchard manager smiled as he placed his straw hat on his head. "Then we better get it done."

Ellie went into the house, and rushed upstairs into the room she'd had since she was a teenager. The soft butter walls and the blue accent colors on the bed were welcoming. Grabbing clean clothes, she ran into the bathroom, knowing all that she'd been used to all of her life might be changing very soon.

Twenty minutes later Ellie made her way to the orchard—to find Hugh there. He was picking alongside the other day workers. Her first feeling was that he was invading her domain, and she wanted to chase him off. But another side of her knew she needed all the help she could get, and that if Papa were here he'd put Hugh to work. Silently, she took a basket and walked up to the trees where the branches had been trained to grow across a trellis, much like her grapes.

The fairly new system had helped to increase the trees' density…and fruit. She blinked back the threatening tears, hoping Papa would soon be able to return to what he loved so much.

Hugh appeared next to her. "Did you get some breakfast?"

He'd showered, too, but hadn't shaved. He looked even sexier with his dark-shadowed face. "Just coffee." She continued to twist a pear stem, then placed the fruit carefully in the box. "How about you?"

"I grabbed some coffee and a bagel off the breakfast tray."

She watched him do his task. He gently picked the

fruit. She recalled that touch, knew what it could do to her. She shook it away.

"You know, Hugh, you're a guest here. You don't need to do this."

"Even a cold-blooded tycoon like myself wants to help out occasionally. You're just lucky I'm so willing." He smiled, and her heart skipped a beat. "Does it bother you that I'm here?"

More than he'd ever know. "Of course not. But this is a lot of work."

He frowned. "You act like I've never had to roll up my sleeves and pitch in. I'll have you know that I had a paper route when I was twelve. At fifteen I worked in a hamburger joint, and I waited tables in a restaurant all through college."

Ellie had trouble believing that. "I thought your father… I mean, he has the means to…"

"Pay for everything I ever wanted?" he finished as he carefully picked and placed a still-green fruit into the basket. "Hardly. Mac and my mother divorced when I was ten. Besides him not being around much, he didn't believe in handing things out for nothing. 'Hard work builds character', Mac preaches." Hugh smiled. "So I have a lot of character."

It dawned on her that he'd probably worked in a lot of those factories he'd downsized. "How many factory jobs have you done?"

He gave her a sideways glance. "Plenty. You can't improve anything without testing it yourself. So I've had to work for my lucrative salary."

They carried their full boxes and put them into the

special bins on the truck. Grabbing an empty, they returned.

"So, when you downsize a business, is it because it's truly needed, or is it strictly for more money?"

He stopped. "If I have to lay off employees, believe me, I don't do it without studying the pros and cons. Otherwise, a plant might be shut down, and then all the workers would lose their jobs, instead of only twenty or thirty percent."

"Your investors still make a lot of money."

"Of course they do. We're all in this to make money."

She frowned. "Not all. Some of us do it because we love what we do."

"I love what I do. But I also love the money I make at my job."

Ellie eyed him closely. "It can't always be about the money. You need more in your life."

Hugh realized he'd enjoyed the morning. He'd liked even more spending time with Ellie.

By noon, they'd loaded the truck, and Ellie now planned to drive it to the packing house. He was surprised when she asked him to go along.

They made the twenty-mile trip without any problems, but the trip back was a different story. The old truck was suddenly temperamental, and decided to quit running.

Ellie coasted to the side of the highway and parked. "So, do you know anything about engines?"

"I'm pretty good at calling a mechanic," he teased. "Or at least a tow truck."

Thirty minutes later they were at a mechanic's shop,

with at least an hour to wait while the truck got a new fuel pump.

"We'll be back in a few hours," Hugh told the mechanic. "If there's a problem, call my cellphone number." He took Ellie's arm. "Let's go have some lunch, I'm starving."

Ellie started to argue, but her stomach growled rudely. They both laughed.

"God, you're beautiful when you smile."

She froze. "I'm a mess."

They walked across the parking lot toward a hamburger place. "Good Lord, woman, if I said it was night, you'd say it was day."

"That's because I'd probably be right."

"Just to warn you, arguing turns me on."

She blinked. "I'm sure that makes things interesting in the boardroom."

He threw his head back and laughed. "Okay, I'll rephrase it." He leaned close and whispered, "I get turned on by *you*."

She honestly didn't have a comeback. Especially with his heated gaze on her.

Once inside, they ordered their food at the counter, then found a table and sat down.

Ellie felt strange, sitting across from this man. What was she thinking? She had slept in the same bed with him. He'd kissed her, touched her…and had her wanting more.

"What's the matter, Ellie? Having second thoughts?"

"Second thoughts?"

"About letting the enemy get close to you last night?"

She glanced away, hating the fact that he could read her. "Nothing happened."

"Ah, but we wanted it to, and that's your problem." He leaned forward and whispered, "You wanted me as much as I wanted you."

"Maybe we should talk about something else."

"Look, you had a rough time last night with your grandfather. And I'm just glad I could help you today." He arched an eyebrow. "But that doesn't change the fact that there's an attraction between us."

She grew serious. "Well, I'm not going to get involved with a man who plans to take the Flanagan land."

He didn't answer, but instead went up to retrieve their food order. He set the tray on the table and she took her hamburger.

"I want you to know, Ellie, with Cullan in the hospital I'm going to back off until he's recovered from the procedure."

"What did Mac say about that?"

"To be honest, I haven't talked with my father in a while. This is strictly my decision."

"Papa…Papa…" Ellie said as she stood next to his hospital bed. "It's over, and the doctor said you did great." She had trouble keeping the tears out of her voice.

Finally Cullan opened his eyes. "Then why are you so sad, lass?"

She forced a smile. "Because you're leaving me with all the work."

"Then I better get out of here."

"Tomorrow is soon enough," she told him. "You still need to take it easy, even when you get home."

"I know…but the picking."

"Ben's there," Ellie insisted. "Hugh has helped me, too."

Papa gave her a half-smile. "That doesn't surprise me. He's a good man."

Ellie had to agree. "Ben had him picking pears this morning. He even went with me to the packing house. The old truck broke down on the way back. The fuel pump. It's all fixed, so don't go worrying."

"Told you he's a good man." He closed his eyes a moment. "Now, give me a kiss goodbye, then go home and get some rest, lass."

Ellie did as she was told, then walked out into the hall.

But maybe he could make her forget for a little while.

He took her by the arm and directed her to the elevator. The bell chimed and the door opened. They stepped inside the elevator and the doors closed, leaving them alone. "Let's go get an early dinner."

She blinked at him. "You want to go out?"

"It wouldn't hurt to get away from everything for a few hours."

"Hugh, I don't think it's wise."

He stared at her, not ready to give her up yet. "You slept in my bed last night and you think us sharing a meal isn't wise?" He hesitated. "I'm only talking about a few hours."

"That's what I mean," she began. "I stepped over the line last night with you when I went to your cottage. It's dangerous for us to continue this—"

"This attraction between us," he finished. "Yes, Ellie, I'm definitely attracted to you."

The bell chimed again and the doors opened. They walked off down the corridor. "I enjoy spending time with you. Is that so wrong? Besides, any discussion of the sale is off-limits."

Ellie knew someone was still going to get hurt. And it was probably going to be her.

"And if this sale goes through, I'm going to be around the place."

She didn't like that he was so confident. "It's not final, yet. You never know what might happen." She had a couple of ideas. They were long shots, but she wasn't giving up so easily.

They stepped outside into the cool evening. "Could we call a truce for tonight?"

She had to smile. "I thought you liked heated discussions."

"Come have dinner with me and I'll give you a list of all the other things that get me heated up."

Ellie couldn't remember the last time she'd gone out to dinner with a man other than her grandfather. It was embarrassing, but she hadn't had the time, or met any interesting men, to accept a date.

Hugh surprised her when he drove her to a place called Porters, a historical train depot that had been converted into a restaurant. It was casual enough for families, but nice enough to take a date. The hostess led them across the dimly lit room to a secluded booth. The bench seats were high-backed, with red curtains tied back to add to their privacy.

"The food here is excellent," Ellie told him.

"So you like the place?"

"I love it here. Although they don't serve our label."

"Well, we should leave, then." He started to get up.

She smiled and placed her hand on his arm. "It's okay, I think I'll manage. Besides, their rosemary roasted prime rib makes up for it."

"So that's your recommendation?"

She nodded. "I've had several dishes here. They're all good."

The waitress came by for their order. Hugh ordered the prime rib for both of them. He let her pick the wine, a Cabernet Sauvignon '03 Del Rio from a local winery.

When the waiter brought the bottle, he opened it, poured red wine into a glass, then gave it to Hugh.

He picked up the goblet and sniffed the bouquet. "I'm following Jillian's instructions." He swirled it, then finally took a drink. He raised an eyebrow. "It's very good. Not as good as the Irish Rogue, but enjoyable."

The waiter smiled and filled a glass for Ellie, leaving the bottle.

She leaned forward. "Have we created a monster?"

"No, but I do want to pick your brain about wine. I am truly out of my element here. This project was supposed to go to someone else—Matt Hudson. He's studied the wine business."

"And you're into manufacturing plants?"

"I'm more into production efficiency."

She played with the stem of her glass. "So if I had a winery it would be easier for you?"

He hesitated. "I think so. I'm good at things like crunching numbers, the depreciation of equipment, efficient use of personnel. Yes, that's my area of expertise."

"So if I ever need someone like that, I'll know who to call."

Hugh wanted to change the direction of the conversation. He reached for her hand. "You don't need a reason to call me, Ellie."

She didn't pull away. "You're a busy man, Hugh McCutcheon. You travel all over the country."

He laced his fingers with hers, feeling her warmth. It was warming him. "I plan to change that. Hopefully, I'll be in San Francisco permanently. Not so far from Medford, Oregon." His gaze met her incredible green eyes, causing feelings he'd never before had for any woman. "You could visit me, too." He was acting crazy, mixing business with…pleasure.

She smiled. "I've visited your city. It was while I was in college."

"I hope you'll want to come back, then. I'd like to take you to The Wharf for some great seafood." There were so many places he wanted to take her.

He didn't wait for an answer as he refilled their glasses, not wanting reality to intrude into this magical evening. Soon their food arrived, and the easy conversation continued all the way though dessert—classic crème brulée—and coffee.

When they left the restaurant, Hugh took her hand and walked her through the parking lot to his car. When they got to the passenger side, he didn't open the door right away.

Hugh gazed into her eyes. "I'm sorry, but I can't wait any longer." He bent his head and captured her mouth. The kiss was controlled, but just barely. It didn't change his need, or the desire he felt for her, but they were in a public place.

He finally tore his mouth away. "Oh, Ellie, you're driving me crazy," he groaned, as he nibbled his way down her neck, then pulled back. "I think I better get you back to the hospital."

Then, with another leisurely kiss, he finally pulled away and opened the door. She climbed in.

Hugh found he was a little shaky as he walked around the car. He got into the driver's seat and started the engine before he succumbed to temptation again. He blew out a breath. Trouble was, even if Ellie Flanagan did come with a warning label, he still wanted her.

And that made for an impossible situation.

About twenty minutes later, Ellie walked into her grandfather's room, wanting to check before heading home. "I don't want you to worry about anything but getting better," she whispered, and placed a kiss against his forehead.

"The same goes for you, Ellie," he murmured as he opened his eyes. "Things will work out."

She knew that was true. Now that she had finally discovered what was most important. "Go back to sleep and I'll see you tomorrow."

"I need to see Hugh first."

"Papa, this isn't the time to talk business."

"Stop worrying, lass." He waved his hand "Now, give me another kiss, then go and send him in."

Ellie did as she was told, then walked into the hall. "Papa wants to talk with you," she told Hugh.

With a nod, Hugh pushed himself off the wall and

went in. He couldn't figure out what Cullan could have to say to him.

Lying flat against the white sheet, Cullan Flanagan looked older, and his skin was pale.

Hugh touched his hand. "Cullan..." he whispered.

Ellie's grandfather opened his clear blue eyes. "Hugh..." He raised a limp hand. "I need a favor..."

Hugh leaned closer. "What is it?"

"Ellie... She acts tough...but if something happens to me...she's all alone." He swallowed. "And because of me she's losing something important to her. You've got to help find a way for her to keep at least part of the vineyard. Maybe the original vines her daddy planted..."

Hugh didn't want to hear this kind of talk. "Whoa, Cullan, you're not to worry about any of that now. I promise I won't discuss anything about the sale until you're well." He squeezed his hand. "We'll discuss this then. And I'll make sure Ellie is fine."

A faint smile appeared across Cullan's face. "I knew I could depend on you. You're a good man." He closed his eyes and was asleep.

A good man? He didn't feel like a good man at all. What kind of man would take advantage of this situation...of a woman? He turned to see an anxious Ellie in the hall. His heart pounded. He knew he wanted to take her in his arms and tell her everything was going to be all right. He couldn't. He couldn't offer her one damn thing—except maybe some honesty.

## CHAPTER SEVEN

ON THE drive home, the car was filled with music, but not much conversation. Ellie was almost afraid to ask what her grandfather had said, but she knew that something had changed the moment Hugh walked out of the hospital room.

Hugh parked in front of the house and got out, started to walk her toward the porch. She stopped him.

"Please, I don't want to go in just yet," she said. "I need to walk."

He nodded, and she led him toward the rose garden. Soft exterior lights lit their way along the path and through the gate. Ellie immediately caught a whiff of the familiar rose fragrance. She felt her grandmother's presence.

"I like to come here when I can't sleep or I need to think about things..." She looked up at him. "Thank you for taking me to dinner tonight."

Hugh didn't want her gratitude. "It wasn't a big deal," he lied. Every minute he spent with Ellie Flanagan was a big deal...but that was about to come to an end.

"I guess that's the difference between us. You're

probably used to going out, sharing wine and a few casual kisses… I'm not."

"There is nothing casual about you, Ellie," he insisted. "And I don't make a habit of taking out potential clients and seducing them."

She took a step closer and slipped her arms around his neck. "Are you trying to seduce me, Hugh McCutcheon?"

He closed his eyes, feeling her soft feminine body pressed against his.

"I think you're the one doing the seducing," he told her, then lost any resolve as he lowered his head and captured her mouth. Wrapping his arms around her back, he dragged her even closer against him. He wanted a permanent imprint of her… He wanted to remember the taste of her on his lips…

But he couldn't allow it to happen… He broke off the kiss. "We should stop."

"Why?" she breathed.

"I don't want to take advantage, Ellie. I know you're worried about Cullan…"

Ellie paused and studied his face, then moved back. "Does this have anything to do with what my grandfather said to you at the hospital?"

"Not in the way you think," he told her. "But he made me see things differently." He caught the wariness in her mesmerizing eyes. "Look, Ellie. This whole situation with Emerald Vale makes it impossible for anything… between us."

She glanced away, then back at him. "That could change."

He froze. "I don't see how?"

"I've changed my mind about a lot of things since

Papa's health scare. I've discovered what's important. My grandfather is my main concern now. I know the pressure of this loan has to be making his life miserable." She sighed. "I'm selfish enough to want him to hang around for another dozen or so years. I'm willing to give up the land."

Hugh stared at her.

Hugh was caught off guard by Ellie's decision. He knew how much she'd looked forward to building a winery. "What about your dream? You're a winemaker."

She shook her head, but she couldn't hide her emotions. "If I have Papa and some of the old Flanagan land, I'll be happy."

They both knew it was a lie, but Hugh wasn't going to argue the point now. "Let's hold off on this decision until your grandfather is out of the hospital."

"I'm not going to change my mind, Hugh. I mean it. I won't fight you about selling." Her voice lowered. "I don't want this to come between us."

"Oh, Ellie…" He pulled her back into a tight embrace, kissed her long and hard, then released her. "God, you're tearing me apart."

"Is that a good thing?" she asked teasingly.

He couldn't go on like this. This was a no-win situation, and he was caught in the middle. "No. Don't you see that business would always come between us?"

"Then walk away from it," she challenged. "The business, I mean…"

"And if I do the bank or someone else will come in here, and you and Cullan will lose everything anyway."

Her mouth was still swollen from his kisses. "So you're saying business comes first?"

"In this instance, yes." He *couldn't* get involved with her, he chanted over and over. His father was ruthless enough to destroy them all.

In the dim light, he watched her blink back tears as her chin came up. "I guess there's nothing more to say."

"I wish it could be different…"

"Please, don't say any more." She stared at him. "Goodbye, Hugh."

With no choice, he had to let her go. He was about to take away her dream…and he knew someday she would come to hate him.

When Ellie got up the next morning Hugh McCutcheon was still on her mind…along with his distracting kisses and his hurtful rejection.

She'd been a fool. Hugh McCutcheon was only after one thing, and it wasn't her. It was the Flanagan property. Now she'd told him she was willing to sell the land, he was moving on.

Well, so was Ellie. She decided she wasn't giving up so easily. She dressed in a print skirt, a royal blue sweater and comfortable pair of sandals, and headed to her car. Ben could handle the harvesting today while she went and brought Papa home. But first she had to talk to a man about getting a loan. She wasn't going to give up everything without finding some other options…

She was determined to fight to keep her heritage.

In the orchard, Hugh emptied another basket of pears into the bin, hoping work would distract him. It didn't. He'd let Ellie get to him. He'd realized that last night when he'd kissed her…and kissed her again. The only choice he had was to cool things off. He had to keep his distance.

Ellie tempted him like no other woman, but he had to find a way to keep focused on his job, because in the end someone would get hurt.

Suddenly his phone rang. He walked away from the other workers and checked the ID to see his father's name. Why not? It had been days. But he couldn't talk to the man now, and let the call go to voicemail.

He cursed. Not at his father, but at the situation. He didn't want Cullan to lose his orchard, nor did he want Ellie to lose the vineyard. It wasn't right. Damn, he hated this. Before he'd come here his job had always been just a building, a business that an owner could walk away from.

How did you walk away from your life?

That evening, Ellie helped her grandfather out to the porch. "Just sit there and rest," she instructed him as she brought him a glass of lemonade. He could watch the sunset over the orchard.

"That's all I've done since I've gotten home."

"And if you want to attend the Stewarts' anniversary party this coming weekend, that's all you're doing—until the doctor says differently."

"Could you at least tell me if Ben finished up today?" he asked.

"I haven't talked to him personally, but he'll be up in a little while to tell you himself." She knew Papa wouldn't rest until he knew everything about the harvest. Since he'd been a boy, the orchard had been his way of life. He'd bragged that he'd never gotten a paycheck for a job.

This was Cullan Flanagan's life. She was going to do everything possible for him to keep it all.

The next evening, Hugh stood on the patio drinking a glass of wine. Ellie was working in the vineyard. Although he was a distance away, he could see the enthusiasm in her movements…her walk. The way she talked and laughed with the workers. No doubt she knew them all by their names… He smiled. She had told him they were all family. Loneliness nearly consumed him as he thought about how he'd walked away from her. It was for the best, he told himself. And he knew he had to keep away. He couldn't get involved with her, then turn around and try to put together a business deal for Mac. Maybe it would help if he honestly felt his father was turning this transaction into something good.

Had Mac always been such a heartless businessman? His father was a millionaire several times over. He didn't have to go after a business—especially one that just needed a little help. Did Mac have to take *everything* from them?

There had to be another way. The Flanagans didn't want to be millionaires, just to keep their family's land. Hugh found he was envious of what Ellie had: her close relationship with Cullan, and her family's history right here in the Valley.

Something he would never have. Not because he couldn't. He just wouldn't allow himself to take a chance at love and a try for a family. The chance his parents had failed at. But that didn't mean he hadn't dreamed about having it all with someone like Ellie.

"I see she hasn't lost her appeal for you."

Hugh turned to see Cullan standing on the path. He was embarrassed that he'd been caught…once again. "It's hard not to stare. She's a beautiful woman."

"Aye, and so much more, too. She has a true heart." Cullan looked back at him. "I thought you could see that, too."

Hugh knew a lot about Ellie Flanagan, but he'd always be hungry for more. "I do. But with everything going on I can't get involved with Ellie."

Cullan continued his journey up the path and stood on the patio beside Hugh. "So you are going to go because of the business between us?"

"That's a valid enough reason," he told him. "I've already come between you two. Ellie loves you, Cullan, and I can't be the cause of her unhappiness."

Cullan studied him for a moment. "Did I misjudge you, lad? I thought you were smart enough to figure out what you truly want and what Ellie needs."

Hugh doubted Cullan was talking about the regional director's job at McCutcheon.

"You need to figure out what is truly important in life." Cullan turned back to the woman in the vineyard. "It might be right in front of you."

Oh, yes, he wanted Ellie Flanagan. "I know what I want, sir. I just can't have it."

"So you give up so easily on love? Maybe you should just work harder on a solution."

* * *

That following Saturday, Ellie was still trying to add the final touches to the scheduled event. She walked around the garden, checking each decorated table. White linen with red roses as the centerpieces. Usually she loved doing weddings and parties in the garden, but it had been an overwhelming week.

Still, Ellie needed to make the Stewarts' fiftieth wedding anniversary party something special. It had been scheduled for nearly a year.

Of course she hadn't foreseen the fact that her grandfather would have heart trouble, or that the property was going to be up for sale.

Speaking of the vulture, where *was* Hugh McCutcheon? Not that she was looking, she reminded herself. But over the last few days she'd barely seen the man. Not since their so-called date. The last time he'd kissed her… The last time she'd dared to hope that he was going to be on their side. She'd been crazy enough to believe that something had happened between them. That Hugh could possibly be the man she'd dreamed about…the man she might fall in love with. But he had made his choice, and that told her he wasn't the man she'd thought he was.

The soft music from the quartet brought her back from her musings. She stood back to check that everything was coming together, and noticed the arrival of some guests. Thanks to Jillian, they were being escorted into the tasting room for now.

She brushed off her dress. It was sleeveless, with a scooped neck and a bias-cut tea-length skirt of teal and pale yellow. Her ivory sandals were high-heeled, with thin straps that fastened around her ankles. She wore her hair up and her grandmother's pearls around her neck.

She looked up, and a man caught her eye as he walked through the gate. Hugh. He looked devastatingly handsome, dressed in a dark suit and a snowy-white shirt with a conservative burgundy tie.

She wasn't happy that he could still set her pulse to racing, making her entire body aware of him. What was he doing here? Then her grandfather walked in and stood next to him. She smiled, seeing how distinguished he looked in his navy suit. Her gaze moved back to Hugh, then to her grandfather. Both men were handsome, had stubborn streaks, and both had plenty of charm. She suddenly realized she loved them both.

"Now, lad, don't do anything to rile her," Cullan warned him, then smiled at Ellie.

Hugh wasn't convinced coming tonight was a good idea. "She isn't going to want me here."

"Then I guess you better change her mind."

He glanced across the garden to see Ellie in a soft floral dress that showed off her shapely body. Although he liked her hair down, wearing it up exposed her lovely neck.

She approached them. "Papa, you look so handsome." She worked to straighten his tie. "Remember, just don't overdo it."

"I feel fine, and I've already promised Amanda Stewart a dance." He winked. "I want one with you, too."

"A slow one." She turned to Hugh. "Hugh, are you dressed up for some reason?"

"I hear there's a party tonight. I've been invited by Cullan."

He watched her expression. She wasn't happy.

"I introduced him to Jim and Amanda," her grandfather told her. "They insisted he come to the party. So put him at our table." Papa waved at someone. "Excuse me, I see some friends." He strolled off, leaving Hugh with Ellie.

"Sorry to mess up your table arrangements…" he began. "I'll sit anywhere you put me."

She raised her chin a notch. "I can't understand why you want to attend anyway."

He shrugged, but he was far from indifferent. "I guess I'm discovering what's important—friends and family celebrating a milestone."

"I wasn't even sure you were still here," she told him.

"I had some business to tie up."

She sighed. "Isn't it always about business with you?"

"I guess it has been…in the past. But can't a guy change?"

"You can do what you please, Hugh. I have no hold on you."

"You might be surprised." He smiled.

"I'm not sure I know what you mean."

He took a step closer and caught a whiff of her perfume. "How about we just enjoy the evening and see where it leads?"

He saw her face flush. She was interested. "I have to work."

"I can help. Show me what you need done."

When those big green eyes locked with his, it nearly brought him to his knees. His chest tightened with the sudden rush of feelings he'd never experienced before.

She didn't seem to be able to break the contact either.

"Ellie…"

She shook her head. "Okay…you can help. Go find Father Reyes. He's in the tasting room, but we should have him here, and ready to begin with the renewing of the Stewarts' wedding vows."

Hugh smiled. "So I look for a guy with a white collar and bring him to the garden? I think I can handle that." He started to walk away, then turned back to her. "Ellie, I said some things last week that I didn't think through."

She blinked. "You don't owe me any explanation."

Yes, he did. And he would tell her everything very soon. He nodded. "Will you save me a dance?"

"Hugh…I'm working. Besides, there'll be plenty of women here to dance with."

"But they're not you. I want you, Ellie."

The party was going perfectly, Ellie thought as she watched the older couple on the dance floor. They'd renewed their vows, and there hadn't been a dry eye in the place. The large wedding cake had been cut by the bride and groom, and they'd playfully fed each other the sweet confection. And many, many kisses had been shared between them.

And now the dancing had started, with the big band sound that Jim and Amanda Stewart had fallen in love to. They looked so happy as they moved smoothly around the floor. She knew that over their fifty years there had been problems and fights, but to see how they looked at each other today was so heartwarming. They had four adult children and eleven grandchildren who were cheering them on.

Someday would she be dancing with her husband? Ellie wondered. Would she have children? She'd been so busy working that the years were quickly passing by, and she was getting pretty close to thirty.

"They look happy."

Ellie turned around to see Hugh. "They are. I've known the Stewarts since I was a child. Jim has always treated his wife as if they were newlyweds."

"That's rare—especially with the divorce rate so high."

He was so cynical. "It was a different generation. They survived the Depression and the Second World War."

"Are you saying our generation gives up too easily?"

"Maybe," Ellie conceded. "Seems we've become a disposable society these days. We need to hold on to some of our past."

He paused a moment, knowing she was talking about her situation. "Not all people work hard for what they want." He leaned closer. "When I find something I want, you can bet I'm going to work hard to keep it."

"A wife isn't a possession," she argued. "She needs to be partner…in everything. That might be the reason so many marriages don't survive. A lot of men can't accept that."

"Whoa…" He grinned. "Don't put me in that category. I happen to like strong women, but I'm not so sure marriage is a great union."

She saw a flash of pain in his eyes before he masked

it. His parents' divorce had caused scars. "I hope you change your mind. Look around. There are a lot of happily married couples right here."

To her surprise, he did glance around at the couples dancing. And when the music changed to a romantic 1940s ballad, Hugh escorted her to the dance floor and pulled her into his arms. "Maybe it's contagious." His breath was against her ear.

"It's also a slower pace here in the valley." She leaned back and looked up at him. "A simpler life."

His grip tightened as her body fit against his. "Is that the secret, Ellie?"

She looked at him. "No, Hugh. The secret is to love someone so deeply you can't live without them…no matter what happens."

## CHAPTER EIGHT

"NOTHING is ever perfect," Ellie told Hugh as they swayed to the music. "But if you find someone you want to share your life with, it can feel perfect."

Hugh didn't want to get into an argument with her. All he wanted was to spend time with her, enjoy this time together. "Having you in my arms feels pretty perfect to me," he whispered, close to her ear. Tightening his hold, he pressed her softness against his body, and heat shot through him.

He wanted to forget everything else but them. That would be an ideal world. To have Ellie close to him always. The admission threw him. But it was true. He did want Ellie more than he'd ever wanted any woman.

"You're a good dancer," she said.

"Thank you," he said. "We fit together pretty well."

Her rich green eyes met his. "Yes, we do."

Her candor surprised him. "Thanks for letting me crash the party."

"I had nothing to do with it. You were invited."

He raised an eyebrow. "That's not exactly true. Cullan told Jim I was your date."

She blinked. "My date? But why? Why did you want to come to the party?"

Hugh took her hand and led her off the dance floor. He stopped at the side of the house, beside the high hedges and away from the crowd. He turned to her as the moonlight reflected off her hair and her pretty face. The sound of music and guests' voices began to fade as he was mesmerized by her.

"Ellie, I wanted to come to the party…to be with you."

"With me… But you were the one who walked away."

He stepped closer. "And I've stayed away because I thought it was the best thing to do. But there was one thing that I didn't figure on."

She swallowed. "What was that?"

"How much I would miss you…miss talking with you…joking with you…even arguing with you."

She lowered her eyes and timidly admitted, "I've missed you too…"

He released a breath. "So tonight… I want to forget everything else and be with you."

"Be we can't…" she said.

He pressed his forehead against hers. "We have this week…we can forget about business." He wanted more time with her, but he'd take what he could get. "Believe me, when I'm around you I'm definitely not thinking about acquisitions." He released a breath. "How can I when all I have on my mind is how badly I want to kiss you?"

Ellie ran her hands up his shirt, over his shoulders,

and locked them behind his neck. "Tell me how bad," she teased, and pressed her mouth against his briefly.

"Bad." He dipped his head and attempted to kiss her, but she pulled back.

"Do you think about me all day?"

He nodded. "And all night…" He cupped the back of her head and held her close. "I dream about you… ache for you. All I can think about is holding you in my arms, touching you…making love to you."

"Oh, my…"

Hugh gave her a smile. "Is that all you can say?"

Her wide eyes roamed over his face. "Kiss me, Hugh."

He didn't make her wait. He bent his head and captured her mouth. His tongue ran over her lips, then delved inside and tasted her sweetness.

"Oh, Ellie. I could get addicted to this…to you." He wanted her, and one night would never be enough. He kissed her again and again, trying to memorize her taste…her touch.

Then their private world was interrupted, when someone called Ellie's name. She looked up to see one of the workers.

"I need to get back to the party." She pulled away, but he stopped her.

"I'll let you go if you promise to come back. I want more time with you, Ellie." He paused. "I think you want the same thing."

She hesitated. "The party will go on for a few more hours."

"Let me help you."

She shook her head. "I'll never get anything done. It

probably won't be until about midnight before I can get away."

"I'll be at the cottage…waiting for you." He kissed her again and finally released her. She hurried down the path, and it took every ounce of his will-power to keep from going after her.

Hugh followed the path to the cottage, realizing that, as much as he'd tried, he'd gone and fallen hard for Ellie Flanagan. And that meant if he wanted a future with her…something had to give. He had to make sure Cullan and Ellie didn't lose Emerald Vale.

The only problem was he could lose everything he'd worked for. But that didn't seem to matter to him anymore.

Hugh stopped, noticing a light on the cottage patio. When he got closer, he found a man sitting at the table. It wasn't just any man. It was his father.

"Well, it's about time you got here," Mac said as he stood.

"Hello, Mac." Hugh wasn't going to give in to the man. "It would have been nice if you'd let me know you were coming."

"I wasn't sure myself," Mac told him. "But you've been dragging your feet, boy. So I thought you needed to be set straight."

Great. At the age of thirty-two, he was getting lectured. "Set straight? I'm not a child. And I don't appreciate you looking over my shoulder while I do my job."

"I'll look when it concerns me," his father warned. "Especially if you aren't doing what you were sent here to do."

Hugh remained silent as he studied Mac. Funny, people always said they looked alike, but he hoped the similarity didn't go any further than appearances. Mac McCutcheon was condescending, rude and arrogant. He treated people with disdain.

"I can't force Cullan Flanagan to sell the land."

"But you can pressure him."

"The man just got out of the hospital," Hugh told him. "I'm not going to do anything to harm his recovery."

"Then maybe you aren't the man for the job."

Hugh tried not to react. Not to protect himself, but he knew Mac wouldn't hesitate to send another vulture to hound Cullan. He had to handle this his way. "Don't worry, Mac. I'll get you results."

Ellie quickened her pace to the cottage. Thanks to Jillian, who'd offered to handle the clean-up for her, she was free to go be with Hugh.

She tried to contain her excitement, but it wasn't possible—not even with all the warning signs that popped up. Nothing could curtail her resolve to be with Hugh tonight.

It would more than likely be their only time together. There was no possible future for them. Once Papa signed the papers the vineyard would be gone, along with her dream…and Hugh.

Ellie reached the patio, realizing that he was the one she didn't want to end things. Did he feel the same? Could they come up with some sort of long-distance relationship? She walked to the door, found it open, and heard voices—men's voices.

Who was with Hugh? She peered inside to see an older

man, with thick gray hair. He was trim and well dressed, in a dark suit. Hugh's father. Mac McCutcheon. They were involved in conversation and didn't notice her.

"Don't worry, Mac. I'll get you results."

"Don't drag this out any longer. I've seen Flanagan's granddaughter, and it seems to me you could make her agreeable to this deal."

Hugh nodded. "I said I would handle it."

Ellie suddenly felt sick. But before she could get away, Hugh saw her.

"Ellie… What are you doing here?"

The look on his face would be almost laughable if she wasn't so hurt. "I was invited. But I see you already have a guest."

Mac McCutcheon immediately came to her. "It's a pleasure to meet you, Ellie. My son has told me so much about you."

He extended his hand to her. She refused to take it.

"Stop with the phony charm, Mr. McCutcheon. I'm not falling for it. And if I have any influence with my grandfather, he'll never sell the land to you or your company."

The man didn't even blink. "I'm sorry to hear that. I can guarantee you the McCutcheon Corporation will give you the best deal, and a large amount of money."

She hated this, and had to fight to keep from running away. "It's not always about money, Mr. McCutcheon." She finally looked at Hugh. "But I couldn't get that through to your son…so I'm not going to waste my time with you."

She squared her shoulders. "Emerald Vale is not for sale…to you." She turned and marched out.

She heard Hugh calling her, but she didn't stop. He finally reached her.

"Please, Ellie. You have to listen to me. I had no idea he was coming here."

"Sorry to spoil it." She fought her tears. "Tell me, Hugh, was seduction part of your plan?"

"Please, Ellie. What happened between you and me had nothing to do with business. I told you the truth. Until your grandfather was well, I wouldn't discuss the deal with him."

She crossed her arms to try and stop her trembling, to stop her pain. What a fool she'd been. She had given her heart and love to this man and he'd thrown it back at her. "But there wasn't anything stopping you from softening up the granddaughter."

Hugh felt as if she'd slapped him. He wished for physical pain, because what he felt inside was killing him. "If that's what you truly believe of me then I'm wasting my time."

She didn't speak. "What am I supposed to believe, Hugh? Your father shows up here…and I find you collaborating with him."

The pain grew worse. "I'll be packed and gone by morning. Goodbye, Ellie."

He turned and headed back to the cottage. The only thing worse was Mac being inside.

"So you couldn't get her to listen?" his father asked.

"No, I couldn't get her to listen. But I haven't given up."

"Don't tell me you've fallen for the girl?" Mac began to pace. "That could be good."

"Just stop. This is not about business anymore. I want you to leave."

"I'll leave when I'm good and ready."

Hugh closed his eyes. He was so tired of this. "No, you're not giving orders now. Not here. I'm going to protect Cullan and Ellie from you."

"How dare you talk to me—?"

"It's time someone stood up to you." He moved forward. "All during my childhood I wanted your attention, your love. Later I would have settled for your acceptance. I never got it. Not even in the last eight years I've worked for the company."

"Don't you see I had to be harder on you because you were my son? I couldn't show favoritism."

"You didn't have to worry about that. I've never been your son. Not truly. You only wanted me around because I produce so well. And I was stupid enough to do anything to try to please you." He paused. "It's never going to happen. Because I'm not trying any more. I quit."

"You can't be serious. You're giving up everything you've worked for because of a woman?"

Hugh clenched his fists. "Yes, because of a woman. And because I found a conscience."

Mac looked him over and paused. "It seems you've found your backbone, too. It's about time. You're the kind of man I want as my regional director." He grinned. "The job's yours, son."

Hugh couldn't believe it. For the past year the man had dangled the position under his nose and he'd worked his butt off trying to earn it.

Funny thing was, he didn't want it anymore. "No, I

don't want it." He leaned closer. "I don't think I need to tell you what you can do with the regional director's job. Goodbye, Mac."

Ellie hid out in her bedroom, praying that Hugh wouldn't come looking for her. She fought the tears. She wouldn't give Hugh McCutcheon the satisfaction. Not even if her world was crumbling and she could do nothing to stop it.

A soft knock sounded on her door, then her grandfather's voice.

She sat up. "Come in."

He peered in the door and smiled. "What's wrong, lass? Are you sick?"

She shook her head. "I'm just tired. So many things have happened the past few weeks. Your illness and…" Hugh's deception, she added silently.

He sat down on the bed. "You shouldn't have to worry about these things, Ellie. I never meant for this to happen."

"Please, Papa. It's not important. We have our home and the old orchard." She forced a smile. "And we have each other. We're still a family. You always taught me family is everything. The love and pride of the Flanagans."

They both laughed. "Your grandmother would be so proud of you."

"And I was proud of her."

Papa touched her chin. "I wish she was here now to help you. I'm not very good with matters of the heart."

She blinked, but, seeing the knowing look in Papa's eyes, she couldn't deny anything. "It's okay. There's nothing to worry about. I misjudged Hugh. He'll be leaving soon."

"Can you tell me what happened?"

"After the party…I was to meet him at his cottage." She saw the gleam in her grandfather's eye and she blushed.

"What? You think you kids invented love?" he asked her. "Your grandmother and I sneaked around more than once to find time alone." He sighed, as if remembering that time. "Her father was pretty strict. But I was heading off overseas during the war, so we had to meet when there was opportunity. I told her I loved her the day I got on the train, and that I'd be back for her. She was there waiting for me. Then I went to her father and asked for her hand in marriage."

Ellie had heard the story many times, but she loved hearing Papa tell it. "Not all love stories turn out that happily."

He studied her a moment. "Have you listened to Hugh's explanation?"

"I overheard what Hugh said to his father. He said he'd get *results*."

"Maybe he was talking about the business deal?" Papa told her. "I'm a pretty good judge of character. I believe that Hugh has feelings for you. Everything he's done here shows me that he isn't just out for the almighty dollar. I saw him watching you in the vineyard. He looked heartsick. He even came to me and asked about coming to the party…to be with you."

Ellie wanted to be hopeful, but she knew what she'd heard. "Then why did he say those things to his father?"

"I don't know. But maybe you should ask him. Give him a chance to explain."

Ellie was tired of explanations, excuses. He was going to take her land. There couldn't be any future for them. Not ever.

The doorbell rang, and her grandfather got up. "It's probably Jillian leaving me the key." He leaned over and kissed her. "Get some sleep. We'll deal with this tomorrow."

Ellie rolled on her side and closed her eyes, but it didn't change anything. She couldn't shut off her feelings for the man, probably never would.

Hugh was about to pound on the door when Cullan opened it. "I need to see Ellie."

"I don't think she's ready to talk to you right now."

Cullan stepped aside to let him into the entry. There was a large oriental rug covering hardwood floors. The staircase leading upstairs had a carved railing that swept up gracefully to the second floor. He wished for Ellie to appear, to let him tell her his feelings.

"I need to talk to her…to explain what happened. I had no idea my father would show up."

"Is that the real problem?"

Hugh raked his hand through his hair and cursed. "No, it's not. That the reason I'm pulling out of the deal. And I quit my job. I can't take the vineyard away from Ellie. I know how much she loves it."

Cullan nodded. "I know, but your pulling out isn't going to stop the sale. I still can't meet the balloon payment. And I'm a proud man, Hugh. Flanagans have always paid their debts…and I owe that money."

Cullan took Hugh into the parlor. He suddenly felt as if he'd stepped back fifty years. There was an ornate loveseat and matching chair in front of a marble fireplace. The centerpiece of the room was a grand piano, and on top was a cluster of pictures. Some very old.

Cullan picked one up. "This is my Eleanor."

In the sepia-colored picture Hugh couldn't tell hair or eye color, but there was no doubt that Ellie was the image of her grandmother. "Ellie looks so much like her."

"I know. They're so much alike. Both women loving and giving…and maybe a little stubborn." He replaced the picture and began to point out some other members of the family.

"Through the decades there have been some colorful characters who've worked this land. I just hate that I have to lose it for future generations."

"If you're willing to listen, I've come up with some possible ideas on how to handle the loan payment."

The older man studied him a moment, then grinned. "I knew you'd come through."

Hugh raised a hand. "I haven't, yet. I still have to iron out some things. So don't say anything to Ellie. I don't want to get her hopes up."

"I think the only thing that would get Ellie's hopes up would be if you didn't walk out of her life."

Hugh's chest tightened. Was there still hope for him? Would she forgive him? "Then I'm going to fight for her, Cullan."

The older man slapped him on the back. "I knew you were the right one for my girl."

"Let's pray she feels the same way."

* * *

The next week was terrible for Ellie. She had wanted Hugh to leave, and now he was gone. No goodbye, no *I'll see you,* just an empty room…and her aching heart. The only thing she could do was to try and stay busy in the vineyard with the upcoming harvest. This would be her last for Irish Rogue.

Her grandfather seemed healthy…and happy. There were only a few weeks left until the payment was due. She'd expected to have her grandfather make a decision on selling. Since there hadn't been any more offers for the property, she figured he was selling to the McCutcheon Corporation. She hated that. So much so, she wanted to move off the property completely. She didn't want to be anywhere around Hugh. But she couldn't leave Papa.

She needed to concentrate on looking for a job. Henry Blackford had been asking her for years. Maybe she could go to work for Blackford Winery. Maybe she could do something completely different and get a job in town. There wouldn't be much to do around the old orchard.

Of course she still had a schedule of weddings the following weekend, and several more until the end of the summer. The weddings and parties provided a good income, and they still needed the revenue.

Ellie stood on the hill and looked down at the rows of vines woven around trellises heavy with clusters of grapes. It was going to be a good harvest this year.

Her last. A tear fell.

"Are you okay, lass?" her grandfather asked.

She wiped her eyes. "I should be asking you that. But, yes, I'm okay. I'm just making peace."

Papa drew her close. She loved his strength and the fact he'd always been there for her. He'd never let her down.

"I love you, Ellie." He hugged her tighter. "And it's going to be okay. Please believe me."

She wanted to, but not much could restore her faith.

"Okay, I'll admit I was wrong," Mac said.

Hugh actually stopped clearing out his desk in the San Francisco office, and looked at him. "What?"

"I said I was wrong. You could have handled the Flanagan deal. I never should have showed up in Medford. There—I said it."

"You're only saying that because you lost."

"There's no reason to rub it in my face. I still have three other vineyards."

"But you want the Emerald Vale land."

He shrugged. "I just don't like to lose."

"You can't have everything."

"I know I want you as regional director."

Mac was too late for that. "That's one of the things you can't have. I've resigned."

"Think of the money you're passing up."

"I have a lot of money. And it hasn't made me happy. There's got to be something else out there."

His father studied him. "So you let her get to you?"

"If you mean Ellie Flanagan, oh, yes, she got to me all right. And I'm going to do everything I can to win her back."

Mac shook his head.

"Come on, Dad. Don't you get lonely sometimes? I

mean, it can't be all about the thrill of running a business."

He shrugged. "Maybe. But no woman could put up with my work schedule."

Hugh saw a flash of a different man. "Maybe you should seek some counseling; it might help you. All I know is I don't want to end up like you."

"Hey, it's not so bad."

Hugh tossed the last of his files in a box and glanced around one more time, then looked at his father. "That's because you were never the kid who longed to spend time with his father. No, I'm never going to be like you. And if I'm lucky enough to have a family, I'm going to put my wife and kids first. Too bad you didn't, Dad. I might not be leaving now."

# CHAPTER NINE

THE following week Hugh drove his rental car along Interstate 5, just outside Medford, Oregon. It was hard to believe it had been a month since he first came here.

Since the first time he'd seen Ellie.

It had taken him a while, but he'd finally realized she was everything he could ever want, and he didn't want to live without her. Now all he had to do was convince her they could make a life together.

He turned off at the exit and drove down the highway until he saw the road leading to Emerald Vale. Soon rows of vines appeared on one side of the road, then the orchard came into view on the other side.

A strange feeling came over him, as he realized this was where he wanted to be. He drove through the gate, passed the house and the general store, then parked and climbed out of the car. He had the papers on the seat beside him—the contracts that could help everyone get what they want.

He closed the door and walked into the empty store. He continued to the tasting room, and saw Jillian working behind the counter.

She smiled. "Well, look what wandered in."

"Hi, Jillian."

"Welcome back, stranger. Are you just stopping by? Or are you hanging around awhile?"

Hugh opened his mouth, but he didn't get a chance to talk. Someone else spoke for him.

"He won't be staying at all."

Hugh turned around to find Ellie. She was dressed in her usual work clothes of jeans, boots and blouse. Her hair was braided, but some curls had pulled free. She looked beautiful.

God, he'd missed her. "Hello, Ellie. It's good to see you again."

"I can't say the same," she announced. "I think it would be best if you leave. This is still Flanagan property."

"I'm here to talk with your grandfather."

She folded her arms over her chest. "I'm not interested in anything you have to say…and I doubt he is either."

Hugh caught the trembling of her hands. He hoped it was an indication that he still had an effect on her. "I seem to recall you saying nearly those same words to me the first time I came here."

She raised her chin. "You should have listened then. It would have been better for all of us."

"As I said before," he began again. "I came to see your grandfather."

"I won't have you causing trouble for him again—"

That hurt. "Give me some credit, Ellie. Since when have I intentionally hurt Cullan? And if you think I don't care about the man, then you haven't been paying attention." He drew a breath. "But I can see I'm wasting my breath." He stormed out of the store.

"Wait," she called. "Hugh, wait."

He was beside the car before he turned around. "What? You remembered some more choice words for me, huh, Ellie?"

She shook her head. "I'm sorry. My grandfather is in the orchard." Then she hurried off.

Hugh wanted to call her back. But not yet. He didn't have it all finalized. He needed to talk to Cullan first.

He grabbed his briefcase off the front seat, and was headed toward the orchard when Cullan appeared.

They met halfway. "Good to see you, Hugh. Let's go to the house and you can tell me what you came up with."

"It's not exactly what we talked about, but I think it might work."

Cullan smiled. "I already like the idea that you tried to help." He paused on the porch step. "I'll never forget that, son."

Hugh nodded, unable to speak.

Once seated at the dining room table, Hugh opened the briefcase and took out the first agreement.

"You have good neighbors and friends, Cullan. And you're well respected here in the community. I talked with—"

"Grandfather…"

They both looked up to see Ellie standing in the doorway. "Does this meeting have anything to do with the loan payment?"

"Yes, it does, lass."

"Then I have a lot at stake here, too. So may I sit in on the meeting?"

"I would never make any decision without you, Ellie. Hugh just has some ideas that might help us."

She turned those sultry green eyes on him. "Hugh, may I stay?"

He couldn't deny her anything. When he nodded, she walked in and sat down across from him at the table.

Hugh didn't want to look at her. He didn't need the distraction. He placed the contract in front of Cullan.

"I talked our idea over with Henry Blackford last week, and after he discussed it with his lawyer he got back to me yesterday. His lawyer drew up this contract."

Ellie frowned. "What did you discuss with Henry?"

Hugh spoke. "I offered Henry an option to buy the vineyard…at the same price as the bank loan."

She gasped. "But the vineyard is worth so much more."

Hugh nodded. "Before you get upset, let me explain."

She sat back in her chair.

"Here's the stipulation," he began, turning his attention to Cullan. "Henry owns the land for the next five years, and takes half the profits of the wine. But after the agreement term ends, he sells the vineyard back to you—and only you."

Ellie couldn't believe it. "Why would Henry want to do that? He never said he wanted to buy our vineyard."

"There's a couple of reasons. First of all, excluding any violent act of nature, he'll make money from your wine sales. And at the going interest rate this investment will make more money for him than if it sat in the bank. And most important to Blackford is to keep the small family vineyards going." He turned to Ellie. "He's also agreed to keep this business transaction private."

Ellie knew that losing half of the income from their wine would hurt, and they wouldn't be able to pay all their workers. "What about the—?"

"The workers?" He interrupted her. "According to my numbers, you should be able to keep your regular employees. It'll work out, Ellie." He handed her the spreadsheet. "Without the large loan payments the money from the orchard, the cottages and the special events should be enough so you'll be able to have a comfortable life."

It looked great on paper, Ellie thought. "Is Henry still willing to keep our agreement to use his winery?"

"If you want. Although this could change somewhat." He turned to her grandfather. "After that five-year period, your vineyard will be yours once again. Now, you and Ellie have a couple of options here. Henry needs to update his equipment, and he wants to enlarge his winery production. For that he needs a larger winery. He would like to keep the same agreement he's had with the Irish Rogue label."

Her heart was pounding. She hated to be selfish, since she'd gotten her vineyard back. But her dream... She'd already lost the most important one. She glanced at Hugh. The winery was all she had left.

"What's the other option, Hugh?" Cullan asked.

His gaze went to Ellie as he leaned back in the chair. "Build your own winery."

Her heart raced. "But how can we afford it? We can't go into such debt again."

Hugh's gaze never wavered. "You take on another partner."

She sighed. "Who would want to invest…? Oh, no. Not McCutcheon. I won't have your father…"

"Not my father," he corrected. "Me. I want to invest in the winery."

"You? You know nothing about the wine business."

"I know the production end. I looked over the vineyard's profits for the last five years. It's a solid company…well run. Why wouldn't I want to invest?"

Ellie couldn't do this. Didn't he know how much it would hurt her to work with him, knowing they would never be together?

She looked at Papa. "You do what you want."

"No, Ellie. I can't do anything without your okay. In fact I'm signing the vineyard over to you. It's always been yours anyway. And any decision about what happens to it is yours, too."

"Thank you, Papa." She turned back to Hugh. "I want to thank you for all that you've done. And, yes, I'll accept Henry's offer for the vineyard. But…I'm sorry, Hugh, I can't let you invest in the winery."

She stood, and with the last of her composure she made it out the door. By the time she made it to her refuge, the vineyard, the tears were already falling.

Normally Hugh didn't give up so easily, but this time his heart wasn't in the fight. Ellie had made it clear. She didn't want him anywhere around her, whether it be business or personal.

"I'm sorry, Hugh," Cullan said. "She's been under a lot of stress lately."

"And she can't forgive me. She thinks I used her."

"Her feelings run deep." The older man stood. "She cares for you."

Hugh hadn't realized her rejection would hurt so much. "Oh, yeah, I can tell. She can't stand to be in the same room with me."

"Then tell her how you feel… Tell her why you really want to be her partner."

In the beginning he wouldn't even admit it to himself. But he wanted Ellie, wanted a future with her. "So she can throw it back in my face?"

"No, so she knows the truth." He placed his hand on Hugh's arm. "I know my granddaughter. Do you think if she didn't care she would raise such a ruckus?"

Hugh didn't know what to think. He was in love with Ellie Flanagan, but he couldn't make her feel the same way. Yet, if he didn't try to tell her… "Where is she?"

"My bet is she's up on the hill, probably talking to her grandmother." Cullan frowned. "She's lost a lot of people in her life…and she thinks she's lost you, too. Go to her," he said, giving him a nudge. "I'll have one of the workers put your things in the cottage."

"So you think I'm staying around?"

"I know you are, lad. For a long time."

Ellie stood, overlooking the vineyard. She wanted to push everything out of her head and just feel grateful to Henry Blackford for helping save Emerald Vale. But it wasn't the vineyard that was on her mind now.

She wondered if Hugh had left yet. Was he gone for good? After what she'd said to him she wouldn't blame him. She brushed away a wayward tear. She didn't need him anyway. Papa was here for her. And someday she'd build a winery. Why didn't that dream satisfy her any more?

"Ellie…"

She jerked around to see Hugh. She tried to draw a breath, but her chest was too tight.

"What are you doing here?"

He came closer. "Because of you. I'm here because of you."

"Please…Hugh. We said everything…"

"Not everything. At least let me tell you that I had no idea my father would show up that night. Also know that I wouldn't push your grandfather into selling. I didn't want him to have to sell Emerald Vale. I'd already approached Henry Blackford about the deal…two weeks ago."

Her eyes widened, but she couldn't speak.

"I no longer work for the McCutcheon Corporation. I resigned when I returned to San Francisco. So you see, Ellie, I wouldn't have been involved in the deal anyway."

"But what about you and your father?"

"Father, huh?" He chuckled. "Funny thing is, I never had a father growing up. I tried for a lot of years. I even went to work for him. But that didn't work, either. Worse, I realized I was turning into the same selfish man. I found I didn't like myself very much." He shrugged. "And I still didn't get my father's attention."

"Oh, Hugh, I'm sorry."

He shook his head. "It's okay, Ellie. You can't miss what you've never had. Or that's what I thought. Then

I met you and Cullan and saw what a family truly was. As bad as things had gotten, Ellie, you and Cullan hung together. You would have survived anything because you had each other." His eyes met hers. "I envied that. For a time, I thought I could fit in here. You were quickly becoming my dream."

"Hugh."

"Let me finish. At first I never thought I'd want all this. It was the big city…the big job." He glanced around, then back at her. "Now I want all this. But only with you. From the first moment I saw you, you took my breath away. You were so beautiful. Your grandfather saw it, too. He said he felt the same way about his Eleanor." He reached for her and drew her closer. "I love you, Ellie Flanagan. I want to share your dreams and build a life with you."

Her heart soared and she began to tremble. "I love you, Hugh. I'm sorry—"

He covered her mouth with a kiss that quickly had her aching for him. He finally released her. He grinned. "Say it again."

She smiled. "Oh, Hugh, I love you."

He picked her up in his arms and kissed her again and again. "Wait a minute. I just realized that I don't have a job. Do you know of anyone who needs a business analyst?"

She doubted that he was broke. "Yes, I just happen to know someone. Please, Hugh, you could work for Emerald Vale Orchard and Irish Rogue Vineyard…soon to be winery." She smiled. "You told me you're good with numbers."

"That's not all I'm good with." He captured her mouth in a searing kiss, giving her a sample.

Business could wait. There were more important things to deal with…like a future together.

# EPILOGUE

IT WAS early summer in the vineyard. The rose garden was in full bloom, with a rainbow of color. White chairs had been set up on either side of the aisle that the bride would walk down to a flower-covered archway…and her groom.

Ellie stood in the back behind a screen. She was wearing her grandmother's wedding dress: antique white lace draped over a satin fitted gown that ended with a long train trimmed with tiny pearls. Her hair was pulled back and woven with fresh flowers attached to an elbow-length veil.

She drew another breath and turned to her grandfather. He looked handsome in his dark tuxedo.

"You look as beautiful as when I saw your grandmother on our wedding day." Tears filled his blue eyes. "She would be so happy you wore her dress."

"I couldn't wear anything else on my special day."

Their eyes met, and she wanted to say so many things, but realized he already knew them. "I love you, Papa."

"I love you, too, lass," he told her. "I hate giving you

away today, but I know Hugh is a good man." His smile widened. "And I'll be waiting for those great-grandkids. Be happy, Ellie."

"I plan to, Papa."

The music changed, giving them their cue to begin. They stepped out onto the runner and started down the aisle. Ellie smiled as she saw all her friends and neighbors gathered there. Even Hugh's father was in attendance today.

Mac and his son had worked through some problems over the last months. They might never be close, but maybe they could be friends.

She gripped her bouquet of pink roses and raised her gaze to the man standing under the arbor. Her heart raced, as it did every time she saw Hugh McCutcheon. He looked handsome in his tuxedo adorned with a pink rose on the lapel.

She loved him with all her heart. Maybe even from that first day months ago, when Hugh had first arrived at Emerald Vale. But they'd decided to wait before they wed. It had given them time to work together and learn about each other. They'd even fought, and the making up had been wonderful. They had survived the remodeling of her parents' home, where they planned to begin their lives together…and start their own family.

Smiling, she reached the front of the garden. Her grandfather gave her a kiss, then gave her hand to Hugh. "Cherish her, son."

"I already do," Hugh said, and his eyes were on her. "You're so beautiful."

They turned to the priest.

The ceremony lasted a short time, and then came

congratulations from well-wishers. The party moved on to the tables set up for the reception and dancing. It wasn't until hours later that they said their goodbyes to their guests and headed to the cottage. Tomorrow they would leave on their honeymoon—a week in Hawaii.

Hugh swung his bride into his arms and carried her over the threshold, inside the beautifully decorated room. There were flowers and lit candles everywhere.

"Oh, Hugh, it's so…romantic." He set her down. "Did you do this?"

"It was my idea, but Jillian helped me."

She frowned. "Should I be jealous?"

"Not in the least, Ellie Flanagan McCutcheon." He came to her and kissed her, long and deep. Then with his bride in his arms he began to dance to the soft music that filled the room. "I'm glad we're alone," he whispered against her ear.

She looked at him. "So am I."

"I'll always remember the time I danced with you at the Stewart party. That was the first time I dreamed about us sharing our lives together."

They'd come a long way in just a few months. The bank loan was paid off, and Henry Blackford had pretty much left the operation as before. One good thing about the years Hugh had worked for his father: he'd made a lot of money. Money he'd invested wisely. Now they'd start making plans for the new Irish Rogue Winery.

"We're going to share a lot more," he told her. "We're building something for future generations." He kissed her. "A place that will always have love…and family. We're not just partners in business, but in life."

"Oh, my. I guess I can't call you the Hatchet Man

anymore." Her arms tightened around his neck. "You're the Family Man now."

"Sounds wonderful to me." Hugh suddenly realized that after all the years he'd been searching he was home. With Ellie.

0708/25/MB130

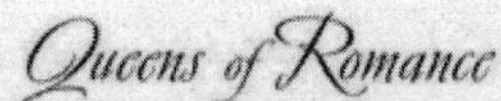


## *An outstanding collection by international bestselling authors*

4th July 2008 | 1st August 2008 | 5th September 2008

3rd October 2008

7th November 2008

One book published every month from February to November

## *Collect all 10 superb books!*

M&B™

www.millsandboon.co.uk